PENGUIN MODERN CLASSICS

NARZISS AND GOLDMUND

Hermann Hesse was born at Calw, Germany, on 2 July 1877. Having begun his career as a bookseller in Tübingen and Basle, he started to write and to publish poetry at the age of twenty-one. Five years later he enjoyed his first major success with his novels on youth and educational problems: first *Peter Camenzind*, then *Unterm Rad* (*The Prodigy*), followed by *Gertrud*, *Rosshalde*, *Demian*, and others. Later, when as a protest against German militarism in the First World War he settled permanently in Switzerland, he established himself as one of the greatest literary figures of the German-speaking world. His humanity, his searching philosophy developed further in such novels as *Der Steppenwolf* and *Narziss und Goldmund*, while his poems and critical writings won him a leading place among contemporary thinkers. The Nazis abhorred and suppressed his books, the Swiss honoured him by conferring on him the degree of Ph.D.; the world, finally, by bestowing upon him in 1946 the Nobel Prize for Literature, an award richly deserved by his great novel *Das Glasperlenspiel* (*Magister Ludi*). Hermann Hesse died in 1962, shortly after his eighty-fifth birthday.

HERMANN HESSE

NARZISS AND GOLDMUND

Translated from the German
by Geoffrey Dunlop

PENGUIN BOOKS

Penguin Books Ltd, Harmondsworth, Middlesex, England
Penguin Books Australia Ltd, Ringwood, Victoria, Australia

—

First published jointly by Peter Owen and Vision Press 1959
Published in Penguin Books 1971

—

Copyright © Hermann Hesse, 1959
All rights reserved

—

Made and printed in Great Britain
by Hazell Watson & Viney Ltd,
Aylesbury, Bucks
Set in Linotype Granjon

CHAPTER ONE

ISOLATED here in the North, planted long ago by a Roman pilgrim, a chestnut grew, strong and solitary, by the colonnade of rounded double arches at the entrance to the cloister of Mariabronn : a noble, vigorous tree, the sweep of its foliage drooping tenderly, facing the winds in bold and quiet assurance; so tardy in spring that when all glowed green around it and even the cloister nut trees wore their russet, it awaited the shortest nights to thrust forth, through little tufts of leaves, the dim exotic rays of its blossom, and in October, after wine and harvests had long been gathered, let drop the prickly fruits from its yellowing crown; fruits which did not ripen every year, for which the cloister schoolboys fought one another, and which Gregory, the Italian sub-prior, burned amid the logs of his fireplace. The lovely tree, aloof and tender, shadowed the entrance to the cloister, a delicate, shuddering guest from a warmer clime, secretly akin to the slender double columns of the gateway, the pillars and mouldings of the window arches, loved by all Latins and Italians, gaped at, as a stranger, by the inhabitants.

Many generations of cloister schoolboys had trooped past beneath this stranger tree, laughing, gossiping, playing, squabbling, shod or barefoot, according to the season of the year; each with his writing-tablet; boys with a flower between their lips, boys cracking nuts, boys with snowballs. Always there were new ones; every second year brought its fresh faces, though most – tousled and yellow-haired – were very like the boys that had passed. Some stayed and turned into novices, then monks, and their yellow hair was shorn.

They wore the habit and the cord, read books, taught boys, grew old and died. Others, at the end of their school-days, were fetched back home by their parents, into knights' castles, merchants' or craftsmen's houses; they were let loose into the world, to run wild or work in it. Sometimes, turned into men, they would come back and look at the cloister, bringing little sons to put them to school with the patres, stand smiling for an instant, full of thoughts, as they saw the chestnut, and then go out again and vanish. In the cells and schoolrooms of the cloister, between the strong double redstone pillars and rounded arches, monks lived, taught, administered, studied, ruled. Every branch of science was pursued there, and inherited by each new generation: divine and worldly lore, the dark and the light. Books were written and annotated, systems evolved, the writings of the ancients collected, missals illuminated, the people's belief fostered, the people's credulity smiled upon. Here there was all, and room for everything, belief and learning, depths and simplicity, the wisdom of the Greeks and the Evangelists, black magic and white – all had their uses. There was room for repentance and solitude; room for good living and company. It depended on the ruling abbot, on the tendency prevalent at the time, which of these came uppermost for the moment, eclipsing the others. For a while the cloister of Mariabronn was renowned for its exorcists and devil-chasers; for a while for the beauty of its plain chaunt; then for a saintly father who healed and wrought miracles; then for its pike broth and stag's liver pasty – each in its time. And ever in this throng of monks and scholars there were lukewarm and fervid fasters and rioters; always, among the many who lived and died there, there had been, here and there, an individual, one set apart from all the rest, whom all loved, or all feared, one who had seemed of the elect, who for long was remembered and talked of when the rest of his generation had been forgotten.

And in this age also there lived in the cloister at Mariabronn two set apart and chosen, one old, one young. Of
the many monks who had thronged the church, the dormitories and study-rooms, there were two, remarked by all,
whom all were watching – Abbot Daniel and the teaching
novice, Narziss, only recently entered in the novitiate, yet
already, against all tradition, and because of his exceptional
gifts, employed, in Greek especially, as a teacher. These
two, the novice and the abbot, were respected and heeded
by all the house. They were watched and aroused curiosity,
admired and envied, slandered in secret.

Most brothers loved the abbot; he had no enemies. He
was full of goodness, humbleness, simplicity. Only the
learned in the cloister strewed a pinch of scorn into their
love of him. This abbot, they would say, might be a saint;
certainly he would never be a scholar. His was that simplicity which is wisdom, but his Latin was poor, and Greek
he altogether lacked.

Those few who were ready on occasion to smile at the
simpleness of the abbot were all the readier therefore to let
themselves be charmed by Narziss – the wondrous boy, the
beautiful young man with the elegant Greek, the manners
and bearing of a knight, the penetrating, quiet eyes of a
thinker, the thin, shapely, firmly outlined lips, whose bril-
liant dialectic attracted scholars. Almost all the others loved
him for the sake of his fineness and nobility. He enchanted
many : many took no offence at the fact that he was always
so still and self-contained, so full of courtesy.

Abbot and novice, each in his fashion, bore on him the
signs of special grace. Each in his own way ruled, each
suffered with his own peculiar pain; each felt drawn to the
other, more akin to him than to any in the cloister.

Yet neither, though he sought, could find the other,
neither could be quite thawed by the other's presence. The
abbot treated the novice with perfect courtesy, with every

7

gentle consideration, chiding him as one might a younger brother, a strangely delicate, perhaps too dangerously precocious younger brother. The novice, in perfect obedience, heeded the abbot's every rule and counsel; he never disputed, never sulked, and, if his superior's judgement of him was right, and his only temptation was to pride, he could hide this sole fault to perfection. Nothing could be brought against him. He was perfect, but self-contained. There was only this: that few save scholars could be close friends with him; that his own distinction seemed to wrap him round, like a chill breath.

Once, when he had confessed, the abbot said: 'Narziss, I am guilty of having passed rash judgements on you. I had thought you proud, and perhaps I did you an injustice. You are much alone, brother; you have many to admire you, but no friends. I wished to find the pretext to chide you a little. But I find none. I wanted to see you as disobedient as young men of your age so easily are. But you never disobey. Sometimes, Narziss, you make me uneasy.'

The young man turned his dark eyes on the old.

'Father, I want above all to bring you no sorrow. And it may well be that I am proud. I beg you to punish me for that. At times I have a longing to punish myself. Send me into solitude, father; or let me do the work of a lay brother.'

'You would be too young for either, dear brother,' the abbot answered, 'and you are wonderfully gifted, my son; in speech and thought. By giving you the tasks of a lay brother I should misuse and desecrate these high gifts. You seem made to be a teacher and scholar. Is that your own wish?'

'Forgive me, father; I am not very clear as to my wishes. I shall always take pleasure in science; how could it be otherwise? But I do not think that learning will be my only service. It may not always be a man's wishes that determine his destiny and his action. He may be predestined.'

The abbot grew more serious. Yet his old face smiled as he answered. 'In so far as I have learned to know men, I have seen that in our youth we are all of us a little inclined to call our own wishes predestination. To what do you feel yourself predestined?'

Narziss half-closed his dark eyes, till they vanished into the shadow of the lashes. He did not answer. There was a long silence.

'Speak, my son,' the abbot commanded him. In a low voice, his eyes to the ground, Narziss began his answer:

'Father, I feel sure that above all else I am destined to the life of this cloister. I know that I shall become a monk, a priest, a sub-prior; perhaps an abbot. My own wish is not for dignities, yet I know they will be laid upon me.'

They both were silent.

'What gives you this belief?' the old man asked, uncertainly. 'Apart from your learning what can it be in you that warrants you to speak these words?'

Narziss was slow with his reply: 'It is because I have in me perception of the ways and dispositions of men: not mine only, but those of others. This quality in me forces me to serve men by ruling them. Had I no vocation to the habit I should have to become a judge; a ruler.'

'That may be so,' the abbot nodded, 'but have you proved this faculty of yours for knowing men and their fates by any instance? Are you ready to give me an example?'

'Yes, I am ready.'

'Good, then – and since I would not pry into the hearts of the brothers without their knowledge, perhaps you will tell me, your abbot, what you know of me.'

Narziss raised his eyes to fix the superior.

'You command me, father?'

'Yes, I command.'

'It is hard to speak, father.'

9

'And I too, brother, find it hard to command your obedience in this matter. And yet I do. So speak, then.'

Narziss hung his head and whispered.

'I know very little of you, father. I know that you are one of God's servants; that you would rather herd goats, or ring in to matins in a hermitage and shrive the peasants, than rule as the head of a great cloister. I know your especial devotion to Our Lady, and that it is to her you pray the most. At times you pray that the Greek and other learning in this cloister may not draw the souls under your care from God; at others that you may be patient with Gregory, the sub-prior. And at times for a peaceful end. In this I think you will be heard, and that your end will be a gentle one.'

It was very still in the abbot's little parlour, till at last the old man began to speak.

'You are a dreamer who has visions,' he answered in a friendly voice. 'Even pious and fair visions can trick us. I put no trust in them, nor must you. Now, brother dreamer, can you see how I feel all this in my heart?'

'Father, I can see you think very pleasantly of it. This is how you think: "This young scholar is in some small peril; he has had a vision, and perhaps he meditates too much. Perhaps it would do him no harm if I laid a penance on him, and I will take the same on myself." That is what you have just been thinking.'

The abbot rose. He dismissed the novice with a smile.

'It is well,' he said. 'Do not take your visions too much in earnest, young brother. God requires much besides visions of us. Let us say you have pleased an old man by telling him he will have an easy death, and that the old man's heart rejoiced for an instant to hear your promises. That is enough. Tomorrow, after early mass, you will say a rosary, and say it with humility and devotion; and so will I. Now go, Narziss, we have said enough.'

On another day Abbot Daniel had to sit in judgement on

Narziss and the youngest of the teaching-fathers, who could not manage to agree on a certain point in the plan of studies. Narziss urged, very zealously, the necessity for certain alterations, and could, moreover, defend them on persuasive grounds. But Pater Lorenz, spurred on by a kind of envy, refused his consent to them, till their every conference was followed by uneasiness, sullenness, and silence, when Narziss, feeling himself in the right, would broach the subject afresh. At last, sore at heart, Pater Lorenz said to him:

'Well, Narziss, let us end our dispute. You know that in this not you but I should decide. It is for you to bend yourself to my will, who are not my fellow-teacher, but my helper. Yet since this matter seems to weigh so heavy on you, and since, although I am your superior, I am beneath you in knowledge and in gifts, I will not pretend to have the last word, but let us take our dispute to our father, the abbot, and ask him to settle between us.'

This, therefore, they did, and Abbot Daniel heard these two scholars kindly and patiently, as they argued on the teaching of grammar. When both had spoken all their thoughts the old man looked at them humorously, and shook his white head a little as he spoke.

'Dear brothers, you can neither of you suppose that I know as much as you of these things. It is very commendable in Narziss that the school should lie so close to his heart, and that so he seeks to better our plan of studies. But if his superior thinks otherwise, Narziss has only to obey and be silent, since all betterment in the school would weigh as nothing if good order and obedience in the house were destroyed by it. I blame Narziss for not having known how to subject himself; and my wish for you two young scholars is that you may never lack a superior whose wits are duller than your own. No salve for pride is better than that.'

With this pleasant jest he dismissed them, yet certainly

did not omit in the following days to observe the two very carefully, and himself discover if between them peace and good understanding reigned once more.

Then it came about that a new face appeared in the cloister, which had seen so many faces come and go, and that this new face was not among those that pass unnoticed, and when they are gone, are soon forgotten. It was a little boy, long since announced by his father, who brought him, on a day in spring, to put him to school in the cloister. Under the chestnut tree they tethered their horses, and the porter had come out through the gate to meet them. The boy looked up at the still bare branches of the tree. 'I have never seen such a tree as that till now,' he said, 'a rare, beautiful tree, and I wish I knew what they call it.'

The father, an elderly man, with a peaked, care-lined face, did not heed the words of his little son. But the porter, pleased already with the boy, told him the name of the tree. The little boy thanked him graciously, gave him his hand, and said to him : 'My name is Goldmund, and I am to go to school here.' The porter smiled and led the new-comers through the gates and on up the broad stone steps. Goldmund entered the cloister without dismay, feeling that here he had met two beings, the tree and the porter, with whom he could easily be friends.

The Pater who governed the school received them, and towards evening, the abbot himself. To both of these this knight, in the service of the Emperor, presented Goldmund, his son, and was asked to stay a while in the guest house. But only for one night would he use his privilege, saying that next day he must ride back. As his gift to the cloister he left one of the horses that had borne them to it, and this was accepted by the monks. His talk with the priests was smooth and cold, but both Pater and Abbot looked with pleasure at the silent, respectful Goldmund; this pretty, fine-bred boy had pleased them at once. Next day, with few regrets, they watched the father ride off again, and were glad indeed to think they kept his son. Goldmund was taken to see his teachers, and given a bed in the scholars' dormitory. He took leave of his sire with fear and reverence in his eyes, standing and gazing out after him, till horse and rider had gone from sight through the narrow arch in the wall of the outer court, between the mill and the granary. A tear still hung on his long, gold lashes as he turned; but the porter, who had stayed there waiting for him, clapped him on the shoulder pleasantly.

'Lording,' he said, to comfort him, 'don't be sad. Most begin here with a little sorrow for father, mother, and their brethren. But you'll soon see! You can have as good a life here as anywhere.'

'Thanks, brother porter,' said the lad, 'but I have no mother and no brethren. I have only my father.'

'Well, here you'll find playfellows and learning, and new sports you never knew before; and this and that. You'll see fast enough. And if you need one that means well by you, come to me.'

Goldmund smiled. 'Oh, many thanks, brother porter. And now, if you would be my friend, show me quick the little horse that bore me hither. I would like to greet him, and see if he too is glad to live here.'

The porter led him at once into the stable, near the granary. There in the soft dusk it smelt sharp of horses, of oats and horse-dung; and Goldmund found his little brown horse in its stall, the horse that bore him to the cloister. He put his arms around the beast's neck; it had known its master already, and stretched out its head to him. And Goldmund set his cheek to the wide dappled forehead of the pony, which he stroked softly, and whispered in his ear. 'God keep you, Bless, my little horse, my brave one. How is it with you? Do you love me still? Do you think of our home? Have you your bellyful? Little Bless, my little horse, my friend, how glad I am to have you stay with me. I will often come to see you.'

He took from his wallet the piece of morning bread, which he had kept for his horse, and broke it to give him. Then he took leave, following the porter through the court-yard, as wide as the market-place of a great city, and grown about with its lime trees. At the inner gate he thanked and gave his hand to the porter, then found he no longer knew the way to his schoolroom, though yesterday they had shown him the direction. He laughed a little and flushed red, turned, and begged the porter to guide him, and he was very glad to do so. So Goldmund came among his mates, where a dozen of lads and junkers sat on benches, and the teaching-novice, Narziss, turned his head. 'I am the new scholar, Goldmund,' said the boy.

Narziss gave him a short greeting, pointed, without a smile, to a place on the hindmost bench, and continued at once with his lesson.

Goldmund sat down. He was astonished to see so young a teacher, not many years older than he; astonished, too, and very glad, to find this young teacher so handsome, so grave, with such fine manners, and yet so winsome and worthy his love. The porter had been very kind to him, the abbot had welcomed him with gentleness; there in his stall stood Bless, and a little of home along with him, and here was this wonderful young monk, as grave as a scholar, as fine as a prince, with his cold, clear voice, compelling his hearers. Goldmund listened gladly, though not understanding what the matter was. He felt at peace. He had come among good men, and was ready to love them in exchange, and strive to make of them his friends. This morning in his bed, after he woke, he had felt so ill at ease, still weary with the long journey, and constrained to weep as he said God-speed to his father. But now all was well and he was happy. Again and again he eyed the teacher, rejoicing in his strength and slimness, his cold, yet glowing eyes, his firm-drawn lips which uttered each syllable so clearly, his soaring, never-wearying voice.

But when the lesson was done, and the noisy scholars started up, Goldmund awoke to know with shame that he had sat there dozing a long while. Nor was he the only one to mark it; his neighbours on the bench had seen it, too, and whispered it around to their fellows. Scarce had the young Magister left his schoolroom than Goldmund's shouting companions surrounded him.

'Awake yet?' said one with a grin.

'A fine scholar,' mocked another. 'Here's one will be a shining Church light. His first lesson sends him to sleep.'

'Carry the babe to bed,' proposed a third, and they pounced on his arms and legs, and lifted him high, with shouts of mockery.

They had scared him so that Goldmund began to grow angry. He struck out around him on all sides, trying to free himself, and earned some clouts, till he ended by sprawling on the ground, though one still had him by the foot. From him he kicked himself loose, and was soon engaged in a bout with him. His enemy was a tall, strong lad, and all gathered in to watch the battle. But Goldmund stood his ground; he had several times clouted his strong enemy, and won himself friends among his fellows before any so much as knew his name. Suddenly they all ran off and were scarce gone than along came Pater Martin, the brother-schoolmaster, and stood looking down on Goldmund, left alone. He gazed in doubt at the boy, whose blue eyes answered him perplexed, his face a little flushed and dismayed.

'Well, and how is it with you?' he asked him. 'You are Goldmund – are you? Have those scamps been doing you any harm?'

'Oh no,' said the boy, 'I held my own with them.'

'But with which?'

'How can I tell? I know none here yet. One of them fought me.'

'Oho! And did he begin it?'

'How should I know? No, I think it was I began it. They set on me, and so I grew angry.'

'Well, sir, this is a fine beginning. Listen to me. If you fight again in the schoolroom you'll be whipped for it. And now – be off with you to supper.'

With a smile he stood looking after Goldmund, as the boy ran off, abashed, after the others, trying, as he ran, to smooth down his yellow hair with his fingers.

Goldmund himself agreed that his first deed here in the cloister had been a very rash and rebellious one. He felt ashamed, as he sought and joined his fellows at supper. But they welcomed him among them with respect, he made knightly peace with his enemy, and from that day on knew himself well liked by the scholars.

CHAPTER TWO

THOUGH he made good friends with all Goldmund could not at once find a true friend. There was none among his companions to whom he felt closely akin, though they themselves were all amazed to discover a very peaceful companion in this bold fighter, who had struck out right and left.

But now this Goldmund seemed to strive to become the best scholar in the school. There were two in the cloister to whom he was drawn to love, who pleased him and filled his thoughts, for whom he felt deep admiration and reverence: Abbot Daniel and the teaching-novice Narziss. The abbot he felt to be holy; his good and simple ways, his humble rule, commanding as though it offered service, his still gentleness and peace – all these drew Goldmund powerfully to him. He would have liked best of all to become the body-servant of this saint, would have brought him, as a perpetual offering, the young lad's urge in him to sacrifice, and longed to learn of him how to live a chaste and noble life, a life conformable with sanctity. Such was his will, and such had been his father's wish and command, and so it was as though God had ordained it. Though none in the cloister had marked it there seemed to be a burden laid on the shoulders of this pleasant and radiant lad, some secret inclination to atonement. Even the abbot did not see it, although Goldmund's father had hinted that it was so, telling him plainly his wish that his son should remain for ever in the cloister. A hidden stain on Goldmund's birth appeared to require its expiation. But the knight had not pleased the abbot, who answered with the smoothest courtesy his cold, somewhat arrogant words, not heeding his suggestions overmuch.

That other who had aroused Goldmund's love saw sharper, and could perceive more of all this. But Narziss held back. He had felt well enough how clear a golden bird had flown to him. He, all alone in his fine being, had known himself akin to Goldmund, though in every outer thing the lad was his opposite. Narziss was dark and thin of face, and Goldmund open and radiant as a flower. Narziss was a thinker and anatomiser, Goldmund a dreamer and a child. Yet things common to both could bridge these differences. Both were knightly and delicate; both set apart by visible signs from their fellows, since both had received the particular admonishment of fate.

Narziss took an ardent share in this young soul whose ways and predestination were so well known to him; and Goldmund glowed with pleasure at the sight of his beauteous, meditative teacher. But Goldmund was timid, and could think of no other way of pleasing Narziss than to wear himself out with industry as a skilful and patient scholar. More than his shyness held him back: his love of Narziss was checked by a feeling that this master was a danger to him. How could he take the good and saintly abbot for his ideal and at the same time love this subtle scholar, the learned, the penetrating Narziss?

Yet with all the strength of his youth he pursued these two incompatibles. Together they caused him great suffering, and often, in the first months of his schooldays, Goldmund felt such confusion in his heart, and his mind so torn this way and that, as to come into sore temptation to break from the cloister; or else, by fighting with his mates, still his inner need and quench his anger. For some small plaguing or saucy word this good, easy comrade would flame up, wild for no reason, so wrath that only with many struggles could he manage to rein in his ire, while, pale as death and with closed eyes, he turned from his tormentors in silence. Then he would run off to the mangers, seek out his pony Bless, lean up his cheek against his forehead, kiss him, and sob out his heart. This pain laid hold of him by inches, and at last was visible to all. His cheeks thinned, his eyes were often dull, the laugh in which all rejoiced grew ever rarer.

He could not himself have said what he lacked. His deepest wish seemed this : that he should grow into a good, trusty scholar, soon to be received in the novitiate, and so live on to the end, as a quiet, devout brother of the cloister. He believed that his whole faculties and strength were centred in these simple, peaceful aims, and had no thought nor knowledge of other strivings. How strange and hard it seemed to him, therefore, that even this, his fair and quiet purpose, should be so difficult of achievement. From time to time he would lose heart, as he found himself guilty of sinful longings, idleness at study, day-dreams, lazy fancies, or drowsiness as he sat in school; rebellious impatience with his Latin master and groundless quarrelling with his fellows. But what caused most turmoil in his soul was his knowledge that his love of Abbot Daniel could never sort with his other longing for Narziss, though he was sure all the while that Narziss loved him, could feel with his pain, and would succour it. Far more than even Goldmund dreamed were Narziss' thoughts engaged about him. He wished this fresh and lovely boy, his friend, could sense in him his opposite and completion, longed to see into his soul, lead him, and enlighten his mind, cherish him and bring him to blossom. Yet many reasons held him back, and of these almost all were known to him. Most was he impeded by his scorn of those many monks and scholars in the cloisters who made favourites of their pupils and novices. He, often enough, had felt with repulsion the longing eyes of elder men upon him, had encountered often enough with dumb rejections their proffered friendship and caresses. Now he could understand them better. He, too, could feel in him the urge to cherish and instruct the pretty Goldmund, evoking his clear, bright laughter, brushing his pale gold hair with tender fingers. But he would never do it. As a teaching-novice, invested with the dignity of a master, yet without a master's office and authority, he was schooled to especial prudence and self-vigilance. He had kept such distance between himself and scholars only a few years younger than he, as he might had he been twenty years their senior: always he had checked most sternly any particular liking for a pupil, while with those who were naturally repugnant to him he had forced himself to particular care and justice. His was a service of the intellect, to which his rigid life was wholly dedicated, and only in his secret mind, at moments when his thoughts were the least guarded, had he given himself up to the vice of pride, of delight in his own knowledge and keen wits. No – no matter how much any friendship with Goldmund might seem to offer him, such a bond could only be perilous: he must never let it touch the core of his life, fashioned to serve the spirit through the word; the life of a quiet and meditative guide, leading on his scholars, and not them only, to higher reaches of perception, oblivious of his own pleasure or pain.

Goldmund had been a year or more at school. He had played many games with his fellows beneath the limes of the outer court and under the lovely chestnut by the gate; games of ball and games of robbers, and snowball fights. Now it was spring, yet Goldmund was dispirited and weary: his head often ached, and in school he found it very hard not to drowse, but to mark his lesson well.

Then one evening Adolf came up to him, that scholar with whom his first encounter had been a fight, and who, in the course of this winter, had begun to study Euclid at his side. It was in the hour after supper, a play-hour, when scholars played in their dormitories, gossiped together in the

20

schoolrooms and, if they chose, might walk in the outer courtyard.

'Goldmund,' said Adolf, taking his arm and leading him down the cloister staircase, 'I have something to tell you, something to make you laugh. You are a pattern scholar and must certainly want to be a bishop, so promise me truly before I tell it you that you'll be a good companion and not breathe a word of it to the teachers.'

This Goldmund promised him at once. In Mariabronn there was honour among the scholars and honour between the monks that taught them, and at times these two came into conflict. But here, as in every other place, the unwritten law prevailed over the written, and never, since he became a scholar, had he broken the law and honour of his kind.

Whispering, Adolf drew him on; out through the gate and under the lime trees. Out here, he said, was a band of good resolute companions, of whom he, Adolf, was the leader. They had taken from earlier generations the habit of remembering, little by little, that they themselves would never be monks, and so, for a night, would break their enclosure, going in secret into the village. This was a pleasure and adventure which no good scholar should deny himself, and, in the thick of night, they would all creep back again.

'But then the gates will be locked,' said Goldmund.

Of course the gates would be locked, but that was what gave salt to the escapade: there were secret ways by which the adventurers could return; it would not be the first time they had done it.

Goldmund remembered a scholars' saying: 'To go out to the village' – a word he had often heard them use. By this was meant the escape by nights of schoolboys to every sort of joy and adventure, and such transgression meant a sound whipping from the fathers. But he knew well enough that among these resolutes of Mariabronn it was a point of honour to dare such consequence, and considered as a mark of high esteem to be asked to share in such transgression.

He would have answered 'no,' run back through the gates and to bed, he felt so sick and heavy at heart. That whole long day his head had ached. Yet now he felt abashed before Adolf. And who could tell? Perhaps out there there would be adventures, some new and beautiful thing to rouse him out of his dullness, the pain in his head and all his heaviness and sorrow. This was an escape into the world, furtive and forbidden, a little dishonest, and yet perhaps a release, a way to happiness. He stood there listening to Adolf, then suddenly laughed and answered 'Yes.'

Unmarked he and Adolf crept out of sight, into the shadow of the limes on the wide courtyard, already dim, its outer gates already fastened. His comrade led him into the cloister mill, where, through the dusk, and muffled by the clamour of the wheel, it was easy enough to escape unheard, unseen. They clambered in through its windows onto a damp and slippery heap of planks, one of which they would have to draw out, and lay it across the stream to make them a bridge. Then they were outside the enclosure, standing together on a high road, that stretched off pale towards the twilight, into dark woods. All this was full of secrecy and excitement, and pleased Goldmund very much.

A companion awaited them at the wood's edge – Conrad: after long waiting another came hurrying to join them; the big Eberhard. The four trooped on through the woods, above them the cries of nightbirds; two stars glittering far off, wet and clear, between still clouds. Conrad gossiped and laughed, and at times the others laughed with him, yet none the less felt solemn and scared of the night, and their hearts thumped and thumped within them.

On the far side of the wood, within a short hour, they reached a village. There all seemed to be asleep; the low white gables shimmered through the darkness, cross-hatched with dark ribs of timber. No lights anywhere. Adolf led them on past the silent houses; they climbed a wattle-fence and stood in a garden, their feet in the soft mould of beds, lurching down steps, and halting by the wall of a house. Adolf tapped at the shutter, waited and then tapped again: within somebody stirred, and soon a beam of light shot through the chinks: the shutter opened and one by one they clambered through the window, into a kitchen, with sooty chimney and earthen floor. On the hob was a little oil lamp; up its thin wick climbed a weak flame. There stood a girl, a scraggy peasant, who held out her hand to the newcomers, while behind, out of the darkness, crept another, a young maid, with long, dark plaits. Adolf had brought them gifts; half a loaf of white, cloister bread, and something wrapped in parchment, a handful of stolen incense, Goldmund thought, or wax from the altar tapers, or what not. The maid with the plaits stole back into the shadow, and went off, feeling her way, unlighted, to the door; was a long while gone, but returned with a grey stone pitcher, painted with blue flowers, which she gave to Conrad. He drank, and passed it to the others: all drank; it was a strong brew of cider.

They sat together in the flicker of the tiny flame; the two maids on stiff little stools, and around them, on the earthen floor, the scholars, whispering and drinking cider, Adolf and Conrad leading their talk. From time to time one would rise and stroke the scraggy peasant's neck and hair, whispering secrets in her ears, though the maid with the plaits they never touched. Perhaps, Goldmund thought, the elder was the servant of the house, and the little, pretty one the daughter. But that was all one to him, since he never meant to come back here again. Their secret creeping out of the mill, and stealing on through the dark wood, had been rare and fine, although not perilous. True it was all forbidden, and

23

yet he could feel no remorse at breaking a rule. But this, he felt, this visiting maids by night, was sinful. Though it might mean nothing to the rest, to him, who would be a monk and live chaste, all commerce with maids was very evil. No, he would never come back here again! Yet his heart beat faster and faster in the flickering light of the poor kitchen.

His comrades bragged to the two maids, striving to over-awe them with Latin tags, with which they adorned their speech. All three seemed in favour with the girls, to whom they crept closer and closer, with little sly love-words and fondlings, though the most they ever dared was a fearful kiss. They seemed to know to a hair what was permitted them; and, since their talk was all in whispers, the scene had in it something foolish, though Goldmund did not feel it to be so. He crouched very still on the floor, staring at the little flickering light, without a word for any of them. At times, with a kind of longing, he would peep round the corner of his eyes at the timid fondlings of the others. Then he would look out stiffly in front of his nose. But at heart he would fain have none of them, save only the little dark maid, though her especially he denied himself. Yet again and again his will forsook him as, when his eyes strayed back to the quiet sweetness of her face, he found hers fixed on him immovably. She sat and gazed, as if enchanted.

Almost an hour slipped by – never had Goldmund known so long an hour – the scholars were at the end of their jokes and Latin; it grew quiet, and they sat a little uneasily. Eber-hard yawned. The scraggy maid warned them it was time to go. All rose to their feet, all gave this serving-wench their hands, Goldmund the last. They reached out their hands to the little one, and again Goldmund was the last. Conrad led the way through the window, with Eberhard and Adolf after him : but when Goldmund made as if to follow he felt a hand on his shoulder draw him back. Yet he could not stay. Only when he found himself in the garden did he linger, and not avert his eyes. Out through the window the maid with the dark plaits bent down to him.

'Goldmund,' she whispered, and he stopped.

'Will you come back?' she asked him. Her shy voice scarcely needed a breath. Goldmund shook his head. She stretched forth her arms and took it between her hands, and he felt her little palms warm on his temples. She bent far down, till her dark eyes were close to his. 'Come back,' she whispered, and her mouth touched his in a child's kiss.

He darted off through the little garden to the others, stumbling over beds, pricking his hand on a rose bush, clambered the wattle paling, ran through the village after his fellows. 'Never again,' his will commanded him: 'Tomorrow! Tomorrow,' sighed his heart.

No one surprised these nightbirds; darkness sheltered their return. They reached their cloister-wall, bridged the stream, and climbed into the mill, swung down under the lime trees into the courtyard, and so, by silent ways, over penthouse roofs, through double-columned windows, to their dormitory.

Next morning the tall Eberhard slept so heavily that his room-mates had to rouse him with pillows. They were all in time for early mass, their morning broth, and so their schoolroom. But in school Goldmund was so pale that Father Martin asked if he were sick. Adolf warned him with a look, and he answered that he felt no pain.

Towards noon, in the Greek school, the eyes of Narziss never left him. This master, too, could see that Goldmund was sick, but asked nothing, and only watched him very closely. When the lesson was done he called to him, and, to escape the eyes of other scholars, sent him with a message into the library. Thither he followed him.

'Goldmund,' he said, 'can I serve you? I see you are in some sort of need. You are sick perhaps. If so we will put you to bed, and order you sick man's broth, and a cup of wine. You had no head for Greek today.'

He waited long for his answer. The pale boy looked up with puzzled eyes at him, hung his head, then raised it again, and strove with twitching lips to form a word. Strive as he might he could not answer. Suddenly, sideways, he sank down, leaning his forehead against a lectern, between two oaken faces of little angels, and broke into such a storm of weeping that Narziss, bewildered and ashamed, had for a while to turn away his face. Then he embraced the sobbing lad, and raised him.

'Now! Now!' he said, in a kinder voice than Goldmund till then had ever heard from him, '*amice*, weep as long as you will, and soon you will have wept out all your tears. So now – sit: you need not speak. I see you have had enough. Perhaps you have been striving all the morning to stand straight and let nobody mark you. Weep – it is the best you can do. Already dry, and able to stand up again? Come with me, then, to the sick-ward, and stretch yourself out, and tomorrow you will wake and be well again. Come, boy.'

He led him gently to the sick-ward, avoiding the rooms of the scholars, placed him in a quiet cell, in one of the two empty beds, and when, in obedience, Goldmund was beginning to strip his clothes off, went out to call the brother physician, and tell him that the boy was sick. As he had promised he went to the refectory, where he ordered him a broth and a cordial; these two *beneficia* of the cloister were considered a great boon by those scholars whose sickness was not a very grave one.

Goldmund lay in bed and strove to recover his wits. An hour ago he might have told himself clearly what it was that had tired him so that day, what fearful struggle in his heart had made his eyes so hot, and his head so empty. It was his mortal effort, again and again, with each new minute, to forget the night he had passed outside the cloister; or rather not the night itself, with its slippery climb across the mill-stream, its wild and glorious roamings in dark woods, its running here and there over hedges and ditches, through windows, down passages – but one instant of it: that instant only in the night when he had stood in the dark, at the kitchen window, feeling the maid's breath and hearing her words, touching her hand, and knowing her kiss on his lips.

And now, to all this, was added another terror, with new knowledge. Narziss felt for him in his heart. Narziss loved him, and had him in his thoughts; he, the delicate and wise, the teacher with the fine, mocking lips. But Goldmund had been foolish and wept before him, shamed, and unable to say a word; he had stood and sobbed before his eyes. Instead of doing as he had hoped, and subduing this learned man with the noblest weapons, with philosophy, Greek, feats of the spirit, and worthy stoicism, he had trembled and whimpered like a child. Never would he forgive himself that! Never again without shame could he look Narziss in the eyes. Yet, with his tears had gone the worst of his grief. This solitude, and the good bed, healed him; more than half the sting was drawn from his despair. Within the hour there came a lay brother with his broth, a piece of white bread, and a little cup of wine to go with it, such wine as scholars drank on feast-days. Goldmund ate and drank, and soon he had half-emptied his bowl, although, before it was done, he pushed it aside, and strove to think again. But he could not, so seized his bowl of broth, and ate it all up to the end. Later, when the door softly opened, and Narziss stole in to visit the sick scholar, Goldmund lay there asleep, and his cheeks were red again. Narziss stood with curious eyes, staring quietly down, in a kind of envy. He saw: Goldmund was not sick; no need to send him wine next morning. Now the ban was lifted, and they could be friends. Today it was the boy who needed him, and so he had been able to do him service. Next time he perhaps would be the weak one, needing love, comfort, and help, and then from this scholar he would take them, if ever it should come to such a pass.

CHAPTER THREE

It was a strange friendship that grew up between Narziss and Goldmund, one which pleased few, and, at times, almost seemed to displease the friends. Narziss the thinker had at first to bear the heavier burden. To him all was thought, even love. In their love he was the guiding spirit, and, for long, only he of the two was conscious of the depths, scope, and meaning of their bond. For long, although he loved, he was alone, knowing that his friend could not in reality be his till he had led him into the knowledge of himself. Goldmund gave himself up to this new love with eager joy, playing unconsciously like a child. Narziss, responsible and conscious, accepted and pondered their high destiny.

To Goldmund, Narziss brought relief and freedom. His first desire had been awakened by the sight and kiss of a pretty maid: all his longings to be cherished had been roused, and yet scared to desperation, and driven back. This had been his deepest fear: that everything he had dreamed till then of life, his hope and belief in his vocation, the future to which he felt predestined, had been imperilled at its root by that kiss given at the window, and the sight of the maid's dark eyes. Destined by his father to be a monk, and accepting the behest with his whole heart, aspiring with all the fire of his young ardour to the pious heroism of chastity, he had known, at this passing touch, this first call of life to his senses, that here was his enemy and demon; that women were his worst and constant temptation.

Yet now fate had seemed to save him; now, at the height

of his need, this friendship showed his longing a garden in flower, in which to erect new altars to his reverence. Here he might love without reproach, transmuting all the perilous fires of sense into clear, sacrificial flame.

Yet even in their earliest spring of friendship he encountered strange, unlooked for, impediments, sudden coldness, terrifying demands. It lay so far from his nature to see in his friend a contradiction and opposite. To him it seemed that only love was needed, only sincere and unconstrained devotion, to make one of two, and quench all differences, to build a bridge between all opposites. Yet how dour and certain, clear and inexorable was this Narziss. To him the harmless, natural gifts of love, a pleasant vagrancy together through the lands of friendship and desire, seemed things unknown, or never sought. This joy in paths leading nowhere, in dreamy straying without a purpose, was one he refused, and would not tolerate. True that when Goldmund was sick he had been troubled, that in matters of school and learning he helped and advised him on many points: he would construe difficult passages in books for him, open out new paths in the realms of grammar, logic, and philosophy; but never did he seem truly satisfied, and never at one with his friend. Often indeed he appeared to scorn him, and treat his words as a jest.

And Goldmund felt that this was more than pedantry, more than an elder and wiser, showing his power; that something far deeper lay behind it. Yet what this deep thing was he could never fathom, and so friendship often made him restless and sad. In reality Narziss knew well enough how much there was of worth in Goldmund. Nor was he blind to the fresh delicate loveliness of the boy, his natural power and zest for life, the sap and promise of his youth. He was no pedant, to feed a fresh young soul with Greek, or answer innocent love with logic. Rather he cherished this yellow-haired boy too much, and that to him seemed a danger, since love, for him, was not in the natural order, but a miracle. He must not, he felt, even satisfy his spirit with this freshness, never allow his affection to stray an instant into any pleasure of the senses. Since, if Goldmund fancied himself predestined to the life of a monk and an ascetic, a life-long striving after sanctity, Narziss was really framed for such a life, and only love at its highest was permitted him. Nor did Narziss believe that Goldmund had any vocation for the cloister. He, more than most, could read men's souls, and here, in the soul of one he loved, he read with redoubled clarity and perception. He had seen into the depths of Goldmund's nature, which he understood completely, despite their difference, as the other, lost, half of his own. And he saw this nature heavily encased; set about with the boy's own false imaginings, faults in his upbringing, things he must have heard his father say, and had long unravelled the whole simple secret of this young mind. His duty therefore was clear: to make known this secret to its bearer; to free his soul from its husk, restore this nature to itself. This would be hard, and, worst of all, perhaps, he would have to lose his dearest friend by doing it.

Slowly, with infinite care, he neared his goal. Months slipped away before any serious trial of his friend, any searching test, was essayed between them. So far, in spite of friendship, were they from each other, so taut the bowstring had been drawn. One of them saw, and one was blind, and so they went together, side by side. That the blind knew nothing of his blindness was a comfort only to himself. Narziss tried his first assault by attempting to discover what experience had caused Goldmund's weakness and tears, at the moment which drew them together. It was easier to unearth than he had thought. Goldmund had for long felt the need to confess the happenings of that night, but for this he trusted none save Abbot Daniel, and the abbot was not his confessor. When therefore Narziss, at a moment when it seemed to him good to do so, reminded his friend of the first occasion of their friendship, and gently touched on the causes of that grief, the boy answered without denials.

'I wish you were a consecrated priest, and that so I could make my confession to you. I should be glad to free myself of a sin, and very willing to do my penance for it. Yet I cannot say it to my confessor.'

With caution Narziss inquired more nearly; his path was found.

'You remember,' he began, by way of trial, 'that morning when you seemed to be sick. You cannot have forgotten, since that was the day which made us friends. It has often been in my mind. You perhaps may not have perceived it, but I was very helpless that day.'

'You helpless!' answered Goldmund, incredulous, 'I was the helpless one. It was I that had to stand there sobbing, and striving to bring out a word, until at last I howled like a baby. Oh – I am still ashamed when I think of it! I thought I should never be fit to show myself to you again. To think you ever saw me look so pitiful!'

Narziss pressed him very cautiously.

'I can understand,' he said, 'that you felt ashamed by it. Such a fine brave fellow as you, and to stand there weeping before his friend – more, before his teacher. That was unlike you. But then I supposed you to be sick. When ague shakes him even Aristotle may say strange things. And yet all the time it was not sickness. Not even a fever. So that was why you were so ashamed! Who feels any shame because he is shaken with a fever? You were ashamed because something had conquered you, because some enemy had you down. Had anything unusual happened then?'

Goldmund did not answer him at once. Then he said slowly: 'Yes, it was something out of the common. Let me suppose you my confessor. After all, I shall have to say it one day.'

With eyes cast down he told his friend the story of that night. Narziss answered with a smile:

'Well, it is forbidden "to go to the village". But many forbidden things may be done by us, and yet we scarcely trouble to even think about them. Or else we confess and are absolved, and so become free of our guilt. Why should not you, like almost every scholar, join in such a small escapade? Is that so bad then?'

Goldmund grew angry, and poured out a torrent of words.

'In truth you talk to me like a pedant. You know quite well what happens "in the village". Naturally I count it no great sin to break a few set rules of the cloister, and run out with a couple of schoolboys – though even that sorts ill with preparation for the life of a monk.'

'Hold,' exclaimed Narziss sharply, 'do you not know, *amice*, that for many of the greatest saints just such infringements have been necessary? Have you not heard that one of the shortest ways to sanctity may be a life of carnal riot?'

'Oh, enough,' Goldmund defended himself. 'I wanted to say that it was not any small infringement of rule that weighed me down that day, and caused me to weep. It was something else; it was the maid! It was a feeling which I could never make clear to you; a feeling that if I yielded to that temptation, if once I stretched out my hand to touch her, I should not be able to come back here, that hell would suck me in, like a swamp, and never let me go again. And I felt that then there would be the end of all fair dreams, all virtue, all love of God and His goodness.'

Narziss nodded very thoughtfully.

'The love of God,' he said, weighing his words, 'is not always one with our love of virtue. Oh, if it were only so easy! We know the good, for it is written. But God is not

33

only in what is written, boy. His commandments are the smallest part of Him. We may keep the commandments to the letter, and yet be very far from God.'

'But don't you see what I mean?' Goldmund complained.

'Certainly I see. You feel that in women, in carnal love, there is contained all that you think of as "sin", and "the world". Of all other sins you suppose yourself incapable, or, if you committed them, they would not weigh you down like this. They could all be confessed and atoned except this one sin.'

'Yes, that is how I feel.'

'Well, you see, I can understand you: nor are you altogether wrong. The story of Eve and her serpent is certainly not an idle tale. And yet, *amice*, you are wrong. You would be right, perhaps, if you were Abbot Daniel, or a patron saint, like your St Chrysostom; or if you were a bishop or a priest, or even a simple little monk. But you are none of these. You are a young scholar, and even if it be your wish to stay for ever here in the cloister or if your father wished it in your stead, you have taken no vows as yet; you are not consecrated. If today or tomorrow you found yourself seduced by a pretty wench, and so gave way to her temptation, you would have broken no oath, and done no sacrilege.'

'No written oath,' cried Goldmund very hotly, 'but one unwritten, and the holiest. The oath I have taken to myself. Can you not see that what may be valid for many others is yet invalid for me? Are you not you yourself still unconsecrated? You took no oath to live chaste, and yet you would never touch a maid. Or am I deceived in you? Are you not truly what you seem? Are you not what I think you? Have not you too long since made a promise in your heart, although you never swore it openly, before your brothers and superiors? And do you not feel bound by it for ever? Are you not like me then?'

34

'No, Goldmund, I am not like you; or rather not as you imagine me. It is true that I have taken a silent oath. There you are right. But in no other way am I like you. Today I will say to you a thing which one day I believe you will remember. It is this: our friendship has only one meaning, only one object — that I should show you how much you differ from your friend.'

Goldmund stood perplexed. The look in Narziss' eyes, the tone in his voice, had been such that they could not be withstood. But why did Narziss say such words? Why should Narziss' unspoken oath be more inviolable than his? Did he see in him only a child, to be teased and humoured? All the perplexities and sadness of their strange bond again assailed him.

Narziss no longer doubted the nature of Goldmund's secret. Eve, the eternal mother, lurked behind. But how had it ever come about that so joyous and beautiful a boy, so full of rising sap and nascent desire, should find in himself so bitter a resistance? Some demon must be at work in him, a hidden fiend to whom it was permitted to divide this noble being against itself, in the essence and primal urge by which it lived. Good then — this demon must be named, exorcised and made visible to all, and, when this was done, he could be conquered.

Meanwhile Goldmund, more and more, was neglected and shunned by his companions: or rather, in a measure, it was they who felt him to be shunning and avoiding them. His friendship with Narziss pleased none of them. The evil-tongued, those who had themselves loved one of the friends, slandered it as a vice against nature. Yet even those who could see plainly that here there was no vice to be reproved still shook their heads. None granted these two friends to one another. By this close friendship, it was said, they had set themselves apart from all the brotherhood: their fellows were not good enough for these noblemen; their spirit was against the community, was against the charity of the cloister, was unchristian.

Rumours of the two, complaints and slanders against them, began to reach the ears of Abbot Daniel. In his forty years and more in the enclosure he had watched many friendships between young men. These had their place in the general life of the monastery, were sometimes a jest and sometimes perilous. He kept apart, watching them carefully, without any direct interference. Such warm exclusive friendship as this was rare, and certainly not without its danger. Yet, since he could not doubt its purity, he put no hindrance in its way. Had Narziss not been as he was, placed midway between the scholars and teaching monks, the abbot never would have hesitated to lay on him commands that should separate them. It was bad for Goldmund that he had ceased to mingle with his fellows, consorting with an elder, and a teacher. But would it be just to prevent Narziss, the learned, the youth set apart and marked by intellect, Narziss acknowledged as his equal, nay superior, by every other teacher, from going the path which he had chosen; impede his mission to instruct? Had Narziss not taught as well as before, had his friendship led him into sloth, the abbot would have parted them at once. But nothing could be brought against him; only rumour, and the jealous mistrust of others. Moreover Daniel was aware of Narziss' unexampled gift; his penetrating, strange, perhaps presumptuous, knowledge of men. He did not rate such faculties too high: others would have pleased him better in Narziss. But he never doubted that this teacher had seen some especial virtue in his friend, and knew him better than any other. He himself had perceived in Goldmund nothing unusual, besides his winsomeness and grace, save a certain eager, almost owlish zeal in him, with which this mere young scholar, and guest of the cloister, already seemed to consider it his home, and himself a fully professed monk. Nor did he fear any danger that Narziss would spur on and encourage this touching but somewhat callow zeal. What he dreaded most for Goldmund from his friend was that Narziss might infect the lad's spirit with a certain learned pride and darkness of soul, although, for this particular scholar, the danger did not seem so great that such risk could not be incurred. No, he would not let mistrust infect him, nor show himself unthankful that great souls were sometimes given into his care.

Narziss pondered much on Goldmund. His faculty to perceive and recognize the characters and desires of human beings had long achieved its purpose with the other. Already he had found what he sought. All this glow and fervour of youth spoke clearly to him. Goldmund bore on him every sign of a strong and highly gifted man, rich in his body and his mind; at least of a man with unusual power of love in him whose desire and happiness lay in this: that his flame was easily kindled, that he had in him the gift of self-forgetfulness. But why was this young being, formed for a lover, this youth of the delicate perception, he who could love, and rejoice so well and fully in the scent of a flower or morning sunshine, a horse, a flight of birds, a stave of music – why was he set so firmly in his wish to become a priest and an ascetic?

Narziss pondered the matter long. He knew how Goldmund's father had encouraged this purpose in the boy. But could he have created the wish? What sorcery had he used upon his son to make him believe in such a vocation as his duty? And what kind of a man could this father be? Although purposely he had often turned their talk to him, and Goldmund had spoken of him frequently, Narziss had formed no clear image of this father: he could not see him.

Was not that unusual and suspicious? When Goldmund told of the trout he had caught as a child, when he painted a butterfly in words, aped the cry of a bird, spoke of a comrade, told of a dog or a beggar, their images arose, and could be seen. But when he spoke of his father there was nothing. No, if indeed the father had been so strong and powerful, so dominant over Goldmund's early life, his friend would have described him far better, would have brought him to life with far more joy. Narziss did not esteem this father much: the knight displeased him, and at times he would even doubt if this could be Goldmund's father after all. He was an empty idol. Yet whence had he derived such power? How had he filled Goldmund's soul with dreams so foreign to the boy's innermost being?

Goldmund often thought of Narziss. Certain as he was of his friend's deep love there remained the constant, irksome, suspicion that this friend was treating him as child. What did it mean that Narziss should for ever be telling him how unlike they were to one another? Meanwhile there was better to do than think, and this scholar had no taste for close thinking. There were many things to fill up the long bright days with. He would often hide with the brother-porter, since with him he felt quite at his ease, and from him would cajole permission to ride again on Bless, his pony. He was much beloved by the two laymen who dwelt in the cloister, the miller, and the miller's boy. With these he chased otters in the mill-stream, or would bake a loaf of fine prelate's bread with them, the scent of which Goldmund could pick out with his eyes shut from every other kind of meal they used. Though still he spent long hours with Narziss there were many when he renewed old joys and habits. High Mass and vespers were a pleasure to him, it pleased him to sing in the scholars' choir, he loved to say his rosary at a side altar, and listen to the solemn church Latin, watch, through an incense-cloud, the gleam of ornaments and chasubles, gaze up at the stiff and reverent images of saints along the arches of the nave: the Evangelists, each with his beast, St James, with his pilgrim's hat and staff.

These images seemed to entice him: he rejoiced to feel, in their stone or wooden shapes, some secret understanding with his mind; to think them, after a fashion, the undying, all-seeing patrons, guides and protectors, of his life. So too he felt a kind of love, a hidden, deep attraction, to the pillars, the scrolls over windows and doorways, and every garnishing of the altars; to the fair and clear-cut garlands, stems, and branches, flowers, and clumps of growing leaves, which burst forth from the stone of every plinth, entwining so persistently and vividly. To him it seemed a deep and precious secret that here, outside Nature, her plants and beasts, there should be this dumb second life, devised by men, and men themselves in stone: men, beasts, and plants in stone and wood. Often he would pass a free hour in taking copies of these devices: beasts, men's faces, clusters of leaves; and at times would strive very hard to draw them again out of his head, or from real horses, flowers, and live men's masks.

He loved their songs in the cloister-church, especially the canticle to Mary: the sure, stern lilt of these chaunts, returning on itself again and again to praises and bursts of supplication. He could either follow their severest sense with his prayers or, careless of what the words might mean, heed only the stately measure of the music, allowing its virtue to sink into him, its long, deep notes drawn out in plangent, resonant supplication, with pious reassurances of love. In his innermost heart he did not love learning, had no taste in him for grammar and logic, although these also had their beauty: his soul was given to the image, and sound world of the litany.

From time to time he would overcome his estrangement from his companions. It is sad and irksome to live long in the midst of coldness and despite. Again and again he made a sulky neighbour laugh in school, led on a silent roommate to gossip at night in the dormitory, strove for an hour together to gain love, and so win back a few eyes, faces, and hearts. Twice, much against his will, such proffered friendship was rewarded with the proposal that he should go 'to the village'. Then he took fright, and again shrank back into himself. No, he would go no more 'to the village'. He had managed at last to forget the dark-haired girl; never to think of her – or seldom.

CHAPTER FOUR

For long Goldmund's secret remained proof against all the siege that Narziss laid against it. For long, or so it appeared, Narziss had striven in vain to give this hidden thing its voice and teach his scholar the word by which to vanquish it. Goldmund in their talks gave no clear picture of his home, of the life whence he had come into this cloister. He had told of a shadowy father, deeply respected but ill-defined, with a misty tale of a mother, long dead and vanished, who remained as a pale name and nothing more.

Narziss, the skilled reader of other men, had come by degrees to see in Goldmund one of those who have had to lose a part of their lives; who, forced by some need or sorcery in themselves, cannot think of certain matters in their past. He saw he would gain nothing by teaching or questioning, saw he had trusted too much in the power of reason, and spoken many vain and useless words.

But his love of Goldmund had not been vain, nor their custom of being much together. In spite of the depths that sundered them each had learned much from the other's company. Between them, beside the language of reason, there had slowly come into being another tongue; a speech of signs and of the soul; as, between two dwellings, though there be a high road for waggoners, on which litters pass, and riders may jog from place to place, there are also set around it many lanes, field-tracks running in and out, hidden paths on which children play, walks under trees for lovers, the half-seen trails of cats and dogs. By degrees Goldmund's magic power of speaking his mind in images had found ways into the thoughts of his friend, creeping into all they said together: so that Narziss, without aid of words, learned to feel for himself and to define much of Goldmund's nature and perceptions. Slowly, in the light of these, a bridge of love was built from soul to soul, and words could find a way along it. So that at last, when neither was expecting it, as they sat on a feast-day in the library, there arose a talk which led them on to the very heart and meaning of their friendship, and illumined its whole future course.

They had sat discussing astrology, a forbidden science, and not pursued in the cloister. Narziss had said that it was a striving to order and arrange after their kinds the many divers sorts of human beings, their predestined character and their fates. Here Goldmund broke into his words.

'You speak of nothing but differences! I have slowly begun to see that they form your own particular whimsey. When you speak of this great difference between us I always feel that it lies in nothing, save in your own strange hankering to find differences.'

Narziss: 'Right. You have hit the nail on the head. That is what I mean — that to you differences mean little, while to me they are the most important things. Mine is the nature of a scholar, and my branch of scholarship is science. And science, to quote your own words, is nothing else than a "strange hankering after differences". Her essence could not be better defined. For men of science nothing is so important as the clear definition of differences. To find, for instance, on every man, those signs which mark him off from all other men: that is to know him.'

Goldmund: 'But how? One has peasant's shoes and is a peasant; another a crown on his head, and is a king. There are your differences! But these are seen by children, without any science.'

Narziss: 'Yet when peasant and king are clad alike children can no longer distinguish between them.'

Goldmund: 'No more can science.'

Narziss: 'Perhaps it can. I admit that science is not any cleverer than a child: but she is more patient. She works more nearly, and sees more than the coarsest of differences.'

Goldmund: 'And so does every clever child. He could know a king from his look and bearing. But to be plain: you fine scholars are proud, and you always think us duller than yourselves. We can sharpen our wits without science.'

Narziss: 'I am glad to see you have noticed that. Soon you will have noticed, too, that I do not mean skill or cunning when I speak of differences between us. I do not say: "Your wits are sharper, or you are better or worse than I." I only say: "You are not I".'

Goldmund: 'That's easily understood. But you do more than speak to me of differences in outward signs; you speak of a difference in fate and predestination. Why, for example, should your destiny be other than mine? You, like me, are a Christian; we are both resolved to live as monks. And you, like me, are the child of our good Father who is in heaven. Our goal is the same – eternal happiness; our resolves the same – to return to God.'

Narziss: 'Very good. It is true that in books of dogma one man is the same as any other. But not in life. I think that the Redeemer's beloved disciple who laid his head upon His breast, and that other disciple who betrayed Him, had not both been framed for the same destiny.'

Goldmund: 'You are a sophist, Narziss. Along such paths we shall never come together, you and I.'

Narziss: 'There is no path by which we can come together, Goldmund.'

Goldmund: 'Don't speak so, Narziss.'

Narziss: 'It is my earnest. It is not our task to come together; as little as it would be the task of sun and moon, of sea and land. We two, my friend, are sun and moon; sea

43

and land. Our destiny is not to become one. It is to behold each other for what we are, each perceiving and honouring it in his opposite; each finding his fulfilment and completion.'

Goldmund hung down his head, discomfited: his face had grown sad. At last he answered:

'Is that why you so often mock my thoughts?'

Narziss delayed with his reply. Then, in a clear, hard voice, he said:

'Yes, that is why. And you must learn to bear with me, dear Goldmund, for not taking your thoughts more seriously. Believe me I mark and study your every accent, and all your gestures, each smile that comes into your face. All that in you seems essential and necessary is real to me. Why therefore should I give your thoughts the place of honour in my mind – you, who have so many other gifts?'

Goldmund smiled sadly: 'I said you always think of me as a child.'

But Narziss was still inflexible: 'Some of your thoughts seem to me the thoughts of a child. Yet remember what we said a while ago; that a sharp-witted child need never be stupider than a scholar. It is only when children speak of science that scholars need not take them seriously.'

Goldmund became impatient: 'But when I do not speak of science you mock me! You speak as though all my piety, and wish to make progress in my studies, and my longing to be a monk, were so much babbling.'

Narziss eyed him very gravely: 'When you are truly Goldmund you do not babble. But you are not always Goldmund. I long for nothing so much as to have you Goldmund through and through. You are no monk – no scholar. Scholars and monks may both be hewn of coarser wood. You fancy you are not learned enough for me, have too little logic, and are not pious enough. None of all these. Only – you are not enough yourself.'

44

Though here in their talk Goldmund, in perplexity, left his friend, with anger against him in his heart, not many days had passed before he himself wished to continue. And this time Narziss succeeded in showing him, in a clear, vivid image, such as he himself would use and accept, the true difference in their natures.

Narziss had talked himself hoarse: yet today, he felt, Goldmund had heard him more willingly, had let his words sink deeper into his soul, and already he began to have power on him. His success made him yield to the temptation to say even more than he had intended: he let his eloquence bear him onwards.

'Listen,' he said, 'I am only your superior in this: I am awake, whereas you are only half-awake, and at times your whole life is a dream. I call that man awake who, with conscious knowledge and understanding, can perceive the deep, unreasoning powers in his soul, his whole innermost strength, desire, and weakness, and knows how to reckon with himself. The task that brings us together, the whole aim and purpose of our friendship, is that you should learn from me how to do it. In you, Goldmund, nature and intellect, consciousness and the world of dreams, are set very far from one another. You have forgotten your childhood, which still strives up from the depths of your being, to possess you. It will always make you suffer till you heed it. But enough: awake, as I said, I am your superior. There I am stronger than you, and so I can help you. But in all things else, *amice*, you are mine, or rather you will be so when you know yourself.'

Goldmund had listened keenly till the words 'You have forgotten your childhood.' On these he started and flinched, as though an arrow had pierced his body, though this was not perceived by Narziss, who spoke, as he often did, with half-shut eyes, or staring far away into the distance, as though, if he did not see, the words came easier. He had not

45

observed how Goldmund's lips were shaking, nor how his face had begun to pale.

'Your superior – I?' stammered Goldmund; but only to have something to answer: it was as if his whole body had been lamed.

'To be sure,' Narziss concluded. 'Men of dreams, the lovers and the poets, are better in most things than the men of my sort; the men of intellect. You take your being from your mothers. You live to the full: it is given you to love with your whole strength, to know and taste the whole of life. We thinkers, though often we seem to rule you, cannot live with half your joy and full reality. Ours is a thin and arid life, but the fullness of being is yours; yours the sap of the fruit, the garden of lovers, the joyous pleasaunces of beauty. Your home is the earth, ours the idea of it. Your danger is to be drowned in the world of sense, ours to gasp for breath in airless space. You are a poet, I a thinker. You sleep on your mother's breast, I watch in the wilderness. On me there shines the sun; on you the moon with all the stars. Your dreams are all of girls, mine of boys —'

Goldmund had heard him open-eyed, and Narziss spoke with a kind of oratorical self-abandonment. Many of his words, like blades, had entered the heart of his friend. In the end the boy turned pale and closed his eyes, and when Narziss saw, and rose in sudden fear, Goldmund, white as death, could only whisper:

'Once I broke into sobs and wept before you; you remember. That must never happen again. I should never forgive myself, or forgive you either. Quick now, leave me! Let me alone! You have said some terrible words to me.'

Narziss was sick at heart. His thoughts had borne him away, since he felt that he spoke better than usual. Yet now he perceived, in consternation, that something in what he had just said had struck his friend a deathly blow; that in some way he had pierced to the quick of him. He found it hard to leave him at such a time, and so, for an instant, he lingered on, till the frown on Goldmund's forehead warned him. Then he went off in great confusion, leaving his friend in the solitude he needed. Though Goldmund wept, his tears were not enough to release the pent-up grief in his soul. In the agony of the deepest wound, and no hope at all of ever healing it – as if his friend had suddenly knifed him to the heart – he stood alone, panting heavily : his breath constricted as though by death, his face waxen, his hands limp at his sides. This was the old pain, only sharper; the old confusion in his spirit, the feeling that he must look on something horrible, something, it might be, too fearful to bear. And now there was no sobbing storm of tears to ease the anguish in his mind. Holy Mother of God, what was it then? Had something happened? Had he been struck to death? Had he killed a man? What terrible thing had they been saying?

He gasped like one that has drunk poison, was filled to bursting with the thought that now he must shake free of something deadly, some barb, stuck in his heart. He stumbled from the room, flinging his arms out like a swimmer, wandered, without knowing it himself, into the stillest, emptiest part of the enclosure, along corridors, down steps, into the air. He had come to the inner heart of the monastery, the central cloister; in the cool light a sweetness of roses lay on the warm air, chilled by stone.

Narziss in that hour had done unwittingly what for long it had been his conscious wish to do: he had named and exorcised the demon inhabiting his friend. Some one or other of his words had stirred a secret in Goldmund's breast, and his demon had reared up in agony. For long Narziss strayed through the schoolrooms, seeking his friend, but found him nowhere.

Goldmund stood in the shadow of the arches that open

onto the little cloister garden: from the pillar above three heads of beasts peered down on him, three stone heads of dogs or wolves, and leered. His pain raged through his mind, finding no way to light, no way to reason. A shudder, as of death, clipped at his gullet: he looked up, not knowing what he did, at one of the capitals, saw over him the three heads of beasts, and at once it seemed that three wild heads crouched, grinning and howling, in his entrails.

'Now I must die at once,' he knew with a shudder. And then, shaking with his fear: 'Or else go mad, and so these beasts will devour me.'

Twitching and shuddering he sank down, huddled at the foot of the column; his pain too great, he had reached its uttermost limit. His face sank between his hands, to his mind came the darkness that he craved.

Abbot Daniel had had a bad day. Two of the elder monks had come before him, peevish, chiding, slandering one another to him, their father; complaining of some old, trivial, rankling difference, born of their spleen, which now, again, had roused them both to bitter strife. He had listened, though all too long, to their bickerings, admonished them, as he feared without success, and in the end sent them sternly away, each with his somewhat heavy penance. Then, worn out, he had gone down to pray in the nave, had said his prayer, and stood up unrefreshed, and so wandered forth to the inner cloister, led on by its faint scent of roses, to stand a minute snuffing in the air.

He came upon the scholar, Goldmund, stretched out there senseless on the flags, gazed down in horror and astonishment at his deathly quiet, the pallor of his cheeks, whose young body was, as a rule, so full of life. Today had surely been an evil one. And now this, to add to it all! He tried to raise the boy, but found himself too feeble for such a load. Then, sighing deeply, he went off, to call for two of the younger brothers to take him up, and carry him to the sick-ward, sent for Father Anselm, the leech, and lastly for Narziss to come before him, who soon was found, and did his bidding.

'You know already?' he asked him.

'Of Goldmund? Yes, father. They told me he was sick, or had injured himself, and I saw them carry him along.'

'Yes. I found him in a swoon, lying where he had no leave to be, in the inner cloister; and he is not injured, although unconscious. This does not please me. And I feel that you have a share in it, or at least that you must know how it came about. It was for that I sent for you. Speak.'

Narziss, as cold as ever in speech and bearing, gave a short account of what he had said to Goldmund, and how some unlooked-for power had wrought its effect in him. The abbot shook his head, displeased.

'That was strange talk,' he said, and forced his words to be calm. 'You have just described such a talk as might be called an attack on another soul. It is, I might even say, the onslaught of a superior, a confessor. But you are not Goldmund's confessor: you are not confessor to any; you are not consecrated! How comes it then that you permit yourself to talk with this scholar as though you had spiritual warrant to instruct him of things which only a confessor has power in? As you see, the issue has been evil.'

Narziss answered softly but steadily:

'It is still too early, father, to judge the issue. I was somewhat startled by the violent effect of what I said, but I do not doubt that the issue of my talk with Goldmund will be to heal him.'

'That is to be seen. It was not that I sent for you to speak of, but your own action. What impelled you to say such things to this scholar?'

'He is my friend, as you know. I bear him a particular love, and feel I understand him very well. You tell me I spoke to him like a confessor. I only did so because I felt I know him better than he himself.'

The abbot shrugged:

'I know you have particular gifts. Let us hope you have done no lasting harm with them. Is Goldmund sick? Had he a fever? Had his nights been restless, or had he not been eating enough? Was there any pain in his body?'

'No, till today his body has been in health.'

'And otherwise?'

'His soul was ailing, father. You know he has long reached the age when men begin to struggle with carnal longing.'

'I know. He is seventeen.'

'Eighteen, father.'

'Eighteen. Well, late enough, then. But these are merely natural struggles, which every man encounters in his life. They would not be enough to make you call him sick in soul.'

'No, holy father, in themselves they would not be enough. But Goldmund's soul was sick already, had long been so, and, therefore, for him, such struggles are more dangerous than for others. I think that he is suffering now because he has forgotten some of his past.'

'Indeed. Which part of it, then?'

'His mother, and all that went along with her. I know no more of her than he. I only know that with her must lie some of his grief. He seems to know nothing of his mother; only that he lost her early, and yet he makes me feel he is ashamed of her, though from her he must have inherited most of his talents, since nothing of what he tells me of his father ever shows me that father as the man to beget such a fair and goodly son. None of what I tell you is hearsay, father, I draw my own conclusions from certain signs.'

These last words set the abbot thinking. At first Narziss had seemed to him foolish, and arrogant, he had even smiled a little as he listened. Now he thought of Goldmund's father, the knight with the wizened face and tricking speech, and remembered, as he searched his mind, some words he had said of the boy's mother. She had shamed him, he declared, and run from him; in his son's mind he had striven to wipe out all memory of the vices which might be her legacy. And in this, said the knight, he had succeeded, and his son was ready to give himself to God, to expiate the sins of his mother's life.

Never before had the abbot been so little pleased with Narziss. And yet, how this thinker had hit the mark; how well he seemed to know his friend! He began to question him further, of all that had happened in their talk.

'It never was my intention to rouse in Goldmund the heavy grief and pain that assail him. I reminded him that he did not know himself, and said he had forgotten his mother, his childhood. Something in my words must have pierced his spirit, forcing its way down into the darkness in him, with which I had been struggling so long. He was as though beside himself: he stared at me as if he no longer knew me, as if he had forgotten his own name. I had often said to him that he slept, and had never in all his life been wideawake. Now he is awake, there can be no doubt of it.'

Here he was dismissed, without a penance, though with the command not to see his friend at present.

Father Anselm had had them lay the boy in bed, and now sat by his side to watch him. It seemed to him best to use no powerful means for bringing Goldmund to his senses, who looked as white as death, the old man thought, peering down, out of kind, wrinkled eyes. He felt the pulse, and laid his hand on the heart. This lad, he said to himself, must be gorged with some monstrous dainty, a bunch of wood-sorrel, or some such thing. They were all alike! He could not look at his tongue.

Anselm was fond of Goldmund, though he never could abide his friend, Narziss, that puffed-up novice, too young to have ever been made a teacher. There was the mischief! That Narziss must have some share in this silly mishap. What need had such a fresh and pleasant scholar, natural and open of heart, to consort with that arrogant pedant, so vain of his Greek that it seemed to him the only thing in the world!

When, long after this, the abbot opened the door of the sick ward, he found old Pater Anselm still peering anxiously. What a young, pretty, guileless face: yet all he could do was to sit and study it, longing to bring it back to life, yet unable to give any aid. To be sure the lad might have the colic; he would prescribe him rhubarb and a cordial. But the longer he watched those sallow, distorted features, the more suspicious grew Pater Anselm. He had had his experience! Several times in his long life he had been with those possessed by devils. He hesitated, even to himself, to formulate the whole of his thought: he must wait and examine before he spoke. But, he reflected grimly, if this poor lad is struck down and bewitched, we shall not have far to seek for the culprit: and he shall answer it in full!

The abbot came to the bed, bent gently down over the boy, and drew back one of his eyelids.

'Can you rouse him?' he asked.

'I would rather wait a little longer. His heart is sound. Nobody must approach him.'

'Is he in danger of death?'

'I do not think so. No wounds on his body, or trace of any blow or fall. He has only swooned. Perhaps it is the colic. Great pain will often rob us of our senses. If he had been poisoned there would be fever. No, he will come to himself and live again.'

'Might it not have come from his mind?'

'I would not say no. Is nothing known of it all? Some

one may have caused him to take fright: some news of a
death, or an insult and a violent quarrel. Then it would all
be clear.'

'We know nothing. Have a care that none be let in to
him. I beg you not to leave him till he wakes, father; and
if he seems in danger call me, even in the middle of the
night.'

Before he left the old abbot bent again over the boy. He
thought of the knight, his father, and the day when this
pretty little yellow-head had been left here for schooling
in the cloister, where they all took to him at once. He too
had been glad to see him come. But in one thing Narziss
had hit the mark: in no way did this boy resemble his
father. Alas, how much grief there was in the world! How
vain and useless all our strivings! Had he neglected the care
of this poor boy? Had he even given him the right confessor?
Was it in order that, in their house, no other should know
this scholar so well as Narziss? Could Narziss help him —
a novice; neither monk nor consecrated priest? He, whose
thoughts and opinions seemed all so arrogant, so full, almost,
of hate? And God alone knew if this Narziss had not himself long been mishandled: God alone could tell if all his
obedience were not a mask, if at heart he were not a mere
heathen. He, the abbot, would have to answer for everything that might one day come to these two young men.

When Goldmund woke it was dark. His head swam, no
thoughts came into it. He could feel himself lying on a bed,
but where he knew not. He strove, and yet nothing came to
him. How had he travelled here: from what strange country of new knowledge? He had been in some far-off place,
where he had seen some rare and glorious sights, terrible,
and never to be forgotten. Yet now he was forgetting them
all. When was it? What was this thing that had risen up
before him, so dolorous, mighty, full of beauty, to fade out
again? He strove to see far down into himself, to the deeps

out of which this thing had come. What had it been? A covey of vain images swirled around him. He could see beasts' heads, three heads of dogs, and caught a whiff of roses in his nostrils. What pain he had felt! He shut his eyes. The terrible pain! He fell asleep.

Then he woke and saw the thing he sought, through a swiftly melting fog of dreams: saw the image, and hunched himself together in a pang of agony and joy. He could see – his eyes had been opened – the tall, shining woman, with full, red lips, her hair blown by the wind: his mother! And in that instant he heard a voice, or seemed to hear it, speak these words: 'You have forgotten your childhood.' He listened, thought; then remembered. Narziss' voice. Narziss! In a flash it was all before his eyes, he could see it all, it was all known. Oh, mother – mother! Mountains of rubbish had been levelled, oceans of forgetfulness dried up: from blue, shining eyes, like a queen, the lost woman smiled at him again, her image unutterably loved.

Pater Anselm, who had fallen asleep in his chair, beside the bed, awoke. He had heard the sick boy stir and draw in a breath. Gently he rose: 'Who's there?' asked Goldmund.

'Don't be scared. It's I – Father Anselm. I'll strike a light.'

He set a flame to the wick; it lighted up his kind puckered face.

'But am I sick?' questioned the boy.

'You fell into a swoon, sonny. Give me your hand, and let me take your pulse. How do you feel yourself?'

'Well, thanks, Pater Anselm. You are very kind to me. I need nothing? I am only weary.'

'To be sure you are weary. Soon you'll drop off again. Take a mouthful of spiced wine first, though. Here it is, all ready waiting for you. We'll empty a glass together for friendship's sake, lad.'

He had ready his pitcher of cordial, and the water boiled

to go with it. 'You and I have both slept sound this long while,' chuckled the leech. 'You'll say I'm a fine surgeon to watch the sick, and too old to keep awake to do it. Well there¯ – we're all of us human. And now let's drink this magic draught together. There's nothing so good as a tipple together in the night. Good health to you.'

Goldmund laughed, clinked cups, and drank with him. This hot cordial was spiced with cloves and gilliflowers, and sweetened with fine sugar-beet: he had never known so good a drink.

He remembered how once before he had been sick, and then Narziss had taken care of him: now it was Pater Anselm, and he was very gentle and kind. It made him laugh, it was all so fine and pleasant, to lie there in the night by lamplight and empty a cup of wine with the old physician.

'Have you a bellyache?' said the father.

'No.'

'And I who said you must have the colic! That's nothing, then. Put your tongue out. Well, once again, old Anselm has shown himself a fool! Tomorrow you'll stay warm in your bed, and I'll come along and take a look at you. Have you finished your wine? Good may it do you! Let's see, there may be a drop more of it. Well, if we share and share alike there'll be another half-cup for each of us. You scared us all finely, Goldmund. You lay out in the cloister like a corpse. Are you certain, now, you haven't a bellyache?'

They laughed, and shared the dregs of sick man's wine: from eyes that were clear and tranquil Goldmund looked up, happily and merrily. The old man went off to bed. Goldmund lay awake a while longer. Visions rose up slowly again in him, again there came to life in his soul the radiant, yellow-haired image of his mother. Her presence filled him through and through, like the sweet breeze blown across a hayfield; a breath of warmth, of life, tenderness, courage. Oh, mother, how could I ever have forgotten you?

CHAPTER FIVE

Till now, though Goldmund had always known something of his mother, it had only been through other folks' stories. Her image had faded from his mind and, of the little which he believed himself to know of her, he had always kept something hidden from Narziss. 'Mother' had become a thought of which it was forbidden him to speak. Once she had been a dancing woman, had been beautiful and wild, noble, but of bad and heathenish kindred. Goldmund's father, or so he told his son, had raised her up from poverty and shame. Since he could not be sure she was a Christian he had had her baptized and instructed in her faith; had married her, and made her a great lady. But she, after a few years of submission to him, and ordered life, had returned to her old arts and practices, arousing dissensions, and tempting men; strayed from her home for days and weeks together, gained the ill-repute of a witch, and, at last, gone her ways for evermore, though her husband had many times pardoned her, and taken her back into his favour.

For some while longer her fame had lived, like an evil fire, flickering in the trail of a comet, till that too had died, leaving no trace. Slowly her goodman had recovered from years of terror and mistrust, shame, and ever-fresh surprises. And, in place of his evil wife, he had loved this son, very like his mother in face and bearing. The knight had grown grizzled and penitent, instilling into Goldmund the belief that now he must offer himself up, in expiation for his mother.

Thus Goldmund's father would talk of his lost woman, although he was not easily brought to speak of her; and when he delivered Goldmund at the cloister he had given the abbot certain hints of it. His son had known it all, but only as a mean and evil tale, which he must put for ever from his mind; strive with all his might to forget.

But what indeed was lost and forgotten was his own true memory of his mother; that other, different mother, in his soul, not built of the sayings of the knight, or the dark, wild rumours of serving-men. This reality, seen by his heart, had soon been forgotten; yet now her image, the star of his babyhood, arose in him.

'I cannot tell how ever I managed to forget her,' he cried one day to his friend. 'Never in all my life have I loved as I loved her, with a love so glowing, and unwithheld. And never have I honoured another like her, or thought any other so beautiful. To me she is the sun and moon. God knows how it ever should have been possible to dim this shining love of her in my mind, and so make of her at last the evil, pale, formless witch she became for me, and was to my father for many years.'

A short while since, Narziss had ended the novitiate, and would soon be a clothed and consecrated priest. His bearing towards his friend had changed, though Goldmund, who, before his swoon, would chafe at Narziss' questions and admonishments, as irksome pedantry and arrogance, now, since his pain had brought back memory, was full of ever-wondering gratitude for the skill and wisdom of his teacher. How deeply had this uncanny scholar read in him: how exactly probed his hidden sore! And then, how cunningly healed it! Not only had his swoon left no trace, but something seemed to have melted out of his nature; some vain, owlish, longing to be a saint, a certain solemn, over-devout frivolity; his belief that it was his bounden duty to be more of a monk than monks themselves. Goldmund seemed both older and younger since the day on which he discovered his true self. And for all this he had to thank Narziss.

But now Narziss, for some short time, had been very prudent with his friend. He watched him humbly, no longer as his teacher and superior, though he had gained a very willing disciple. But he saw Goldmund endowed from a hidden source with gifts for ever denied him. It had been granted him to foster their growth, yet he himself would have no share in them. He rejoiced to see his friend made whole and free, and yet in his joy there was some sadness. He felt himself a husk, to be sloughed aside: a surmounted rung on the ladder of perfection; could see the near conclusion of their bond, which had brought such gladness to his heart. And he still knew Goldmund better than the boy himself, who now, though he had found his soul again, and was ready to follow where it would lead him, could not tell as yet which way it might beckon. But Narziss had perceived that his friend's path led through lands he himself could never travel in.

Goldmund was less eager for learning; his itch for disputation had left him utterly. Now, in all their talks, he would speak with shame of many of his former arguments.

In the meantime, since he had ceased to be a novice, or else because of what he had done to Goldmund, these last days had roused in Narziss a need for retirement and self-questioning, askesis, and devotional exercise; the urge to fast much, and say long prayers, often confess, and lay voluntary penance on himself. Goldmund tried hard to share these inclinations. Since his cure all his instincts had been sharpened. Though as yet he had not any inkling of what the future might have in store, he could feel every day more clearly, and sometimes with terror in his heart, that now his real destiny was upon him, a time of respite and innocence at an end, and the life in him rose to meet its fate. The omens at times seemed full of happiness, keeping him awake half the night, like a sweet, bewildering caress, but often they were dark and terrible.

His mother, the long-forgotten, had come again. She had brought great joy, but whither did her siren-call entice him? Out into the unknown world, into enthralment, need, perhaps to death. She would never lead him back to safety; to the peace of cloister schools and dormitories, and a life-long fellowship with monks : her call had nothing in it of the commands laid on him by his father, which for so long he had imagined his own wishes. Yet this new emotion, at times as strong, poignant, and full of life as any sensation in his body, awakened all the piety in Goldmund. In repetitions of many prayers to God's Holy Mother in the sky he poured forth the too-great emotion in himself, which drew him back to his own mother. But many of these prayers would end in strange, haunting dreams of delight and triumph, day-dreams of the half-awakened senses, visions of her in whom all his senses had their share, and then, with its scents and longings, the mother-world would lie about him : its life calling enigmatically; his mother's eyes were deeper than the sea, eternal as the gardens of paradise, she lulled him with gentle, senseless words, or indeed with all the gentleness of the senses : life would taste sweet and salt upon her lips; his mother's silky hair would fall around him, tenderly brushing his mouth and longing eyes, and not only was this mother all purity, not only the skyey gentle-ness of love, the clear, serene promise of smiling happiness; in her, somewhere hidden beneath enticements, lay all the storm and darkness of the world, all greed, fear, sin, and clamouring grief, all birth, all human mortality.

Her son would lose himself in these dreams, in the many-threaded woof of his living senses. More than the past which he had loved came alive, as by magic, in his mind, than babyhood and his mother's tenderness, the twinkling dayspring of his life : these thoughts held promises and threats, enticements and dangers to come. He would wake at times from such a vision of his mother as both madonna and ravisher, as filled him with a sense of horrible sin, sacrilege, and vilification of God, death from which he could never rise again. At others all was harmony and release. Life full of her secrets lay about him: a magic garden grown with enchanted trees, flowers bigger than any in the world; deep, misty hollows. In the grass there were glittering eyes of unknown beasts, smooth powerful snakes glided along the branches: from every bough hung clusters of glittering berries which, when he plucked them, swelled within his hand, spurted soft, warm sap, like blood, or had eyes on them, and slithered cunningly. He would lean against a tree and feel its trunk, clutch down a branch and stare at it, touch, between bough and stem, a cluster of thick, wild hairs, like the hairs in an armpit. Once he dreamed himself his patron-saint, the holy Chrysostom, the golden-tongued, whose mouth was gold, from which he uttered golden words, and the words were a swarm of little birds, rising and flying off in glittering bands.

And once he dreamed he was grown to manhood, yet could only sit on the ground, like a child, had clay before him, and kneaded it like a child, till the clay began to shape itself in images: a little horse; a bull; a little woman. This kneading of clay delighted him, and he gave his little men and women the biggest genitals he could fashion, since, in his dream, that seemed to him very witty. He grew tired of his game, stood up and left it, and suddenly felt something behind him, something huge and noiseless, and, looking back, saw in great amazement and terror, yet not without some pleasure in his work, that his little clay men and women were huge and alive. Powerful, dumb giants, they came marching past him, growing, and growing as they went; out into the world, high as towers.

He lived more truly in this dream-world than in the real.

The school, the courtyard, the dormitory, the library, the
cloister chapel, had become only the surface of reality, a
trembling outer film, encasing the image-world of dreams,
the deep intensity of life. Any trifle served to rend this
outer veil; some sound of a Greek word, in the midst of the
dullest lesson, a whiff of scent from the herb-stuffed wallet
of Pater Anselm, the simple-gatherer; a glance at the clustered leaves which twined over the arches of a window;
such nothings as these could dispel the illusion called reality,
opening up, beneath its sober peace, the whirling depths,
torrents, and starry heights of the world imagined in his
soul. A Latin initial would frame the radiant eyes of his
mother, a long-drawn note in the Ave open some inner gate
in Paradise, a Greek letter become a galloping horse, a rear-
ing snake, sliding in and out among flowers, till it vanished
and left him staring down at the dull page of a grammar
book.

He never told all this; only now and then would he hint
of it to Narziss. 'I believe,' he said to him once, 'that the
cup of a flower, or a little, slithering worm on a garden-
path, says more, and has more things to hide, than all the
thousand books in a library. Often, as I write some Greek
letter, a theta or omega, I have only to give my pen a twist,
and the letter spreads out, and becomes a fish, and I, in an
instant, am set thinking of all the streams and rivers in the
world, of all that is wet and cold; of Homer's sea, and the
waters on which Peter walked to Christ. Or else the letter
becomes a bird, grows a tail, ruffles out his feathers, and
flies off. Well, Narziss, I suppose you think nothing of such
letters. But I tell you this: God writes the world with them.'

'I esteem them highly,' said Narziss sadly, 'they are magic
letters, and every dream can be conjured up with them.
But, alas, they cannot be used for learning sciences. Thought
loves definitions, and clear forms, and needs to be able to
trust its signs for things: it likes what is, and not what is to

be, and so it cannot bear to call an òmega snake or a theta bird. Now, Goldmund, do you believe what I told you, that we should never turn you into a scholar?'

Oh yes, Goldmund had long since agreed with him, and long since known himself resigned to it.

'I no longer care to strive after your learning,' he said, almost with a laugh, 'and I feel now for all learning and intellect what once I used to feel for my father. I used to think I loved him very dearly, hoped that I had made myself very like him, and swore by everything he said. But my mother came back, to show me what true love is, and, beside her image my father's memory shrank to nothing. It displeased me; I came near hating it. And now I almost think that all learning is like my father; that it hates my father, and has no love in it, and so I begin to despise it a little.'

Though he jested in saying all this he could not bring any smile to his friend's sad face. Narziss studied him in silence, his glance almost a caress. Then he said:

'I understand you well. Now we have no need to dispute: you are awake, and so you have seen the difference between us, the difference between men akin to their father and those who take their destiny from a woman; the difference between spirit and intellect. And now too you will also soon have perceived that your life in the cloister, and longing to be a monk were a misprision; a device of your father, who sought to purge your mother's memory, or perhaps only to be revenged on her. Or do you still imagine it your destiny to stay here all the days of your life?'

Goldmund considered a while, studying the hands of his friend, thin, delicate, white hands; soft and yet resolute. Every one could perceive in them a monk's hands.

'I do not know,' he replied, in the slow, singing, voice in which he had spoken for some time, a voice which seemed to pause on every syllable. 'How can I tell you? You may be judging my father a little harshly. He knew much grief. But perhaps in this too you may be right. I have been many years in this cloister, and yet he has never come to visit me. He hopes I shall stay here always. Perhaps it would be best if I did, since I, too, used always to wish it. But today I no longer know myself, nor my real wishes and hopes. Once everything seemed so easy, as easy as the letters in a grammar-book: and now nothing is easy, not even those letters. I cannot tell what is to become of me, and, for now, I don't want to think about it.'

'Nor need you,' answered Narziss. 'Your way will soon lie clear before you. It has begun by leading you back to your mother, and will bring you even nearer her than you are. As for your father I do not judge him too harshly. Do you feel you would like to go back to him?'

'No, Narziss, that I should not! If I felt I could, I would do it, as soon as I was clear of school. Or even now, perhaps, since I never intend to be a scholar. I have learned enough Greek and Latin and mathematics. No, I do not want to go back to my father.'

He gazed out abstractedly; then, with a sudden cry:

'But what trick do you use to question me thus again and again, in words that illumine my mind, and make me see into myself? Now again it is only your question if I want to go back to my father which makes me perceive that I do not. How do you do it? You seem to know everything. You have taught me so many things about our friendship which I did not understand at the time I heard them, and later they seemed full of meaning and consequence. It was you who told me I take my life from my mother; you discovered first that I lay under a spell, and had lost the memory of my childhood. How is it you can know me so well? Could I learn that from you also?'

Narziss smiled and shook his head.

'No, *amice*, that you could never learn. There are men

who can learn many things, but you are not one of them. You will never be a learner. Why should you be? You have no need of it. You have other gifts, and far more than I: you are richer, yet not so strong as I am, and your life will be fairer than mine, and harder. Often you did not want to understand me; you jibbed away like a young colt. It was not always easy, and I must have made you smart. But you were asleep, I had to wake you. It hurt you even to be put in mind of your mother, and your pain was so great that they found you stretched half-dead in the inner cloister. It had to be – no, leave stroking my hair! No, stop I tell you! I can't bear it.'

'So you think I shall never learn! All my life I shall be stupid, like a child.'

'There will be others there from whom you can learn. You, child, I have taught you all I could, and now the lesson is over.'

'Oh no,' cried Goldmund, 'it was not for that we became such friends. What kind of friendship would that be, that ended at our first milestone. Have you known me so long that I weary you? Have you had enough of me?'

Narziss paced quickly up and down, his eyes to the ground, and came to a halt before his friend.

'Let be,' he whispered, 'you know very well you do not weary me.' He eyed him as though in doubt, then started his pacing to and fro again; stopped again, and stared at Goldmund, with firm eyes from his stern face. In a low, clear, resolute voice he spoke: 'Listen, Goldmund. Our friendship has been a good one: it has had its particular goal, and reached it, since now you are roused from your half-sleep. But now we have no more to achieve. Your purposes are still uncertain, and I can neither lead you nor accompany you. Ask your mother; ask her image, and listen. My aims are not misty and far-off; they lie here around me in the cloister, demanding fresh efforts with every hour. I can be your friend, I can never love you. I am a monk, and have taken my oath to God. Before I make my final vows I shall ask to be relieved of my office as teacher, and go into retreat to fast and do penance. Throughout that time not a word of earth must pass my lips; not even to you.'

Goldmund understood. He answered sadly:

'So now you will do as I should have done had I entered the order as a monk. But when your retreat is over, and you have fasted, watched, and prayed long enough – what will your goal be then?'

'You know that,' Narziss answered him.

'Yes. In a few years you will be the teaching-superior, then, perhaps comptroller of the school. You will better the teaching, add many new scrolls to the library: perhaps you will write books yourself. Will you not? You shake your head. What will you do then?'

Narziss smiled rather sadly: 'What shall I do in the end? Who knows? I may die as head of the school, or as abbot or bishop. That is all one. But my aim is this: always to be where I can serve best, where my disposition, talents, and industry may find their best soil and be most fruitful. That is the only aim in my life.'

Goldmund: 'The only aim for a monk. Is that what you mean?' Narziss: 'Oh yes; and object enough. A monk's whole life may be spent in learning Hebrew; or he may live to annotate Aristotle, to decorate his cloister church, or shut himself up and meditate on God, or a hundred and one other things. But none of all these are final aims. I neither wish to multiply the riches of the cloister, nor reform the order, nor the Church. What I wish is to serve the spirit within me, as I understand its commands, and nothing more. Is that an aim?'

Goldmund considered this:

65

'You are right,' he said. 'Have I hindered you much in its achievement?'

'Hindered? Oh, Goldmund, no other has helped me more than you. You sometimes set difficulties in my way, but I am not one to shrink from difficulties. I learnt from all of them, and, in a sense, I overcame them.'

Goldmund interrupted him almost mockingly:

'You have conquered them all. But tell me this. By helping me and giving me back my memory, and freeing my soul, and so restoring me to health – were you truly serving the spirit? Have you not robbed the cloister of a zealous and obedient novice, and perhaps raised up an enemy of the spirit, one who will do and feel the opposite of all that you consider holy?'

'Why not?' said Narziss very gravely. '*Amice*, you still know so little of me! True that in you I have spoilt a future monk, and in place of him have opened out a path in you which may lead you to no common destiny. But even if tomorrow you were to burn down this whole fair cloister, or propagate some wild heresy in the world, I should not feel an instant's remorse for having helped you to it.'

He laid friendly hands on Goldmund's shoulders.

'Listen, little Goldmund, this too is part of my ambition! Whether I become a teacher or abbot, confessor, or whatever else it may be, I never wish to be of such a sort that when a strong man crosses my path – a man of high worth and real capacity – I find myself unable to understand him, find myself his enemy in my heart, unable, if I will, to further his purposes. And this I say to you: You and I may turn into this or that; we may meet either good or bad fortune; but you never shall lack my help if you truly ask for it, and feel in your heart that you need me, since my hand will never be against you. Never.'

These words had the ring of a farewell, and indeed they were the foretaste of their leave-taking. As Goldmund stood gazing at his friend, with his resolute face and eyes that seemed to see far beyond him, he could feel, past all deceiving, that now they were no longer brothers and comrades, no longer one another's kind: that their lives had sundered them already. This man who faced him was no dreamer, waiting — as he must wait, on some hidden admonition of destiny: he was a monk who had inscribed himself on the roll, accepting his strict duties and rule; a soldier in the service of his order, of God and the Church. But now Goldmund knew for a certainty that here was no place for such as he: he was homeless, and the unknown world awaited him. So also had it been with his mother. She had left house and court, man and child, company and all fair pastime, good order, reverence, and duty, to go forth into the huge, uncertain world, and in it had certainly perished. She had had no aim, as he, too, had none. Aims were set to others, not to him. Oh, how well Narziss had seen all this, long ago: how right he had been!

And already, soon after this, Narziss seemed to have vanished from his life. It was as though he were suddenly wrapt away. Another teacher gave his lessons: his lectern in the library stood empty. Still hovering, not altogether invisible, he would sometimes pass quickly through the cloisters; at others his murmuring voice could be heard at a side-altar, as he knelt praying on the stones. He had entered his retreat for his final vows; it was known he kept strict fasts and rose three times in the night for office. He was still there, yet half in another world, could be seen, though seldom, but never reached. They could not speak, and now there could be nothing more between them, and though Goldmund knew that Narziss would return, would sit again at his desk, his place in the refectory, and his voice be heard again in the schools, yet nothing of what he had been would ever return with him. Narziss would not belong to him any more.

So that, with this thought, it grew clear to him that Narziss alone had made him love the cloister and the monks, with their grammar and logic, study, and intellect. It was Narziss who had given all this its meaning: Narziss's example had enticed him; to become as Narziss had been his aim. It is true that the abbot was still there, and he, also, Goldmund had honoured; he had loved him, too, and seen in him his example. But the others, the teachers, his fellow-scholars, the dormitories, the cloisters, the refectory, the lessons and exercises in syntax, the service of God – the whole of Mariabronn – without Narziss it all meant nothing. Why did he still remain here? He waited under this cloister roof like an undecided shelterer from the rain, taking cover under any tree or penthouse; a guest who still delays because of the unfriendliness of the world.

Now Goldmund's days were nothing but a lingering farewell. He would seek out all the things that had meaning for him, all he had grown to love in the cloister, beginning, in amazement, to perceive how few of the faces that surrounded him would cost him any pain after he left them. There was Narziss and old Abbot Daniel, and the good, gentle leech, Pater Anselm; and then, perhaps his friend, the brother-porter, and perhaps the miller, their jolly neighbour. Yet even these seemed half-unreal to him. Far harder to say farewell to the great stone virgin in her chapel, the apostles over the arch of the gateway. He would stand for an hour together examining them, or the beautiful, intricate carving of the choir-stalls, gaze at the cloister fountains, the pillar with its three beasts' heads, and, in the court, would lean against the lime-trees and the chestnut. Soon all these would be a memory, a little picture-book in his heart. Even now, though still they surrounded him, they were beginning slowly to fade out. With Pater Anselm, who liked his company, he would go forth, gathering simples, or gossip with the men at the mill who sometimes asked him into their mill-loft, to a platter of baked fish, and wine. But already it was strange, and half a memory. As over there, in the twilight of the church and of his cell, Narziss, withdrawn to fast and pray, had taken on the dimensions of a ghost, so too was this reality fading round him: it all breathed autumn and the past.

Now there was only one thing left that mattered: the wild beating of his heart, an anxious pricking of desire in him, the joy and terror of his dreams. To these he now belonged, and let them master him. As, one of many class-mates, he seemed to study, he could sink down into himself and forget his fellows, plunge through the murmuring tor-rent in his heart, and let its current swirl him away with it; into deep pools echoing with dark music, clouded depths of fairy sounds and happenings, all calling him with the voices of his mother, their thousand eyes his mother's eyes.

CHAPTER SIX

One day Pater Anselm called Goldmund into his pharmacy, a little sweet-smelling room, where he felt at home. The old man showed him a dried plant, neatly laid up between two sheets of parchment, and asked if he knew its name, and could describe it, as it looked out there, growing in the fields. Yes, said Goldmund, he knew it well, and the name of the plant was John's Wort. He was asked for an account of all its particulars, and the old monk seemed satisfied with his answers. He therefore commanded the scholar to go out that afternoon, and gather him an armful of these simples, giving him exact direction of the places where they most delight to grow. 'You will have half a play-day for your pains, and so lose nothing by your trouble, and I think you have nothing to say against it. It takes some study to know herbs as well as all your silly grammar books.'

Goldmund thanked him for such a pleasant errand to spend a few hours plucking flowers, instead of fidgeting on a bench: then, that his pleasure might be complete, he begged for the loan of Bless, his horse, from the brother-ostler, and, after dinner, led it from its stall. It neighed him greetings, he jumped on its back, and galloped off, through the warm summer's day, rejoicing. He rode here and there for more than an hour, sniffing the fresh air and scent of the fields, and very pleased to be on horseback. Then he remembered his commission, and sought a place which Pater Anselm had described to him. This found, he tethered his horse in the shade of a maple tree, talked to him for a while and gave him bread to eat, and so set out to gather simples. Here were some strips of fallow land, grown about with every sort of herb, little wizened poppy-stalks, with their last faded petals still upon them; and already many ripening seed-pods stood there among the withered vetch, and wild succory, blue as the sky, and spotted knotweed: green lizards ran in and out upon the heap of stones between two fields, and there, too, already, stood the first yellow clumps of flowering John's Wort, and these Goldmund started to gather.

When he had a good armful he sat down to rest, on the heap of stones. It was hot, and he looked with longing at the deep blue shade that edged a far-off wood, though he did not care to stray so far from his plants, and from Bless, his horse, whom he still could see, from where he sat. So there he stayed, on his heap of stones, sitting very still, in the hope that a lizard would run his way, sniffing his John's Wort, and holding its little petals against the light, to see the hundred pin-points in each.

'How wonderful,' he thought, 'that each of these thousand tiny leaves should have a whole starry heaven hidden in it.' It was all a miracle and a mystery; the lizards, plants, stones, all of it together! Pater Anselm, who liked him so well, had grown too stiff to come out gathering leaves: the rheum took him in his legs, and now there were many days when he could not stir, though none of his own simples would heal him. Perhaps he would soon be dead, and the herbs in his closet still give out their fragrance, though old Pater Anselm was gone for ever. But he might live many years yet, another ten or twenty years, still with the same thin white hair and criss-crossed wrinkles under his eyes: and what would Goldmund be in twenty years? Oh, it was all hard to understand, and all sad, although it was so beautiful. Nobody really knew anything. People lived; they went here and there about the earth and rode through forests; so much seemed to challenge or to promise, and so many sights to stir our longing: an evening star, a blue harebell, a lake half-covered in green reeds, the eyes of beasts and human eyes; and always it was as though something would happen, something never seen and yet sighed for, as though a veil would be pulled back off the world; till the feeling passed, and there had been nothing. The riddle was still unsolved, the hidden magic unrevealed, so that, in the end, people grew old, and looked comic, like old Father Anselm, or wise like old Abbot Daniel, though really perhaps they still knew nothing, still waited, pricking up their ears.

He picked up an empty snail-shell; it had rolled, with a tinkle, off a stone, and was warmed through and through by the sun. Sunk deep in thought, he stared at the notched spirals, the curious twist of the little crown, the frail, empty house, in which light was pearly. He shut his eyes, to know it with his fingers only. That was an old game he often played with himself: holding the shell gently between his fingers, he stroked it lightly round and round, not pressing it, rejoicing in all shape, all magic of corporeal things. It seemed to him that, with our minds, we are inclined to see and think of everything as though it were flat, and had only height and breadth. Somehow or other, he felt, this denoted the lack and worthlessness of all learning, yet he could not seize his thought, and define it. The snail-shell slipped through his fingers: he felt very drowsy, and longed to sleep. His head fell forward over his plants, which gave out a powerful scent as they started to wither, and so he fell asleep in the sunshine. Over his shoes swarmed ants; the bundle of fading herbs lay on his knees. Bless champed and whinnied under the maple.

Then some one came from the far-off wood, a young peasant woman, in a pale-blue, faded gown, with a scarlet kerchief bound round her dark hair, and her face tanned brown by the summer, a red gillyflower gleaming between her lips, and paused in her stride to watch the sleeper. For long she stood some distance away, to examine him, curious, and full of mistrust: then, convinced he was asleep, came cautiously nearer, on bare feet. Her fear of him melted away. This pretty sleeper pleased her well, and now he did not seem to her dangerous. How did he come to be out here in the fields? He had been plucking flowers, she saw with a smile, and already his flowers were almost faded.

Goldmund opened his eyes, returning from a forest of dreams. Now his head was pillowed on softness, since it lay in a woman's lap; down over his sleepy, wondering eyes, two strange eyes bent, warm and brown. He did not start, there was no danger, the two warm, brown stars shone down on him. The woman smiled at his astonishment, and in her smile he saw such gentleness that suddenly he, too, began to smile. Down to his smiling lips she bent her mouth, and, in a flash, as their lips joined, Goldmund remembered again that night in the village, and thought of the little maid, with her dark plaits. But their kiss had not ended yet; her mouth still lingered upon his, drawing out its love, enticing, stroking against him, till at last the lips fastened with greedy power, firing his blood, and sending it coursing through his body, while in a long, dumb act, the brown woman taught him to love, letting him seek her and find her, letting her love flame up in him and stilling it.

Their clear, brief transport flickered and died out between them, glowing like a swift gold flame, bending upon itself, and dying down. With closed eyes they lay there together, his head on the peasant woman's breast. There was no word said between them: she stirred no muscle in her body, only gently stroking his hair, letting him come slowly to himself again. At last he opened his eyes.

'You!' he said. 'Where do you come from?'

'I am Lisa,' she answered him.

'Lisa,' he said it after her, delighting in it. 'Lisa, you are very beautiful.'

73

She bent her mouth down to his ear:

'Did you never love before me?'

He shook his head. Then suddenly sat up and stared about him, across the fields, and at the sky.

'Oh, the sun is almost down,' he cried, 'and I must get back —'

'Where then?'

'Back to the cloister. To Pater Anselm.'

'In Mariabronn? Is that your home? Oh, stay with me a little longer.'

'I would stay if I could.'

'Well, stay then.'

'No, it would not be right. And now I have to pluck some more of these —'

'But are you a brother in the cloister?'

'No. But I am a scholar. I shall not stay there. Could I come to you, Lisa? Where do you live. Where lies your house?'

'I live nowhere, my heart. But tell me your name. So, Goldmund is what they call you. Give me a kiss, little Gold-mouth. Then you may go.'

'You live nowhere? Where do you sleep, then?'

'If you like I'll sleep with you in the forest, or in the hay together. Come tonight.'

'Oh yes, I'll come. Where shall I find you?'

'Can you hoot like a little owl?'

'I never tried it.'

'Well, try it now.'

He tried. She laughed and was pleased.

'Well, come to me tonight, out of the cloister, then, and cry like an owlet, and I'll be waiting for you. Do I please you then, little Gold-mouth, pretty one?'

'Oh, Lisa, yes, you please me greatly. I will come. God keep you: I must go now.'

On his steaming horse Goldmund galloped back to the

cloister, and was glad to find Pater Anselm very busy. A brother had been paddling in the mill-stream, and had cut his foot on a flint in it.

Now he must seek out Narziss. He asked of him from the lay-brother who waited at supper in the refectory. No, said the brother, Narziss would eat no supper that night. He had fasted all day long, and must be asleep, since during the night he would have a vigil. Goldmund made haste. Now, during his long penitence and retreat, his friend spent his nights in the penitents' cells, in the inner cloister, and without thought of rules, he ran thither, stood at the door of Narziss's cell and listened. But no sound came from within. He stole in on tiptoe. He had no thought that all this was strictly forbidden him.

There, on his narrow pallet, lay Narziss, like a corpse stretched out in the twilight, stiff, on his back, his pale thin face to the ceiling, his hands crossed on his breast. But he did not sleep, his eyes were wide. He stared, without a word, at Goldmund, not angry, but with no sign of life, so wrapped, it seemed, from outer things, and sunk in contemplation beyond time. He had some pains to recognize his friend, and grasp the sense of what was said to him.

'Narziss, Narziss! Forgive me for having roused you. But I did not do it in idleness. I know it is forbidden you to speak to me, but I beg you to forget that, and answer.'

Narziss raised himself up, blinking a minute in astonishment, as though it cost him an effort to come to life.

'Is it necessary?' he asked in a dead voice.

'Yes, very necessary. I am come to bid you farewell.'

'Yes, then it is necessary. And you shall not have come to me for nothing. Come now, sit here beside me. A quarter of an hour will be enough, and then the first vigil will have begun.'

He sat, thin and haggard, on his plank: Goldmund came over to his side.

'Forgive me,' he said, in a guilty voice. This cell, the pallet, Narziss's face, worn with concentration and lack of sleep, his eyes, half-conscious of the world, all told him clearly that he was troublesome.

'There is nothing to forgive. Don't heed me. I lack for nothing. You say that you come to take your leave of me. So you are going away from the cloister?'

'I am; this very day. Oh, how shall I say it to you? Suddenly it has all been decided.'

'Is your father there, or any messenger from him?'

'No, nothing. Life itself has come to me. I shall creep off, without the abbot's leave or my father's. I shall break from the cloister, Narziss, and bring shame on you.'

Narziss stared down at his white fingers, issuing, thin as ghosts, from the wide monk's sleeve. There was no smile on his stern, exhausted face, yet a kind of smile in his voice, as he answered:

'*Amice*, our time is very short. Tell me all I need to know, and say it as briefly and clearly as you can. Or must I tell you what has happened to you?'

'Tell me,' begged Goldmund.

'You are in love, boy. And already you have known a woman.'

'How you always read me.'

'This is easy. Your face and bearing, *o amice*, show every mark of that drunkenness which men call "being in love". But say it yourself, please.'

Goldmund shyly touched his friend's shoulder.

'You have told yourself. And yet, Narziss, this time you did not say it well or accurately. This is all quite different from drunkenness. I lay out there in the fields, and fell asleep, and when I woke my head lay on the knees of a woman, whose beauty was such that I felt my mother had come back to me, and taken me back into herself. Not that I held this woman to be my mother. She has dark brown

76

eyes, and dark hair, and my mother's hair was gold a
mine, her face was altogether different. And yet it was
she. She called me, and this woman was her messenger, who
cradled my head in her lap, and kissed as softly as a flower,
and was gentle with me, so gentle that her first kiss made
me feel as though something in me had melted, till my
whole body thrilled with wonderful pain. All the longing I
had ever felt in my life, all secrets and sweet fears that had
lain asleep in me, came to life, transformed and renewed,
with another meaning in them. In a little time she had made
me older by many years. Now I know much, and of this I
was suddenly quite certain : that now I can live here no
longer, not another day in this cloister. I shall escape as soon
as it is dark.'

Narziss listened, and nodded.

'It has come upon you suddenly,' he said, 'but this is
what I had always expected. I shall think of you often, and
long to have you back, *amice*. Can I do anything to help
you?'

'Yes, if you can bring yourself to do it, say a word in
my excuse to our abbot, so that he does not condemn me
utterly. You and he are the only two in the house for whose
thoughts and good opinion I care anything. You and he.'

'I know. And is that all?'

'Yes – though I would ask this : when later you think of
me, pray for me. And . . . thanks, Narziss. . . .'

'For what, Goldmund?'

'For all your patience, and your friendship. Also for having listened to me today, when everything outside you is
so difficult. And thank you, too, for not having tried to
hinder me.'

'Why should I? You know my thoughts about all this.
But where will you go, my Goldmund? Have you any aim,
you who are going to your woman?'

'Yes. I shall go along with her. I have no other aim

part from her. She is a wanderer, a homeless one, or so he says; perhaps a gipsy.'

'I understand. But listen, Goldmund: your way with her may be a very short one. You should not trust her too much, I think. Perhaps she has a husband and kindred. Who knows what kind of welcome they may give you!'

Goldmund bent closer to his friend.

'I know all that,' he said, 'although, till now, I had not thought it. But as I told you; I have no aim. This woman is not my aim, although she was very tender and gentle with me. Though I go to her it will not be for her sake. I go because I must; because it calls me.'

He sighed and was silent, and they sat close up to one another, sad, and yet happy together in their knowledge that their friendship would never end. Then Goldmund spoke again:

'Don't think me altogether blind and reckless. I am glad to go because I am sure I cannot stay; because today I have seen a miracle. But I do not deceive myself, or fancy that outside these walls it will all be pleasure and junketing. I can feel that my way will be rough: but, rough, or smooth, I hope it will be beautiful. It is very fine to love and know a woman, and give her love. Don't laugh at me if what I say sounds crazy to you. But tell me this: to love a woman, and comfort her with my love, entwine my body with her body, and feel myself altogether hers – all which you would call "to be enamoured", the thing you seem to scorn a little – why is it to be scorned? For me it is my path into life.

'Oh, Narziss, and now I must leave you. I love you, Narziss, and many thanks for giving up your sleep today for my sake. Now it is very hard to say farewell. Will you forget me?'

'Don't grieve yourself for that, or me either, Goldmund. I shall never forget you. You will come back to me. I will pray that you come, and I shall be waiting. And if you eve[r] find things go hard with you, come to me, or send me your messenger. God speed and keep you, my friend.'

He had risen. Goldmund embraced him. They did not kiss, since his friend shrank from all caresses, but he stroked his hands.

Darkness had gathered. Narziss closed his cell door after him, and went along the cloister into the church, his sandals clattering on the flags. Goldmund, with love in his eyes, watched the lean figure go from him and vanish, swallowed up round a bend in the corridor by the gaping darkness of the church. How confused everything was, how infinitely glorious and unknowable. This, too – how terrifying and strange: to have come upon his friend at such a moment, when, worn almost to death with fasting and long meditation, he had nailed his senses to a cross, bowed his head to the stern rule of obedience, resolute to serve only the spirit, offering his body as its sacrifice; had become, through and through, *minister verbi divini*. There like a corpse he had lain, half-dead from weariness, with white face and pale thin hands, yet ready to give his clear, attentive sympathy to the friend about whose hair and body there still clung the savour of a woman, ready even to sacrifice the short time of rest between two penances, in order to listen to his hopes. It was a glorious thought that there should be such love in the world, love that is all spirit and selfless joy. How different from that love in the sunny field, the drunken, reckless love of flesh and blood. And yet both were love. Alas, now Narziss had gone from him, having shown him again so clearly, in this last hour together, how far apart their natures lay. Now Narziss would be kneeling before the altar on aching knees, summoned and prepared for a night of vigil in which only two hours sleep were granted him, while he, Goldmund, would steal off and, somewhere under trees, meet Lisa, to play again the sweet game of beasts.

Narziss would have found some notable things to say of it. But — he was not Narziss. It was not for him to unravel these fair and terrible enigmas, with notable sayings to explain them: he could only follow his own mad path as Goldmund, not knowing whither it would lead. All he could do was to give himself up to his own fate, and love his praying friend in the dark church no less than Lisa's tender warmth, who awaited him.

As now, in his heart a thousand conflicting longings, he stole away beneath the cloister limes, and climbed into the mill to escape, he could only smile at the sudden memory of that evening long ago with Conrad, when they had used this same secret passage out of the cloister, stealing off together 'into the village'. How scared he had been, for all his excitement, as they crept out, one by one, through the little hole! Now he would wriggle out through it for ever, onto far more forbidden, dangerous ways, yet now he felt no fear, had no thought for the abbot, had forgotten the brother-porter, the teachers.

This time there were no planks in the mill, so he had to cross without a bridge. He stripped, and flung his clothes to the opposite bank, went naked through the deep, cold, swirling mill-stream, up to his chest in icy water. As he dressed again his thoughts returned to Narziss. Now, utterly shamed, he could see clearly that he, at this moment, only did what the other had led him to and foretold for him. That clever, mocking, Narziss came back, all too distinctly, into his mind, the thinker to whom he had said such foolishness, the friend who had opened his eyes at the cost of such sharp pain in an hour of destiny. He could hear again, as though Narziss were saying them, some of the things his friend had told him: 'You sleep on your mother's breast, I watch in a desert.' 'Your dreams are all of girls, mine of boys.'

For an instant his heart seemed to freeze; he stood alone

in the night, and fearful: behind him the cloister, an unrea
home, yet one he had loved and long inhabited.

Yet, with his fear, came another feeling: that now Narziss
had ceased for ever to be his superior and guide, the friend
whose eyes were used on his behalf. Today, he felt, he had
strayed into a country in which he must find his way alone,
through which no Narziss could ever guide him. He
rejoiced to think that he knew it: it shamed him and
troubled his heart to look back to the days of his discipleship.
Now he could see; he had ceased to be a scholar and a
child.

It was good to know: and yet, how hard to take his leave.
How hard to remember Narziss, on his knees over there in
the dark church, to have no more to give him; not to be able
to help, to be nothing to him. And to leave him for so long,
for ever perhaps; not to feel him there any more, hearing
his voice, seeing his clear and beautiful eyes.

He shook it off, and went on down the pebbled road.
A hundred paces clear of the cloister wall he stopped, drew
in a breath, and let out as good an owl-cry as he could
muster. Another owl-cry answered, away down the stream,
out of the distance.

'We call to each other like beasts,' was the thought that
came to him, as he remembered their loves, that afternoon.
Only then did he remember clearly how few had been
the words that passed between them, how neither he nor
Lisa had thought to speak until their sports were at an end.
Even then such words as they had used had been hurried,
and of no account.

What long talks he had had with Narziss! But now, it
seemed, he had entered a world where words meant nothing,
where they called to one another with bird-cries, and never
spoke. He was ready for that, since today he had had no
need of words or thoughts, only of Lisa, of her blind caresses
without words, her desire and its sighing consummation.

Lisa was there already, coming towards him from the wood. He stretched forth his arms to touch her, stroked her head with gentle, feeling hands, her hair, her throat, her shoulders, her slim young body to her hips. His arm slid round her waist, and they went off together without a word, nor did he think to ask where she was leading him. Her step was sure, through the dark wood, and he had some trouble in keeping up with her, she seemed to see, like a marten or a fox, with night-eyes; went forward without once stumbling or running her head against dark branches. He let her lead him on to the thick of the wood, through the night; into blind, secret places without words, in a land without any thoughts. His had all fallen asleep, even thoughts of his home, the cloister, and thoughts of Narziss.

Without a word they sped on together through woodland darkness, over soft-springing moss and hard clusters of roots. At times between two high, sparse, tree-tops, a pale glint of far-off sky, and again the darkness was pitch-black. Branches whipped his cheeks, brambles caught his clothes and held him. She, in every place, knew her way unerringly, never lost her trail, seldom stopped, seldom delayed. In a long while they came out on an open space where, over widely separated pines a wan sky stretched away before them and around them, lay a valley clothed in meadows. They waded through a little, silently trickling, stream. Here in the open it was even quieter than in the woods: no rustle among the bushes, no scurry or call of birds and beasts in the night; no crackle of twigs. Lisa stopped by a big haystack.

'We'll stay here,' she said.

They lay down together in the hay, glad at first to lie side by side and rest, stretched out to listen to the silence, with both their bodies a little tired, feeling the sweat dry slowly off their foreheads, their cheeks cool. Goldmund crouched happily weary, hunched up his knees in sport, and spread his legs again, breathed in the night, and the scent of hay, in long deep breaths, thinking neither of past nor future. Or, by slow degrees would he let himself be drawn into love by the magic warmth and odour of his beloved, repaying, little by little, her stroking hands with his caresses, suddenly happy as she too began to take fire, and wriggled up closer at his side. No, there was no need here of words or thoughts; clearly he felt whatever was needful for this delight, the young sap rising in his body, the clear, gentle loveliness of the maid, her joyous warmth and clinging greed, knowing at once that she asked of him another way of love than that which she had shown him in the sunshine; that now she would not teach or entice him, but lie there tense, to receive his onslaught and his longings. Quietly he lay, and let her current of passion flow through his body, the little, gently rising flame which, in exultation, came to dancing life in both together, making of their gipsy's sleeping-place a richly glowing canopy of splendour, set in the wide, silent night. As he bent over Lisa's face to kiss her lips in the dark, suddenly a pale, lost shimmer surrounded her eyes and forehead: he stopped in wonder, as the light glowed up to quick intensity. Then he understood, and turned his head. The creeping moon had climbed to the open sky over long, black, straggling battlements of forest. He watched the pale light flow gently onwards, down across her forehead and cheeks, over the round, warm throat, and whispered his delight in her ear: 'Oh – you are beautiful!'

She smiled, as though for a gift: he rose on his elbow and gently pulled away her garment, helping her to cast the stuff aside, and strip off her husk till breast and shoulders lay shining in the soft, cool light. Held in enchantment, he followed the tender shadow with eyes and lips along her body, kissing and gazing. She lay like death, as if bewitched; her eyes cast down, and on her face a look of ceremony, as though in that instant, even to her, her beauty lay revealed for the first time.

CHAPTER SEVEN

W HILE the moon stole on over fields, higher and higher hour by hour, the lovers lay on their pearly bed together, lost in their games, waking and sleeping, and, as they woke, turning towards each other, ever to renew the fire between them, wreathed into one another, and so to sleep again. Their last embraces done they lay worn out, Lisa with her face deep in hay, Goldmund stretched on his back, staring up at the milky sky. A deep sadness rose in both of them, from which they turned for refuge to sleep. When he woke, Goldmund saw Lisa, busy with her long dark hair. He watched her for a while through sleepy eyes.

'Already awake?' he said at last.

She turned with a start, as though he had surprised and terrified her. 'I must leave you now,' she said in a low voice, a little guiltily. 'I did not think to wake you.'

'But now I am awake. Must we go on our way already, then? We have no home.'

'Yes, yes, we have,' said Lisa. 'You come from the cloister.'

'I shall never go back to the cloister. I am like you; I am all alone and have no home. Of course I will go along with you.'

She looked away from him.

'Goldmund, you cannot come with me. I must go to my husband. He will beat me for staying out the night. I shall tell him that I lost my way, but of course he will never believe me.'

Then Goldmund remembered how this had been predicted by Narziss. Now it was upon him.

He stood up and gave her his hand.

'I have made a mistake; I thought we should stay together always. But did you truly mean to let me sleep, and run off without another word?'

'Oh, I thought you would take it ill, and beat me perhaps. My husband beats me, but that is his right, it is in order. I did not want you to beat me.'

He kept tight hold of her hand.

'Lisa,' he said, 'I will never beat you. Neither today nor ever. Would you not rather come with me than go back to your husband who beats you?'

She pulled away from him.

'No! No! No!' she cried in a whining voice. And he, since he felt that in her heart she was already striving to be gone from him, that her husband's beatings were sweeter than his good words, let go her hand, and she started weeping. But as she wept she ran. With her hand to her wet eyes she escaped from him. He said no more, and watched her go. In his heart he pitied her, as she scurried away through new-mown meadows, drawn off and called from him by some power, an unknown power, the thought of which had set him thinking. He pitied her, and also himself, a little: his luck was out, it seemed, in this case; and he sat alone, somewhat forlorn, moping and left in the lurch. But he was still very tired and longed for sleep, never had he felt such weariness. Later there would be time for grieving: already his eyes had closed again; nor did he rouse himself up till the sun, high in the heavens, shone him awake.

Now he was rested. He sprang up and ran to the stream, washed himself in it, and drank. Then memories came upon him, pictures like flowers from a strange land, drew him back to the joyous garden of the night, sensations of tenderness and beauty. His mind followed and retraced them as he went his aimless way over fields: every joy he had felt he knew again; over and over again he touched and savoured. How many dreams this fair brown maid had given him, how many buds she had brought to flower, how much restless longing stirred, how much re-awakened!

Wood and heath lay before him; dried fallow land and dark brown wood, and beyond it there would be mills, castles, and villages, and then a walled town. Now the world lay open to him at last, waiting, ready to take him into itself, give him his share of joy and pain: he was no schoolboy now, to stare out at the world through narrow windows, his way not a summer walk whose appointed end was a return. The whole vast earth was his reality, he was part of it, in it lay his destiny, its sky was his, its weather his. He was a small thing in a great world, running over fields like a hare, speeding on his way through blue and green eternity, like a cockchafer, with no bell to drag him from his bed, and send him to church and school and dinner. How hungry he felt! Half a loaf of barley bread, a bowl of milk, and meal broth – what magic memories! His belly howled like a wolf. He had come into a cornfield, standing half-ripe: he fleshed the ears with teeth and fingers, scrunched the small, glittering fruit in ecstasy, gathered more and more, crammed all his pockets, with ears of corn. Then he found hazel nuts, still very green, cracked their shells with delight, and of these, too, laid in a store.

The wood began again; pine trees, with oaks and ashes here and there, and here there was abundance of bilberries; he halted, and lay down to cool. Blue harebells grew in the spare coarse tuft-grass of the wood, brown, sunny butterflies fluttered past him, and disappeared in ragged flight. In just such a wood had lived St Genevieve, a saint whose face he had loved. How he would have liked to talk to her. Perhaps here in the wood there was a hermitage, with an old, bearded Pater in a hollow of the rocks or a wattle hut. There might be charcoal burners in this wood,

and with these he would gladly have spent his time. The
might be robbers, and yet they would do him no harm. I
was good to meet men, no matter which. But he knew he
might wander long in this wood — today, tomorrow, and
many days to come, and meet none. This, too, he would
accept, if such were his fate; too much thought was bad, it
was easier to take things as they came. He heard a woodpecker tap and tried to stalk it. For long he tried in vain
to get a sight of it, succeeded at last, and crouched there a
while to watch it, as it bored and hammered at the trunk of
its tree in solitude, preening its busy head this way and that.
Why had he no speech to talk to beasts in? It would have
been so pleasant to bid good morrow to this woodpecker,
pass the time of day, and hear of his work among the trees,
his life and his friends. Oh, if a man could change his
shape! He remembered how, in many idle hours, he had cut
figures on wood with a stilus, leaves and flowers, trees,
beasts, and men's heads. He had often played this game
with himself, sometimes, like a little God Almighty, fashioning his own creatures after his will, giving the cup of a
flower eyes and a mouth, turning the leaves jutting out from
a twig into fingers, and setting a head on a tree. This game
had kept him happy for hours, drawing a line and letting
himself be surprised when it shaped into a leaf or a fish-
head, a fox's tail or the eyebrow of a face. He should be able
now to wander the world, he told himself, as easily as then,
in his game, the lines he drew in sport had turned into
shapes. Goldmund longed to be a woodpecker, perhaps for a
day, perhaps a month living high up in tree-tops, flying
around the summits of smooth trunks, picking them with
his strong, sharp beak, and balancing against them with his
tail feathers. He would have spoken woodpecker's speech
and dug out good things out of the bark. The hammering
beak rang sweet above him.

Goldmund met many beasts on his way through the forest,

many hares that shot like arrows out of the ferns as he approached them, stared at him, turned and scurried off, their ears down, white under their scuts. Once, in a little clearing, he came upon a long coiled snake, but it did not slither away, it was no living snake, only an empty skin, which he took and examined. Beautiful pattern ran along it, brown and green; the sun shone through; the skin was as frail as a spider's web. He saw ouzels with yellow beaks, staring at him through round, black, scared little eyes, and they darted off in a flock, close to the ground. There were many redbreasts and finches; at one place in the forest there was a pool, a deep stagnant puddle of green, thick water, over which ran industrious, busy spiders, chasing one another as though possessed, deep in some mysterious sport, and over them a pair of dragon flies, darting here and there, on dark blue wings.

Once, as night came on, he saw something – or rather there was nothing there to see, only a scurry and stir through the undergrowth; he could hear a crackling of twigs, a thudding of scraped-up earth, and a huge, half-invisible beast, grunting and hurtling through the leaves, perhaps a stag, perhaps a wild boar, he could not tell. He stood a long while, panting with fright, his ears strained with panic, listening to the thudding, scurrying feet and, when all had long been still again, remained quiet and tense, with a thumping heart.

He could not find his way out of the wood, so there he had to spend the night. As he looked about him for a sleeping-place, and plucked up heaps of moss for his bed, he tried to think how it would be if he never found his way out of forests, but were forced to live on in them for ever. It seemed to him that this would be terrible. In the end he might grow used to living on berries; he could sleep on moss if he chose, and no doubt he would soon manage to build a hut, or even, perhaps, to make a fire. But to be alone for ever and ever, housed between the quiet, sleeping tree-trunks, with beasts as his only companions, who would scurry off at the sight of him, and with whom he could never exchange a word – that would be unbearably sad. Never to see another man; never to say good night or good morrow; not to be able to look again into human faces and human eyes, not to see a maid or woman, feel her kiss, and play the joyous, secret game of lips and limbs with her – oh, it was an unbearable thought. If such were to be his lot, he told himself, he would have to strive to change into a beast, a bear or a stag, even though he should lose his immortal soul by it. To be a bear and love a she-bear, that would not be such a bad life, and would, at least, be a far better one than to keep his reason and his thoughts, with all the rest that made him human, and yet live on alone, unloved, in sadness.

On his bed of moss before he fell asleep, he listened, curious and afraid, to the many new, incomprehensible, and eerie night-sounds of the forest. These were his comrades now, and he must house with them, become accustomed to them all, measure himself against them, and bear with them: now he was made one with deer and foxes, with pines and firs; he must live their life, take his part of sun and air with them; with them await the day, go hungry with them, and be their guest.

Then he fell asleep, and dreamed of beasts and human kind; became a bear, and ate up Lisa while he loved her. In the thick of night he woke in terror, could not tell why, felt horrible grief in his heart, and for long lay pondering uneasily. He remembered then how yesterday and tonight, he had fallen asleep without having said his prayers. He stood up, knelt beside his moss-bed, and said his evening prayer twice through, once for last night and once for this. Soon after this he fell asleep again.

At daybreak he sat up amazed, unable to remember where he was. His fear of the wild had soon grown less, and so, with new joy in his heart, he trusted to the life of the woods, though still he strove to find his pathway out of them, and strayed on and on, turning his face towards the sun. Once he found a track through the forest, a smoothed-out path, with little undergrowth, the wood around it made of very thick and ancient pine trunks, soaring straight up into the sky. When he had gone a little way under these trees they began to remind him of the pillars of the great cloister church in Mariabronn, into which, so recently, he had seen Narziss swallowed up. When had that been? Was it really only two days ago?

For three days and nights he strayed in the forest. Then, with delight, he saw that he had come back to human kind – ploughed land, on which stood oats and barley; meadows, over which, here and there, a little further on, he could see a field-path. Goldmund plucked some rye and munched it, the tilled land welcomed him in fellowship, every sight encouraged and befriended him, after his long wanderings under trees. The little path, the he-goat, the shrivelled, silvery cornflowers. Soon he would come to men and women. In a short while he saw a ploughed field, a crucifix planted at its edge, and he knelt beneath it and said a prayer.

His path, round the bend of a hillock, led him out into the shade of a lime, where he heard, with delight, a splashing stream, its waters tumbling out through a wooden pipe into a trough: he drank of this clear, lovely water, and saw with joy a cluster of straw roofs among elder trees, the berries of which were dark already. But better far than all these friendly sights was the lowing of a cow, as warm and kind as if it had been a human welcome.

He spied about round the hut from which the cow had greeted him. There in the dust before the house door, sat a little red-headed boy with light blue eyes: near him an earthen pitcher, full of water, and, with water and dust together, the boy made mud-pies, his bare legs all smeared with his mud. Happy and solemn, he kneaded mud, watched it squelch out through his fingers, and made pellets of it, using his chin to help on the work.

'God keep you, little son,' said Goldmund softly. But when the boy looked up to see a stranger he opened his mouth wide for a bellow, puckered his little face, and shinnied away through the house-door, roaring. Goldmund followed into a kitchen, where the light was so dim that he, coming from bright sunshine, could at first see nothing of it clearly. But, to be on the safe side, he gave Christian greeting to all the house. He got no answer, though above the bellowing an old, thin voice had begun to make itself heard, speaking to comfort the baby. At last a little old woman came through the dark, shading her eyes to see the stranger.

'God keep you, mother,' said Goldmund, 'and may all the saints in heaven bless your good face. For many days I have met no human kind.'

The old woman eyed him with simple cunning.

'What is it you want?' she asked uncertainly.

Goldmund gave her his hand, and stroked hers a little.

'Only to say "God keep you," little mother, and to rest a bit here in your kitchen, helping you to build up your fire. I would not say no to a bit of bread, if you could spare it me, though you need make no haste with that.'

He saw a bench, let into the wall, and sat down to rest, while the old woman cut a bit off her loaf to give the urchin, who now grown eager and curious, though ready still to burst into sobs and run away, stood beside her, gazing up at the stranger. She cut a second bit, and gave it to Goldmund.

'Thanks,' he said, 'God will repay you.'

'Is your belly so empty?' she asked him.

'Not that, but full of bilberries.'

'Well, eat then. Where did you come from?'

'From Mariabronn; from the cloister.'

'Are you a shaveling?'

'No, but a scholar on my travels.'

She peered at him, half-jeering, half-simple, her head shaking a little, on her thin, wrinkled old neck. She left him to munch a couple of mouthfuls as she led out the urchin into the sun again. Then she came back, all curiosity, to ask:

'Have you any news?'

'Little news, mother. Do you know old Pater Anselm?'

'No. But what of him?'

'He is sick.'

'Sick? And will he die?'

'Perhaps: who knows?'

'Well, let him die if he must. I have my broth to cook. Help me to chop up my kindling.'

She gave him a log of pine, well dried at the hearth, and a hatchet. He cut her all the kindling she needed and watched her lay it on the ashes, hunched over them, bending and wheezing, till all her sticks of fireing were alight. In her own exact and secret fashion she piled up her pine-twigs on the flames; the fire burnt clear in the open hearth, and on it she set a big black pot, that hung from a rusty nail over the hearthstone.

At her orders Goldmund went to the stream for water, skimmed off the milk from her pails, and then sat down in the smoky twilight to watch the dance of flames and, over it, the old woman's bony, wrinkled face, in the red glow, coming and going. Nearby, through the wooden wall, he could hear cows, pushing and rubbing in their stalls. It all pleased him greatly. Everything here was fair and good, speaking to him of peace and a full belly: the lime-tree and the brook beside it, the leaping flames under the pot, the stir and snuffle of champing cows, and their clumsy rubbings against the wall. There were two goats besides, and a swine-stall, so the old woman told him, away on the other side of the hut. She was the master's grandam, she said, and great-grandam to the little howling boy. Cuno was his name: he wandered in and out, but would say no word, and glanced up timidly at Goldmund, though he did not bellow any more. Then came the goodman and his wife, and were all amazement to see this stranger. The man was surly at first; he gripped the scholar's arm mistrustfully, and led him forth to see his face by daylight. But then he laughed, gave him a clap on the shoulder, and bade him come in and break bread. They sat together, each dipping his bread into the milk-dish, till the milk ran low, when the goodman took the dish and drank the sops. Goldmund asked could he stay with them till morning and sleep as guest under their roof. No, said the man, there was no room for it, but out there was hay enough, and there he could easily make a bed.

The wife had her little boy beside her, and took no share in their talk. But, as she ate, her eyes grew curious, and she could not look enough at this fair young scholar: his hair and eyes alike had caught her fancy; then she saw his fine, white neck, and the noble shapeliness of his hands, as they flew so deftly here and there. This stranger was a townsman and a noble; and so young. But what drew and charmed her most was his young man's voice, which seemed to sing to her, warm in its notes, pleading gently, its sound as sweet as a caress. She would have liked to sit there long and listen to it.

Their eating done the goodman went to work in his cow-stall. Goldmund had gone outside to wash his hands in the running stream, and now he sat on the low trough's edge, cooling his face and listening to the waters. He was perplexed; he had all he needed of these folk, and yet he did not want to leave them yet. Then came the wife with her pitcher, which she set down under the jet to let it fill itself. She said in a low voice:

'If you are still around here tonight, I'll bring you out a bite for your supper. Over there beyond the long barley-

93

ield, there lies the hay, and they won't get it in before to-morrow. Will you be there still?'

He looked into her freckled face, watched her strong arms as she raised her pitcher, and felt all the warmth in her wide, clear eyes. He laughed and nodded his head, and she was already away, with her brimming pitcher, into the door-way. He sat on for a while, glad at heart, listening to the rushing brook and thanking her: then he entered the hut, sought out the goodman, gave him and the old granny his hand, and thanked them both. The hut reeked of smoke, soot, and milk. A minute ago it had been his home and shelter, now it was already a strange place. He greeted and left them.

Away beyond the huts he found a chapel, near it a pleasant copse, and a group of strong old oaks, with turf beneath them. He lingered on in their shade, wandering in and out among thick stems. It was strange, he thought, how women loved, and truly they had no need of words. This woman had needed only one with him, to tell him the place where he should meet her, and all the rest was said without speech. How had she told it him? With eyes, and a certain note in her low voice; and then, with something else, some emana-tion, a tenderness shining through her body, a sign by which all men and women know without telling that they please each other. It was all as strange as some very subtle, secret tongue, and yet he had learnt it so easily. His heart leapt up to think of the coming night, longing for the time when he would know how this strong, yellow-haired woman could love, how her limbs would feel to his touch, and how she would move with him and kiss him: surely she would be very different from Lisa.

Where was Lisa now, with her straight black hair, her brown skin, her quick, short sighs? Had her husband beaten her yet? How swiftly all that had come and gone; pleasure lay waiting on every highway, an ardent, passing joy, soon

94

over. It was all sin, it was adultery, and not long since he would have killed himself rather than have such sin on his conscience. Yet here he was, awaiting his second woman, and his heart was clear, his mind at peace. Or rather, perhaps, not at peace, though it was not from lust or adultery that at times he felt uneasy and weighed down: it was something else, he could not give it a name – the feeling of some guilt he himself had done nothing to incur, some sorrow men bring into the world with them. It was perhaps what theologians define as original sin: the sin of being alive, that might be it! Yes, life itself has a kind of guilt in it; or, if not, why should so pure and wise a man as Narziss have submitted to penance like a felon? And why should he, Goldmund, even, be forced to see this guilt, deep down in him? Was he not happy? Was he not sound and young, not free as any bird in the sky? Did not women love him? Was it not fine to know that he, their lover, could give to any woman he loved the same deep joy he knew himself? Why then was he not entirely happy? Why should this strange, deep sorrow sometimes rise in him, infecting his young and careless happiness as much as ever Narziss' wisdom and chastity – this slight fear, this hankering for the past? And what was it that so often set him thinking, cudgelling his brains, although he knew well he was no thinker?

Yet it was good to love. He plucked a purple flower from the grass, held it to his eyes, and peered into the tiny narrow chalice, over which the veins ran in and out, around little pistils, fine as hairs. How life moved, trembling with desire, as much in a woman's lap as a thinker's forehead! Oh, why must men know scarcely anything? Why could he never talk to this flower? But not even two men could really talk: for each to know the other's thoughts they had need of a moment of special happiness, close friendship, and willingness to hear. No, it was fortunate indeed that love had such small need of speech, or else love itself would have been

95

...tter, full of misunderstandings and craziness. How Lisa's eyes, half-shut in a thrill of pleasure, had seemed as though dying of their ecstasy, showing only a thin gleam of their whites through the slit in her trembling eyelids: ten thousand learned words, or words of poets would never be enough to tell that feeling. Nothing – nothing at all, could ever truly be spoken or thought of from beginning to end; and yet each of us was for ever longing to speak, each felt the never-ceasing urge to thought.

He examined the leaves of the little flower, as they rose, one over another, along the stalk, so curiously and beautifully set on it. Virgil's lines were beautiful, and he loved them, but Virgil had many lines not half so beautiful, so clearly and yet cunningly wrought, so full of meaning and delight, as this spiral of tiny leaves along a stalk. How glorious, noble, and joyful a piece of work were any human being to make such a flower. But none could do it, neither hero, emperor, pope, nor saint.

He rose when the sun was low, to seek out the place the woman had named to him. There he awaited her. It was good to wait, knowing all the while that a woman, full of love, was on her way.

She came with a linen bundle, into which she had tied a great manchet of bread and a cut of bacon. She undid the knots, and set it out.

'For you,' she said to him, 'eat.'

'Later,' he answered her, 'I am hungry for you, not for bread. Oh, show me the beauty you have brought me!'

She had brought him his fill of beauty, strong thirsty lips, and gleaming teeth, strong arms, browned by the sun, though within her clothes, down from below her neck, she was white and tender. Of words she knew little, but deep in her throat could sing with a note of clear enticement, as she felt his touch upon her skin, his hands more sensitive and gentle than anything she had known in all her life, till she shuddered with delight and purred like a cat. She had learned few sports, fewer than Lisa, but with marvellous strength she pressed her love, as though she would have crushed out his heart. She was full of greed, like a child, simple and, for all her strength, ashamed. Goldmund and she were very happy.

Then she went from him, tearing herself away with a sigh, since she dared not linger. Goldmund sat on alone, happy yet sad. It was long before he remembered his bread and bacon, and fell to alone; it was quite dark.

CHAPTER EIGHT

GOLDMUND had long been a wanderer, seldom sleeping twice in the same place, everywhere desired and appeased by women, tanned by the sun, made thin by trudging and spare diet. Many women had left him at daybreak, many had gone in tears, yet often he thought:

'Why is it that none ever stays with me? Why, if they love me so that they break their marriage vows to still their need of me for a night, must they all go running back to their husbands, from whom mostly they fear to be whipped?'

None had truly begged him not to leave her, and not one to take her along with him: none, for the sake of love, had yet seemed ready to share his joys, and the need of a vagrant's life. Nor indeed did he ever long to propose it to them, or urge the thought on any of his loves, and, when he examined his own heart, he found that his freedom was very dear to him, and did not remember a single mistress so sweet he could not forget her with the next. Yet it seemed a little sad and puzzling that love should be so fleeting in every place, both his love and the love they bore him, and no sooner kindled than it died. Was there nothing more? Was it always and everywhere the same? Or did all the fault lie in him: was he, perhaps, fashioned of such a sort that, though a woman might hanker for his beauty, she could wish to stay with him no longer than for a brief, wordless space on hay or moss? Was it because he loved as a vagrant and they, secure in their homes, were scared by the thought of homeless life? Or was the lack all his, a defect of beauty, for which, though women craved as for a doll, pressing it hard, they then ran back to their husbands, even though a whipping awaited them? He could not tell.

But he never tired of learning from women. True he was more drawn towards young maids, those maids too young to have a husband, and in these he might have lost himself for longing. But such maids were mostly out of his reach, the protected, the cherished, the shy. Yet from women also he could learn : each left him something of herself, a way of kissing, a gesture, the fashion in which she defended herself or gave. Goldmund would play at any game with them, as eager and pliable as a child, ready to give himself up to every enticement. His beauty alone would never have sufficed to draw them so easily : it was his way of making himself their baby, open in his mind, curious and innocent in his greed, his perfect readiness to comply with whatever a woman cared to ask of him. He, without himself having known it, was, with each love in turn, what she had dreamed of, the sure fulfilment of all her hidden longing; tender and patient with the one, eager and full of fire with the next, as fresh and innocent, at times, as a boy at the end of his virginity; at others all art, and all design. He was ready to play or fight, to sigh or laugh, to be very bashful, or shameless. He did nothing to which a woman was unwilling, nothing she herself had not first coaxed him to. It was this that many, of quick perceptions, could see or feel in him at once, and so they made of him their darling.

Thus he learned much. Not only, within a short space of time, had they shown him many ways and arts of love, making him the master of wide experience. He had also learned to perceive the multiplicity of women : his ear was attuned to every voice, and with many its sound was enough to let him know to a hair her needs and amorous limitations. He observed, each time with more delight, the endless ways in which heads spring from shoulders, a forehead ends in piled up tresses, a knee-cap moves beneath a gown. He had learned to feel in the dark, with stroking fingers, the many sorts of women's hair, to distinguish one skin from another. Even then he had begun to perceive that perhaps this refining of his senses was the true, hidden purpose of all his wanderings; that in this might lie his deepest thought, driving him on from love to love, so that his faculty of distinguishing and perceiving might grow ever finer and more multiple, and ever profounder for its use. Such may have been his deep intent, that he should get to master women and love in all their thousand modes and differences, as some musicians become the masters of three or four instruments, or of many. But what might be the purpose of all this, and whither it was leading him, he knew not.

Though able enough to learn Latin and logic, for neither had he any surpassing gift: but for love, and the game of loving, he was gifted. Here he could learn without pains, forgetting nothing, and every lesson sorted itself for ever in his mind.

One day, when already he had been a year, or two years on the roads, Goldmund came to the castle of a rich knight, with two young daughters. It was late autumn, soon there would be frost after sundown, and last winter had given him a rough taste of it. His mind was a little troubled by the thought of these coming months of frost, as he asked for food and shelter at the castle, since winter has no tenderness for vagrants. Here he was well received, and when the knight had learned that this vagabond had studied, and could read Latin and Greek, he sent for him to come up from the servants' table, and treated him almost as his equal. His daughters sat with drooping eyes; the elder eighteen, her sister scarce sixteen; Lydia and Julia.

Next day Goldmund wanted to go further. He saw no hope of gaining love from either of these fine, yellow-haired maids, and there seemed no other woman in the castle for whose sake he would have cared to remain. But the knight, when their fast was broken, came to him, and led him aside, into a room furnished to suit a special purpose. The old man spoke modestly to the young one of his love of scholarship and books, showed him a box with the rolls of parchment he had assembled, and a desk he had specially caused to be built for his reading, with pens and sheets of the finest paper. This pious knight, as Goldmund later discovered, had been a scholar from his youth, but had turned, forgetting his scholarship, to the life of the world, and to the wars, till once he had received God's bidding, in sickness, to forget his sinful past, and set out on pilgrimage. He had trudged to Rome, and even to Constantinople, returning to find his father dead, and an empty house, in which he had settled, taken, and since lost, a wife, brought up his daughters, and now, in the beginning of his age, set himself down to the task of writing a true account of all that he had seen on his journeys. Of this he had even contrived the first beginnings, but, as he admitted to the vagrant, his Latin had in it many gaps, and hindered him in all he strove to relate. He offered Goldmund new clothes and long hospitality, in exchange for correcting what he had written. He must copy the beginning out afresh, and be of service for the remainder.

It was autumn, and Goldmund knew what winter means to a vagabond. A new suit of clothes was not to be scorned. But what pleased his youth above all else was the thought of housing so long with the two young daughters, and, without another thought, he consented. In a few days the housekeeper was ordered to open her wardrobe: in it lay a length of fine brown cloth, and from this they made a dress and cap for him. The knight himself had wanted a black gown, cut as near a scholar's gown as might be, but of that his guest would hear nothing, and knew how to make him alter his mind: so that now he had fine new clothes on his back, half-page, half-huntsman, and of a colour sorting with his complexion.

With Latin, too, it all went smoothly. Together they read over what had been written, and not only did Goldmund set to rights all the many wrong words and mistaken case-endings of his master, but here and there would build up into fine rolling periods the short clumsy phrases of the knight, in solid construction, with clear *consecutio temporum*. The old man was overjoyed, and praised unstintingly. Each day they would spend at least two hours at work together.

In this castle (which in truth was more of a farm, strengthened with certain fortifications) Goldmund found much to pass the time. He went out with the others on every hunt, and learned to shoot cross-bow from Heinrich, the huntsman, made friends with all the dogs in the place, and could ride a horse whenever he wanted it. He was seldom alone, either talking with a dog or a nag, or with Heinrich, or Lea, the porter's wife, a fat old dame, with a man's voice and a love of jesting; or else with the shepherd and the kennel-keeper. With the miller's wife who lived beyond the gates he easily might have had his way, but from her he held aloof, playing the innocent.

He rejoiced in the sight of the two young maids, of whom the younger was the fairer, and yet so coy and hard to please that she scarce would say a word to Goldmund. With both he was very courtly and reserved, yet both were ever aware of his proximity. The younger drew away, defiant from shyness. Lydia, her elder, adopted a strange demeanour with Goldmund, half of respect and half of mockery, as though he were some curious monster of learning: she would ask many eager questions of their way of life in cloisters, yet always with the hint of a jest in them, and the scorn of a high-bred lady, sure of herself. He bent himself to every fancy, respecting Lydia as his liege, Julia as a holy little nun, and whenever, in his tales and talk of the cloister, he could manage to lure on these two maids to sit longer than was their custom after supper, or when Lydia, in court-yard or garden, said a passing word and mocked him a little, he felt some advancement had been made.

Autumn leaves clung late that year to the branches of the tall ash in the courtyard, and for long there were roses in the garden. Then, one day, came a visit; a neighbouring knight, with his dame and a squire attending them. The mildness of the season had lured them out on this unaccus-tomed jaunt, so far from home, and now they rode to the castle, craving hospitality for the night. They were wel-comed; Goldmund's bed was shifted at once from the guest-room to the room where he did his scrivening, and his bed made ready for the newcomers. Some hens were slaughtered and a messenger sent for fish to the mill. Goldmund rejoiced in all this bustle and feasting, and could feel at once how eagerly the strange lady eyed him. Yet scarcely, by her voice and manner, had she shown how he pleased and roused her longing than he saw too, with rising excitement, that Lydia's whole demeanour to him had changed, how still and reserved she had become, how closely she watched him with the guest. When, at their festal supper, the lady's foot be-neath the table began to find a way to Goldmund's, it was not her sport alone that delighted him, but much more the silent anger and constraint with which Lydia sat, watching them both, with curious and glittering eyes. At last he could let his knife fall under the board, and so, in bending to pick it up, stroke the feet and legs of his new paramour : he rose again, and saw how Lydia paled, how she bit her lip, as he told his stories of the cloister, though he felt the strange lady to be less eager for them than for the voice and accent of the narrator. The others also sat listening : the knight, his patron, with great benevolence, the other with a wooden face, though even he took fire from the young man's words.

Never had Lydia heard such eloquence: he had flowered, desire trembled in the air, his eyes shone, in his voice was all delight: he begged for love. This the three women felt, each in her fashion: little Julia in panicked defence against him, the knight's wife radiant with pleasure, Lydia with pain in her heart; pain made of the deepest longing, her frail effort to shield herself against it, sharp jealousy narrowing up her face and smouldering behind her eyes. Goldmund felt all these emanations, the secret answers to his striving. They flowed back into him; love thoughts darted like birds about his head, birds that came to his hand and fluttered off again, fighting and pecking at each other. Julia after supper withdrew (it had long been dusk) with her rushlight in an iron sconce, as cold and quiet as a religious. The others sat an hour longer, the knights discussing the emperor and the bishops, while Lydia, with flaming cheeks, listened to all the merry, trivial talk spun out between Goldmund and the lady. Beneath its shimmering words they had cast a skein of intermingled glances and accents; little gestures running between them, heavy with love. Lydia breathed this air in greedily, shuddering as she knew, or felt, how Goldmund's knee, under the table, brushed against the knees of the dame. Each touch ran through her like a blade. Later she could not sleep, but lay with a beating heart half the night, sure she had heard them together, completing, in her mind, what was forbidden them, seeing them lie clasped, hearing their kisses, fearing, even though she wished it done, that soon the stranger knight would surprise them, and stab this catiff Goldmund to the heart.

Next day the sky was overcast; a damp wind sighed, yet the guests, refusing all persuasions, seemed very impatient to set off again. Lydia stood watching them mount; she pressed their hands and wished them God's speed, all the while scarce knowing that she did it, since every sense was in her eyes, as she saw Goldmund's hand at the lady's foot, helping her to climb her palfrey: the hand gripped the foot, broad and firm, and for an instant it closed on the lady's shoe.

The guests had ridden away: Goldmund had to be off to his scrivening. Within half an hour he could hear the imperious voice of Lydia, calling to the grooms in the courtyard, the clatter of hoofs as they led her pony from the stall. His master went across to the window, and looked out with a smile, shaking his head. Together they watched Lydia ride off. That day their Latin seemed to rust, and they made less progress than before, since the scholar was at pains to keep his mind on it. His master, with a friendly smile, dismissed him earlier than usual.

Unseen by any in the castle, Goldmund led his horse into the courtyard, and rode into the teeth of an autumn wind, over brown moorland, faster and faster. He felt his horse grow warm beneath him, and its warmth firing his own blood. Over heath and moor, stubble and fallow land, grown about with shave-grass and sedge, he rode into the grey, fresh morning, past clumps of alders, through dark pine woods, and out again, on to brown, empty heath. On the brow of a hill far off, sharp against the pale, cloudy sky, he saw the little shape of Lydia, set high on her slowly cantering palfrey. He spurred on to reach her, but the instant she knew herself pursued, she whipped up and galloped away from him. At times she vanished, then he could see her again, her hair in the wind. He galloped after, like a hunter, his heart leapt as he urged his horse, with little soft words of encouragement, happily noting the country as he rode, the alders, the slanting fields, the maple-clumps, and the muddy brinks of pools, yet never losing sight of his quarry.

When Lydia knew he was upon her she ceased her flight, and let her palfrey walk. She would not turn to her pursuer. Proud, to all seeming unaware of him, she went on as though alone, and nothing had happened. He drove his horse to come up with her, and the two beasts walked peace-fully together, though both they and their riders glowed with the chase.

'Lydia,' he said to her gently.

She would not answer.

'Lydia.'

Still she sat dumb.

'How fair to see you riding in the distance; your hair was like gold lightning behind you. Oh, you were beautiful. It's a fine thought that you should fly before me: this has shown me first that you can love me a little. I did not know, and even last night I was still in doubt. Only now, as you were trying to escape me, have I suddenly begun to understand. My sweet, my beauty, you must be weary! Shall we rest ourselves?'

He swung to earth and caught her bridle, so that she should not run from him again: her face was pale as snow as she looked down at him, and as he lifted her down she started to weep. There she sat, struggling with sobs, valiantly, until she had mastered them:

'Oh,' she began, 'why are you wicked?' It was hard for her to bring out her words.

'Am I so wicked?'

'You are a lecher, Goldmund. Let me forget the words you have just said: they were shameless words, and it does not beseem you to say such things to me. How did you ever think that I could love you? Let us forget them. But shall I ever forget what I saw last night?'

'Last night? What did you see then?'

'Oh, don't feign so, and lie to me! All that you did last night was shameless and cruel, before my very eyes, with that woman. Goldmund, have you no shame? Why you even stroked her leg under the table — my father's table — before me! And now when she is gone you come hunting me. In very truth you cannot know what shame is.'

Goldmund was already sorry that he had spoken before helping her from the saddle. What a fool he had been not to keep his mouth shut; words were not needed in love.

He said no more, but knelt beside her and, since she looked so fair and sorrowful, soon found himself sharing her grief. Even he felt a little to be pitied. Yet, in spite of all she had said against him, he could see the love in her eyes. Even the grief on her trembling lips was love; her eyes he could believe more than her words: But she had been expecting his answer. Now, since none came, Lydia drooped her lip still further, her eyes bright with tears, gazed, and repeated:

'Have you no shame, then?'

'Forgive me,' he answered her humbly, 'these are matters none should ever speak of. It was all my fault, so forgive me. You ask me if I have no shame. Yes, to be sure, I can feel shame: but I love, I love you, and love knows nothing of it. Don't be angry.'

She seemed scarcely to hear him. There she sat, pulling a sad face, staring away into the distance as though she had been all alone. This he had never known before: it all came from words.

Gently he laid his face against her knee, and at once her touch was as a salve to him. Yet still he was a little restless and sad, and she too seemed sadder than ever, sitting still, holding her tongue, and gazing far away beyond him. What heaviness now, and what discomfort! But her knee felt friendly to his cheek, and did not seem to long to thrust him off: his face, with closed eyes, lay against it. Slowly he drew its long, fine shape into himself, thinking with trembling pleasure how worthily this young and delicate knee completed and set off the firm, beautiful arch of her finger-nails. He nestled close up against it, letting his cheek and lips talk in their fashion: at last he could feel her hand, like a soft, shy bird, alight on his hair. 'Lovely hand,' he felt. How fearfully, like a child, she stroked him! He had often studied her hands, and wondered at them, till he knew them almost as his own, with their long fingers, tapering down to the swelling, rosy hills of the nails. And now these tapering, gentle fingers spoke shyly and gently to his hair, their words soft, greedy, children's words; they were words of love. Gratefully he nestled up his head and, with his cheek and neck, rubbed her palm. At last she spoke:

'We must go; it is time.'

He raised his head and looked up at her, softly kissing the slim fingers.

'Get up, please, now,' she said, 'we must go home.'

He obeyed at once: they stood up, mounted their horses, and rode.

Goldmund's heart was full of happiness. How beautiful Lydia was, how clear and tender, like a child. He had not so much as kissed her cheeks, and yet he felt so peaceful and satisfied. They rode hard, and only in the courtyard, almost at the castle door, did she turn, with a little start, to say to him: 'We should not have come back together. How mad we are.' Not until the very last minute, as already the stable-boys came running, could she whisper in quick, burning words: 'Tell me, did you sleep last night with that woman?'

He shook his head several times, and fell to patting down his horse. That afternoon, when her father had gone out riding, the lovers came together in the workroom:

'Was that the truth?' she asked at once, and he, without further speech, knew what she asked him.

'Then why did you play that horrible game to make her love you?'

'It was for you,' he said; 'believe me I would rather ten thousand times have had your foot to stroke than hers. Yours never came to me under the table to ask me whether I could love.'

'And do you really love me, Goldmund?'

'Oh yes.'

'But what is to come of it?'

'How can I tell you, Lydia? What do we care. I can only be happy that I love you, and what will come of it never troubles me. My heart leaps up to see you ride, to hear your voice, and feel your fingers in my hair. I shall be full of joy when I can kiss you.'

'Goldmund, a man may only kiss his bride. And did you never think of that, then?'

'No, I never thought of that. Why should I? You know as well as I that you can never be my bride.'

'So that is it; and since you can never be my goodman, and stay for ever at my side, it was very wicked of you to speak of love to me. Did you really think you could entice me?'

'I thought of nothing, Lydia, but you only. I think much less than you suppose. And I ask nothing, except that one day you should kiss me. We talk too much; lovers should never talk. I think you do not love me, Lydia.'

'This morning you said the opposite.'

'And you did the opposite then.'

'I? What do you mean?'

'First you rode off as you saw me coming, and then I thought that you loved me. When you began to sob and weep I thought that you were weeping for love. My head lay on your knee, you stroked it, and I thought that was love. But now you will do nothing kind to me.'

'I am not that wanton whose feet you stroked beneath the table. You seem only to know such women as that.'

'No, God be praised, you are far more beautiful, and finer.'

'That was not what I meant.'

'No, but it is so. Do you know how beautiful you are?'

'I have my looking-glass.'

'Did you ever look and see your forehead in it, Lydia? And your shoulders and your little finger-nails; and then your knees? And have you seen how all these things belong to each other, how all has the same long, beautiful shape? Have you seen it?'

'How you talk, Goldmund! No, I had never seen it before; but, now that you tell me, I can see it. Listen, you are a lecher, and now you come to make me vain?'

'I wish I could make you very vain. But why should I want so much to make you vain? You are beautiful, and I want you to see your beauty. You force me to tell it you in words, but I could say it a thousand times better. With speech I have nothing to give you. With speech I learn nothing from you, or you from me.'

'What could I ever learn from you, then?'

'I from you, Lydia, you from me. Yet you refuse, you only want to love one man, the man who is to be your husband. He will laugh when he sees you have learned nothing, not even to kiss.'

'So, master-scholar, you would give me lessons in kissing?'

He smiled, although these words did not please him; yet behind the malapert false ring in them, he could feel the sudden longing in her maidenhead, and her struggle to keep off her desire.

Nor would he answer her again. He smiled, holding her restless eyes with his, and while, although she resisted, she submitted to the enchantment within her, he bent his face down slowly until their lips met. Then he pressed her mouth very softly, and it answered him with the kiss of a little maid, parting, as though in agonized astonishment, when his lips refused to let her go. Gently enticing he followed her lips as they moved back, until, with hesitation, they met again, and he taught the enchanted, without forcing her, to give and return kisses, until, exhausted, she leaned her head against his shoulder. He let it rest there happily, savouring the long yellow hair, whispering little words of comfort to her, remembering how he, an innocent scholar, had been taught this secret once, by Lisa the gipsy. How dark Lisa's hair had been, how brown her skin, how the sun had burned them, as the fading John's Wort gave out its scent! But now, from what a distance the picture shone on him! Everything withered so soon, almost as soon as it had blossomed: Lydia slowly stood upright again; her face had changed, her eyes were wide and serious lover's eyes.

'Goldmund, let me go,' she said. 'Oh you, my love, I have stayed too long with you.'

Each day they found their secret hour together, and Goldmund gave himself up to his new love. This maiden's love danced in his heart and soothed him. Often she had only one thought; to keep his hands in hers for an hour together, look in his eyes, and leave him with the kiss of a child. At others she would kiss and kiss, yet, even then, he might not touch her body. One day, blushing very deep, with a mighty struggle against herself, to give him a great joy, she showed him her breasts: shyly she unlaced her bodice, to let him see the small white fruit concealed in it: when he had knelt and kissed she put it carefully away again, her cheeks, and all her neck, still crimson. They would talk, but after a new fashion, not as they had done on the first day, inventing many names to call each other. She told him of her childhood, her dreams and games. Often too she would say that her love was wicked, since she and Goldmund never could be wed. She would speak of it in a low, submissive voice, and set this secret grief on her love like a gaud, or as though she had been wearing a black veil.

For the first time Goldmund knew himself beloved, and not only desired, by a woman.

Once Lydia said:

'You are so brave and look so merry. But deep in your eyes there is no merriment. There there is only sadness, as though your eyes could see that there is no happiness, and nothing loved, or lovely stays with us long. You have the most beautiful eyes any man could have, and the saddest. I think it must be that you are homeless. You came to me out of the woods, and one day you will go back to them again, to sleep on moss, and wander the roads. Where is your real home, then? When you go I shall have a father and sister, I shall have my turret-room with its window, at which I can sit and remember you: but I shall not have a home any more.'

He let her speak, and often smiled at her, although at times her words made him sad. Nor would he ever comfort her with words, only with little gentle strokings, holding her hands against his heart, humming soft magic in her ears, as nurses comfort babes when they cry. Once Lydia said: 'I would very much like to know what will become of you, Goldmund; and I often think of it. You will have no easy life, and not such a life as other men. Oh, how I wish you may be happy! I often think you should be a poet, whose head is full of dreams and histories, and who knows how to speak them in beautiful words. Or else you will wander through the world, and every woman you meet will love you, yet all the while you will be alone. Better go back to your cloister, to the friend of whom you tell me so much. I will pray for you, that you need not die alone in the forest.'

She could say such things in deepest earnest, with eyes that seemed not to see the world around her. But often they would be merry together, riding over the brown, autumn heath, she telling him riddles to make him laugh, or pelting him with sticks and acorns.

One night Goldmund lay waiting for sleep, his heart weighed down with a new, poignant heaviness: it beat full and heavy, pregnant of love, heavy with restlessness and sorrow. He could hear November winds creak in the rood; he had long been used to lying a while before he slept, but now sleep refused to come to him. Softly, as his habit was at night, he whispered a chaunt to the Blessed Mary:

Tota pulchra es, Maria,
Et macula originalis non est in te,
Tu, lætitia Israel,
Tu, advocata peccatorum.

This chaunt sank into his mind like a sweet music: but out there he could still hear the wind, as it told of restlessness and wanderings, of winter forests, and all the rough adventures of vagabonds. He thought of Lydia, then of Narziss and of his mother: his restless heart was brimfull of its grief.

Then he sat up with a start, and stared incredulous. The door had opened, and through the dark, in a long white shift, came Lydia, noiselessly moving across the flags, with bare feet, to reach his bed. She had closed the door very quietly, and now came over to sit beside him.

'Lydia,' he whispered, 'my white flower, my little doe. Lydia, how do you come to me?'

'I have come,' she said, 'for a minute only. I only wanted to see how my Goldmund lies in his bed, my Goldheart.'

She stretched herself out beside him, and they lay still, their hearts beating hard. She let him kiss, let his marvelling hands go where they would about her, but more than this she still refused him. In a little while she put his hands gently away, kissed him on his eyes, stood up without a word, and stole off again. The door creaked; the wind clamoured and pressed upon the roof, all was bewitched and full of mystery, of secrecy, sadness, threat and promise. Goldmund did not know what he thought, or what he should do. After a short, restless sleep he awoke again, to find his pillow wet with tears.

In a few days the tender ghost came back to him, to lie at his side for a while, just as before. She whispered to him, held in his arms; she had much to say, and to lament. He ened tenderly, she lying with his left arm about her, hile, with the right, he stroked her knee.

'Little Goldmund,' she said, pressed close to his cheek, in a tiny voice: 'it is so sad I cannot give myself. This little secret, our little happiness, will not last. Already Julia suspects, and soon she will force me to tell it her: or else my father will get wind of it. Should he find me here in your bed, oh little Goldmund, it would go ill with me. Your Lydia would have to stand and weep, look up at trees, and watch her little Goldheart dangling, and soon the wind would be sighing through him. Oh, run, my love – run at once; it were better not to let my father catch you, and tie you up, and string you to a tree. I have seen one hung already; a thief. I could never see you hang, little Goldmund, so run far away now, and forget me. Oh, you must never die, my Goldheart, birds must never eat your blue eyes. Oh, no, my dear, you must go from me; and what shall I ever do when you are gone!'

'Come with me, Lydia.'

'That would be very fine,' she smiled, 'oh, it would be fine and merry to run off with you into the world. But I cannot do it. I could never sleep in the wood, and lie in fields with straws in my hair. I could never do it, and never shame my father. No, don't talk; these are only fancies. I can't do it: I could no more do it than eat off a dirty platter, and sleep in rags that crawled with lice. Oh no, we two are born to sorrow, and everything fine and beautiful is forbidden us. Goldmund, my poor little love, I shall end by seeing you hanged. And then I shall be locked up and sent to a cloister. My sweet, you must run far off, and sleep again with gipsies and peasants' wives. Ah, go! go! before they take you and bind you. We can never be happy; never.'

He stroked her knee very cunningly, and gently he touched her maidenhead.

'Little flower. We could be so happy.'

'No,' she said, 'no, you must not! That is forbidden me. You, little gipsy, perhaps could never understand. But I am a wicked maid, and have done wrong. I bring shame on my whole house. Yet somewhere in my soul, though I do it, I am still as proud as I ever was, and into my pride there must be no breaking. You must leave me that, or I will not come again and lie beside you.'

Never had he refused a command, a wish, or any hint of a wish from her. He himself was amazed by her great power on him. Yet he suffered, his senses were unappeased, and his heart would often struggle against this bondage. Sometimes he strove to shake it off, and then with many fine words, he would pay his court to little Julia, though in any case it had now become most necessary to keep her in the dark as much as possible.

Yet the very strength of this enchantment in which both the sisters held his senses had made him aware, to his amazement, of the difference between desire and love. First he had coveted both equally, had longed for both, but found Julia the sweeter of the two, the maid it would be pleasanter to lie with: he had courted both without distinction, ever keeping both in his mind's eye.

Now Lydia had him in her power: he loved her so that he even could renounce full possession of her. Her soul had grown familiar and beloved, in its childish gentleness and melancholy it seemed to him a part of his own. He was often surprised and overjoyed to see how her body expressed her essence. She would say or do a thing after her fashion, utter a judgement or a wish, and her words, with the form of her soul in them, seemed set in the very mould that informed her fingers and her eyes. These instants, like a revelation of the laws and basic forms by which her essence, both soul and body, had been devised, often aroused the longing in Goldmund to seize and retain some beauty of this design. He strove, on many sheets of paper, which, after, he would careally hide, to retrace in pen the outline of her head, her knees, her hands, the arch of her eyebrows, as he remembered them.

Julia had become a danger. Well aware at heart of the air of love her sister breathed, though all her senses drew her to this paradise, her stubborn mind refused to give them leave. She treated Goldmund with strained hostility and coldness, though her eyes, at unguarded moments of curiosity, would stray and linger about his body. With Lydia she was often very tender: sometimes she would creep into bed beside her, hinting to her of love and carnal knowledge, all greed and silent curiosity, prying capriciously at this longed-for, and forbidden, secret thing. Then almost shrewishly she would hint that she knew Lydia's secret and despised her for it. This lovely, capricious child, a delight and hindrance, darted upon the short joy of the lovers, spying them out in greedy fantasy, pretending at times that she knew nothing, at others making them see in her a danger. She had ceased to be a child, and become a power. Lydia suffered more from her than Goldmund, who only saw Julia at supper. Nor could it escape Lydia's knowledge that Goldmund was alive to Julia's beauty, since she often saw his eyes appraise her. She could not speak, it was all too hard, too dangerous. Julia must not be crossed and her anger roused. Alas, any day or hour might bring the discovery of their loves, the end of this hard-won, fearful happiness; perhaps a terrible end.

Goldmund would often wonder why he had not long since run off again. It was hard to live as now he lived, his love requited yet with no hope in it, either of a blessed and lasting happiness or the short fulfilment which, till then, had never been withheld from his desires: and all the while in mortal danger. Oh, why did he stay to bear all this; all these smothered longings and blind constraints! Were not such fine feelings and scruples proper to safe, legitimate, rich men, men living snug in their warm houses? Had not vag-

rants the right to stand aside from all such courtesies a
laugh at them? He had this right, and was a fool to seek
kind of home in this castle, and pay for it with so much pain
and disquiet.

And yet he lingered on and suffered willingly, finding a
kind of happiness in his pain. It was hard and senseless to
love in such a fashion, set about with traps and full of obstacles, yet it was glorious. The dark, sad beauty of this love,
its craziness and hopelessness, had glory in them: each
heavy sleepless night of unstilled longing had its beauty: his
days were all as full of rare delight as the tremblings of
desire on Lydia's mouth, the lost surrender in her voice, as
she spoke to him of her love and fears. In a few weeks sorrow had entered her face, whose lines it gave him such
pleasure to trace with a pen that, as he did it, this alone
seemed of significance, and he felt that in these few weeks
he had changed and grown older by many years; less cunning yet more deeply experienced; not happier, yet much
richer in soul. He had ceased to be a boy any more.

In her lost gentle voice Lydia said to him:

'You should not be sad for my sake, Goldmund. I would
only make you happy and see you merry. Forgive me that I
taint your heart with my grief. Each night I have the strangest dream. Always I seem to be straying in a wilderness, so
dark and huge I could never tell you of it, and I go on and on
through it, seeking you. You are never there. I know I have
lost you, and so I must go on for ever to find you. Then
when I wake I think: "Oh, how good to know he is still
with me, that I may see him still for a few more weeks or
days; it is all one to me since I have him." '

One morning, soon after daybreak, Goldmund woke and
lay awhile thinking. The images of a dream surrounded him,
but without any sequence or meaning in them. He had
dreamt of Narziss and of his mother, and still saw their
shapes clearly before him. When he had shaken off these

gering figments he perceived a strange new light in the
room, glittering with another sort of clarity through the
little round window, set deep in its wall. He jumped out of
bed and ran to look out: the window-moulding, courtyard,
stable roof, and then the whole wide country-side beyond,
shimmered blue-white, before his eyes, the first snow of the
year spread over them. This contrast with his heart's hot
restlessness of the still, surrendered world, made him uneasy. How quietly, how touchingly and devoutly, did
moor and forest, hill and ploughland, give themselves up to
sun or wind, rain, snow or drought. With what fair and
gentle pain ashes and maples bent under their white winter's
burden. Could men never grow as patient as these, never
learn the secret of their tranquillity. He wandered forth,
abstracted, into the courtyard, wading in snow, filling his
hands with it; went across to the garden and peered through
the high privet hedge at rose-bushes, laden with whiteness.

For breakfast they ate a meal broth, all chattering of the
first fall of snow. All, even the maids, had already been out
in it. This year the snow was late, Christmas was near. The
knight told of lands in the South where no snow fell.

But what made this first day of winter unforgettable in
Goldmund's life did not take place till late that night. Lydia
and Julia had quarrelled, though of this Goldmund knew
nothing. When all was still and dark in the house, Lydia
crept as usual to his bed, stretched herself out in silence at
his side, close up to him, to feel his heartbeats. She was sad,
full of fears for Julia's treachery, yet could not bring herself
to tell her lover, and cloud his mind with her grief. She lay
still, close to his heart; from time to time he whispered and
caressed her, running his fingers through her hair. Suddenly
– they had not been long together – her body shuddered
from head to foot, and she sat bolt upright with open eyes.
Goldmund himself grew scared as he watched the chamber
door pushed open by inches, and a shape, which first his

terror did not recognize, creep across the stones to his bed. Not till it was close up beside them, and hovering over them, did he see, with pounding heart, that it was Julia. She let a cloak, flung round her shift, slip to the ground. With a moan, as though she had been stabbed, Lydia sank back and clung to Goldmund. Then Julia, with joy and malice, though her words trembled as she spoke them:

'I will not lie all alone in my bed,' she whispered. 'Either you take me into yours and let us three lie close together, or I go now to rouse my father.'

'Well, come then,' Goldmund answered, and flung back the coverlet, 'or your feet will freeze to the stones.'

She crept in; he found it hard to make a place for her, since Lydia lay like death, her head in the pillow. Then the three lay side by side, Goldmund with a maid on either hand, and for a moment he could not banish the thought of how, not so very long since, this would have seemed his heart's desire. With reverence and fear, yet a secret joy, he felt Julia's hip against his side.

'I had to see for myself,' she began again, 'how soft and downy is this bed of yours, to which my sister creeps so eagerly.'

Goldmund, to still her, gently brushed his cheek against her hair, his cunning hand stroking along her hip and knees, as men please cats; he felt her magic steal into his senses, reverenced her yet would brook no resistances. Yet all the while he strove to comfort Lydia, whispering little love-sounds in her ears, and slowly brought her to such a point that at last she raised her head and turned to him. Noiselessly he kissed her eyes and mouth, though his hand, as he did it, subdued her sister, and the strange peril of these moments rose to an unbearable pitch in his mind. It was his left hand taught him the truth, as it learned the quiet, the expectant beauty of Julia's body, so that now he could feel for the first time, not only all the bitter delight and hopelessness this love that held him bound to Lydia, but also how much foolishness there was in it. He should, so now he began to think, as he gave his lips to one, his hand to the other, either force a surrender from Lydia, or leave them both, and go his way. To love her as he did, yet renounce her, had been too meaningless and unjust.

'My heart,' he sighed in Lydia's ear. 'We suffer with no reason. How happy we might be, all three together. Let us do what our blood demands of us.'

As she shuddered at this and drew away from him, his desire leapt up to meet the other, and his hand began to give her such delight that she answered it in a long trembling sigh. When Lydia heard this it pinched her heart, as though some poison had been dropped in it. She raised herself up, flung back the coverlets, started to her feet, and cried aloud:

'Let us go, Julia.'

Julia trembled: the sudden shrillness of this cry, loud enough to bring ruin on them all, had waked her to their danger, and she rose quietly. But Goldmund, deceived and wounded in all his senses, had clasped her quickly as she rose, kissed her two breasts, and whispered burning words:

'Tomorrow, Julia, tomorrow.'

Lydia stood barefoot in her shift, her toes pinched with cold on the bare flags. She caught up Julia's cloak and flung it about her: in a motion of such humbleness and pain as, even in the dark, her sister could feel, and which moved her heart, making them friends again. Together they stole off on tiptoe. Goldmund lay, at odds with himself, scarce daring a breath till the house was still as a grave.

So these three were flung back from this strange unnatural contact into sad meditations and loneliness, since even the two maids, lying together, could not bring themselves to speak a word, and each lay there without sleep, defiant and speechless. A spirit of strife and ill-luck, some demon of solitude, misrule, and the dire confusion of souls, seemed to have been let loose upon the house. Goldmund could g no sleep until long after midnight, nor Julia until close o. daybreak: Lydia lay watching, full of grief, till the pale day came stealing across the snow. At once she rose, put on her gown, knelt long before her little wooden crucifix, prayed till she heard her father's step on the stairs. She went out to him and begged him to hear her. Without having made any effort to sunder two emotions in her mind, jealousy, and her care for Julia's maidenhead, she had resolved to bring it all to an end. Goldmund and Julia were still sleeping when already the knight had heard from Lydia whatever she thought good to tell him. Of Julia's share she did not speak.

When Goldmund, at the appointed hour, attended his master in the workroom, he found the knight, as a rule clad in his frieze gown and slippers, and busy with their writing for the day, with his sword girdled on, in a leather jerkin; and he knew at once what this would mean for him.

'Put on your cap,' the knight commanded, 'I have a little way to walk with you.'

Goldmund took his cap from the nail, and followed his lord down the stairs, out over the courtyard, to the gates. Their feet crunched the lightly frozen snow: the morning red was still faint in the sky. The knight went on in silence, the young man at his heels turning back, now and then, to look up at the castle, the little window of his chamber, the snowy inclines of roofs and gables, till all had been blotted into the distance. Never again would he see that window or those roofs, never again his workroom or his sleeping place, never again the knight's two maids. He had long since accustomed his mind to the thought of this sudden separation, yet now his heart was full of anguish, and the parting seemed a bitter sorrow.

For an hour they walked on thus, the knight leading, both in silence, and Goldmund began to consider his own fate. The knight was armed, perhaps he would strike him down,

d yet somehow he did not fear it. The danger was small:
e need only take to his heels, and there was an old man,
with his sword, helpless. No, he was in no danger for his
life. But this silent walk behind the ceremonious old man,
this dumb submission to be led, had grown more painful
with every step. The knight halted at last.

'And now,' he thundered, 'you will go alone, always in
this direction, and lead your vagabond's life as before. If I
ever see you near my house again I will have you shot to
death with arrows. I want no vengeance. I should have been
wiser than to let so young a man come near my daughters.
But if ever you dare return, that is the end of you! Go now
and may God pardon your sin.'

In the livid, shimmering brightness of the snow his face,
with the grey beard, seemed dead and extinguished. He
stood there waiting like a ghost, and never once shifted his
ground till Goldmund was lost to sight behind a hillock.

The red gleam had faded out of the sky; no sun came up;
thin lingering snowflakes swirled about him.

CHAPTER NINE

GOLDMUND knew this country from many rides. Away beyond that frozen pool stood a barn, owned by the knight; further, a peasant holding where he had friends: in one or the other he might have to seek shelter and a sleeping-place, and all the rest could keep till tomorrow. Little by little there stole upon him the old sense of freedom and fresh adventure, which for a while had almost been forgotten. True that on this surly winter's day adventures looked frozen and uninviting, true they would be pinched, famished, and difficult, and yet their hard, untrammelled necessity came as a kind of salve, almost a balm, to his blunted senses and all the confusion in his heart.

He ran on until he was tired out. No more riding now, he said to himself. Oh, wide world! The snow had almost ceased to fall. Ragged lines of woods away in the distance seemed to mingle with the grey clouds above them, stillness to stretch on and on, as far as the end of the world. What had become of poor, frightened Lydia now? He pitied her from his heart, and thought with tenderness of her, as he lay down to rest by a frozen stream, beneath a bare, solitary ash. The cold pricked him up; he rose, stiff in every limb, and by degrees fell into a run, since the grey, dull light seemed already fading.

He thought of nothing, as he tramped over empty fields. What was to be gained by thoughts or feelings, no matter how fair and tender they might be? He must keep warm, and find some refuge for the night, keep alert, as a fox or marten, in the rigour of this frozen world, and, if he could t let himself perish in icy fields: nothing but that was vorth considering.

He turned in surprise, and peered about him, since he seemed to hear a horse's hoofs, far off. Had they sent out to hunt him down, then? He drew his little hunting-knife from his pouch, to ease the blade in the wooden sheath. Then he caught sight of the distant rider, and recognized a horse from the knight's stable. It cantered stubbornly in pursuit of him: any attempt to fly would have been useless, so he waited, without actual fear, yet tense with expectation and curiosity, his heart beating faster and faster. A thought leapt into his brain. 'How good if I could manage to kill this rider! I should have a horse, and so the world would be mine.' But when he saw the horseman, Hans, the stableboy, with his light, watery-blue eyes and silly moonface, he laughed at himself. He would have to have been made of stone to slay such a kind, honest simpleton. He greeted Hans as a friend, and gently patted Hannibal, his horse, which knew him at once, as he stroked down its warm, damp neck.

'Whither away, Hans?' he asked the lad.

'To you,' grinned Hans, with flashing teeth. 'You've tramped a bit already, haven't you? Well, now I've found you, I can't stay. I was only to greet you, and give you this.'

'From whom do you greet me?'

'From Mistress Lydia. Ah, you've brought us a sour day, Magister Goldmund. I was glad to be able to get off for a bit. Master must never know I've come forth with a message, or he'd string me up as soon as look at me. Well, take it, then.'

He held out a package to Goldmund.

'Tell me, Hans, have you any bread in your wallet?'

'Bread? I dare say there's still a crust.' He rummaged and drew out a chunk of rye-bread. He turned his horse.

'How is it with Mistress Lydia?' Goldmund asked. 'Di she send you no message, nor a letter?'

'No. I only spoke with her a short while. Bad weather at home, I tell you. The master walks up and down like King Saul. Well, I have this to give you, and no more, Master Goldmund. Now I must hurry back.'

'Yes, but only a minute. Hans, could you give me your hunting-knife? I have only my little one. If wolves come out and – well, it would be better for me if I had a good knife in my hand.'

But of this Hans would hear nothing. He would take it very ill, he said, should any misfortune befall Magister Goldmund. But his jack-knife, no – he could never give that, no, not for gold, not even in exchange for a better one. Oh no, he could never give it, not if good Saint Genevieve were to ask it of him. Now he must urge his horse, he wished Godspeed, and he was sorry.

They shook hands, and the lad rode off again, while Goldmund stood looking after him, with an odd grief in his heart. Then he undid the package, pleased with the good, stout, neat's-leather cords that bound it. It was a woven undershift, of strong, grey wool, and seemingly Lydia's handiwork, made to his measure. Wrapped in the wool was something hard – a side of bacon – and, in the bacon, a little slit, and, stuck into the slit, a clear gold ducat. No letter came with all of this.

He stood in the snow with Lydia's gift, and hesitated: then he stripped off his jerkin, and pulled on the woollen shift, which warmed him, wrapping his cold body. Quickly he pulled his jerkin over it, and the ducat he hid in the deepest pouch, bound the leather strings tight round it, and went on his way over snowfields. It was time to seek out some sleeping-place, since now he was feeling very weary. He would not go to any peasants' huts, although he might find a warm shelter in them, and a bowl of milk to his supper: he had no wish to gossip, and answer their questions.

He slept in snow, rose up at daybreak, and trudged over frost in a sharp wind, urged to forced stages by the cold. For many nights he would dream of the old man with his sword, for many days loneliness and sorrow would gripe his heart.

In a village where poor peasants had no bread, but only millet broth to give him, he found a shelter, some few days later, at nightfall. Here new adventures awaited him. A woman, whose guest he was, dropped her child in the night, and Goldmund was present at the birth. They had roused him up from his straw to help them, although in the end they had no work for him, save to hold a rushlight, while the midwife did her business. That was the first birth he had ever seen and, suddenly made rich with a new experience, he stared with surprised and shining eyes at the face of this woman in labour. It seemed, at least to him, that what he saw in the mother's face was worth the noting. Something he would never have looked to see was revealed to him there in the torchlight. As this groaning mother screamed her pain, the twisted lines of her face differed little from those he had seen in the moment of love's ecstasy, on the faces of the women he had clasped. True the look of agony in this face was more strongly marked, and therefore clearer than any of supremest pleasure. But what lay beneath was the same: the almost grinning drawing together of the features, the same glow, the same extinction. He marvelled much at his sudden thought: pleasure and pain can be as like as sisters.

He had another experience in this village. For the sake of a neighbour's wife, whose eye caught his on the morning following this childbirth, and who speedily heard his supplication, he lingered a second night in the village, pleasing her well, since this was his first appeasement, after all the deceptions and longing of many weeks. And this delay brought his adventure. Because of it, on his second day's sojourn here, he fell in with a tall, bold fellow, Victor, seemingly half-cleric, half-vagabond, who greeted him with a Latin tag, and proclaimed himself a wandering scholar, though long past the age for universities. This fellow, with his stubbled, pointed chin, met Goldmund with a kind of comradeship, a vagabond's humour, which soon had won him a young companion. On Goldmund's asking where he had studied, and whither his journey might be leading him, this strange brother ranted out the following:

'By my poor lost soul I have frequented enough high seats of learning. I have been in Paris and Cologne, and seldom has a more pregnant word been uttered on the true metaphysics of the horse-sausage than by me, in my dissertation at Leyden. Since then, *amice*, I have wandered, a poor scholar, through German lands, my little soul racked and tormented by unappeased hunger after knowledge. I have been called the peasant-wenches' scarecrow, and my mystery is to instruct young harlots in Latin, and exorcise the sausages from their chimney-pieces into my belly. The King of Bohemia is my brother, and the All-Father nourishes us both, though in my case, I have the most labour of doing it, and, two days since, hard-hearted as are all fathers, he intended so to misuse me as to save the life of a famished wolf with my poor carcass. Had I not struck down that wolf, Master Colleague, you would not now have had the honour of making my reverend acquaintanceship. *In saecula, saeculorum, Amen.*'

Goldmund, still unversed in the gallows-humour of this sort, felt drawn towards something in this tough vagrant, although he misliked the harsh laugh in which the man applauded his own jests, and the long, unshaven face scared him a little. Still he was easily persuaded to take him as companion on the roads since, whether or no his tale of the slaughtered wolf had been a brag, two were always stronger and safer than one. But Victor refused to set out again till, as he said, he had taught a little Latin to the peasants, so he quartered himself in the village for one more night. His way of going to work was not like Goldmund's in all his wanderings till that time, when he asked for shelter in a village. Victor slunk along from hut to hut, gossiping with a woman at every doorway, poking his long nose in stalls and kitchens, loath to go on his way until he had taken tribute at every house. He had tales of the wars in Italy for each goodwife, squatting beside her fire, and bawling out the song of the fight at Pavia, with a certain cure for the grand-dam's falling teeth and rheumy legs, stuffing his jerkin down to the belt with nuts, shavings of pear, and bits of bread. He had been in every place, it seemed, and knew all know-ledge. Goldmund sat watching him open-mouthed, as he fought his unending fight for victuals, flattering some and scaring others, bragging to set them gaping, ranting Latin tags and playing the scholar, fuddling their wits with chequered knaveries, his sharp eyes straying all the while from face to face, noting each half-open cupboard, each loaf, the nail for every key. Young Goldmund saw that this was a seasoned vagabond, weathered to sun and frost, and one who had lived in many climes, gone cold and hungry for many years, and so grown insolent and cunning, in the bitter fight for perilous, uncertain life. Such was the end of those who stayed too long on the highways. Would he, too, be like it one day?

Next morning they jogged out together and, for the first time, Goldmund had a companion. By their third day he had learned many things. To satisfy the three first needs of vagrants; security from mortal danger, shelter from the cold, and a full belly, had grown less a thought, with Victor, than an instinct. Long years on the roads had taught him much, and so he was past master of many arts; could tell from imperceptible signs the nearness of any human habita-tion, even in the dark, or in deep snow; knew to a hair which place in a wood or field it were best to sleep or sit to rest in; could see, the very instant he entered a room, the exact degree of its owner's riches or poverty, how good-hearted he was, or curious, or fearful. His young companion listened eagerly, but when Goldmund once answered his advice by telling him he made a mistake to approach human beings with so much guile, and that he, although quite ignorant of these arts, had seldom been refused hospitality when he asked for it in friendly words, the tall, spare Victor laughed, and answered good-humouredly:

'Well, little Goldmund, you are in luck, no doubt. You are so young, and look so brave, and seem such a handsome, innocent seraph, that your looks make you worth keeping for the night. You please the women, and the men say: "There's no harm in him. Why, he couldn't so much as hurt a fly". But, listen, my young friend, youth fades; the angel's face gets a stubble on it; wrinkles come, and hose need patching, so that, before a man knows where he is, he has turned into an ugly, ill-looking guest, with only hunger in his eyes, in place of all the sweet, pretty inno-cence: and then he must know something of the world, or soon he'll be lying out on the dung-heap, with every cur in the village to come piss on him. But I think you'll not stay long on the roads. You have too dainty hands and fine yellow hair. You'll soon creep off where you find you can have a better life, into some large, warm marriage bed, or some fine, fat little cloister, or a warm, snug scrivener's room. Why, with that good cloth on your back you might be a junker.'

Still laughing he passed his hands over Goldmund's jer-kin, who felt his fingers, touching and seeking in every pocket. He drew off, remembering his ducat. Then he told of the knight's castle, and how he had earned these good new clothes with his Latin, till Victor could not understand how he had left such a snug nest in midwinter, and Gold-mund, unused to lying, let him know a little of Julia and

Lydia. This brought these two companions their first quarrel. In Victor's eyes Goldmund had been a fool without his fellow, to run off so, with no more ado, leaving the castle and its maids in the keeping of their good Father in heaven. This must be remedied, and soon he would have a plan for doing it. Together they would seek out that castle, and though Goldmund, of course, must never show himself, Victor, his friend, would care for all the rest. He must write a little love-message to Lydia: with that as his warrant his friend would be welcomed, and by God's wounds! would never leave the stronghold again without this or that in gold or gear as his recompense. And so he gossiped; till Goldmund, having refused, at last grew angry, and would not hear another word of the matter, or let Victor learn the knight's name, or where his castle might be situated.

When Victor saw him so ruffled he laughed again, and feigned good-fellowship. 'Well,' he grinned, 'bite all your teeth out if it pleases you. All I will say to you, young sir, is that you make us both miss a good catch, and that is not the way of a kind colleague. But you'll hear nothing, it seems; you are a rich knight, and will ride back again, storm the castle, and carry off the wench on your charger. Boy, your head's stuffed full with humours and foolery. All's one: I'll be content to jog at your side until our shoes freeze off our feet.'

Goldmund sulked until evening. But since, at sundown, they had no shelter, nor could see any trace of human kind, he was thankful enough to let Victor pick their sleeping-place, help him build their couch with pine-branches, and rig up a shelter by the wood's edge, between two tree-trunks, against the wind. They munched good bread and cheese, out of Victor's bulging wallet. Goldmund, now ashamed at his anger, showed himself tractable and helpful, offering his companion his woollen shift for the night, and undertaking the first watch, when they agreed to watch by turns, and keep off wolves. The other lay down to sleep on their bed of twigs. For a while Goldmund leaned against a pine-trunk, very quiet, not to trouble his fellow's sleep. Then, since he froze, he paced the wood. The circle of his steps grew ever wider; he looked up at the pointed tips of pines, like spears, thrust at the leaden sky, his heart a little sad and afraid of the deep, still, freezing night around him, as though his own warm, living heart beat solitary, in a world of never-answering silence. Then he stole back, to listen to his sleeping comrade's breath. Deeper than ever before, did he feel the disquiet of the homeless, who have set no wall of castle, house, or cloister, between themselves and the great fear; who go naked through a world of strangers and enemies, alone under icy, mocking stars, with prowling beasts, among the patient, resolute trees.

No, he thought, he would never become like Victor; not if he strayed the roads his whole life long. Never could he manage to assume that vagabond's defence against the fear, his sly, thief's tricks, to hunt up a living; his bold, ranting kind of foolery, the mouthing gallows-humour of Bramarbas. Perhaps this trickster was right, and Goldmund could never be his colleague, never the completed vagrant, and would one day have to creep back to the shelter of walls. But whether or no, he would always know himself a homeless one, nowhere really secure and well-protected: the world would be a riddle to the end; a gruesome, fair, unanswerable riddle, and, to the end he must listen to its silence, in the midst of which his heart thumped so wildly, and seemed so transitory and frail. A few stars glittered high above him: no wind, though distant clouds seemed to drift.

Victor did not wake for many hours since Goldmund had not ventured to rouse him. At last he shouted:

'Come, you must get some rest, or tomorrow you'll be fit for nothing.'

Goldmund obeyed, lay on the branches, and shut his eyes.

e was worn out, yet no sleep came. His thoughts kept him awake, and a new sensation along with them, one that he himself could not explain, as though he were uneasy for his comrade. Nor could he understand how he ever brought himself to speak of Lydia to this ruffian, with his strident laugh, his bawdry, and impudent beggary. He was enraged with Victor and with himself, and pondered with a heavy heart on his best means of parting company. Nevertheless he must have dozed, since suddenly he knew with a start, that Victor's hands were fumbling on his body, straying here and there with quick caution, and thrusting into the pockets of his jerkin. In one lay his knife, in the other the ducat. Victor would steal both if he could find them. He pretended still to be asleep, and as if in the heaviest slumber, shifted his arm. Victor drew back. Goldmund, with fury in his heart, resolved to go from him next day.

But when, perhaps an hour after this, Victor bent over him again, and began to rummage in his pocket, Goldmund grew cold for very rage. He lay quite still, but opened his eyes, and said scornfully:

'Go now! You'll find nothing here to steal.'

The thief, in terror at this, gripped Goldmund's throat between his hands, who struggled, and strove to fling him off. But the other pressed down tighter and tighter, setting his knee against his chest. Then Goldmund, as his breath was extinguished, wriggled and tore with his whole body, made suddenly wary and alert, as he could not manage to break loose, by the instant fear of death that entered his mind. At last he brought his hand round to his pocket, as the grip tightened upon his throat, whipped the little hunting-knife far out, and struck down, quickly and blindly, several times, on the kneeling Victor. An instant later Victor's grip fell loose, and there was air again. Goldmund drew a deep, wild breath of delight, exulting in his rescued life.

Then he strove to scramble up, but the long thin comra~
fell in a heap on him, crumpled, with a rattling groan, h~
blood streaming down on Goldmund's face. Only then could
he thrust him aside and rise. There, in grey light, the long,
spare carcass sat hunched up, slippery with blood, when
Goldmund clasped it. He raised its head: it dropped again
like a soft, heavy sack. The blood still oozed from his nape
and back, while from his mouth, in a wild sigh, that soon
diminished, the life ebbed out of him.

'Now I have slain a man,' thought Goldmund, and
thought it again and again as he knelt above the dying Victor, watching the pallor stiffen out his face. 'Holy Mother of
God, now I have slaughtered.' He could hear his own voice
saying the words.

Suddenly to remain became unbearable. He caught up
his knife, and wiped it on the woollen shift, still worn by the
other, woven by Lydia's hands to keep her love warm;
sheathed it in its wooden case, and thrust it away into his
pocket: sprang up, and ran off with all his might.

This merry vagrant's death was a heavy grief to him.
Shuddering, as the sun arose, he cleaned all the blood from
off his body: for a day and night wandered aimlessly. It
was hunger at last that spurred him up, and ended his
remorse and terror.

Lost in the empty snow-bound country, without shelter,
path, or bite to stay his entrails, he grew wild and desperate
at last, howling his need like a beast, sinking again and
again, worn out; longing only to sleep, and die in the snow.
But famine would grant him no peace. He ran madly on,
avid to live, quickened and spurred by the bitterest hunger
and despair, by soulless strength and wild desire, the sheer
stark force of naked life in him. From juniper-bushes, laden
with their snow, he clawed, with stiff blue fingers, the
shrivelled berries, chewed up the bitter fruit, strewn with
pine-needles, whose sharp taste maddened him, devoured

133

ndfuls of snow to still his thirst. Blowing in his frozen
ands, he sank down to rest upon a hillock, eagerly spying
out the land. Only heath and woodland within sight, nowhere any traces of men. Over him flew two ravens; he
eyed them maliciously. No, they should not get him for
their supper, not with an ounce of strength still in his legs,
a spark of human warmth still in his blood. He stood up,
to fight again with mighty death, ran on and on, while in
the fevered exhaustion of this last effort, a thousand strangest
thoughts possessed his mind, and he cracked wild jests
with himself, half in his head and half in words. He shouted
to Victor, whom he had stabbed, taunting him in harsh
scorn of his death: 'How is it with you, sly brother?
Does the moon shine clear through your ribs yet? Are two
foxes snuffling round your ears, lad? You told me once you
killed a wolf. Did you bite out his throat or tear his tail off?
So you wanted my ducat, you old guzzler! But you see
little Goldmund was your match – eh, Victor, he tickled
your ribs finely! And all the time you'd a wallet of cheese
and sausage, you swine, you gormandizer.' Such jests as
these he proclaimed, howling and panting, mocking the
dead, and crowing over him, laughing the fool to scorn, for
letting himself be slaughtered like a fool, the poor knave, the
silly swaggerer!

Then he thought no more of poor, lean Victor, since Julia
seemed to run in front of him, just as she had left him that
night. To her he cried out little love-words, tempting her
with lewd, jocund cries, asking her body; let her come to
him, strip off her shirt, and they'd go to heaven together,
for one hour only before they died, an instant only before
they stank and rotted. Begging her, enticing her on, he told
of her little jutting breasts, her legs, and the rough, gold
hair under her armpits. And again, as he stumbled on his
way, in the snowy tuft-grass of the moorland, with stiff legs,
and drunk with pain, triumphant with the flickering greed

for life, he began to whisper to another. This time it w
Narziss he talked with, telling him new thoughts, new jests
new wisdom.

'Do you fear, Narziss,' he asked him, 'has your blood
run cold? have you not seen it? Yes, my friend, the world
is full of death, he sits on every hedge, and stands in wait
round every tree-trunk, so there's no help to be got by
building stone walls and dormitories, and churches, and
chapels of ease. He'll spy you out through any window;
he can smile, he knows each of you so well, and at midnight
you can hear him chuckle, calling your name outside the
house. Sing your psalms and light up your tapers on your
altars, hurry to your matins and vespers, gather your herbs
in the stillroom, pile your books together in your libraries.
Do you fast, *amice*? Do you watch? None of it all will do
you good: friend Bones will take it all away from you,
strip off the flesh, and leave you rattling. Run, Narziss,
make haste. There's junketing out in the fields: run – only
keep your bones together, man, they'll fall apart unless you
look to them. Bones won't stay tight for any man! Alas for
our poor bones! Alas for our poor soft gullet and belly, alas
for our poor bit of brain under the skull. All that melts
away like the snow. It all runs off to the devil, while crows,
like black priests, croak on their branches.'

For long the wanderer could not tell what place he was
in, or where he went – if he spoke, if he ran on, or lay on his
face. He tripped on tufts, ran against trees, clutched, as he
fell, at brambles, thick with snow. Yet the will to run from
death was strongest in him, ever hunting him up, and urging him forward, chasing the blind runner over his ground!

When at last he fell in a long swoon this happened in the
very same village where, some days back, he had met the
wandering scholar, and held his rush-light over a groaning
birth. Then he lay still; the folk came out and stood around
him gossiping, but he could not hear them any more. The

man he had pleased with his love knew his face again, and shuddered to see it, took pity on him, let her husband scold, and lugged his half-dead body into her cow-stall.

It was not so long before Goldmund was on his feet, and ready to take the roads afresh. His long sleep, the warmth of the stable, the goat's milk given him by the woman, had soon brought back the strength to his body. And all the rest was half-forgotten, his trudging at Victor's side, the sad, frozen night under the pines, his fellow's fearful end, his days in the wilderness. But though it had half-faded something was left of it. Some fear he could never name refused to leave him, although he put it from him into the past: a terror, and yet a precious thing, sunk deep in him but still a part of his mind, an aftertaste, a lingering thought, an iron ring about his heart. In scarce two years he had learned all there was to learn of vagrants' lives: solitude, freedom, the instinct to spy out beasts and trees, fleeting love, without any faith in it, need, bitter as death. For days he had been the guest of summer fields, for days and months the guest of forests; days in the snow, and days with the fear of death on him.

And in all the keenest, strongest feeling had been that he must fight off death; that, small and miserable as he knew himself, he yet, in this last desperate encounter, had felt the glorious, terrible hold of life in him. The echoes of this battle still rang through him, his heart was graven with it indelibly; as deep a knowledge as that other, of the gesture and expression of desire, so like to those of the dying, and bearing mothers.

How short a time since that mother had lain, groaning and puckering; how short a time since Victor had crumpled together with a groan; how softly, quickly, his blood had dripped!

Oh, and he too, how those days of hunger had taught him to keep guard against death; how they had torn at his en-

trails, freezing him almost to ice! And how he
struggled against it all, striking death full in the face; w
what mortal fear, what grim exultation, he had guarde
himself! There was not much more to be learnt in the
world, he felt. He might perhaps talk of it to Narziss. Nobody else would understand.

When Goldmund, on his straw bed in the cow-stall, came
to his senses again for the first time, he missed the ducat
from his pocket. Had he lost it in that terrible half-swoon?
He pondered the matter long. He loved his ducat, and
would not willingly have lost it. Money might mean very
little, since he scarcely knew how to value it, but this gold-
piece had grown dear to him for two reasons. It was the only
gift of Lydia that remained, since her woollen shift, on
Victor's body, lay in the forest, stiff with blood. Then, above
all, it had been this piece of gold he would not relinquish;
for its sake he had struggled with Victor, and killed him
for it. If now his ducat should be lost his cruel deed, in a
sense, would have lost its meaning. After long cogitation he
decided to speak his mind to the peasant-woman.

'Christine,' he whispered, 'I had a gold ducat in my
pouch, and it isn't there any more.'

'Oh, then you've noticed,' she said, with an odd, tender
smile, yet sly, which pleased him so that, weak as he was,
he slipped an arm about her waist.

'You're a funny lad,' she said gently, 'so fine and clever,
yet so simple. Does any but a fool wander the roads with a
gold ducat loose in his pouch? I found your ducat in your
jerkin, as soon as I laid you in the straw.'

'Did you? And where is it now, then?'

'Seek it,' she laughed; and did indeed let him search a
long while, before she showed him the place in his jerkin
into which she had sewn his piece of gold. To this she added
a whole string of good, sage, motherly counsel, which he
forgot as soon as she gave it, though he never would forget

over's service, or the sly, kind look in her peasant's
.

He strove to show her that he was grateful, and when, in
a short while, he could take the roads again and was eager
to get up and go his ways, she held him back, saying that
soon the moon would change, and then the weather must
certainly be warmer. So it was. When Goldmund went his
ways the snow lay, sick and grey, on the roads; the air was
heavy and damp, and spring winds moaned in the sky.

CHAPTER TEN

ONCE more the ice drove down the streams, and violets thrust up through the earth, scenting the air where leaves had rotted, and Goldmund trudged again through the pied seasons, his senses drinking their fill of woodland, mountain, and cloud, as he strayed from village to village, castle to castle, wench to wench, sitting to rest in the cool of many evenings, sad at heart, under lighted windows, where far off, in a gleam of candle-light, there shimmered, clear, remote and unattainable, all that the night can show to vagrants of this world's comfort, happiness, and peace.

Again and again it all returned – once, twice, thrice – all he had believed he knew so well. Yet each time he saw it it had changed: the long trudge over field and moorland, or on stony paths; the summer's sleep in forests; the loitering up a village street, at the heels of wenches arm in arm, on their way back from haymaking or hop-picking; the first shudder of autumn, and evil nip of early frost: it all passed and returned, like an endless particoloured ribbon across his eyes.

Much rain and snow had fallen on Goldmund when he clambered one day to the summit of the steep side of a beechwood, full of light, yet thick already with clear, green buds, and above, through branches at the crest, peered down on another country-side, stretching away before him, rejoicing his heart, filling him with desire and expectancy. For days he had known himself near it, and had spied about for what he saw. Now, on this midday tramp, it had come when he least awaited it, delighting him and strengthening his longing. He looked down from between grey trunks gently-stirring foliage on the brown and greenish valley ..ead beneath, in its midst a wide, blue, glassy river. Now ..e would be done with field-paths, with straying here and there across the land in the mystery of forest and heath, with only very rarely any castle or some poor village to receive him. There, through the valley, flowed the river and, stretching away along its banks, the finest, broadest, most famous highway in the Empire, with rich, fat country on either side, and rafts and galleons on its waters, while the road led on into fair villages, to castles, cloisters, and wealthy towns.

And whoever would might walk for days along it, with no fear in his heart of losing it suddenly, in the thick of woodland, or in a marsh, as he might the wretched field-tracks of the peasants. Here was a new thing to please his heart.

And by sundown he had reached a merry village, set between the river and red vineyards, its fair timbers and gables striped in scarlet, with many arched doors to the houses, and narrow alleys, built up steps. A smithy threw its glow across the street, with a clear ring of hammer on anvil. The vagrant looked in every nook and corner, snuffing up the musty reek of wine and casks at tavern doors, the cool, fishy smell off the river-bank, visiting God's house and His acre, not forgetting to spy out a warm barn for the night. But first he would beg his victuals at the priest's house. There he found a fat rosy priest, who asked him of his life, which Goldmund told, adding a little here and there, and leaving out whatever he felt unseemly. On this he was given an honest welcome and, with good fare and wine in his belly, had to pass the evening with the reverence, telling him stories of this and that. Next day he jogged on along the highway, beside him the river with its rafts, and barges laden up with merchandise, which he haled, and some took him a stretch of his way. Spring days sped past him,

crowded with images: villages, and little towns welcor
him, women smiled through garden trellises, or knelt
the brown soil and dug-in plants: girls sang at sundown ir.
village streets.

A young miller's wench pleased him so greatly that he
stayed two days in her neighbourhood to court her: she was
always ready to laugh and chatter with him, and he longed
to be a miller's boy, and live in the mill with her for ever.
He sat with fishermen, and helped the carters to feed their
beasts and comb them, earning meat and bread, and a lift,
for his pains. This friendly traveller's world rejoiced him;
he was pleased, after so much loneliness and deep meditation in the woods, to gossip with well-fed and garrulous
people, eating his fill every day, after many months of spare
diet. He let the smooth, gay stream bear him along and, the
nearer they came to the Bishop's city, the richer and jauntier
grew the high road.

Once, as night drew in, he loitered down a village street
by the river's edge, under fair trees, thick with their leaves.
The river flowed calm and mighty, sighing, and lapping
the bank beneath their roots: over a hillock rose the moon,
glittering on the stream, and drawing out shadows from the
trees. There he found a girl, who sat weeping. She had had
a quarrel with her boy, now he had run off and left her.
Goldmund sat beside her, hearing her plaint, stroking her
hands, and telling her of the deer out in the forest, and she
did not say no to a kiss. But then her boy came back to seek
her, who had cooled down, and was sorry for their strife,
found Goldmund sitting with his love, and flung himself
on to him at once, pummelling him hard with both his fists.
Goldmund had some trouble to beat him, but managed in
the end to fight him off, and the lad ran cursing through the
village. The girl had long since run away.

Goldmund, not trusting this peace, gave up all thoughts
of finding himself a sleeping-place, and walked on half the

by moonlight, through the quiet, silvery world, very
tent, rejoicing in the strength of his legs, till dew cleaned
e dust off his shoes, and he, grown suddenly weary, lay
down under the first tree to sleep.

The sun had long been bright when something tickled his
cheek and roused him. He brushed it off with a sleepy hand,
turned over and settled himself again, but was soon roused
up by this same tickling. There stood a girl looking down at
him, and tickling his face with the tip of an osier switch.
He stumbled up; they stood and laughed at each other,
and she led him to a barn, where he might sleep better, if he
would. They lay together for a while, till she ran off, and
came back with a bowl of milk for him, warm from her cow.
He gave her a blue ribbon for her hair, which he had picked
up on the road a while since, and they kissed and tumbled
again before he went further. Francisca was her name, and
it grieved him to part from her.

That night he begged for shelter at a cloister, and there,
next morning, he heard a mass. A thousand memories came
to life in him, born of the cool dank air from the vaultings,
the clattering of sandals along the aisles. Most strangely he
remembered his home in Mariabronn. When mass was done
and the cloister church all quiet again, Goldmund still remained on his knees, his heart marvellously stirred. The
night before he had had many dreams; now he felt a need
to confess, and rid himself of his past, if he could do it;
somehow to change his way of life, though how he could
not truly say: perhaps it was only the cloister, bringing
memories of his fervid youth in Mariabronn, and these had
stirred his soul a little. He longed to assoil himself and do
penance, telling of his many minor vices, but, above all else,
of Victor's death, which still lay heavy on his mind. So he
found a Pater, to whom he confessed it all, and especially
his cruel dagger-thrusts, into poor Victor's nape and back.
Oh, it had been long since his last confession: the number

and weight of his sins loaded him so, that gladly he would have accepted any pains for them! But this confessor seemed to know the lives of vagrants, and showed neither horror nor surprise, hearing him quietly to the end, gravely and gently warning and admonishing him, without once saying he would be damned. Goldmund stood up with a light heart, prayed, and said his penance, as the Pater had directed, at the high altar, and was already on his way out of the church. Then a shaft of sunlight streamed through the window into a side-chapel, and he saw a statue, which seemed so to speak to his heart and call him to it, that he turned as though to greet a love, and stood, struck to the heart, and full of reverence. It was a Blessed Mother of God, in wood, standing there so tranquil and tender, with her blue cloak spread from her little shoulders, her soft maiden's hand stretched out to him, her eyes so bright, above the sorrowful mouth, her pure forehead curved in such living guise, so deeply lovely and half of earth, that he felt he had never before seen anything like it. He would never have done gazing at that mouth, at the tender, loving bend of the neck.

He knew that something had sprung to life in him, something half-known, and yet often seen in dreams, something he had longed for all his days. He tried many times to leave the statue, but again and again it drew him back to it. When, at last, he had torn himself free he turned, to find his confessor standing behind him.

'You think her beautiful?' asked the priest.

'Unspeakably beautiful,' said Goldmund.

'Many say that. And others that she is no true Mother of God, that she is too new-fangled and worldly for them, and everything about her false and overwrought. We hear much disputation on the matter. Well, she pleases you, and I am glad of it. She has only stood a year in our church; a donor of our house made us the gift of her. She is by Master Nicholas.'

Master Nicholas: who is he? Where does he live? Father oh, do you know him? Oh, I beg you, tell me what you know! He must be a great, wonderfully gifted man to be able to make a thing like that.'

'I know very little about him. He is a carver in wood, who lives in our bishop's city, a day's journey off, and has great fame at his craft. Such artists are not usually saints, nor is he, I think, but certainly a fine and gifted man. I have often seen him. . . .'

'You have seen him? What does he look like?'

'My son, you seem to be bewitched by him. Well, seek him out yourself, then, and give him a greeting from Pater Bonifazius.'

Goldmund poured forth his thanks. The Pater left him with a smile, but he stood on a while longer, held by this mysterious image, whose breasts seemed to breathe, and in whose face such pain and sweetness dwelt together that both were clutching at his heart. He went from the church transfigured, out into a world utterly changed. Since his sight of this sweet and blessed Mother of God, Goldmund had a thing he had never known, a thing he had often smiled at, or envied, in others: an aim. Yes, he had an aim, and would reach it, and so, perhaps, his whole confused existence might take on new meaning and unity. The knowledge brought both joy and fear. The fair road was no longer what it had been, a playground, a good place to enjoy, and loiter in; it was nothing now but a road to the city; to the Master! He hurried on, and by sunset the city lay before him, its towers glittering above walls. He saw painted shields and chiselled escutcheons over the gates, ran under them with a pounding heart, scarce heeding the bustle of the streets, the mounted knights, the carts and litters. Neither knights nor litters, city nor bishop, were of worth to him. He asked the first citizen at the gate to direct him to the house of Master Nicholas, and was bitterly grieved that he knew nothing of

him. Then he came out on a square of lordly houses, some
gilt, some painted and decked with images. Tall and mag-
nificent over a doorway, was set the statue of a lansquenet,
painted in strong and glorious colours. He was not so beautiful as the image in the cloister church, yet he stood with
such an air, jutting his calf, thrusting his bearded chin into
the world, that Goldmund almost knew for certain that
here was a work of this same Master Nicholas.

He ran into the house, fell down steps, knocked at doors,
and so came into the presence of a gentleman, in a velvet,
fur-trimmed gown, who asked him his business. He
inquired for the house of Master Nicholas. What errand
had he for him? the gentleman asked, and Goldmund had
pains to master himself, and answer merely he had a message for him. The gentleman named the street the Master
dwelt in, but when Goldmund had found his way there it
was night. Overjoyed, but still uneasy, he stood before the
Master's house, and would much have liked to go straight
into it. Then he remembered that it was late, and he all be-
grimed and sweating from his journey, so forced himself
to tarry a little longer, though for a while he could not bear
to go from the door.

He saw light come into the window and, just as he was
about to turn away, a figure came over to lean out of it, a
very beautiful girl, with yellow hair, through which the
light of the tapers, in the room behind her, shimmered down.

Next day when the town was awake and noisy again,
Goldmund washed his face, in the cloister where he had
slept, knocked the dust off his clothes and shoes, and found
his way back to this same street. He beat on the house-door:
there came a serving-woman, who seemed unwilling to
lead him straight in to her master, but he managed to soften
her old heart, and in the end she led him through the house.
In his little work-room stood Master Nicholas, a tall,
bearded man in a leather apron; of forty or fifty odd, it

eemed to Goldmund. He stared with sharp, light blue eyes
at the stranger, and curtly asked what was his will. Goldmund gave him greeting from Pater Boniface.

'And is that all?'

'Master,' said Goldmund, sick at heart, 'I saw your
Mother of God, out there in the cloister. Oh, I beg you not
to look so unfriendly; it is sheer love and reverence brings
me to you. You do not scare me. I have lived too long on
the roads in frost and snow, and known too much hunger
for that. There is no man in the world could make me afraid.
Yet I fear you, Master. ... Oh, I have only one great wish,
and my heart is so full with it that it pains me.'

'And what kind of wish may that be?'

'To be your apprentice, and learn from you.'

'You are not alone in that, young man. But I want no
apprentices in my house, and already I have two journeymen to help me. Where do you come from, then, and who
are your parents?'

'I have none, and I come from nowhere. I was a scholar
in a cloister, where I learned Latin and Greek. Then I ran
off, and, since, I have lived on the roads.'

'And what is it makes you feel you would be a wood-
carver? Have you tried your hand at anything like it? Have
you any drawings to show me?'

'I have made many drawings and lost them all. Yet I can
tell you why I would learn your craft. I have watched many
faces and shapes, and afterwards thought of them. Some
of my thoughts have never ceased to plague me, and still
they give me no peace. I have seen how always, in every
shape, a certain form, a certain line, repeats itself; how a
forehead seems to tally with a knee, a hip with a shoulder;
and how the essence of all this is the very being and temper
of the person, who alone could have such a knee, or shoulder, or forehead. And this, too, I have noted, which I saw
one night, as I helped a woman bear her child: that the

146

sharpest pain and sweetest pleasure seem to have almost one expression.'

The Master glanced keenly at Goldmund.

'Do you know what you say?'

'Yes, Master, and so it is. It was just this which, to my own delight and commotion, I found expressed in your Holy Mother of God, and that is why I come to you now. Oh there is such grief in that pure face of hers, and yet all her pain is as though transmuted to smiles and joy. When I saw that it ran like a fire through me. All I had thought or dreamed for years seemed confirmed by it. Suddenly my dreams had ceased to be idle, and I saw at once what to do, and where I must go. Good Master Nicholas, I beg you from my heart not to turn me from you.'

Nicholas was surly still, and yet he had listened very carefully. 'Young man,' he said, 'you can talk astoundingly well of image-making, and at your age, too, I am amazed that you have such things to say of pain and pleasure. I should much like to sit out an evening with you, drink a cup of wine, and discuss all this. But hear you: to talk well and pleasantly together is one thing, to live and work together for years, is another. This is my workshop, and here I work, I do not gossip. Here it matters nothing what one has thought, or how well he knows how to speak of it, but only what he can do with his two hands. You seemed to mean what you were saying, and so I will not send you packing at once. Let us see if there is anything behind it. Did you ever try to model in wax or clay?'

At once Goldmund thought of a certain dream, dreamed by him a long while since, when he had made little clay men and women, that rose up and grew into giants. But he did not tell it, only saying humbly that he had never tried such a work.

'Good. Well, then, you must draw me something. There is a table, you see, and paper and charcoal. Sit there and draw. Take your time with it. If you please you can stay till midday or evening. And now we have talked enough. I must do my work; go and do yours.'

On the bench which Master Nicholas pointed out to him Goldmund sat down before the drawing-table. He could not set to work at once, but remained, like a quiet and eager scholar, eyeing his master with timid reverence, who soon had turned away and forgotten him, standing, hard at work on a small clay figure.

He was not as Goldmund had pictured him: he was grimmer, elder, and more decided, far less delightful and winsome; by no means happy.

His sharp, inflexible eyes were on his modelling, so that Goldmund, freed from his uneasiness, could carefully note the Master's shape. This man, he thought, might also have been a scholar had he wished it; an austere seeker out of truths, given to a work which many predecessors began before him, which one day he must leave to those that would follow; a hard, eternal work, into which the labour and devotion of generations had been poured.

So he read this Master's face. Much patience and painfully got learning, much thought on what was known already, humility, and ultimate doubt of the value of all human seeking, yet, with them, a belief in what he did, all could be seen in the outlines of the head.

Yet again the shape of the hands belied it: between them and the face there was contradiction. These hands touched the clay they moulded with firm, but very tender, fingers, stroking it as a lover might his mistress, full of desire, of dainty, tender compulsion, greedy, yet never distinguishing between what they took and what they gave, at once reverent and lustful, as sure and masterly in their motion as though from some very ancient, deep experience. Goldmund, full of wondering delight, sat watching these inspired, well-graced hands. He felt tempted to make a draw-

ing of Master Nicholas, but would not, because of this contradiction between his face and hands, which lamed him.

When for close on an hour he had watched Nicholas at
his work, striving to unearth the man's secret, his mind full
of questing thoughts, another image shaped itself slowly
in him, coming to life before his soul: the image of the man
he had known best, had loved and reverenced most in all
his life. This image was a perfect whole, without any flaw
or division in it, although it, too, was many-faceted, and
bore on it the scars of a deep struggle. It was that of his
friend, Narziss.

Clearer and clearer its shape defined itself, printing its
lines upon his thought, showing him the hidden law
informing this beloved being: the fair head, chiselled by
intellect, the controlled, beautiful lips, made firm-set and
shapely to serve the spirit, the shadow of pain about the eyes,
the lean shoulders, emaciated in their struggle against the
flesh; the long neck, and gentle, lovely hands. Never since
the day he broke from the cloister had Goldmund seen his
friend so clearly, or known his spirit so complete.

As in a dream, yet full of preparation and foresight, he
began to make a careful drawing, with loving fingers stroking in the outline of the head, as it stood already in his
heart, forgetting the Master, forgetting himself, and where
he sat. He did not see how the light in the workshop slowly
changed, or that Nicholas several times had glanced across
at him. He finished his drawing, like a task imposed by his
love, to raise up out of his heart, and fix for all time, the
picture within him of his friend.

Nicholas came over to the drawing-table.

'It is midday and so now I go to dinner. Come with me if
you like. You have finished something; let me see.'

He stood over Goldmund and glanced down, thrust him
aside and took up the sheet of paper, carefully, in expert
hands. Goldmund, roused up from his dream, now stared

in apprehension at the Master, as Nicholas stood examining his drawing, with a sharp gaze, through light blue eyes.

'Who is this you have drawn?' he asked after a while.

'My friend, a scholar, a young monk.'

'Good. Now wash your hands. The fountain stands out there in the courtyard. Then we will go to dinner. The journeymen do not eat with us today; they have work to do out in the city.'

Goldmund hurried off obediently, found courtyard and fountain, and washed himself. He would have given much to know the Master's thoughts. When he returned, Nicholas had left the workshop, though he heard him move in the next room. When he came back he, too, had washed himself, and now, instead of his leather apron, wore a fine doublet of cloth, and looked very fair and majestic in it. He led the way up a staircase; its banister-posts bore small carved angels' heads in nut wood, over a landing where stood old and new wooden images, and on, through a pleasant room, its four walls and ceiling of hard woods, to a laid table, set in the window. A young girl came running into the room. Goldmund knew her at once for the yellow-haired maid of the night before.

'Lisbeth,' said the Master, 'bring a fresh platter. Here's a guest. His name is – but now I remember he never told it me.'

Goldmund named himself.

'Well, Goldmund, then. Is dinner ready?'

'In a minute, father.'

She fetched the platter, and ran out again, but soon came back with the old serving-woman, who brought them their meat: hog's flesh, lentils, and fine white bread. As he ate the father discussed this and that with his daughter, but Goldmund sat dumb, eating little, and feeling very shamefaced and uneasy. The maid pleased him well; a fine, high-bred maid, as tall almost as her father, but she sat as modest and aloof as though she had been behind glass, not granting either a look or word to the stranger.

When they had done the Master said:

'Now I must rest for half an hour. Go back to the workshop, or into the streets if you will, and then we will talk of this matter.'

Goldmund left him, with a bow. An hour or more since this Master had seen his drawing, and yet he had not said a word of it. And still half an hour to wait! He would not go back to the workshop, since he did not want to see his work again, but out into the little courtyard, where he sat on the edge of the fountain, staring at the tiny thread of water, which came sparkling and splashing from its mouth, down into the deep stone trough, wrinkling, as it fell, into fine waves, drawing a little air to the depths along with it, which for ever forced its way back, rising in pearly bubbles to the surface. Perhaps, thought Goldmund, fear of death is the root of all our image-making, and perhaps, too, of all our intellect. We shrink from death, shuddering at our frail instability, sadly watching the flowers fade again and again, knowing in our hearts how soon we shall be as withered as they. So that when, as craftsmen, we carve images, or seek laws to formulate our thoughts, we do it all to save what little we may from the linked, never-ending dance of death.

The woman from whom this Master drew his madonna is faded perhaps, or dead already: he, too, will soon be dead, others will live in his house and eat at this table. But his work will stand a hundred years from now, or longer still, shimmering in the quiet dark cloister church, smiling with the same lovely mouth, as beautiful, young, and full of pain.

He heard the Master's step on the staircase, and ran back into the workshop. Master Nicholas walked up and down, with a glance, from time to time, at Goldmund's drawing, stood still, at last, at the window, and said, in his dry grudging fashion:

'The usage with our guild is this: that each apprentice should serve at least four years, and his father pay the Master a fee for him.'

Since here he paused Goldmund thought that Nicholas was afraid of his having no prentice-fee to offer him. In a flash he had pulled out his knife, slit the threads round the hidden ducat, and fished it up. Nicholas watched all this in surprise, and, when Goldmund tendered his ducat, began to laugh at him.

'Oho. Is that how you feel?' he chuckled. 'No, young sir, you may keep your gold-piece. I have told you how our guild treats its apprentices. But I am no ordinary master-craftsman, nor can you be any ordinary pupil, since such as they must enter the workshop by thirteen, fourteen, or fifteen years at latest; and for half his time, an apprentice must drudge for his Master, and do any labour he may be set to. But you are a grown man, and should, by your age, have been journeyman, long since, or Master even. We have never seen a bearded apprentice in our guild. Besides, as I said before, I want no apprentices in my house. Nor do you look the kind of fellow who lets himself be told to come and go.'

Goldmund was at the height of his impatience; each care-ful word was like another turn of the rack to him, they sounded unbearably tedious and pedantic. He cried out hotly:

'Why should you say all this to me, since you have no mind to make me your apprentice?'

The Master continued unmoved, as slow as before.

'I have considered your request for an hour, and now it is for you to listen patiently. I have thought of your drawing. It has its faults, and yet it is beautiful. If it were not I should have given you half a gulden, and sent you packing, and forgotten you. I would like to help you become a carver, but, as I say, you cannot be my 'prentice. And whoever has not done his apprenticeship can never be a journeyman of our guild, and so can never be made Master. This I must say to you at once. But, if you can live outside, in the city, you shall try your hand and learn from me as you may. All this must be without indenture, leaving us free on either side. Break a few knives, if you will, and spoil a few woodblocks, and, if I see you are no carver, then you must turn to some other trade. Are you content?'

Goldmund had heard with joy and shame.

'I thank you,' he cried out, 'from my heart. I have no home, and can live here among houses as in the woods. I see you would not have to answer for me. I hold it great good fortune to have you teach me, and thank you from my soul that you grant me this.'

CHAPTER ELEVEN

HERE in the city new sights surrounded Goldmund, and another life spread out before him. As this countryside, gay with its river and villages, had drawn him on and on with its enticements, so too the city held many promises. Though, deep in his heart, his grief and wisdom were untouched, life with all her colours tickled his senses, captivating the surface of his mind. Round him, with all her arts, lay the Bishop's city, rich in a hundred pastimes, with women to love, while ever-increasing skill sharpened his senses. With the Master's help he found a lodging in the Fish-Market, in a guilder's house, from whom, as from Nicholas himself, he learned the craft of working in wood and stucco, colour, varnish, and gold-leaf.

Goldmund was not one of those luckless artificers who, though they bear within them the highest gifts, can find no right craft by which to express them. There are many such who, seeing all the beauty of earth, can find no way to give it forth again, and share with others what they have seen. To him it was easy as sport to use his hands, and attain the perfect deftness of his craft; as easy, as on a feast-day evening, to pick up lute-playing from a journeyman, or dance on Sundays on village greens. He had hardships and disappointments to surmount, was forced to spoil a few woodblocks, and several times cut his fingers to the bone. But these early stages were soon passed, and he had his skill, even if the Master grew impatient, and chid him somewhat as follows:

'It is good you are not my pupil and journeyman, Goldmund – good that we know you are come from the forests,

and that one day you will certainly go back to them. A
man who did not know this of you, that you are no hone.
craftsman and citizen, but only a strolling gipsy off the high
road, might be tempted to set you such tasks as any other
Master asks of his men. You are a good enough workman
when it pleases you : but last week you idled for three
whole days, and yesterday, in the Castle workshop, where I
sent you to polish the two angels, you lay and snored half
the day.'

Such reproaches were just, and Goldmund always heard
him in silence, without a word in his own excuse. He knew
well he was no dependable, busy workman. For so long as
any work held his mind, with such obstacles to surmount as
could give him the joyous sense of his own skill, he was
expert and zealous at his craft. But heavy drudging he always loathed, and those many tasks which go to the making
of a craftsman, which though not heavy in themselves, require great pains and finnicking patience. These were an
unsupportable burden. Often he wondered at himself. Had
a few years on the roads been enough to make an idler of
him? Was the nature he inherited from his mother beginning to master him altogether? Or what did he lack? He
thought of his first years in the cloister, when he had been
such an industrious, fervent scholar. Why had he been so
patient in those days, so willing to give up his mind to Latin
syntax and master all those strings of Greek aorists for
which, at heart, he cared so little? He would often ponder
this enigma, and his answer was that it had been love which
steeled his will, and gave his industry such wings. His dili-
gence had all been nothing save the deep longing to satisfy
Narziss, whose esteem, he felt, was only to be gained by
grateful industry. Then he would toil for days and hours together to earn one smile of recognition, and this, when it
came, had been ample recompense. Narziss had been his
friend : yet strangely it had been this learned Narziss who

shown him his inaptitude for learning and conjured
up a beloved mother-image in his mind. So that, instead
of learning, virtue and monasticism, the strongest primal
urge in his nature had mastered him — lechery and carnal
love, the longing to depend on none, and to wander. Then
came Master Nicholas' sorrowful Virgin, to reveal to him
an artist in himself, with a new way of life, and fetters
again. How were things with him now? Where would life
carry him in the end? Whence came these obstacles in his
mind?

At first he could not understand himself, could only perceive that, deeply as he admired Master Nicholas' skill, he
felt for him nothing at all of the love which he had borne
Narziss — that indeed he sometimes delighted to bait and
cross him. Images from Nicholas' hand, or the best among
them, were to Goldmund the summit of all achievement;
but Nicholas himself he did not reverence.

Beside this artist who had carved such a Blessed Mother
of God, with all the pain and loveliness of earth in her face
— in the heart of this seer and sage, whose hands transformed
to visible shape the deepest perception and experience, there
dwelt a second Master Nicholas, the strict and sober father
of a family, the widower, and Master in his guild, living a
retired, narrowish life, with his daughter and ugly serving-
wench; a man for ever on his guard against the deepest
urge in Goldmund, a master-craftsman, with the thoughts
of a snug, prosperous citizen.

Much as he might honour this teacher, never judge, never
let himself question a stranger, a year in his service had been
enough to show Goldmund all there was to be known of
him, down to the minutest detail. This meant so much: he
both loved and hated him, never let him out of his thoughts,
forced his way with eagerness and mistrust, alert and thirsty
after knowledge, into the secret places of his life. He observed how Nicholas kept neither apprentice nor journey-

man in his house, although there was room enough both; saw how very rarely he went forth, and as rare visited any guests. He watched his jealous passion for hi. daughter, how he strove to hide her from all other men — knew the living urge and desire, lurking behind this widower's seeming continence, his strictness, and premature old age; knew that when a commission caused him to travel, he could, in the space of a few days' journey, be marvellously transfigured and renewed. And once, in a little neighbouring town where they went to set up a carved angel, he had seen how one night on the sly, Nicholas crept out to visit a whore, and then for days was restless and illhumoured.

With these, at times, besides his eagerness to learn carving, one other conjecture kept Goldmund closely watching his master, and it filled his thoughts. It was Lisbeth, the pretty daughter, that engrossed him. He could very seldom get a sight of her since she never showed her face inside the workshop. Nor could he decide if her prudish shrinking away from men were a quality implanted by her father in her, or verily a part of her nature. It was not to be blinked that Master Nicholas had never invited Goldmund to a meal. He did his best to surround his daughter with obstacles. Lisbeth was a dainty sheltered maid. There could be no hope of loving her out of wedlock: more, whoever wanted her as his bride must be the son of rich parents, a member of one of the higher guilds, and if possible own gear and a house.

Lisbeth's beauty, so different from that of vagrant women and peasants' wives, had drawn Goldmund's eyes to her that first day. There was something in her he never fathomed, an aloofness and mystery drawing him powerfully to her, and yet arousing all his mistrust. There was a deeply modest peace and virginity, a purity, but with nothing childlike in it, with a hint of cold reserve and pride,

er all her modesty and fair breeding, so that her inno-
ce did not move and disarm him, but rather challenged
nd rasped his senses. No sooner had her shape begun to
define itself than he felt the impulse to carve her form, not
as she was, but as she might be, with awakened flesh, with
desire and anguish in her face, no little virgin but a Mag-
dalene. He would often long to see her smooth, quiet, passionless features become contorted and alive, till either in
pain or pleasure, they yielded their secret.

But another face had begun to shape itself in his heart,
although it was still not altogether his, a face that his whole
soul longed to capture, and hold in wood, but which still
eluded him and veiled itself.

This face was the face of a mother, though for years it
had lost all resemblance to that vision which arose from the
lost depths, at the end of his talk with Narziss. In nights of
joy and days of wandering, long times of solitude and restlessness, danger and close proximity to death, this mother-
face had slowly changed and renewed itself, become enriched, more set in his mind, more many-faceted. It was no
longer his own dead mother that he saw, since her colour-
ing and features, by degrees, were lost in an impersonal
mother-image, a vision of Eve the mother of all mankind.
As, in his Blessed Virgin, Master Nicholas had set forth
the pitiful, sorrowing Mother of God, with a certainty and
perfection of craftsmanship which his pupil felt he could
never reach, so Goldmund hoped, when he had mastered
the richness and surety of his craft, to shape an Eve, the
mother of the world, as she dwelt already in the deepest
sanctuary of his heart. This face within him was more than
the memory of his mother, since that love was for ever developed and transmuted. Now she had something of the
gipsy Lisa in her aspect, something of Lydia the knight's
daughter, something of many other women, all harmonized
in the one primal shape. And not only had all these faces

of well-loved women gone to build up its composition, every pang, adventure, and fresh experience, completed too, and had left in it traces of themselves. This form, if he could ever make it visible, should not be that of any creature he had known, but of life herself, the mother of all. Yet of her face and what it expressed he could have told nothing, except that in its lines he wished to realize lust and the joy of life, in their secret kinship to death and pain.

Goldmund had learned much in a year, attaining great certainty of design, and from time to time, besides his wood-carving, Nicholas would let him model in clay. His first successful work was a small clay figure, three spans high; the sweet enticing shape of Lydia's little sister Julia. The Master, though he praised this work, refused Goldmund's wish to cast it in metal. It was too unchaste and worldly for Master Nicholas, who had no wish to be its godfather! Then came a figure of Narziss, whom Goldmund set out to carve in wood, as John the beloved disciple, since Nicholas wished, if it succeeded, to make it one of a group of the Crucifixion, commissioned for a long time past, at which his journeymen laboured unceasingly, leaving the last touches to their Master.

At this Narziss-figure Goldmund worked, finding himself again, his soul and best skill in what he did, whenever he had broken away from the workshop. And this would happen very often. Love, dancing, drinking, bouts with the journeymen, dice, and a brawl if he could find it, would tear him loose from the fetters of his life, till for days together he shirked his craft, or stood all day idling and dreaming.

But this figure of St John the Disciple, whose loved and pensive face emerged before him, clearer and clearer from the wood, he only touched at hours when he was ready for it, utterly self-forgetful and absorbed. Then he would be neither gay nor melancholy, think neither of lechery nor

159

past. That first, quiet, happy gentle love with which, rejoicing in his discipleship, he had given his whole being to Narziss, returned to him again, with Narziss' image. It was not he that stood before a wood-block, hewing out a portrait with his will; far rather it was the other, was Narziss, who used the skill in his hands to draw aside from the brittle transcience of time into the clear, abiding life of his essence.

Only thus, thought Goldmund, at times in terror, could any real work be brought to birth. Such had been the birth of Nicholas' unforgettable Virgin which, on many Sundays since first he saw it, he had trudged out to the cloister-church to visit. Thus, in this sacred, hidden fashion, had been carved the best of those old figures which Nicholas stored upon his landing. Thus, too, he would carve his second work, the sole and perfect shape within his heart, more reverent and secret even than this; his Eve, the Mother of all life. Ah, that such shapes alone might ever emerge from human hands; such sacred, necessary works, not blurred by any vanity or striving! But it was not so, he had long known it. Men could contrive quite different works of art — pretty figures, fashioned with intricate skill, their owners' pride, the ornaments of church and council-house — pleasant toys, yes, but never holy, never the true-born forms of the soul! Not only had he seen many such, by Nicholas and the Masters of the Guild — toys, for all the grace of their conception, the skilful labour of their design — he knew, to his own regret and shame, had felt in his own, juggling hands, how carvers will put forth such trumpery, from idle pleasure in their cunning, vanity, and finnicking ambition.

When first such realization came to Goldmund it brought with it the sadness of death. What was the use of being a carver, to make polished angels and such trash, no matter how masterly the workmanship? Others perhaps might find their pleasure in it, handymen, fat, smug, prosperous citi-

zens, quiet little souls, easily pleased – it was not for .
For him all art and artistry were worthless unless t...
shone like the sun, had the might of storms in them – .
they brought only pleasant, narrow happiness. He did not
seek that. To gild some winsome Virgin's crown, intricate
as point-lace, with gold-leaf; that was not the work he had
in mind, even though it happened to be well paid.
What made Nicholas take so many orders? Why did he
stand for hours so attentive to the wishes of burly provosts
and councillors, come to bespeak a doorway or a rood-screen
– so eagerly, with his measuring rod in his hand? He did
it for two shabby reasons – he had set great store on being
a famous craftsman with more orders than he ever could
execute; and then because he wanted to pile up money; not
money for great feasts and enterprises, money for the pretty
Lisbeth, long since already a well-endowed young maid,
money for her costs, for brocade and points, money for her
nutwood marriage-bed with its shining coverlets and fine
linen. As though the smooth disdainful child could not have
learned love as well in any haystack!

In hours when such things were in his mind his mother's
nature rose in the depths of Goldmund, with all the pride
and scorn of the homeless for those who own, and live at
ease. In such hours the Master and his handicraft sickened
him like a taste of cold porridge and often he was near running away.

Nicholas, too, would angrily regret the trust he had
placed in this shiftless workman, who often set his patience
the sorest tests. Nor was he in any way appeased by what he
heard of Goldmund's life, his spendthrift ways, his brawls,
his many women. He had taken a gipsy, an idle apprentice
into his shop, nor did it escape his notice with what eyes the
fellow watched his daughter. If, in spite of all, he showed
more patience than came easy to him, it was born of no
feeling of duty or care for the wastrel, but solely because of

...tatue of St John the Disciple, of which he had seen the ...t design.

Something he would only half-acknowledge, a kind of love and spiritual kinship, stayed Nicholas' hand as he watched this spielmann off the highroads fashion in wood his figure from that drawing, at once so clumsy and so beautiful, so sensitive in its own queer fashion, for whose sake he had taken the fellow as his man – a carving only worked on by fits and starts, slowly and moodily, yet insistently. One day, Master Nicholas never doubted it, in spite of all these whimsies and obstacles, it would be finished, and would be such a work as the greatest masters can put forth only once or twice in a lifetime. In spite of all that riled him in his pupil, no matter how he stormed and chided, no matter how this gipsy's ways displeased him – he never said a word of his St John.

Gradually in these last years the freshness of Goldmund's pleasant youth, that boyish grace that had won him so much favour on the roads, had faded and gone from him for ever. He was a strong, handsome man, coveted by every woman he met, and so not beloved of other men. His turn of mind and inward aspect had also ripened since the years when Narziss had roused him from the slumbering innocence of the cloister. Vagrancy and the world had shaped his spirit. Another Goldmund had long replaced the delicate, well-loved boy. Narziss had awakened him into life, women had given him their wisdom, vagrancy had brushed off his bloom. He had no friends, his heart was all for his mistresses; they could win him easily, one longing glance was enough. He found it hard to resist, had an answer to their lightest inclination. And he, who loved all gentle beauty, longing most of all for those women who came to him in the first sap of their spring, could still be held and stirred by the less beautiful, by women no longer lovely, or very young. Sometimes, on village greens, he would stay

at the side of some old timid spinster, desired of none, ⋯
had won his heart by way of gentleness, and not of gent⋯
ness only, but an ever re-awakened curiosity. When onc⋯
he had yielded to a woman – though his love might last for
days or only hours – she became a beauty in his eyes, and to
her he surrendered his whole heart. And soon experience had taught him that every woman is beautiful and
worth loving; that those least flaunting, the scorned of men,
possess undreamed of ardour and self-forgetfulness, that
withered virgins bear within them a tenderness as great as
any mother, a sweet, confiding gentleness of their own – so
that every woman in the world has her own magic, her own
secret, which to read will bring happiness to a man.

In this all women were alike. Every lack of youth or
beauty found its recompense in some special gesture or tone
of voice.

But not all could hold him equally long. To the youngest,
freshest of them all, he showed himself no whit more loving, no whit more grateful, than to the ugly ones. Although
he could never love by halves there were women who only
rendered up their secret after three or ten nights in his arms,
others who in a single night were fully known, and so forgotten. Desire and love seemed to him the only satisfac-
tions which can warm life, or give it any price. Of ambition
he knew nothing; beggar and cardinal were alike to him.
He despised all ownership, would not offer such things the
smallest sacrifice, and threw his money away with both
hands, now that he often earned as much as he would.
Women and the game of the senses – these seemed to him
the highest goods on earth, while the core of his days of
brooding sadness, of every disgust and weariness of mind,
was his knowledge of the passing of desire.

The quick delighted flame of a passion, its short, wasting
fire and sudden extinction – these seemed to him to con-
tain the heart of all knowledge. To him they were the pat-

of worth, of every joy in human life. He could let their —ness sweep across his mind, with its shudder of eternal —ndings, and surrender to that as fully as to love, since it too was love, it too was desire. As wantonness at the summit of his glory, knows of his own end and quick oblivion, knows that he will perish in the next breath, so is the innermost sadness of this drowned solitude sure of its resurrection in desire, in a fresh awakening of the senses in the lust of the eye, the pride of life. Lust and death were the same to Goldmund. The mother of life might be called either 'Lust' or 'Love', though her other names were 'Death' and 'Corruption'. She was Eve, the fount of death and joy, for ever bearing and extinguishing. Cruelty and love were as one to her, and her form, the longer he bore it in his heart, his holiest allegory and symbol.

He knew, not in thoughts or words, with the sure, deep knowledge of the blood, that all his ways would lead him to the mother; to lust and death. The other, the father-side, of life, the intellect and will, were not his home. There dwelt Narziss, and Goldmund now, for the first time, had grasped all the reach of his friend's saying, and, in his heart, knew himself his opposite. With this new perception he carved his St John the Disciple: he might long until he wept for Narziss, dream of him the most splendid of his dreams, he would never reach him, or be as he.

With some kind of hidden intuition he also knew the secret of his artistry, his innate hankering to carve, his hatred, now and then, of all he had made. Without thoughts he could feel many comparisons. Art was the fusion of two worlds, the world of the spirit and the blood, the world of the father and the mother. Rooted in the grossest senses, she could grow to the clearest abstract thoughts, or take her origin in the rarest, incorporeal world of the intellect, to end in the solidest flesh and blood. All works that truly served their purpose – as for instance, Master Nicholas' Sorrowful

Virgin – all these legitimate, true-born works of art, jugglers' pieces but true craftsmen's – presented this sa... perilous, two-faced smile, this quality both of man an... woman, the living together and intermingling of desire and the clearest, passionless intellect. But more than any work yet born should his Eve set forth this double life, if ever he succeeded in carving her.

In the carver's craft there lay for Goldmund the assurance of reconciling his deepest contradictions. But art did not come as a free gift, certainly she was not to be had for the asking, she cost dear, demanding many offerings. For over three long years she had robbed him of his dearest joys, exacting the very breath of his life, all to which he clung besides desire, the freedom of his vagrant curiosity, his solitude, his dependence on no man. All had been offered up to image-making. Let others accuse him of surliness, call him sullen, feckless, disobedient, whenever he raged, and would not go to the workshop that day: for him this life was bitter slavery, chafing him, and poisoning his heart. It was not that he had a master to obey, not that he was in bondage without a future – it was art herself that riled and embittered him; art, that seeming goddess of the mind, who makes so many small exactions. She must have a roof above her head, needs carving tools, clay, wood-blocks, gold-leaf, colours; exacts industry and patience. To her he had given the savage freedom of the woods, all the boundless joy of the wide earth, the tang of danger, the pride of beggary. And, with growls and clenchings of teeth, he must offer them up again and again.

Sometimes these holocausts were returned to him. He could find some slender compensation for the slavish order and discipline of his days in certain of the adventures that go with love; rivalry, and the brawls to which it leads. To be fallen on suddenly from behind, in a narrow alley on his way to a wench, or back from a dance, feel a few cudgel-

s on his shoulders, turn in a flash to attack, not to de-
..d himself, set his teeth, and clasp his panting enemy,
..rike up with all his strength under a chin, fasten his fingers
into hair, or feel his grip press down into a throat – all this
was good, and cured his surliness for a while. And women
also had their pleasure in it.

Pleasure filled up his nights abundantly, and gave some
savour to his life, for as long as his work on St John the
Disciple lasted. The work prolonged itself, till one by one,
with patient ceremony, he put the last, dainty touches to
face and hands. He had carved it in a small wooden shed,
built behind the journeymen's workshop. Then came the
morning when it was ready. Goldmund went off to fetch a
broom, swept the floor scrupulously clean, softly brushed
the last traces of wood-dust from the modelled hair of his
Johannes, and stood an hour or longer before him.

Deep joy awoke in his heart, the rare delight of a new,
overmastering experience, something which might repeat
itself once in his life, or which he might never know again.
A man on his wedding-day, or the day of his knighthood,
might feel this : a woman delivered of her firstborn. A high
dedication, a deep solemnity, with already secret terror of
the instant when such strange perfection of happiness would
be over, lived through, and fallen into its place, in the ordered rut of everyday. There, before his eyes, stood Narziss,
the friend who had led him out of his boyhood, clad in the
robes and part of the fair disciple, with so quiet a look of
pity and surrender, in the lines of his clear, attentive face, as
might have been the bud of a smile. This lovely, radiant
face, formed by the spirit, the lean, almost hovering body beneath, the long, comely hands, opened in prayer, had
known pain and death, although so full of youth and inner
music. But despair, disorder, rebellion, they had never
known. The soul behind these radiant, gentle features might
be sad or gay, it was a harmony; it suffered from no rift or

discord. Goldmund stood lost in his work. His thoughts, first all reverent devotion to this monument he had give to his youth, ended in a cloud of care and heaviness. There stood his work: this fair Johannes would remain; his gentle grace was fixed for all time. But he, the maker, had lost it. Tomorrow it would not be his, would not grow and prosper under his touch. Even now it no longer needed the love of his hands, had ceased to be his refuge and comfort, the form and purpose of his days. He stood there empty.

And so, he felt, it would be best to take his leave at once – of St John and of Master Nicholas also; of this city, and the carver's craft. There was nothing further for him here; he had no more figures ripe in his mind; his Eve, the mother of all, was still unattainable, and so she would remain for many years. Should he stay here, polishing angels' heads?

With an effort he left Narziss, and went across to the Master's workshop, entered, and stood by the door in silence, till Nicholas noticed him, and called out:

'What is it, Goldmund?'

'My St John is ready. Perhaps you will come yourself and look at it, before you go in to dinner.'

'Gladly. I'll come at once.'

They went over together, leaving the door wide-open, to have more light. For a long while now Nicholas had not seen the St John, letting Goldmund work on it undisturbed. Now he said nothing, but only carefully examined. His stern, secretive face lit up. Goldmund saw delight in the sharp blue eyes.

'It's good; very good,' said Master Nicholas. 'This is your journeyman's piece, Goldmund. You've mastered your craft. I will show this carving to the Guild, and ask that you be given your Master's patent for it. And you'll have earned it.'

Goldmund cared nothing for the Guild, but rejoiced, knowing how much recognition such words as these im-

...ed from Master Nicholas. As the Master viewed his work ...om every angle, walking slowly round about it, he sighed:

'This image is full of peace and stillness, and, although it is sad, it seems to rejoice. One might almost say that the heart of the man who made it had been all happiness and delight.'

Goldmund smiled:

'You know that in this I did not make an image of myself, but of my best friend, Master. It was he who brought the peace and light, not I. It is not really I who have shaped this figure, but he, who brought it to my soul.'

'It may be so,' said Nicholas, 'it is a secret how such figures as this are made. I am scarcely humble, but I'll say this to you: I have made many works in my time that stand far below this St John of yours, not in care and skill, but in their truth. Well, you know it yourself, such a work can never be repeated. It is a secret.'

'Yes,' said Goldmund, 'when this figure was carved I looked at it and said to myself: "You'll never do another like it." And so, Master, I think that soon I'll go back to the roads.'

Nicholas gave him a puzzled, grudging look; his eyes were stern again.

'Later we can talk of that. This is the time when work should start for you in earnest, and truly not the moment for running off. But for today you can have a holiday, and at dinner you shall be my guest.'

Goldmund presented himself at dinner, washed and combed, in his Sunday clothes. This time he knew how rare an honour it was to be bidden to dine with Master Nicholas. Yet, as he climbed the stairs and crossed the landing, crowded with its wooden figures, there was no such joy and anxious awe in him as when last, with a thumping heart, he had entered these pleasant, peaceful rooms.

Lisbeth, too, was pranked out in her best, with a chain of

jewels round her neck, and at dinner, besides their carp and wine, the Master had another favour for him: a leather purse, with two gold ducats, his wage for St John the Disciple. Today he did not sit with his mouth shut, listening to the talk of father and daughter. Both had much to say, and they all clinked glasses: his eyes were busy with the maid, and he used his chance to the full to take a long look at her pretty face, with its high-bred, smooth, disdainful beauty. She was very gracious, yet he wished she could blush and thaw a little, longing as never before to compel this smooth, still face to answer him. He took his leave soon after dinner, paused for a while to examine the statues on the landing, and then, not knowing what to do, loitered about the city streets. He had been honoured past all hope by Master Nicholas. Why should he not rejoice? What made this recompense so mean?

Yielding to a sudden whim, he hired a horse and rode out to the cloister where first he had heard the Master's name. Two years since then, and today they seemed an eternity! In the cloister-church he stood before the Sorrowful Virgin, and again her beauty caught and held him. She was a better work than his St John, equal in magic and profundity, surer far in knowledge and in skill.

Now he noted details in the craftsmanship which only a carver could perceive, softly rippling lines in the mantle, a boldness in the construction of the long thin hands and fingers, the delicate use of accidents in the grain of the wood; and yet all these beauties were as nothing in comparison to the loveliness of the whole, the inspired simplicity of the vision, only possible to some great master who had his craft at his finger-tips. To present such figures a man must have more than imagery in his soul; he must have both eye and hand consummately skilled. Therefore perhaps it was worth while to serve art for the whole of a lifetime, at the cost of freedom and all delight, if the end were one such

auty as this, not only seen and lived, and conceived, in
oy, but carved with the last and surest mastery. It was a
hard question. Goldmund came back late that light, on a
tired horse, to the city. The lights still shone in a tavern, and
there he ate bread, and drank some wine. Then he climbed
to his room in the Fish-Market, at odds with himself, weary
and restless.

CHAPTER TWELVE

NEXT day Goldmund could not make up his mind to work. He loitered about the streets in which he had spent so many unwilling days, watched serving-women and dames on their way to market, stood long by the Fish-Market brook, where vendors, with their lusty wives beside them, hawking and pricing their wares, clutched the cool silver fish out of their tubs, and flourished them at every passer-by.

The terrified fish, with open gills and gold-filmed eyes, surrendered to death, or struggled and slithered in anguish to escape it, and, as often before, his heart was filled with pity for these fish and gloomy detestation of human beings. Why were those people so brutish, so raw, so unbelievably slow-witted? Had nobody eyes, neither men nor fish-wives, nor the cheapening burgesses around them? Why had they never seen these anguished gills, these eyes glazed, with the agony of death, these tail-fins, beating the air so wildly — or felt the bitter, desperate horror of this slithering fight against extinction, this last, unbearable transformation of lovely and mysterious fish, as a shiver ran along their dying bodies, and they lay, exhausted and limp, pitiful meals for the table of some gluttonous burgess? These people were all blind; nothing ever spoke to them or moved them. A poor, beautiful beast might die in front of them, or a master, in some saint's face, have revealed all the pain, the thought, the noble hopes, the dark, clutching fear in a human life, making of it a visible shudder — it all meant nothing; they could not see.

They were all so busy or amused, fussing and scurrying;

bawling, cackling, belching in one another's faces, clattering with pails, cracking their jokes, falling out over a couple of pfennigs: so glossy with civic pride, pleased with their own well-ordered lives, satisfied with themselves and the whole world. Swine! But no, far worse and lower than swine. Well, although his life had seemed so pleasant here, he had lived long enough with them and their kind, slept with their wives and daughters, and made many a jolly meal of good baked fish with them. Again and again, with all the suddenness of a charm, his peace and satisfaction had fallen away. The glib illusions had been defeated, the smooth self-esteem and fatness of soul. Something kept urging him off into solitude, to long meditation and vagrancy, to the sight of grief and pain and death, and the doubtful issue of all men's striving; something had made him long to stare into the gulf.

Often in his blackest desolation at this glimpse of vanity and terror, sudden delight had flowered in his heart; a violent impulse to make love, draw, strike up a song; or else, as he smelt a flower or played with a cat, his boy's acceptance of life had all come back to him. This time, too, it would all come back, if not today tomorrow, or the day after, and the world be as goodly as ever before. Yes, till the blackness came again, the heavy, solitary pondering, his hopeless, stifling love of dying fish or withered flowers, his hatred of the swinish lethargy, the dull, ugly gapings of human beings! Always, at such times as these, he would be forced, with shuddering curiosity, to remember Victor the travelling scholar, between whose ribs he had thrust his jack-knife, whom he had left stretched out on leaves, dripping blood. Then he had to think it all out afresh, wondering what Victor looked like now. Had the foxes eaten him all up yet? Could any traces still be left of him? Yes, there would be something strewn there still — the bones, and then perhaps a handful of hair. But bones? What happened to bones? How long did it take, years or decades, till bones lost their form and became earth?

Ah, he was forced to think of Victor now, as, sick at heart, he watched these fish, hating the market burghers and their dames. He was full of hatred of the world, hatred and pain within himself. Perhaps they had found Victor and buried him. If they had, had the flesh come off him yet? Was it still rotting away, bit by bit? Or had the worms got their bellyful? Was there any hair still on the skull? Were there eyebrows still above the eyes? And Victor's life, so full of histories and adventures, fantastic games and japes and bawdry – how much remained of it now? Did anything save the few shabby thoughts still haunting his murderer's mind, live on of him? Yet, as the world goes, this life had been no ordinary one. Was there still any Victor in women's dreams? No, it was past and done with, and such must be the fate of each and all; we come to swift blossom and shrivel up, and then the snow hides us away. How his whole being had seemed to flower as, two years back, in restless longing to learn a craft, he had hurried along the high-road to this town, to lay his heart at the feet of Master Nicholas. Had anything of that still life in it? Nothing – no more life today than the long, spare carcass of that poor guzzler. Had somebody told him of a day when he would treat Master Nicholas as his equal, and demand his patent from the Guild, he would have felt he had all the joy of the world in his hands. Now it was stale and joyless as withered flowers.

Suddenly, as he thought all this, Goldmund had the vision of a face. It came in a flash, and was gone again, one darting, quivering clarity, that vanished. It was the face of the earliest of all mothers, bent above the whirling darkness of life, looking down, with her sad, unchanging smile, all cruelty, all beauty in her eyes; smiling on births and deaths, on springing flowers and rustling autumn leaves, smiling on art, and on decay. All things were alike to this great mother; over them all her terrible, hovering smile hung like a moon. The surly meditation of a Goldmund was as dear to her as dying carp, slithering on the cobbles of the Fish-Market, dear as the cool, disdainful, Master's daughter, dear as Victor's bones, strewn in the wood, who had longed so much to steal a ducat.

Already the livid glow had died, the secret mother's face was lost again. Yet still its paleness shimmered on, in the very depths of Goldmund's being, as a surge of pain, and life, and stifling longing, swept, breaking and lashing, through his heart. No, he had no more use for the well-fed pleasure of these citizens, fish-sellers, buyers, busy owners. Let the devil take them! Ah, the white gleam of that full-lipped smile of dying summer, around whose eyes the nameless, heavy sheen of death had played like moonbeams or autumn wind!

Goldmund went to the house of Master Nicholas. It was midday or near; he waited till he heard that the Master had finished his work and gone to wash before he dined. Then he went in to him:

'Master, I have something to say to you. You can listen while you wash and change your jerkin. I am dry for a mouthful of truth, and now I have things to tell you which perhaps I can only say once, and never again. This is how it stands with me, Master. I have to speak my mind to somebody, and you may be the only one in the town who could ever understand what I mean. I do not speak to the owner of the famous workshop, who receives so many honourable commissions from every city and abbey in the land. I speak to the Master who carved that Holy Mother of God out in the cloister, the fairest virgin that I know. That is the man I love and honour, and to be his equal seems to me the highest good. I have just finished a work, my St John, and did not make it near so perfect as your Blessed Mother in that church. But let my work be what it is. I have no other waiting to be done. There is nothing in my mind that calls me, forcing me to shape it with my two hands. Or rather, no, there is another; but a very distant and holy image, that one day will constrain me to give it shape, and yet I cannot do it today. To have the power in me to make it I must know and feel far more of life. In three or four years it may be ready for me; or in ten, or longer still, or never perhaps! But, Master, till that time comes I cannot spend my days at handiwork, polishing angels, cutting rood-screens, living as a journeyman in this workshop, earning money, and growing like other workmen – no, I will not ... I want to live, to wander the roads again! I want to feel summer and winter, and see all the beauty of the world, and I want to taste my fill of its pain. I must know hunger and thirst, and forget, and free my mind of all I have learnt here. One day I want to make a statue which shall move men as deeply, and be as fair, as your own Holy Mother of God. But to be as you, and live your life. ... I will not.'

Nicholas had washed his hands and dried them. Now he turned and glanced at Goldmund. His eyes were sharp, but not malicious.

'You have spoken,' he said, 'and I have heard you. Let all that be! I do not expect you in the workshop, although there is so much to be done there. Nor do I consider you my journeyman. You need your freedom. I would like to discuss all this, and much besides, friend Goldmund. Not now, but a few days hence – and, meanwhile, do as you please. Listen, I am much older than you, and have seen this and that in the world. I think in a different fashion, yet I understand what you mean. In a few days I will send to fetch you, and then we will discuss your future, for which I have made many plans. Patience till then! I know well enough how it feels when one has finished a work that lay very close to the heart; I know that emptiness. It passes, believe me.'

Goldmund took his leave dissatisfied. The Master meant him well, but what did he care? He knew a place at the river's edge. There, where the water was not deep, it came rushing on, over a bed full of rubbish and offal, since, beyond the gates, the huts of the fishermen's quarter emptied every kind of waste and flotsam in it. Thither he loitered now, straddled the river-side wall, and sat looking down into the stream. Water he loved, every sheet of water drew him to it; and from here when, through running crystal threads, that rushed and mingled, a man looked down, into the dark, indefinite river's bed, he could see, here and there, some vague quick shimmer of gold gleam up at him; some half-seen thing – it might be the splinter of a dish, a scythe-blade, broken and thrown away, a shining pebble, a glazed tile : perhaps at times it was a mud eel, a fat lote or a roach, wriggling down there, catching a sunbeam for an instant on fins, scales, or glittering belly; he could never be quite certain what had glinted, and every time it was full of magic and delight, this muted sheen of buried gold, down in the wet, dark, unknown chasm.

Every real secret, he thought, all the true-born pictures of the mind, were like this one small secret of water. They had no form, no clear, accomplished shape, would never let themselves be perceived, save as far-off lovely possibility : they were veiled and had many meanings. As there, out of the green river twilight, in tiny flashes, some indefinite gold or silver thing shone for an instant and was gone again, so could the passing outline of a face, half-seen from behind, become the herald of endless grace or endless sorrow : or as, under a loaded waggon at night, a lantern swung, and the giant turning shadows of the spokes spread out their dance over a wall, these, in any one of their movements, might be as full of pictures and histories as Virgil. Of this same flimsy, magic stuff our dreams were woven in the night – nothing, with all the pictures of the world in it; a water in whose crystal the forms of all things, of angels, devils, men and beasts, lived as eternal possibility.

His thoughts returned to the water; abstractedly, through the rushing, purling river, he saw formless shimmerings in the bed; shaped kings' crowns, and women's naked shoulders. In Mariabronn once, he remembered, he had dreamed such magic, ever-changing form into the shape of a Greek or Latin letter. Had he not spoken to Narziss of it? Ah, how long ago was that, how many centuries ago! Alas, Narziss! To see him now, and talk an hour with him, holding his hand and listening to his quiet, level voice, he would willingly have given two gold ducats. What made all these things so beautiful, these glittering mysteries and shadows, all these unreal, enchanted forms – what made them all so unbelievably fair, since, in themselves, they were the opposite of any beauty craftsmen make? If the beauty of these dim, unnameable things enthralled him only by its vagueness, it was all the other way with the works of craftsmen. These were all form, speaking with the clearness of perfection. Nothing was more inexorably clear than the lines of a well-drawn head, or a carved mouth. Precisely as he had seen them, to a hair, he could have shaped again the eyes or underlip of Nicholas' statue of the Virgin. There, there was nothing vague, tricking, impermanent.

Though Goldmund pondered the matter long, in the end he could still see no good reason why these clearest, most defined of forms should work on our spirit in just the fashion of these vaguest, least definite of all. But one thing was clear to him. He could see now why so many faultless works, fashioned by the masters in their craft, displeased him utterly; why, in spite of a certain beauty in their design, they wearied him so he almost hated them. Workshops, churches, and palaces, were full of such fatal works of art;

he himself had helped to make a few. Their bitterest decep-
tion lay in this: that they roused men's longing for beauty,
and left it unsatisfied, since, in themselves, they lacked its
essence – a secret. Dreams and the greatest works both had
their mystery.

And Goldmund thought: 'The thing I love and hanker
for is mysterious. I am on its track. I have seen it in flashes
several times and, as a carver, when I can do so, I mean to
shape it till it reveals itself. Its form shall be the form of the
mother of all things. Her beauty, unlike that of other figures,
shall not consist in any particular, no special roundness
or slenderness, plainness or decorated form, winsomeness
or strength, but in this – that in her the furthest opposites shall be reconciled, living together in my work: birth
and death, pleasure and pain, life and destruction; all which,
outside her, could never make peace in the world. Had I
taken her form from out of my mind, she would have been
no more than any craftsman's whim, and so my vanity
would be worthless. I could see her faults, and forget her.
But this primal mother is not my thought, since I have never
known her with my mind. I saw her! She lives within me.
Again and again I have met her shape. I saw it first in that
village on a winter's night, as I held my torch over the bed
of a peasant-woman in labour, and, from that day on, she
has been part of me. I lose her often, and then I seem to
have forgotten her, till suddenly her image flashes up again,
as it came today. That dearest of all my thoughts, the
thought of my mother, has transformed itself. It has given
life to this new shape, and informs it, like the kernel in a
cherry.'

Now he could feel most clearly how matters stood with
him, and his heart beat now, as it had at no other turning-
point in his life. Today, no less than on the night when he
bade farewell to Narziss and the cloister, his feet were set on
a new road. This mother called: one day perhaps he would

transform her into a work for all to see. He could not tell. But this was certain — to follow her, be for ever on his way to her, feel her calling, leading him on, was good. That was his life. Perhaps he might never carve what he had seen; it would remain a vision to the end, a lure, the gleam of hidden, sacred treasure. However that might be, he must follow it; to her he gave himself, she was his comfort.

So that now the decision was upon him, and everything settled in his mind. Art was a very fine thing no doubt, but art was no goddess, no final aim. He had not to follow art, but his mother's voice. What use would it be to make his fingers more and more skilful? Master Nicholas had shown him where that led a man. It led to a craftsman's fame, to money and a dull, snug life; to a withering and stunting of that essence by which alone the secret yields itself up. It led to carving petty, costly toys for every rich council-house and altar, St Sebastians, and neatly lacquered cherubs, gilded at four thalers the piece. The gold in a carp's eyes, the lovely flicker of silver, round the edges of a butterfly's wing, were endlessly more beautiful, more alive, more precious than roomfuls of such work.

A boy came singing along the river's bank, breaking off in his song from time to time, as he bit into a loaf of white bread. Goldmund hailed him, and asked for a bit of his bread. Then he pulled out the crumb with his thumb and forefinger, and rolled little white bread pellets. Leaning over the wall, he flung his pellets, one by one, far out into the dark hurrying stream; quick fish thronged round them, until they vanished into a mouth. Pellet after pellet he saw vanish, with the same deep satisfaction for each. Then he felt hungry, and went in search of one of his mistresses, the serving-wench in a butcher's house, whom he called 'the pork and sausage maid'. He would hail her with his usual whistle, tell her, when she came to the kitchen window, that he did not care what flesh she offered him. Whatever she gave he would pocket it, and eat it in the vineyards across the river, whose fat red soil glowed with grapes, and where, in spring, there were blue sweet-smelling hyacinths.

But this seemed the day of fresh perceptions. When Katherine came smiling to the window – smiling her rather fat-faced smile – as already he raised his hand to give their signal – suddenly he remembered all her other smiles, all the other times he had stood just in this place, waiting at this window, just as today. And then, with wearisome distinctness, he saw it all before it happened; saw her answer his sign and leave the window, come round in a trice to the back door to him, with her packet of smoked meat in her hand, saw himself take it, and stroke her a little for her pains, pressing her to him – just as she expected. Suddenly it all seemed endlessly foolish, this whole, mechanical series of oft-done things. Why call them back and play his part in them; thank her for her sausage, and kiss her lips, feel her jutting breasts thrust out against him, pressing her a little in exchange? In her good, plump face he could see a look of soullessness and habit, in her friendly laugh hear something bereft of dignity, something he had heard far too often, a clockwork sound, without any mystery in it. His smile froze; he dropped his hand. Did he still care anything at all for her? Had he ever really wanted her kisses? No, he had come here far too often, and seen the same smile far too often, always the same, and answered it far too often – without desire. What yesterday he could have done without a thought, had suddenly, today, become impossible. The maid still stood there peeping out at him, as already he turned his back, and went his way, resolved never to enter the street again. Let some apprentice stroke those breasts of hers. Let someone else eat her good sausage! Oh how these citizens guzzled away their lives! How lazy and dainty were these provosts for whom, day after day, so many sows and calves were put to death, so many shining fish pulled out of the river. And he himself! How like the glossy fools he had become, how lazy and gluttonous! A bit of dirty crust on the moors, a dried-up sloe, tasted better than a whole Guild-banquet in this town. Ah, freedom of dark moors under the moon, traces of beasts, spied out carefully in the grey, wet grass of breaking dawns! These citizens' life was all so flat and cheap – even their love. He had had enough! Life, like a bone, was emptied of its marrow. Once it had been better, had had some meaning in it, in the days when the Master was still his pattern, and Lisbeth a princess in his eyes. Even after that it had been tolerable, while he had his St John to hold his thoughts. Now it was over, the bloom was off it, the little flower had shrivelled up. Like a wave, the sense of impermanence overwhelmed him.

Everything shrivelled, all pleasure ended in a breath, leaving nothing there but dust and bones. Yes, one thing stayed: the eternal mother. Eve the ever-young, yet ever old, with the sad, cruel smile of her desire. Again for an instant, he could see her: a giantess with stars in her hair, crouched dreaming at the edge of the world, idly plucking flower on flower, life after life, and dropping them slowly into space.

While in these days Goldmund, in a melancholy dream of farewells, watched a part of his life fade out and perish, as he strayed through the withering city streets, Master Nicholas was taking endless pains to bind down the vagabond for ever. He had made many plans for Goldmund's future, prevailed on the Guild to grant him his master's patent, thought out a scheme to hold him fast, not as his journeyman but his equal, one whom he would consult on all great orders. Together they would make the designs, and Goldmund should have a share in the gain. There were risks in this, for Lisbeth no less than for her father, since naturally the young man must be his son-in-law. But the best of all the journeymen yet hired by him could never have made the new St John, and he, the Master, was growing old, poorer in conceptions than he had been, and feared to see his famous workshop sink to the level of ordinary carvers' booths. It would not be easy with this Goldmund, but still the attempt would have to be made.

So did the Master reckon, sadly and prudently. He would have the inner workshop rebuilt, and enlarged to house his new assistant; give him the attic floor in his house and a fine new doublet and hose to attend his election to the Guild. Tenderly he sounded Mistress Lisbeth, who, since that noon when they all had dined together, expected some such proposal from her father. And behold, Lisbeth had nothing against it! If the lad could be made a guildsman and a citizen she would not say no to him for a husband. Here, too, there seemed to be no obstacle. If Master Nicholas and his craft had not quite managed to tame this gipsy, Lisbeth would soon have clipped his wings.

So it was all contrived, and the lure well baited for the bird. And so, one day they sent for Goldmund, who had given them no news of himself, and this time, too, he was asked for dinner. He came as before, combed and in his Sunday clothes, sat down again, in the beautiful, rather ceremonious room, with the Master and the Master's daughter till, after dinner, Lisbeth curtsied and left them, and Nicholas made him his great offer.

'You understand,' he added, at the end of his surprising scheme, 'and I need not say that scarcely any other young man, with not even the usual apprenticeship behind him, has been made a Master as you have, and set down in such a warm nest. Your fortune's made, Goldmund!'

Surprised, and very discomfited, Goldmund sat staring at Master Nicholas. He thrust back the cup, half-full before him on the table. He had expected nothing from the Master save a few complaints for idle days, and the offer to make him his journeyman for ever. But now this! It saddened him, and filled him with embarrassment, to sit and face the man without a word. Yet he could not answer him at once.

Nicholas, already a little vexed that no humble thanks had at once requited his generosity, stood up, and continued:

'Well, this seems to take you by surprise. Perhaps you would like some time to consider it. It irks me a little that this is so. I had hoped to give you the greatest pleasure. But, for me, it's all one. Take your time.'

'Master,' said Goldmund, seeking for words, 'don't take it ill of me. I thank you with all my heart for your kindness, and even more, for the patience you have shown me, your scholar. Never shall I forget my debt to you. But I need no time to consider. I made up my mind long ago.'

'And to what?'

'I had resolved it long before you sent for me – before I had any inkling of the noble offer I have just heard. I cannot stay here. I must go on the roads again.'

Nicholas paled, and his eyes glittered.

'Master,' said Goldmund, 'believe me when I say I would not grieve you. I must leave all this. I must wander, and have my freedom. I thank you again with all my heart, and let us take our leave of each other kindly.' He held out his hand, almost in tears. Nicholas would not take it. His face was white. Now he began to pace the room, in quick, and ever quicker strides. But rage seemed to mount up through his body. Never before had Goldmund seen him thus.

'Go then! But go at once. Don't let me have to look at you again. Don't let me speak or do anything which one day I might have to be sorry for. Go!'

Again Goldmund stretched out his hand, Nicholas made as though to spit on it. Now, pale as the other, Goldmund turned, stole from the room, put on his cap on the landing, crept down the stairs, stroking the nutwood angels as he went, and out into the little wooden shed, to take a last farewell of his St John. There he stood for a while; then left the house, with a deeper sadness in his heart than ever he had felt that day in the snow, when he had gone from the castle, and poor Lydia. But this, at least, had ended quickly. At least they had wasted no words. That was his one consoling thought, as he crossed the threshold, and saw the streets take on the new look of familiar things, when our hearts have already taken leave of them. He glanced back once at the house-door ... the door of a stranger's house, for ever closed to him.

Back in his room, Goldmund made ready for the roads. There there was not much to hamper him; he had little else to do but take his leave. A picture he himself had painted, a gentle Madonna, hung on the wall, and many trifles strewed the room. There was a pair of dancing-shoes, a roll of drawings, a small lute, a row of clay figures he had modelled, some wenches' gifts; a bunch of artificial flowers, a drinking-glass, stained crimson, an old, stale comfit, shaped like a heart, and more such rubbish, though every piece had its history. Once they had all meant something, now they were a tedious encumbrance. But at least he could go to the landlord, exchange the glass for a good, strong hunting-knife and whet it on the grindstone in the yard. He could crumble the gingerbread heart, and feed the hens in the neighbour's court with it, give his Madonna to the goodwife, and get from her a useful present, an old leather wallet, crammed with food.

To this he added the two clean shirts he owned, and a couple of his smallest drawings, rolled over a piece of broomstick. The rest of the flimsy he left behind.

There were many women in the city, of whom he might have taken his leave: even last night he had slept with one of them, without saying a word to her of his plans. It was not worth the trouble of taking seriously, so he said farewell to none but his landlord, and of him took his leave overnight, in order to set out early next day.

Yet in spite of this, another was up before him, to bid him into the kitchen for a milk-broth, just as he was about to creep from the house. It was a child of fifteen, the landlord's daughter, a quiet, sickly maid, with beautiful eyes, but lamed in her hip-joint, so that she limped. Her name was Marie. With her face pale for want of sleep, but her hair carefully dressed and combed, to meet him, she set out warm milk for him in the kitchen, and bread to go with it, and seemed very sad to have him leave her. He thanked her with a farewell kiss, and pitied her. She took his kiss with half-closed eyes.

CHAPTER THIRTEEN

On the first days of these new wanderings, the first greedy tumult of new-won freedom, Goldmund had to learn all over again how to live the homeless, timeless life of the roads. The homeless live the lives of valiant children, obeying none, their only lord the changing sky, with no aim before them, and no roof over them, owning nothing, ready for any hazard – their beggarly and stalwart lives. They are Adam's sons, who was turned forth, and brothers of the innocent beasts. From the hand of God, from hour to hour, they take whatever He may send them, sun, rain, mist, snow, heat or cold, famine or bellyful, and never notice how time goes, or consider the future, or man's history. For them there is no striving to be great; they have no knowledge of that strange idol called well-being to which the owners cling so fervently. A vagrant may be savage or gentle, skilled in his life or slow to cope with it, valiant or cowardly, he is a child. He lives for ever in the Garden before the coming of wars and cities, his steps guided on for ever by a few simple needs and longings. Cunning or slow of mind; feeling in the depth of his heart how brittle and fugitive is all life, how meagrely and fearfully living things carry their spark of warmth through the icy universe; or else a poor gluttonous simpleton going in the wake of his gnawing belly – either of these is the deep implacable enemy and deadly rival of safe citizens. They dread him as they dread to be reminded of the running away of all that is, the eternal withering out of warmth and joy into chill inescapable death, which lives in the air and eats up all men.

Summer and autumn died. Goldmund fought his way

through snow again, wandered, full of joy in the sweet-smelling spring, saw seasons tread each other down, the swift sinking to earth of golden summer. So he went on year by year, till at last it seemed he had forgotten all earthly things save thirst, hunger and love, and the quiet, uncanny slipping away of the years. He seemed to have sunk back utterly into the mother, lost in her world of hunger and appeasement, although in every dream or brooding rest, with a view out over flowering or withering valleys, his eyes were open and he a craftsman again, longing to shape this clear and hurrying life, exorcise and inform it with his spirit.

Since Victor's death he had always wandered alone. Yet now one day he found he had a companion, who seemed by degrees to have attached himself, without his ever having noticed it, and for some long time he could not get rid of him. But this new vagrant was no Victor; he was a Roman pilgrim and still young, who bore his pilgrim's gown and wide hat, whose name was Robert, and his home by the Lake of Constance. This pilgrim, an artisan's son, had been for a time to school with the monks of St Gallus, and already as a little boy, had his head crammed full of dreams of a Roman pilgrimage, till at last he had no other thought, and seized his first chance to make it reality. His father's death, in whose shop he had had to work as a joiner, had brought him the liberty he craved. Scarcely was the old man safely buried than Robert announced to mother and sister that nothing now should hold him back, but he would go to Rome for his soul's sake, to pray there for his father's many sins and do penance for them. In vain the women wept and scolded, he set out for Rome, as obstinate as ever, without any blessing from his mother, amid a hail of shrewish chidings from his sister. It was more his longing to wander than any piety in him, though along with this went a kind of shallow devotion, a love of idling in the neighbourhood of priestly shows and cathedrals. His pleasure was to listen to long offices, watch baptisms, burials, masses for the dead, sniff up incense, warm himself at the gleam of candles. He had managed to pick up a little Latin, though not enough to make himself a scholar, but to still the childish fancies of his soul in long, pious, hovering daydreams at side-altars, in the shadow of naves. Goldmund did not mark him very closely, although he liked him well enough, and felt in some small measure akin to him in his urge to wander and see new lands. So that Robert had broken loose and even managed to get as far as Rome, lodged in his time in numerous cloisters and priests' houses, seen the mountains, and the southern land beyond, and felt very happy indeed among Roman churches and the pious foundations of the city. There he had heard a hundred masses, knelt and dreamed at all the most famous holy shrines, received the sacraments, and breathed more incense than he needed to fumigate every sin of his youth, or indeed those of his father's whole life.

He had been away a year or longer, but when at last he came back to his father's house they did not welcome him as a prodigal, since he found that his sister in his absence had made herself mistress of the household, with all the rights and duties that should have been his. She had married an industrious journeyman-carpenter, and ruled with such a rod of iron that Robert, after a short stay among them, knew himself one too many in his home, and nobody pressed him to remain when he talked of fresh journeys and pilgrimage. This did not trouble him overmuch. He begged a few spare groats from his mother, donned his pilgrim's hat and gown afresh, and set out on another holy journey. This time he had no aim, but wandered here and there across the Empire, half-friar, half-vagrant, with copper medals jingling round his neck, from every famous place of pilgrimage, and indulgenced rosaries along with them.

In such guise as this he met Goldmund, trudged at his side for a day, and exchanged many vagabonds' tales with him, vanished in the next little market-town, fell in with him again here and there, and in the end, remained with him for good, as a willing, dependable companion. Goldmund pleased him very well, he admired his daring, wit, and knowledge, loving him for his health, strength, and sincerity. He strove to win his favour with small services; they became good friends, since Goldmund was a very easy companion. One thing only he would not tolerate. When his brooding, thinking fit was on him, he would trudge along in stubborn silence, looking past Robert as though he were invisible; and then there must be no questions and no chattering, no gossiping attempts to comfort, he must be left alone within his mood. This Robert discovered for himself. Ever since he had known that Goldmund knew strings of Latin verses and songs; since one day, at the door of a cathedral, he had heard him explain the structure of the stone images, and watched him once, as they stood and rested by a wall, daub life-size figures in a few quick strokes on it in raddle, he had begun to consider his comrade one of God's chosen, and indeed almost a magician. That women also favoured Goldmund, so much that, with a look or smile he could make them grant him his desire, pleased Robert less, and yet he had to admire it.

Their journey together was interrupted in a way which neither had foreseen. One day they came to the outskirts of a village: with cudgels, flails, and poles in their hands a handful of peasants awaited them, and, from far off, their leader shouted at them to get back, be gone to the devil, and never show their faces there again. Goldmund went on unheeding, curious to see what the matter was, and soon a stone came crashing into his chest. Robert, for whom he looked about him, had scurried away, as though from fiends. The peasants edged nearer, shouting threats, so that nothing was left him but to follow, though not so hastily. Robert awaited him, trembling, under a rood, with the hanging image of Christ, planted in the middle of a field.

'You ran like a hero,' laughed Goldmund. 'But what have those clods got into their thick heads? Is there a war? — are armed watchmen set before their hovels, and none permitted along the road? I marvel what lies behind all this.'

Neither could tell. Not until the following morning when certain adventures awaited them in the yard of an isolated farm, did the secret, piece by piece, reveal itself. The farm, set in the midst of a green orchard, with high grass and many fruit-trees, and composed of hut, stall, and barn, lay oddly quiet, as if asleep. In the orchard stood a cow, and lowed in the grass: it was easy enough to see it was time to milk her. They went to the house-door, knocked, and, getting no answer, to the cow-stall, which stood there gaping and empty, and so to the barn, on whose thatched roof the light green moss glistened in the early morning sunshine. There, too, they could find no living soul.

They turned back to the house, baffled and glum at the emptiness of this homestead, beat again on the house-door with both fists, and still no answer came from within. Goldmund pressed against it to open, found, to his surprise, the door unlocked, thrust it back, and entered the low, dark room.

'God greet you,' he called aloud, 'is no one at home?'

But there was silence.

Robert lingered on outside. Goldmund went in, eager to see. It smelt very bad within the hut, a curious sickening stench. The hearth was piled with ashes, and he blew in them, since a few embers clung to the grey logs. Then, in the twilight of the chimney-corner, he looked up and noticed a seated shape. On a settle somebody sat asleep, and, through the gloom, he saw an old woman. To call was useless, since the house lay as if bewitched, so he nudged the sitter gently and laid his hand upon her shoulder. She did not stir even now, and he noticed that she sat in the midst of a spider's web, its threads spun partly from her hair and partly clinging to her knees. He shivered a little and thought 'She's dead.' To make quite certain of this he worked hard to build up a blaze, raking and puffing until he had a flame and could set a light to a long stick from it. This torch he held above the sitter's face. Under white hair he saw the grey-blue features of a corpse, one eye still open, glazed as if with lead. She had died there sitting in her chimney-corner. Well, there was nothing to be done for her.

Goldmund, with his flaring torch, stumbled here and there about the place. In the doorway to the room beyond he found another corpse stretched out. A boy of perhaps nine or ten, puckered and bloated, dead in his shift. He lay on his belly across the threshold, his two hands clenched into angry fists. 'This is the second,' Goldmund thought, and went on, as through an ugly dream, into a back room, where the shutters were pulled wide, so that the sunny day shone bright on everything. Carefully he extinguished his light, treading out the sparks on the floor.

This back room had three beds; one empty, with ends of straw jutting out under the coarse grey linen sheet. On the second another body; a bearded man stiff on his back, his head thrust up, his chin and beard stuck out. This must be the master of the house. His sunken face glistened dully, with the opalescent hues of death on it, one of his arms hung down to the earthen floor, where an empty pitcher lay on its side, with the long damp trickle not sucked up yet, and some of it run into a little hollow in which a puddle was still standing. In the second bed, buried and muffled in sheets and coverlet, a broad strong woman lay hunched up, her face pressed down into the bedding, her coarse straw-blond hair glittering in the strong sunlight. Beside her, as though sucked down along with her, caught and stifled in tumbled linen swathes, lay a half-grown maid, straw-blonde, with grey-blue splotches on her dead face.

Goldmund examined all these faces. In the little maid's, though already it was puffed and swollen, there was a look of helpless shrinking away from death. This mother's nape and hair, who had burrowed so deeply and wildly, had a kind of rage and terror, of passionate flight, in them. This tousled hair would not be reconciled with death. The man's face was defiant, and set in pain: he seemed to have perished there by inches; his beard was thrust sharp into the air; a warrior, stretched upon the field. His rigid defiant sullen-ness was beautiful. It could have been no ordinary weakling who met his death there. Most moving of all was the corpse of the little boy, lying on his belly over the threshold. His face said nothing, but his boy's fists, tightly clenched, told much, and the place where he lay over the threshold – a rest-less grief, a hopeless shielding of himself against unimagin-able pain. Close to his head a cat's hole had been let into the lintel.

Goldmund examined every detail. No doubt this hut was very terrible, filled with the savage stench of death. Yet, in spite of all, its attraction was powerful enough. It was real and true, so full of magnificence and fate that something in its terror won his love, forcing a way into his soul.

In the meantime Robert outside was calling querulously. Goldmund was fond enough of Robert, yet this voice brought a thought into his mind: how mean and foolish are the living, with their never-ending terrors and curiosities, the puny effort of their lives, when faced with the quiet, kingly dead. He would not answer at once but gave himself up to the spectacle of these bodies, with that strange admixture of deep pity and cold observation that artists use, taking a close look at their stiffened shapes: then back to the sitter in the chimney-corner to scrutinize her head, her eyes, her hands, the posture in which she had frozen up. How still was this enchanted hut. How strange and terrible this death stench. How remote and ghostly this small habitation of living men, possessed by these — though a few pale sparks still clung to the logs — how penetrated and soaked in quiet decay! Soon this flesh would drop off the rigid faces, rats would scurry out and gnaw the fingers. What others did in the decency of coffins, laid up in wood, safe in the earth, covered away for the last, most wretched of all processes, these five must accomplish above ground, dropping away and rotting in their dwelling-place by garish light, with clapping doors around them, untroubled, shameless, un-protected.

Goldmund had seen many dead, yet never in his life met such an image of the unwithstood, eternal work of death. He let it all sink into his mind.

Robert at last broke up these thoughts with his cries. He went outside, his comrade questioned him fearfully.

'What is it?' he asked in a low voice. 'Is any one there? Oh, what a face you have – well, say something.'

Goldmund eyed him coldly.

'Go in and see for yourself. It's a queer-looking house in there. Then we can milk the peasant's pretty cow. In with you.'

Robert obeyed uncertainly, groped his way through the twilight to the chimney-corner, found the old woman be-side her hearth, saw she was dead, and let out a yell fit to wake her. He ran back with staring eyes.

'For God's sake, Goldmund! There's a dead old woman sitting by the hearth-stone. What is it? Why is nobody with her? Why can't they bury her? Oh, God, what a stink there is!'

Goldmund smiled.

'You're a hero, Robert! But what made you come out again so fast. A dead old woman sitting in her chair is a sight worth noting, for any man. And if you go a few steps further you'll see something better still beyond. There are five of them in there, Robert. Three in their beds, and a dead boy in the doorway, besides old granny. The whole family lies there stinking, and the house itself is well-nigh starting to rot. So this was why we found an unmilked cow.'

There was only fear in Robert's eyes, suddenly he cried in a shrill voice:

'Oh – I see now what those peasants were after yesterday when they came to chase us from their village. God! – now I see it all – it's the plague! By my poor wretched soul, the plague! Goldmund! And you've been in there all this while, fingering corpses like as not. Get away from me. Don't come so near. You're poisoned for sure! I'm sorry, Goldmund, but I must leave you. I can't go along with you now.'

Before he could manage to run a yard Goldmund had hold of his pilgrim's gown, and held him, wriggle as he might.

'Young sir,' he said, mocking him gently, 'you're a cleverer fellow than I took you for, and most likely what you say is the truth of it. Well, we shall find that out in time, in the next farm or village. It's likely there's the plague in these parts, we shall know if we escape it and come off again. But to let you run like that, young Robert – oh, no! I'm a soft-hearted man. I couldn't bear to think of you stricken with the fever, as most likely you are, having been in that room with it, and scuttling off by yourself, to lie down somewhere in the fields, and die alone, with no man near you to close your eyes, and none to make you a grave or throw the earth on you – oh, no, my friend, that thought's too sad! So mark me, and mark me well, for what I say I won't say twice: we two run the same risk, it may bite either you or me. So we'll stay together and perish together, or else come through this cursed pest-land. Should you sicken and die I am here to bury you, and I promise it.

If I die, do as you will, bury me or run off and leave me, all's one. But till that time, dear Robert, you don't escape me. Remember that! We shall need each other. Now hold your noise, I want to hear nothing! And off to that stall to find a milk-pail, so then we can milk the cow at last.'

So it was done, and from that instant it was Goldmund who commanded, Robert obeyed, and for both this made things go easier. Robert did not try to escape again. He answered in a soft meek voice:

'You scared me for a minute, Goldmund. You looked so queer, as you came out of that room with all those corpses, and I thought you must be smitten with the plague. Even if you're not, your face is different! Was it so bad – what you saw in there?'

'No, not so bad,' Goldmund hesitated, 'I saw nothing in there but what lies in store for you and me, and every other man and woman on earth, even with no plague to bite us.'

They went further and soon, on every side, had black death round them, that ruled the land. Many villages refused all access, in others they could wander in every street. Farms stood empty, many rotting dead lay out in the fields, or dropped to pieces in their rooms. Cows, unmilked or famished, lowed in the stalls, and cattle ran wild over the country. They milked and foddered many goats, slaughtered and roasted at the wood's-edge many a kid and many a sucking pig, drank the wine and cider in many cellars without any hindrance from the master. They had a good life, yet could only half-taste of all these riches. Robert was in perpetual fear of the plague, his belly heaved to see a corpse; often he was almost mad for fright, again and again declared himself struck down, stood long with his head and hands in the smoke of camp fires (it passed for wholesome) and, even asleep, would feel himself all over to make certain that arms and legs and armpits had no boils. Goldmund sometimes chid, and often mocked him. He did not share Robert's terrors, his sick mistrust of a corpse. With sad abstraction filling all his mind he plodded through this land of death, fearfully drawn by the sight of the great slaughter, his soul full of a vast autumn, his heart attuned with the song of the mowing scythe. Often he could see his mother again, a giantess with the livid face of Medusa, smiling her heavy smile of death and grief.

One day they came to a little town. The place was heavily fortified. From its gates, on a level with the housetops, wide ramparts spanned the town's whole girth; and yet no watchman stood above, and none under the open arch of the gateway. Robert feared to enter this walled town, and begged the other not to venture. Meanwhile came the sound of a death-bell, a priest with a crucifix held aloft, and behind him three loaded wagons, two pulled by horses, one by oxen, each piled high with its dead. A couple of churls in strange cloaks, their faces buried in pointed cowls, ran at the side, to prick the beasts.

Robert's knees were shaking under him, his face was the colour of whey. Goldmund followed after the death-carts, keeping a little distance in their wake. But not to a graveyard. Out on the empty heath gaped a hole, only deep a couple of hands, yet wide as the throne-room in a palace. Goldmund stood and watched the churls tear down the dead from their carts with long hooked poles, and heap them into the earth, as the priest muttered and waved his crucifix, went off again, and left them there, to build great fires around the graves, and run back in silence into their city. He went to the edge and looked down. Fifty or more must be huddled there, one over the other, many naked. Here and there a stiff reproachful arm or leg, the edge of a shift fluttering in the wind.

When he came back Robert went on his knees to him, begging him to hurry away from the place. He had good reason for such petition, since the absent look in Goldmund's eyes, that deep stare, grown all too familiar, revealed to him only his fellow's longing to see more and more of death. He could not prevail over Goldmund, yet would not follow, and let him go alone through the gates.

As he passed under this unwatched gateway, and heard his feet ring out again on cobbles, Goldmund remembered many little towns into which he had loitered off the high-road. How noisy they had been, with children's voices, with boys shouting at their games, women squabbling, smiths hammering music out of anvils and many such delicate, lusty sounds to welcome him, whose intermingled skein had filled his ears with all the manifold pattern of human work, pleasure, accomplishment, companionship. Here, in this hollow-sounding gateway, these empty streets, there was no noise; it all lay dead and rigid with decay, and the music of a gossiping brook came far too loudly, almost disturbingly. Behind one grating he saw a baker, in the midst of his quartern loaves and small-bread. Goldmund pointed to a loaf, and the baker thrust it forth very gingerly, laid on the end of a long baking shovel, and waited for Goldmund's money to be set down. With nothing more than an evil look, as the stranger set no money on the shovel, but went on his way munching the loaf, the baker pulled his grating to again.

Along the casement ledge of a fine house stood a row of earthen vases, where flowers had bloomed, and over which hung shrivelled leaves. From another came sobs and the whining cries of a child. But in the next street, high up in her window, Goldmund saw a dainty girl, combing her hair out of a casement. He caught her eye, and she blushed, but did not turn aside from him, and when he smiled, a poor weak smile crept into her face along with her blushes.

'Soon have finished your combing?' he called up to her.

She bent down smiling over her window-ledge.

'Not sick yet?' he asked, and she shook her head. 'Well, come with me, then, leave this death-warren! Let's go into the woods and have a good life there.'

Her eyes began to question his.

'I mean it!' Goldmund insisted, 'but don't take too long to think it over. Have you father and mother, or do you live here with strangers as their serving-wench? Strangers, eh? Then come, sweet, let the old folks finish their dying! We're sound and young, and want a good life while we can get it. Come, little brown-hair – this is my earnest.'

She took his measure, hesitant and surprised. He loitered on down an empty street, then down a second, and came back slowly. There stood the maid, bent over her window-ledge, and rejoiced to think he had not left her. She beckoned him, he went on past her; soon she had come running to his side and, even before the gate, she had caught up with him, a little bundle in her hand, her brown hair bound in a red kerchief.

'What do they call you?' he asked.

'Lene. I'll come along with you. Oh, it's so bad here in the town – all dying. Let's get away, far away!'

Not far from the gates Robert squatted ill-humouredly on the ground. He sprang up at the sight of Goldmund, and stared when he saw a maid beside him. This time it was not easy to calm his fears, he wailed, lamented, and protested. To bring a woman out of that den of sickness, and force poor Robert to keep company with her – it was worse than mad, it was tempting God, he would not go another step beside them; he must leave them now, his patience was at an end.

Goldmund let him curse and rail himself out.

'There,' he said, 'you've sung your song. Now, you'll come along with us, and be thankful you have such a dainty companion. And listen, Robert, I have good news for you. We'll live awhile now in peace and health, and do all we can to shun this pestilence. We'll find some place in the woods, with an empty hut in it, or build one; and there I shall live with Lene as man and wife, and you, my friend, shall keep house along with us. Let's have a little ease and quiet together. Are you willing?'

Oh, yes, Robert agreed with all his heart. If only he were not expected to give Lene his hand or touch her gown.

'No,' said Goldmund, 'that you need not. Indeed, I forbid you very strictly to put so much as a finger on Lene. So be content.'

All three went on together, at first in silence, till at last Lene began to talk. How glad she was to see meadows again, and trees, and the wide sky; it had been so terrible in the plague-town, she could never say how fearful it had been. But then she began to tell them all, easing her mind of all its dread. She had many stories of horrid sights, evil tales, for the little town had been a hell. One of the two leeches had died, the other would only visit the rich; dead lay and stank in many houses, with no man to take them out and bury them; in others the coffin-bearers had stolen, swilled and whored, and often, along with the corpses, they had pulled the living sick out of their beds, and thrown them with the others into their death-carts. She had many such fearful things to relate. Neither interrupted her words. Robert heard it all with shuddering joy, Goldmund silent and indifferent, letting her pour out all her grief. He made no comment. What was a man to say to all that? At last Lene was tired, her torrent of words had spent itself. Goldmund slackened his pace and, in a low voice, struck up a song — a song with many verses and ritournelles, and with every verse his voice grew louder. Lene had begun to smile, and Robert listened, happy and amazed. Never before had he heard Goldmund sing. Why, he could do anything, this Goldmund! He was a sorcerer. Goldmund sang truly and well, though his voice was muted. And already, with the second verse, Lene had begun to join in, and soon she was with him full-throatedly. The sun was setting; away along the sky-line, over the heath, lay black woods, with far blue mountains behind them, bluer and bluer, as though their hue came from within. Merry or sad, to the beat of their tread, went Goldmund's song.

'You seem very happy today,' said Robert.

'Of course, I am happy today when I have such a fine love to go with me! Oh, Lene, how glad I am that the death churls left you over for me! Tomorrow we'll find a little hut, and in it we can live a good life and be glad that our flesh and bones still fit so well together. Lene, have you seen, in the woods in autumn, the little brown mushrooms the snails love so – and which you can eat?'

'Oh, yes,' she smiled, 'I've seen them often.'

'They are just as brown as your hair, and it smells every bit as good as they do. Shall we sing another catch, or are you hungry? I've still something good in my wallet.'

Next day they found what they were after. In a birch-wood stood a hut, of rough pine-logs, built by woodcutters or hunters. It was empty, the door could be prised open, and Robert thought it a good hut, and felt the place to be healthy. On their way they had met some goats, straying along the road without their shepherd, and had a fine nannygoat along with them.

'Robert,' said Goldmund, 'you may not be a master carpenter, but at least you were a joiner in your youth. We want to live and keep our state here, and you must build the dividing wall of our castle, so that then we shall have two good rooms, one for my Lene and me, the other for you and your nannygoat. We haven't much to eat though, so today we shall have to do with goat's milk whether there's much of it or little. Now you must build us a wall, while we two strew the beds for all three of us. And tomorrow I'll go out after victuals.'

They got to work at once. Lene and Goldmund gathered ferns and moss and dry leaves, Robert whetted his knife on a flint to cut branches and build up a wall. But he could not finish it that day, so for the night he went off and slept in the wood.

Goldmund found a sweet mistress in Lene, shy and young and full of love. He took her gently in his arms, and they lay awake many hours, he listening to the beating of her heart when she, long appeased and weary, had fallen asleep. He smelt her brown hair and nestled against it, thinking all the while of that wide shallow grave into which mumming devils had emptied out their cartloads of dead. Our life is fair, fair and soon over all our happiness, fair and quickly withered our youth.

The wall when it was built was a good one, but before that they had all three worked on it. Though Robert itched to show his skill, he bragged for hours of what he might have managed, if only he had had his tools, his planing bench, his iron rule and nails. Since here he had only his two hands and a knife, he contented himself with cutting a dozen birch stems, and setting them in a firm close row, well planted in the soil of the floor. The spaces in between, so he insisted, would have to be filled with plaited birch twigs. That needed time, but the work went happily, and both the others lent him a hand. Meanwhile Lene went picking berries, and saw to foddering the goat, while Goldmund strayed about the wood spying out the lie of the land for food, and bringing his plunder back home with him. Far and wide there were no men, and this pleased Robert very well, since now there was no danger of being tainted, or having an enemy to fight. Its disadvantage lay in this, that they found very little to stay their hunger. There was an empty peasant's holding not far off, and this time one without any dead in it, so that Goldmund urged that they must move there, instead of keeping to their log hut. But Robert shuddered and made such faces that Goldmund went alone to the empty house, and brought back all the gear along with him, though every piece he fetched must be washed and smoked at the fire before Robert would touch it.

Certainly it was not much he found there; two stout posts, a hatchet and a milkpail, a few iron vessels and, one day, he caught two hens escaped in a field. Lene was beloved and happy, and all three laughed, as they made their little home, adding something better every day. Bread they might lack, but found instead another goat, and near them a bit of ploughland with beetroots. Day after day sped by, the wattle wall was standing finished, their beds were softer than before, and a chimney with a hearth-stone built in the hut. Not far off was a stream where the water was clear and sweet. They would often sing over their work.

Once, as they drank their milk together, and applauded their householder's life, Lene, in a dreamy voice, said suddenly:

'But how will it be in the winter?'

No one could answer her. Robert laughed. Goldmund stared uneasily in front of him. Suddenly Lene grew aware that neither had so much as thought of that. Neither in his heart intended to stay long in this place, and so their home was not a home, and she only a wanderer with vagabonds. She hung her head.

Then Goldmund answered, as one jokes to put new heart into a child:

'You're a real peasant's daughter, Lene, and such have a care for far-off days. Don't be afraid! You can soon find your way back home again, when the plague-time is over and forgotten. Then you can go to your own, or whoever else may be there waiting for you, or back into the town as a serving-wench, and get your bread. But now it's summer still, and here it's pleasant, and life is good. So let's stay here together as short or long a while as pleases us.'

'And after?' cried Lene angrily. 'It will soon be winter. Then you'll jog off alone. And I–?'

Goldmund snatched her plaits and tugged them gently.

'You silly maid,' he said, 'do you forget the grave-churls and the death-carts, and the houses standing empty or full of corpses, or that hole by the gates, with the fires burning? Be glad you're not lying out in a hole, with the rain pattering down onto your shift. That's what you should think. "I've come out of it, and still have sweet life in my limbs, and can sing and laugh still."'

That did not please her yet.

'But I don't want to be off again,' she whimpered. 'You shan't leave me – no! How can I live happily here, if I know that soon it will all be past and over?'

Once more Goldmund answered her gently, but this time with a hint of threat in his voice.

'My Lene, what you have just been saying has plagued every wise man in the world, and all of them have broken their skulls, thinking of it. But if what we have now is not to your liking, or good enough for such as you, I'll fire the hut this very minute, and let us all go our ways. Be content, Lene, I speak my mind.'

She said no more, but a shadow lay across their love.

CHAPTER FOURTEEN

BEFORE the summer was quite withered their life in the huts came to an end, unexpectedly. One day Goldmund cut a sling, and strayed here and there around the clearing with it, in the hope of winging a partridge, or some such game, since their store of food was getting scanty. Lene had come with him to pick berries. Sometimes he would cross her track, and could see her head between the branches, on its brown neck, rising from the linen shift, and hear her singing. Once she came to his side, and they munched some berries: then she went on, and he lost sight of her. He thought of her half-tenderly, half-angrily. She had spoken again of autumn, and the future, and then said she believed herself with child, and would never let him go from her again.

'Now I must end it,' he was thinking. 'Soon I shall be weary of all this, and then I must wander again alone, and leave Robert, too, and see that before the winter comes I get back to the Bishop's city, to Master Nicholas, and there I shall weather out this winter, and next spring buy myself some good shoes, and trudge on till I reach our cloister in Mariabronn, and greet Narziss. It must be full ten years since I saw him. I must see him again, if only for a day, or two days.'

A sudden voice broke in upon his thoughts, and he grew instantly aware how far his mind and wishes had strayed from Lene, as though he had gone from her already. He listened sharply; the same noise startled him again, and he thought he could hear Lene's voice, calling in the bitterest need. Soon he was near enough. Yes, it was Lene. He hurried on, still rather angry, though her cries had roused his dread and pity. When at last he came within sight she was kneeling, or crouching, in the grass, her gown half-torn off her body, screaming and struggling with a man. Goldmund rushed in on them, all the grief, anger, uneasiness in his mind venting itself in rage against the aggressor. He came upon him, just as he had pinned her to earth; her naked breasts streamed blood, and the man held and clasped her greedily. Goldmund threw himself onto him, and crushed his throat with lustful, angry hands, a thin, reedy throat, covered in hair. He throttled with delight, till the man hung limp. Still gripping hard, he dragged his swooning, surrendered enemy over the ground, to a place where grey ridges of stone jutted, sharp and bare, out of the earth. Here he raised him high, twice, thrice, and, heavy as he was, dashed down his head.

He flung the body away with its neck broken, his anger still unappeased; he would have liked to do him a longer injury.

Lene watched it all with delight. Her breasts streamed blood, she was trembling still from head to foot, gasping for air. But now she had stumbled to her knees, and, in ecstasy, watched her mighty lover drag her assailant over the ground, throttle him, break his neck, and fling him aside. He lay like a slaughtered snake, limp and disjointed; his grey face, with the wild beard and matted hair, hung pitifully down over his chest. Lene stumbled, with cries of triumph, to her feet; yet suddenly, now, her face went white, the fear still shook in all her limbs, she turned sick, and fell fainting into the bilberry shrubs. Soon she was recovered enough to let Goldmund lead her back to the hut, where he washed the blood from her breasts, all covered in scratches, and one with the marks of a man's teeth on it. Robert was entranced by this adventure, and eager for details of the fight.

'His neck broken, you say? Wonderful, Goldmund; all men fear you.'

Goldmund had no wish to speak further of it. His rage had cooled, and soon, as they left the huddled corpse, he had had to think of Victor, the poor, dead guzzler, and that here was the second man to die at his hands. To get clear of Robert, he answered:

'Well now, you can do something yourself. Go along, and see that he gets a burial. If you find it too hard to scrape up a hole for him, drag him as far as the pool, and throw him in among the reeds; or cover him well with earth and stones.'

Robert would hear nothing of this. He would have no truck with corpses. How could you ever be certain that a corpse had no taint of plague on him?

Lene had lain down in the hut. The bite on her breast throbbed and burned. Yet, in spite of it, she soon felt better, rose, blew up her fire, and warmed the goat's milk for their supper. She was full of mirth, yet none the less they sent her early to bed, where she went like a lamb, so deep was her admiration of Goldmund.

He however was surly, and would say nothing. Robert, knowing his mood, left him in peace. When, late that night, Goldmund joined Lene on the straw, he bent above her, listening to her breath. She slept; he lay very restless, thinking of Victor, longing to get up and go from the others, feeling that this was the end of playing at houses.

Yet one thing had set him thinking. He had caught the look in Lene's eyes, as she watched him fling aside the throttled churl. That had been a thing worth noting, and he knew he never should forget it. In those wide, horror-stricken, delighted eyes, there had been such a glint of triumphant pride, such a glow of deep and passionate lechery, as he never had seen or imagined in women's faces. But for this one look, he might not have remembered Lene's

face, when he strove, years later, to recall it. It had bee
enough, this single look, to give her peasant's face a terro.
and beauty. For months his eyes had seen nothing which
roused the thought, 'This should be carved.' With this, in
a kind of livid terror, the wish to draw flashed back into his
mind.

Since he could not sleep he stood up at last, and went
outside. It was cold, a breeze sighed in the birches. He
walked up and down in the dark, came to rest on a stone,
lost in his thoughts, deep in sadness. He suffered for Victor's sake, for the sake of the man he had slain today, suffered for the loss of his innocence, the clear, child's beauty
of his soul. Was it for this he had broken out of the cloister,
left Narziss, given such pain to Master Nicholas, scorned
even to marry the pretty Lisbeth – that he might live like a
gipsy on a heath, chase escaped cattle through the woods,
batter out a wretched life on the stones. Had it all any sense
or worth in it? He sank back, and stared up at the pale
night-clouds, till he had gazed so long that his thoughts all
left him. He could not tell if he watched clouds or looked
into the darkness of his own mind. Then, at the instant he
fell asleep, there flamed, in the drifting sky, like a lightning
flash, the great pale face of his Eve, her heavy eyelids
drooping above him. Suddenly these eyes opened wide;
deep eyes, full of longing and lust to kill. Goldmund slept,
till the dew had soaked him.

Next day Lene was sick. They let her lie; there was much
to do. Early that morning Robert had seen two sheep in the
wood, which scampered away as he approached them. He
ran back for Goldmund, they hunted the sheep half the day,
and at last succeeded in trapping one of them. They were
tired out when, towards evening, they reached their hut
with the beast.

Lene felt sick to death. Goldmund bent over her, feeling
her body, and found plague-boils. This he kept to himself,

Robert suspected it at once, when he heard that Lene was still sick, and so refused to come inside. He must find some place to sleep in the wood, he said, and must take the goat, since it too could sicken of the plague.

'Go to the devil,' Goldmund shouted. 'Never let me set eyes on you again.'

But he seized the goat, and led it into the hut, behind the birch wall. Quietly, without his goat, Robert went off, full of dread; dread of the plague, dread of Goldmund, dread of solitude and the night. He lay down to sleep, nearby, in the woods.

Goldmund said to Lene:

'Don't be afraid. I'm with you. You'll soon be better.'

She shook her head.

'Be careful, love. Don't come too near me. And don't you weary yourself to comfort me. I must die, and I'd rather die now than see an empty place beside me, and know you'd gone from me for ever. Every morning I thought of that and feared it. No, I'd rather die.'

By morning it was already bad with her. From time to time Goldmund brought her a drink of water, and then, for an hour or two, he slept. Now as the light came creeping into the hut, he could see death plainly in her face, it looked so soft and shrivelled up. He went outside, to breathe the air and see the sky. The two gnarled fir trunks at the wood's edge were already glittering in the sunrise; the morning tasted sweet and cool, the far-off hills were hidden in a mist. He went a few steps further, stretched his tired body, took a deep breath. The world was fair on this sad morning. Now he would soon be on the roads again. This was a time for leave-taking.

Out of the wood Robert called to him. Was she any better? He would stay with them if only it weren't the plague. Goldmund must not be angry, he had kept the sheep with him all night.

'Get away to hell, and your sheep along with you,' shouted Goldmund. 'Lene's half-dead, and I'm infected.' This last he invented to get rid of him. This Robert might be harmless enough, but Goldmund wanted no more of his company. He was far too timid and mean, did not sort with this hour of fate and horror. Robert went off and never came back. Lene lay asleep when he entered the hut. He too dozed off for a while, and in a dream saw Bless his pony, and the lovely chestnut in the cloister. In this dream he felt that he looked across an endless desert, at a lost home that was still dear to him. Tears ran down his cheeks, and over his yellow beard as he woke.

He heard Lene speak, in a feeble voice. She had called him, and he sat upright on his straw. But she spoke to none, only muttered words to herself, little love-words and words of strife, laughing to herself and sighing heavily, till at last she sobbed, and gradually her voice died out. Goldmund stood up and bent over her tainted face, noting all its lines with bitter eagerness, traced out its forms, twisted and jumbled together, by the shrivelling breath of destruction. 'Sweet Lene,' his heart called, 'my sweet, kind, pretty one – will you leave me, too? Are you, too, weary of me, already?'

He would have liked to run off and leave her. To wander far, breathe in the air, tire himself out, see new sights, would ease his pain, might even perhaps have comforted his grief. Yet he could not leave the maid to die alone.

Lene could drink no more goat's milk, so he drank his fill, since now they had no other food. Several times he led out the goat to pasture, let it run, and get its drink of water. Then he went back to stand by Lene's side, whispering tenderness, gazing very closely into her face, watching her die, disconsolate but attentive. She was conscious still, at times asleep, but when she woke she could only half unclose her eyes, their lids were so heavy and sagging. From hour to hour this young girl aged and aged, wrinkles came round her eyes and nostrils; on her fresh young neck stood the quickly withering face of a grandmother. She said very little; only 'Goldmund' or 'Oh, my love,' striving to moisten her blue swollen lips with her tongue. Then he would set the pitcher to her mouth.

In the night she died, without a plaint, in one short sigh, and then no more breath came from her body. A shudder ran along her skin. This sight caused his heart to swell with grief, as he thought of the dying fish in the market-place, whose death he had so often seen and pitied. That was just how they too had died; one spasm, then a quick, light shudder, running along their bodies from end to end, skimming off the sheen, and the life along with it. He knelt with her a little while longer, then ran out into the air, to lie in bracken. He remembered the goat, and went back for it. It strayed a while, and lay down on the grass. He lay beside it, pillowed his head on its flank, and slept till daybreak. Then he entered the hut for the last time, and there, on the hither side of the wattle, took one last look at Lene's face. He loathed to abandon the dead; went forth again to gather an armful of bracken, dried leaves and boughs, and fling them into the hut; struck fire, and set light to it all. From the hut itself he took nothing but flint and steel. Their wattle fence went up in flame in an instant.

Outside he stood to watch it burn, his face scorched by the blaze, till at last the roof stood in flames, and the first rafter crashed within. The goat leapt about him, bleating wildly. It would have been well to slaughter the little beast and roast himself a morsel of goat's flesh, to get up his strength for the roads, but he could not do it. He drove the goat into the bushes. Smoke from Lene's pyre followed him on his way through the woods. Never had he set forth so disconsolate.

But that which now awaited his sight was worse, far

worse, than he had imagined. It began with the first farms and villages, and never ceased, no matter how far he strayed, more terrible and strange as he found his way into it. A thick mist of decay hung over this land, a veil of cruelty, horror, darkness of soul. The worst were not the empty houses, the farmyard dogs, famished or rotting on their chains, the dead, strewn about the earth, the begging children, the death-holes at city gates. Far worse than any dead were the living, who seemed to have their souls crushed out of them by a load of horror and panic fear of the end. Strange, gruesome tales met him on all sides. Parents had run from their children, husbands from their ailing wives, the instant they knew them to be tainted. Death-churls, hospital servitors, ruled like hangmen, looting the perished houses and, if it pleased them, leaving the dead to fall to bits; plucking the dying from their beds and casting them, alive, into the death-carts. Crazy, mumbling fugitives wandered the roads, shunning every contact with other men, hunted on and on by the thought of death. Others, resolute to live, herded, while still they might, in merry bands, dancing and drabbing, with Death their fiddler. Lost waifs clustered at graveyard gates, or crept into empty, plundered houses. And, worst of all, each sought a scape-goat, to unload this horrible weight of grief; each had his tale of some cursed creature whose guilt had brought this on the land, whose malice had conjured up the pestilence. Devilish folk, they would say to Goldmund, of their hate had spread death here and there, squeezed poison from the boils of corpses, to daub it over walls and lintels, infect-ing well-springs, and the cattle. Any in such suspicion were lost, unless they had been warned and could take flight, since justice and the mob soon made an end of them. The rich had brought the plague, said the poor, and the rich said it was the poor; while many said it was the Jews, and some the Italians, or the leeches. In one city, with fierce disgust in his heart, Goldmund watched the Jews roast in their Jewery, house taking fire from house, while the mob clamoured around and made a ring, to thrust back shrieking fugitives into the flames. Everywhere in this welter of hate and grief, the innocent were burned, racked, or struck down. Goldmund felt that the world was poisoned indeed, since there seemed no innocence or joy, honour or love, on earth any more. Then, since death's fiddle sounded in every place, he would join the merriest of the dancers: he had learnt to hear their notes far in the distance, could strum a lute to their caperings, or himself dance all night long under pitch-pine torches.

He did not fear. Once on a winter's night under the fir-trees, with Victor's fingers round his throat, he had tasted the deep terror of death. He had known it since, out on the moors, in the snow and dearth of many hard days' wanderings. But that had been such death as a man could grapple with; against it he could set himself on guard, and so he had fought death off with weary limbs, with shaking hands and gnawing belly. None could fight this death by pestilence; they must let it rage, and surrender to it, and Goldmund had surrendered long ago. He did not fear, since it seemed to him there was nothing left in life for him, now he had turned from Lene's shrivelling body and wandered so many days in the Kingdom of Bones. Yet a strange, sharp eagerness kept him alert. He could never tire of watching the reaper at his work, or listening to the song of passing life. Nothing could appal his sight; in every place the same quiet passion seized him, to be by, noting with careful eyes each step along the road through hell. He would eat tainted bread in perished houses, sing and share their wine with tipsters, pluck the quickly shrivelling flowers of lust, gaze into the staring eyes of women, the glazed, unanswering eyes of sots, the slowly filming eyes of the dying; loving these fevered, desperate, half-dead harlots; help for a plate of broth to carry out corpses, shovel on the earth for two farthings. The world had grown savage and full of darkness, death howled his song in Goldmund's straining ears, who marked its note with never-sated eagerness.

His aim was the city of Master Nicholas, urged thither by the longing to work again, though the way was long and full of fear, through a shrivelled world, where light had perished. He trudged sadly on, lulled by death-songs, but attentive to the wailing voices of men, sad, and yet aglow with desire, his itch to see it all never appeased.

In a cloister he saw a freshly painted wall-picture, and had to stand there long, before he could leave it. It was a dance of death across the wall: pale Bones dancing folk off the earth, a king, a bishop, an abbot, a count, a knight, a leech, a peasant, a serf, he took them all — and skeletons piped, through hollow bones, to lead them. Goldmund's curious eyes took in this picture. There, from what he had seen of murky death, some unknown fellow-craftsman drew the lesson, crying his shrill-voiced admonition that all must die, in the ears of men. It was good, a very good sermon, was this wall-painting: the fellow had seen the matter well, his savage picture seemed to moan and rattle. Yet none the less Goldmund had felt it otherwise. Here it was the necessity to die that stood painted up so sternly and inescapably. Goldmund would have liked another picture. In him death's wildest song had a different echo, a voice calling homewards into the earth, home to a mother; its sounds not harsh and white, but sweet and enticing. Here, where death thrust forth his hand into life, it was as an iron-tongued warrior that he came. And yet his voice had other notes in it; deep, loving sounds, gentle as sated autumn, so that near him the tiny lamp of life seemed to shine with a brighter, warmer glow. For others death might be a captain, a judge, a hangman, a stern father – for Goldmund death was also a mother and mistress, crooning the enticements of life, touching him with a shiver of desire.

When he had left the painted death-dance, and gone his way, he longed still more for work, and Master Nicholas. Yet every place he traversed had something to hinder him, new sights of death, a fresh experience, and he sniffed their reek with eager nostrils. Face after face demanded an hour or day of this watcher's pity or curiosity. For three days he had a little whimpering peasant-boy at his side, and for hours carried him on his back; a half-famished waif of five or six, from whom he found it hard to rid himself. In the end he left him with a charcoal burner's wife in a wood, whose man was dead, and who wanted some living warmth to comfort her. For miles a stray cur limped at his heels, eating from his hand, warming his sleep; and one morning, when he woke, it had gone its ways. This grieved him, since he was used to speak to the dog, pouring out his thoughts, for hours, on the malice of men, to it; on God's existence, the carver's craft, the breasts and lips of a knight's young daughter, Julia, whom he had known long ago, in his youth. Like many other wanderers through the death Goldmund had become a little crazed. None in this plague-stricken land had all their wits, and many were mad out and out. The young Jewess, Rebecca, may have been mad, the fair, dark maid, with glittering eyes, with whom he passed some days on the roads.

He had found her in the fields, out beyond the gates of a little town, rocking and moaning, by the cinders of a burnt-out heap of logs, beating her face, and tearing at her long black hair. It was her hair first moved his heart, it looked so beautiful, and he caught her wild hands and held them fast, talked to the maid and, as he comforted, saw that her face and body were very fair. She raved with grief for her father whom the balies of the town had burnt to ashes, along with fifteen other Jews. She had escaped, but then returned in desperation, and now lay howling out her grief that she had not let them burn her along with him. Patiently he held her clawing hands, speaking soft words, muttering of pity and protection, and offering to do whatever she would. She asked his help to bury her father, and they gathered all the bones from the glowing ashes, carried them in secret into the fields, and there laid them in the earth. Then it was night, and Goldmund sought out a sleeping-place, heaped up a bed for the maid in a little oak wood, promised he would guard her sleep, and listened as she lay there sobbing, until at last sleep came and stilled her cries. He too slept for a while, and in the morning began to court her, telling her she could not stay there alone, she would be known for a Jewess and struck to death, or vagabonds would come on her, and rape her, and in the woods there were wolves and gipsies. But he, he said, would bear her company, protecting her from beasts and humans, for she moved the pity in his heart; he had eyes in his head to see what beauty was, and never would he suffer those white shoulders and shining eyes to be the food of wolves, or burnt to ashes on a scaffold. She heard him sullenly to the end, then sprang up and ran away from him. He had to chase, and hold her, before she would listen.

'Rebecca,' he said, 'you see I mean you no harm. You are sad for thinking of your father, and will hear no word of any love. But tomorrow, or next day, or later, I'll ask you again, and, till then, I'll shield you, and bring you food, and never touch you. Mourn as long as you must! You can be either sad or merry with me, but always you shall only do what pleases you.'

All this was spoken to the wind. She would do nothing, she said with stubborn rage, that could ever bring her joy again. She would do what brought her the worst agony, and the sooner the wolves had got her the greater her content

215

would be. Let him go his ways; he should never have her. He had said too much to her already.

'Sweet,' he answered, 'can you not see that death is everywhere – that they are dying in all the houses of every town, that the whole world is full of clamour and grief? Even the rage of the fools who burned your father was nothing but their grief and need. It was all born of the same great pain. Listen – soon death will take us too, and then we shall lie out rotting in the fields, and wolves play at dice with our bones. Let us live, now while we may, and love each other. Oh, it were such pity, my love, for your white neck, and little feet. Sweetheart, come with me now, I will only watch you and protect you.'

He begged her long; till suddenly he remembered that it was useless to persuade with words, or any reasoning. Then he was silent, and stared glumly at her. Her dark, proud face was set in hate.

'So are you all,' she said at last, in a voice of utter loathing and derision. 'All you Christians are the same. First you help a daughter to bury her father, slaughtered by you and your like, whose little finger was worth all of you – and have scarce done when the maid must be yours to lie with, and go out junketing at your side. So are you all. At first I thought you might be a good man : but how can any of you be good? Oh, you are swine.'

As she said all this Goldmund watched her eyes, and saw something deeper than the hate in them; a thing which moved him to the heart. He saw death again, there in her eyes; not the death which cannot be escaped, but the freedom to die, the will, the longing for it, the quiet, soft answer of resignation to the call of our mother, the earth.

'Rebecca,' he told her very gently, 'you may be right, and I a wicked man, although I meant only good to you. Forgive me. I have only just understood.'

He took off his cap and bowed very low, as though to a

princess, then left her, with an aching heart. For long his soul was full of pain, and he could not bear to speak to anyone. Little as they resembled one another, this poor, proud Jewess, in some strange fashion, put him in mind of Lydia, the knight's daughter. It brought a man sorrow to love such women, and yet, for a while, it seemed to Goldmund that these were the only two he had ever loved; the poor, anxious Lydia, and this shrinking, bitter Jewish maid.

For days he remembered this dark Jewess, and dreamt, for many nights after, of the fiery, lissom beauty of her body, fashioned, it seemed, for all desire, and yet given over to death. Oh that such lips and eyes should be formed to be the loot of 'swine', and then lie rotting in the fields. Was there no power, no magic in the world, to save such tender blossom of precious joy?

Yes, there was one such magic. This loveliness must re-shape itself in his soul, his hands inform it, and preserve. With delight and fear he perceived how full his mind had grown of images, how many shapes this long, dread journey had left inscribed upon his heart. Forms thronged and jostled within him, till he longed for quiet, to see them all, and release them into living permanence. More eager, more alert, more curious, he went on, with searching eyes, and passionate senses, but restless, now, for clay and wood, for paper, charcoal, and a workshop.

The summer died. Many assured him that with the autumn, or early winter, the plague must end. It was autumn now, but with no joy in it. Goldmund came through empty, desolate country, with none to gather in its harvests, so that fruit dropped from the trees, and covered the grass. In many places it was plundered by savage bands from the town, consorting together to rob the land. Slowly he neared his destination, and would often fear, in these last days, to find himself tainted with the plague, and so be forced to die in a cow-stall. He feared death now, and shrank away from it; he must live, to taste the one delight of standing again before a wood-block, and giving himself up to the carver's craft. Now, for the first time in his life, the Empire was too broad, and the world too wide for him: no pleasant town could hold him now, no wench keep him longer than a night.

One day he came to a church, on whose front, in deep niches, born up by columns, stood many rows of figures, cut in stone, fashioned in a very ancient time – figures of apostles, martyrs, angels, such as he had seen often before, in his own cloister-church in Mariabronn. As a boy he had taken a certain pleasure in them, although they never stirred him very deeply. They had seemed to him beautiful and worthy, yet a little too stiff, patriarchal, ceremonious. Later, at the end of his first great wandering, when he had been so moved to joy and wonder by Nicholas' sweet and sorrow-ful Mother of God, he had found these old, solemn figures clumsy and heavy, too rigid, too remote from life, think-ing with a certain disdain of them, finding this new style of Master Nicholas a far more living, deeper, and rarer art.

But as, today, after long experience, he came back to them, his soul scarred by the world, full of the urgent need for quiet and thought, their old, stern forms suddenly moved him, with a force and power he had never known. Piously he stood before their reverence, in which still beat the heart of a perished day, the fears and raptures of many dead, held in strong lines above the centuries, defying the brittleness of time. A feeling of deep awe and love of them stole into his heart as he gazed, and he shuddered at his wasted, burnt-out life. He did what he had not done these many years; accused himself, and longed for penances, sought out a confessional and a priest.

But, although the church had many shriving-stools, there was not a priest in them all: they were dead, or lying in

218

hospices; they had run far off, fearing the taint. The nave was empty, Goldmund's steps rang in the vaultings. He knelt at an empty stool, and shut his eyes. Then he began to whisper through the lattice:

'Dear God, see what is become of me. I come back to You, an evil, useless man. I have flung away my youth, like a spendthrift, and now very little is left over. I have slain, I have stolen, I have whored. I have idled, and eaten the bread of others. God, why did You make us so? And why do You lead us by such ways? Are we not Your children? Did not Your Son go to death for us? Are there not saints and angels to watch over us? Or is it all a bundle of pretty tales, invented to keep the children quiet, at which shavelings laugh among themselves? Your works have confused me, God the Father. You have made the world very ill, and now You rule it very weakly. I have seen streets and houses full of dead men. I have seen the rich lock up their doors and fly, leaving the poor, their brothers, to rot unburied. I have seen how men feared one another, how they struck down Jews like slaughtered cattle. I have seen so many innocent suffer and die, so many evil men wallow in sloth. Have You turned away, and left us utterly? Are Your own creatures of no more worth to You? Do You want men to perish from the world?'

Sighing he came out through the great doors: dumb rows of saints and angels towered above him, each set high in its narrow space, held in the long, stiff folds of their gowns; unchangeable, unattainable, greater than men. Stern and mute, in their narrow niches, deaf to every question and petition, yet they seemed eternally to comfort; the triumphant conquerors of death, the rigid saviours from despair. They, in their dignity and beauty, had watched the crumbling generations. Ah, that poor Rebecca had been as they, poor Lene, charred to ashes in her hut, poor gentle Lydia, Master Nicholas! One day these, too, should stand and abide: soon he would have fixed their memories, which now meant only love and grief to him, fear, and the longing to hold their shape. They, too, should comfort the living, alive with neither name nor history; the still, mute symbols of human days.

CHAPTER FIFTEEN

At last he had reached his journey's end, and Goldmund, through the same gateway under which, so many years ago, he had hurried first into this city, to find a master and learn a craft, re-entered the place of his desire. He had been told that here, too, they had had the plague, and perhaps it reigned still. There had been risings and tumults, so that the Emperor had sent his Stattholder to quell them, and set up the law in its place again, protecting the lives and goods of honest citizens. The bishop had fled his city the instant he knew that the plague had entered it, and now lived out on the land, in one of his castles. Goldmund paid small heed to all this. Let it all go as it would, if only there were a city still, and his workshop! But when he reached the gates there was no more plague; the burghers were expecting their bishop's return, and with it their settled, peaceful life. He rejoiced to see these streets again, and his heart leapt, as though for a home-coming, so that he had to master himself, and frown a little.

It was all just as he had left it: the gates, the delicate fountains, the old, squat tower of the Minster, the long, slender spire of St Mary's church, the clear, bright chimes of St Lawrence, the wide and beautiful market-place. Oh, how good to feel it had all been waiting for him! Had he not dreamed, out there, that he came back only to find it shrivelled up, one half in ashes, the other full of unfamiliar houses. He almost wept as he passed along the street, recognizing house after house. After all, perhaps these burghers were to be envied for their calm, deep knowledge that they were at home, living their safe and peaceful lives, ensconced in their workshops and houses, with wives and children, journeymen and neighbours.

It was late afternoon, sunlight lay gold over the house-fronts, with their tavern-signs, and signs of guilds, their carved doors, their rows of flowerpots on the balconies. It all looked warm; there was nothing there to remind him that through these pleasant houses death had raged, ruling the panicked fears of men. Cool, clear green and blue, the river ran like glass under echoing arches. Goldmund sat to rest on the river wall: down under layers of greenish crystal the same shadowy fish still glided; or they lay inert, their noses turned against the currrent, and still, out of the shad-owed twilight around them, some pale gold object glittered here and there, promising much, and favouring dreams.

Though other waters had the like, and other towns and bridges were very fair, to Goldmund it seemed that not for years had he met any sight to equal this, nor ever, except here, felt anything like it. Two laughing butcher's pren-tices came driving their cow across the bridge, joking, and winking at a maid who, in a niche in the wall above them, took in her washing. How soon everything changed! A short while ago the plague-fires had burned outside this city, and gruesome death-churls done their will in it. Now life flowed and hurried just as before. People could laugh — and he himself was like them, sitting there, rejoicing to see it all, as though there had been no pain or death in the world, no Lene, no Jewish maid. He felt so glad that he even loved the citizens, stood up with a smile, and went further, and not till he reached the street of Master Nicholas, by alley-ways which he had trodden each day on his way to work, did his heart begin to beat, and his mind grow restless.

He quickened his pace, longing, even tonight, to speak to the Master. He must know for certain, could not brook a second's more delay: to wait another night seemed impos-sible. Was Nicholas angry still? Ah, it was all so long ago, it could have no meaning any more. But if he stormed, Goldmund would mollify and placate him. All would be well if only the Master were still there — he and his work-shop! Running, as though, even in this last instant, he might come too late and lose some chance, he came to the house he knew so well, seized the latchet, and gave a little start, as he found the house-door locked against him. Was this ill-omened? In his day it had never happened that this door was bolted before dark. Trembling he crashed down the knocker, and waited. His heart stood still.

There came the old serving-woman again, who had let him into the house that first time. Now she was no uglier than then, but older, and still more crotchety in her ways, and she did not seem to know who he was. In a low voice he demanded Master Nicholas. She squinted up, mistrust-fully and stupidly.

'Master? There's no master here. Go your ways, man, no one is admitted.' She tried to thrust him back from the doorway, but he caught her arm, and shouted in her ear:

'For God's sake, Margrit, stop your whimpering! I am Goldmund. Don't you know who it is? I must go in now to Master Nicholas.'

'He's dead, I tell you,' she said grudgingly. 'We've no Master Nicholas here. Be off with you now; I haven't the time to stand here gossiping.'

Goldmund, with tumult in his soul, thrust the old woman aside, who hobbled after with many cries, and rushed down the dark passage to the workshop. That, too, was locked. He turned, and ran up the stairs, with the whining, chiding Margrit at his heels, and there in the half-light of the land-ing, stood the figures Master Nicholas had assembled. He stopped, and called for Mistress Lisbeth.

The door into the oakroom opened: Lisbeth came, and when at the second glance, he knew her, the sight of her pierced him to the heart. If, from the apprehension of that first minute when he found the street-door bolted against him, everything in this house had seemed bewitched, a little ghostly, as though in some uneasy dream, now, with his first sight of Lisbeth, a cold shiver ran along his spine. Lisbeth, the proud, the beautiful, had shrunk into a timid, faded gentlewoman, in a black gown, with a yellowish, sickly face, with no jewels now, with uncertain eyes and anxious mien.

'Forgive me, Mistress,' he said to her. 'Margrit did not want to let me in to you. You know me? Surely you must. I'm Goldmund. Say – is it true your father's dead?'

Her eyes said she knew him well, and that here his memory was unwelcome.

'So you are Goldmund, are you?' – in her voice he could still hear something of her pride – 'You have given yourself these pains for nothing. My father is dead.'

'But the workshop?' he had to ask her.

'The workshop? Closed. You must go elsewhere if it's work you need.'

He strove not to let her see his grief.

'Mistress Lisbeth,' he said, in a friendly voice, 'I am not come to ask you for work. I wanted to give you greeting – you, and the Master. It irks me sore to have to hear you. I can see you have had much sorrow. If your father's thankful apprentice can do you a service – name it – it would be my recompense. Ah, Mistress Lisbeth, it breaks my heart to see you so . . . so deeply afflicted.'

She stepped back into the shadow of the doorway.

'Thanks,' she hesitated, 'you can do him no further service, or me either. Margrit will lead you into the street.'

Her voice had an evil ring, half fear, half malice. He could feel that, if she had had the courage for it, she would have railed, and turned him from the house.

Old Margrit slammed the door behind him, and drew the bolts. Now he stood in the street and heard them still, like the double grating-down of a coffin lid.

Slowly he returned to the river wall, and leant again above the water's edge. The sun was down, a chill came off the river, the stone that touched him was like ice. The street behind had grown very silent, the current swirled around the piers; no sheen of gold off the dark waters.

'Oh,' he thought, 'if I could slip off this wall and vanish.' Once more the world was full of death. An hour went by, and the dusk had gathered into darkness. He could weep at last; the warm drops splashed his hands and knees. He wept for Master Nicholas, who was dead, for Lisbeth's beauty that had vanished, for Lene, for the Jewish maid, for Victor, for his own shrivelled, wasted days.

Late that night he found a wine-cellar, where he had often drunk and diced with apprentices. The hostess knew him again: he begged for a slice of bread, which she gave him, and along with it a friendly cup of wine. Neither bread nor wine could he taste. He slept on a bench in her tavern. Early in the morning she waked him, and he gave her thanks, and said, 'God's speed'. On his way he finished the bread she had given him.

He strayed about, and came to the Fish-Market. There stood the house where he had lodged. Two fishwives, by the fountain, hawked their wares. The fair, shimmering fish swam round and round in their tub. He saw it all in a dream, remembering his pity for the fish, his anger against the buyers and sellers. Then, so he thought, he had loitered, just as today, pitying fish, and wondering at their beauty; endless time had passed since then, and water flowed under bridges. He had been very sad, he still remembered, but strove in vain to capture the feeling that had made his heart so heavy, long ago. 'So it is,' he thought, 'sadness withers, and even our despair shrivels up. Pain, like our joys, fades out and leaves us, losing all its depths and worth, till at last a day comes when we have forgotten what stung our hearts so many years before.' Even pain crumbles away and perishes. Would this today lose all its depths and meaning — this despair that Master Nicholas was dead, in anger against him; that now there was no workshop to take him in, bring back his delight in carving shapes, and rid him of his weight of images. Yes, there could be no doubt, even this bitter longing would age and tire, his need would all be forgotten, since nothing stays with us long, not even grief.

As he stood there, watching the fish and thinking all this, he heard a shy, friendly voice, beside him.

'Goldmund,' it said very softly, and he turned to see a timid, sickly girl, with wide and beautiful eyes, who had said his name. He did not know her.

'It is you, Goldmund?' she asked in her small, shy voice. 'Since when have you been back in the city, then? Don't you know me, Goldmund? I'm Marie.'

But still he could not remember. She had to say how she was the daughter of the guilder in whose house he had lodged in the Fish-Market; how, early one morning, before he left them, she had risen from her bed to warm his milk in the kitchen. She blushed in telling him all this.

Now he remembered; yes, it was Marie, the little, sickly maid who had limped, and been so quiet and timid as she served him. He remembered it all; she had come to him in the early morning cool, and been very sorry to see him go from them. She had brought him milk, and when he kissed her in exchange for it she had taken his kiss as reverently and quietly as if it had been the Blessed Host. He had never once thought of her since.

In those days she had been a child. Now she was grown into a woman with beautiful eyes, though still she limped, and seemed a little doleful. He took her hand. It was good to find someone in the town who knew him still, and still had any love for him.

Although he protested, Marie led him into their house. In the living-room, where still his picture hung and his ruby glass stood over the chimney-piece, her parents bade him stay with them to dinner, and pressed him to remain a couple of days. All seemed very glad to see him again. Here, too, he learned how things had gone with Master Nicholas. The Master had not died of the plague, they said, it had been Mistress Lisbeth who sickened of it. She had lain near death; her father had worn himself out with grief and care of her, and died before she was quite well again. Her life was saved, but not her beauty.

'Now the workshop stands empty,' said the guilder, 'and for a good carver there would be a snug home, and money enough. Consider it, Goldmund. She would not say "no" to you. She has no choice now.'

He learned this and that of the plague-time; how first the rabble had fired a hospice, and then burned and looted a few rich houses, till for a while there was no safety or order within the walls, since the bishop and his men had taken flight. But then the Emperor, who happened to be near the city, had sent his stattholder, Count Heinrich. Well, sure enough, this lord was resolute, and had soon brought the city to submission, with his riders, and his band of archers. But now it was time to be quit of him, and the city wanted its bishop back again: this count had laid contributions on the citizens, and they wearied both of him and Agnes, his doxy. She was a proper devil's piece. But soon they would be gone, both he and she; the city fathers had long grown weary of them, and of having, in place of their good bishop, this courtier and captain on their backs, a kaiser's minion, who received ambassadors and churchmen like a prince.

Then the guest was asked to tell of his travels. 'Alas,' he answered them, 'no man could speak of it well. I went on and on, and in every place there was the plague; I saw corpses rotting by the roadside, and in cities the folk were mad, and evil with fear. I came out whole, and perhaps one day I shall forget it. Now I am here, to find my Master dead. Let me bide with you, and rest a few days, before I go on my way again.'

But it was more than need that made him ask it. He stayed because he was sick at heart, and irresolute; because the city, with its memory of better days, was dear to him, and poor Marie's love soothed his heart. He could not love her in exchange, could give her nothing save friendship and gentleness, yet her humble longing seemed to cherish him.

And, more than all, his burning wish to make images held him back: even without a shop to work in, as a journeyman even, he longed to stay in the city.

For two whole days Goldmund did nothing but draw. Marie had procured him pens and paper for it, and now, hour after hour, he sat in his room, filling the wide reams with scribbled shapes, though some were careful and full of thought. He made many studies of Lene's head, as he had seen it after the death of the vagabond, smiling with triumphant love, exulting in the sight of death; of Lene's head, as it had looked on the night before she died, eager to return into the earth, already almost crumbling into formlessness. He drew a little boy he had once seen dead, stretched on the threshold between two rooms, on his way to his parents, with clenched fists. He drew a wagon full of corpses, with three thin jades wearily tugging it, and churls running beside to urge it on, long poles in their hands, and with squinting eyes, glittering through the slits in the black plague-masks. Over and over again he drew Rebecca, the dark slim Jewess, whose eyes were fire, with her small, proud mouth, her face full of misery and defiance, her pure young body, shaped, it seemed, for nothing but love. He drew himself, as a wanderer, a lover, a fugitive, with reaping death hard at his heels; as a dancer at the feasts of the plague-stricken. Eagerly he bent over the paper, to fix, in long, firm strokes, the features of the pretty, disdainful Lisbeth he had known, the broken grimaces of old Margrit, the admired form of Master Nicholas. And several times, in dim, uncertain outlines, he suggested another face, a woman's – mother earth, with hands folded in her lap, the ghost of a smile under heavy lids. This knowledge of the power in his hands, the mastery he had of all these faces, comforted him more than any words. In two days he had covered every sheet that Marie brought him, while from the last he cut out a space, and on this, in a few clear strokes, drew Marie – her face with the beautiful eyes, and lips that renounced. This he gave her.

This work had appeased him. For as long as he could stay there drawing he had not known where he sat, or what he suffered. His world had been nothing but a table, the white paper, a rush-light at dusk. Now he awoke to remember that his Master was dead, and that he must set forth on the roads again, and so began to stray about the city, with a strange sense of welcome and farewell.

On one of these walks he met a lady, whose sight alone resolved the tumult in his mind. A fair woman, with light, gold hair, on horseback; with inquisitive, rather cold blue eyes, beautiful and strong, with a fresh, clear skin, a face all eagerness for life, greed to enjoy and rule, self-reliance, and sensual curiosity. She sat her horse with an air of mastery and disdain, the look of one who commands by habit; yet with nothing reserved or guarded in her face and, beneath the rather cold light in her eyes, nostrils, which seemed flutteringly eager to welcome every savour life could offer her, while her firm beautiful lips seemed to promise that she could give and take without stint. The sight of her made Goldmund feel alert – suddenly eager to measure himself against this woman's pride. To win and master her seemed to him a glorious achievement, nor would he have thought it a bad death to forfeit his head in the attempt. At once he knew this strong, golden woman as his equal, rich in her senses and her heart, with the strength in her to weather any storm, as wild in her loves as she was tender, sensing the very tact and beat of passion from ancient inherited knowledge of the blood. She rode on past him, and he watched her. Between her dark blue bodice and rough gold hair her firm, white neck rose proud and strong, yet cased in the delicate skin of a child. She was, he thought, the fairest woman he had seen, and he longed to feel her neck under his hands, and pluck the cold, blue mystery out of her eyes. Nor was he long in learning her name. He heard at once that she was Agnes, the stattholder's leman, who lived with him in the bishop's palace. The news did not alter his purpose, since she might have been the empress herself. He stopped, to bend over a fountain, and see his image in the water. The face he saw matched hers, as brother to sister, but his was far too wild and unkempt. Within the hour he had hunted up a barber and, by persuasion, had himself oiled and combed, and his beard cut.

He spent two days in pursuit of her. Agnes would ride out of the palace, to see this fair-haired stranger at the gates, who stared at her with longing in his eyes. She would canter her horse around the bastions, and the stranger would be waiting under the elms. Agnes would have been at the goldsmith's and, as she left his workshop, meet the stranger. Her proud blue eyes measured him sharply, yet her nostrils quivered a little as she stared. Next day, on her early ride, she met him again, and smiled a challenge as she passed. With her he saw the count, the stattholder, a bold and stately man, and a serious enemy. But his hair had grey in it already, and creases of care under the eyes. Goldmund could feel himself a match for him.

These days filled him with delight, he rejoiced in a sense of new-won youth. It was very good to draw this woman on, and challenge her, good to risk his freedom for this beauty. Best and pleasantest of all was his sense of setting his life on this one throw.

On the morning of the third day, Agnes rode forth from the castle yard followed by a groom on horseback. She looked at once, a little restlessly, for the stranger, as though she were eager to do battle. Her groom was sent ahead with a message, and she walked her horse slowly after him, under the gateway, to the bridge, and over it. Only once did she look behind her to see that the stranger was at her heels. In the street to St Vitus, the pilgrims' church, at that time of day almost deserted, she reined up, and waited his approach. She had nearly half an hour to wait for him, since he followed her very slowly, refusing to approach her breathless. He came, smiling and radiant, with a little bunch of red hips and haws between his teeth. She had slid from her horse, and tethered it, and now stood with her back against the ivy that climbed up the steep church bastion. She looked her pursuer in the eyes. He faced her gaze, and doffed his cap.

'Why do you hunt me?' she asked him. 'What do you want of me?'

'Oh,' he replied, 'I would as lief make you a gift as take one. It is myself I would offer you, fair woman, and then you shall do as you will with me.'

'Well, I shall see what use I can put you to! But if you thought you could come out plucking flowers without danger, you were wrong. I can only love those who risk their lives for me if they must.'

'Mine is yours to command.'

Slowly she drew a thin gold chain from her neck.

'What do they call you?'

'Goldmund.'

'Goldmund – good; I must taste how golden is that mouth of yours. Now listen well. You are to bring this chain at dusk to the palace, and say you found it. You will not let it leave your hands. I must have it back from you alone. You are to come to me just as you are, even though they

231

take you for a beggar. If any of the palace-rabble come sniffing you, bear with them. Know that only two of my people are trustworthy, the squire, Max, and Bertha, my woman. One of these two you must seek out, and have yourself led to me. Be on your guard against all the others, and the count himself; they are your enemies. You are warned; it may cost you your neck.'

She held out her hand for him to kiss, and he took it smiling, stroked it against his cheek, and kissed it tenderly. Then he hid her chain and left her, walking downhill into the city, with city and river spread beneath him. The vines were already stripped: one gold leaf fluttered past another off the trees. He smiled again and nodded at these streets, lying there so snug and friendly. Only a few days back he had been all sorrow, sick at heart that even pain and grief pass over us, leaving no trace. Now these were gone indeed; they had fluttered down, like the gold leaves off the branches, yet never, he thought, had love promised so much as it did in the eyes of this woman, whose tall beauty and golden fullness of life put him in mind of the image of his mother, as he had seen it long ago as a child in Mariabronn, when first he knew he carried it in his heart. Even two days since he would not have believed that the world could ever again seem young and vivid, nor the sap of life rise in him so mightily, with all the eager pleasure of his youth, setting new fire in every vein. How glorious to know he was still alive, to know that death had passed him by, in all the crazy horror of these months.

That evening he stole into the palace. Its great courtyard was full of stir and bustle, palfreys were being stripped of their trappings, messengers hurried to and fro, while a little procession of monks and ghostly dignitaries followed servants through the doors, and up the staircase. Goldmund tried to enter after them, but found that a porter barred his way.

He brought out his chain, saying that he had commission to give it to none but the Lady Agnes, or her tire-woman. They gave him a groom to take him further, who left him in one of the long passages. Then came a nimble, beautiful woman, who whispered, as she hurried past, 'Are you Goldmund?' – and beckoned him to follow in her wake. She vanished quickly through a side door, came back after a while, and called him in. He found himself in a little room, with a scent of fur and sweet essences, and hung about with robes and mantles; women's hats were set out on wooden stands, and many pairs of shoes in an open trough. Here he stood waiting a long half-hour, sniffed at the scented robes that hung about him, stroking their fur, and smiled inquisitively on all the pretty gauds that dangled down.

At last the inner door was opened and there came, not the tire-woman but Agnes, in a sky-blue robe, with white fur at her neck. Slowly she approached the waiting Goldmund, step by step, and her deep blue eyes measured him gravely.

'You have had to wait,' she said in a low voice, 'but I think we are safe at last. An embassy of prelates is with the count. He must sup with them, and they will have much business together. Priests always draw out their sessions. This hour is yours and mine. Welcome, Goldmund.'

She stood beside him, her greedy lips bent close, and without more words they greeted in a kiss. Softly his fingers stroked her nape. She led him out of the wardrobe into her sleeping-chamber, high, and bright with many tapers. Food had been set out on one of the tables. They sat, and she spread butter on wheaten cakes for him, with flesh, and gold wine in a high, blue-tinged glass. They ate and drank, both from the same azure cup, their hands caressing, by way of trial.

'What made you fly into my nest,' she asked him, 'my pretty bird? Are you a soldier of a spielmann; or are you some poor vagabond off the roads?'

'I am all that you will,' he answered softly, 'and am all yours. I am a spielmann, if you will, and you are my sweet lute, so that when I touch your neck with my fingers, and play on you, we can hear the angels, how they sing! Come my heart – I am not here to eat your wheaten cakes and drink your wine. I came only for you.'

Gently he unclasped the white fur at her neck and unsheathed her body. Though around them priests and courtiers might hold session, servants come creeping up the passages, the sickle moon drop far into the branches in the courtyard, these two knew nothing of all this. For them the trees of Paradise were in blossom. Drawn and clasped to one another, they lost themselves within its scented night, saw the white, shimmering secrets of its flowers, plucking its fruits, for which they thirsted, with gentle, ever-grateful, hands. Never before had spielmann struck such a lute, or lute known fingers so strong and cunning.

'Goldmund,' she whispered, full of ecstasy. 'Oh, what a sorcerer have I found. I would have a child of you, my sweet goldfish. Or better, I would die under your kisses.'

Deep in his throat he hummed a song of joy to her, as he saw the hardness melt in her deep, blue eyes, felt how love weakened all her body. In a gentle shudder, like a death-pang, her eyes drank his love into their depths, filmed, as with the trembling sheen on the glittering scales of dying fish, faint gold, like the magic shimmer in deep water. All human joy seemed gathered into that hour.

Then at once, as she still lay trembling with closed eyes, he stole from the bed, and slipped into his clothes. He bent over her with a sigh, and whispered:

'I must leave you, my jewel. Your count mustn't come and kill me. Why should I die, when first I would make us happy again – once more – a hundred times more.'

She lay there silent till he was ready. He drew the soft coverlet over her, kissed her eyes.

'Goldmund,' she sighed. 'Oh, must you leave me? Come tomorrow. If there's danger I'll send to warn you. Come soon. Come soon.'

She tugged the bell-cord. Her tire-woman came to the wardrobe door to guide him, and led him quickly from the palace. He would have liked to give her a gold ducat; for a minute he was ashamed of his poverty.

Late that night he stood in the Fish-Market, looking up at the windows of his lodging. They would all be asleep, and it seemed he must lie down in the square. But, strangely, he found the house-door open, and crept in, shutting it softly after him. The way to his room lay through the kitchen. There was light there, and he found Marie, sitting, with her tiny lamp, at the table. She had nodded off to sleep as she waited for him. She started up as he came through.

'Oh,' he said, 'Marie – are you up still?'

'Yes,' she told him, 'or else you would have found the house locked up.'

'I'm sorry you waited for me, Marie. It's so late now. Don't be angry.'

'I'm never angry with you, Goldmund. I only feel a little sad.'

'Sad you shall never be. Why sad?'

'O, Goldmund, how I wish I were strong and beautiful. Then you need never go out at night, courting other women in strange houses. You would stay with me; and perhaps you would sometimes be a little kind to me.'

Her gentle voice had neither hope nor bitterness in it, only sorrow. He stood uneasily. She irked him, and he could find no words to answer her. With a gentle hand he stroked her hair, and she was silent, trembling a little as she felt him. She wept a while, then dried her eyes and said shyly:

'Go to bed now, Goldmund. I've only been saying a lot of foolishness. I felt so sleepy. Good night.'

CHAPTER SIXTEEN

GOLDMUND spent a day of impatient happiness in the hills. If he had had a horse he would have ridden out that day to the cloister, to the Sorrowful Madonna of Master Nicholas. He longed to see her again, and seemed to remember that in the night he had had a dream of the dead Master. Well, he must go back to her later. Even should this happiness soon be over, should Agnes' love prove evil in the end — today she was in his blood, he could not miss an instant of her.

This morning he wanted to speak to nobody, but to spend this warm, autumn day with trees and clouds. He said to Marie that he wanted a day in the woods, and might not come back till late that night. Would she give him a good loaf to take with him, and not sit up, this time, for his return? She did not answer, only filled his pockets with bread and apples, brushed down his old, shabby jerkin, which she had patched the first day he came back to them, and let him go.

He crossed the river and climbed through empty vineyards, up, by their steep earthen steps, into the hills, losing himself, above, in the woods, and never stopped till he stood high up at the summit. The sun shone warm through bare branches, ouzels scurried off as he passed, to sit in the midst of their thickets, staring timidly out, through round, black eyes; while far below, in a long, blue curve, flowed the river, and the city lay, like a little, built-up toy. No sound of it could reach him here, save only the bells, tolling to prayers.

Here at the summit there were mounds grown over with

turf, from the old heathen days, long ago; fortresses perhaps, or graves. On one of these he stretched himself out in
the sunshine, where he could lie in the dry rustling autumn
grass and see out across the whole wide valley, with hills
and mountains over beyond the river, chain after chain, till
peaks and sky hovered in a misty uncertainty. Through all
the wide country stretched beneath him, and further still,
his feet had strayed: all that, now memory and far off, had
once been close, and in the present. He had slept a hundred
times in those far woods, eaten berries, hungered in them,
and frozen, toiled over the brows of those hills, been gay or
merry, tired or vigorous. Somewhere, away among those dis-
tances, lay the charred bones of poor dead Lene; somewhere over there his companion, Robert, must wander still,
if the plague had not stayed his feet: there, out of sight,
Victor lay dead. Somewhere, enchanted and far off, there
stood the cloister of his boyhood, somewhere the castle of
the knight, in which he had lain with two young daughters: there, in rags and hunted, ran poor Rebecca, or else
lay dead. These many places, set so far apart, these moors
and forests, villages and cities, walled towns and cloisters –
all these people, who might be either dead or still alive – in
him were ever-present, and reunited. They dwelt together in
his memory, his love, his longing, his regret. If he died tomorrow they would all separate, be lost again, and the pictures in the book wiped out, of women, love, and winter
nights, and summer mornings. Oh, it was high time to
accomplish something, carve out some figures to leave behind him; something with longer life in it than he. Small
fruit was born of all these wanderings, these years since he
escaped into the world. He had saved so little from time; a
few figures, carved and left in a workshop, the best of them
all his Johannes – and now this unreal picture-book in his
head, his fair and agonized image-world of memories.
Could he ever manage to rescue some of them, setting them

forth, for all to see? Or would his life go on like this to the end, always with new cities, new country, new women, fresh experience, other pictures, one piled up over the other, from which at last he would have nothing, save the restless, painful beauty in his heart? Life tricked so shamelessly. It was enough to make men laugh or weep. A man could live, letting his senses have free rein, sucking his fill at the breasts of Eve, his mother – and then, though he might revel and enjoy, there was no protection against her transcience, and so, like a toadstool in the woods, he shimmered today in the fairest colours, tomorrow rotted, and fell to dust.

Or he could set up his defences against life, lock himself into a workshop, and seek to build a monument beyond time. And then life herself must be renounced; the man was nothing but her instrument: though he might serve eternity he withered, he lost his freedom, fullness, and joy of days. Such had been the fate of Master Nicholas.

And yet our days had only a meaning if both these goods could be achieved, and life herself had not been cleft by the barren division of alternatives. To work and yet not pay life's price for working: to live, yet not renounce the work of creation. Could it ever be done?

Some men could do it, perhaps. There might be husbands, and honest fathers of families in the world, whose senses had not been blunted by their fidelity. There might be industrious burghers whose hearts had not been tamed and rendered barren, by their lack of danger and its freedom. Perhaps. He had met none yet.

All being, it seemed, was built on opposites, on division. Man or woman, vagabond or citizen, lover or thinker – no breath could be both in and out, none could be man and wife, free and yet orderly, knowing the urge of life and the joy of intellect. Always the one paid for the other, though each was equally precious and essential. Perhaps it was easier for women. Nature had made them so that, with them, their passion brought its fruit, and so a child was born out of their happiness. Men had no such simple fruitfulness, but instead, an eternal craving, never appeased. Was the god who fashioned all this malicious and evil – did he laugh at the pain in his own creation? No, it could be no evil god who had made the roes and harts in the forest, fishes and birds, trees and flowers, spring and autumn. And yet this cleft ran through his work, whether it were less perfect than his intention, or he, the god, had a hidden purpose in this lack, this never-satisfied hunger in all his kind. Perhaps it was a seed, sown by the enemy: original sin. But were not all beauty and sanctity born of this same 'sin' in human beings, all that man had fashioned with his hands, and then given it back to the god?

Sad with these thoughts, he turned his eyes upon the city, spied out the market, and the fish-market, the bridges, churches, and council-house. Then he saw the bishop's stately palace, where now Count Heinrich held his court. Among these towers, beneath these long, sloping roofs, dwelt Agnes, fairer than any queen, who looked so proud, and could be so lost and humbled by her love. He remembered last night with grateful joy. To have felt the glory of that one night every love in his past had been necessary, all his schooling in women for this one woman, all that he had learned in need and wandering, every night through which he had had to tramp in snow, his kinship with beasts and flowers, trees, and waters, butterflies and fishes. It had needed all the quickened lust of senses sharpened by danger as by love, all the cravings of a lonely wanderer, the image-world, graven within him by the years, to bring this woman so much joy. For so long as his days remained a garden in which such flowers as Agnes still could flourish, he need not complain.

He wandered the whole day long on autumn summits, walking, resting, eating bread, thinking of Agnes and the night. By sundown he was back in the city, before the castle. It was chilly now, and houses stared with fixed red eyes through the dark. A troop of little boys came singing past him, carrying turnips, cut into faces, on poles, which they waved aloft, with flaming torches stuck in the heads. This little rout of mummers brought winter with it, and Goldmund let it pass him with a smile. For a time he loitered outside the palace. The embassy of prelates was still with the count, and, here and there, at one of the high windows, a ghostly father stood, looking out. Goldmund, at last, succeeded in creeping through the door and, within, found the tire-woman, Bertha. Once again she hid him in her wardrobe, till Agnes came, and led him softly into the bedchamber. Tenderly her beauty welcomed him, but she was sad, her mind was full of cares, and he had great pains to cheer her a little. Slowly, under his kisses and love-words, she roused herself, and began to take comfort.

'You can be so gentle,' she told him gratefully, 'you have such deep, sure notes in your voice, my bird, when you prattle and chirrup, deep in your throat. I love you, Goldmund. Oh, if we were only away from here! I hate it here, though soon it will be over, anyway. The count is summoned back to the Emperor, and the silly bishop will soon be here again. But today the count is surly, the priests have angered him. Oh, Goldmund, never let him see you! You would not live another hour. I fear so much what may happen.'

He remembered a half-forgotten voice – surely he had heard this song already! Lydia had said such things to him, with the same gentle, fearful, loving sadness. It was thus she had come stealing to his bedside, full of love yet restless with her fears. It pleased him, this anxious, tender song. What worth were any love without its secrecy? Could there be any love without love's dangers? Gently he drew her close, stroking her, holding her hands, murmuring small enticements in her ears, kissing her eyebrows. It touched, and filled him with delight, to find her so uneasy and full of care. Gratefully, almost with humility, she took and answered his caresses, preening herself against him, full of love, although she could find no merriment or peace. Suddenly she started wildly: somewhere, not far off, a door slammed to, and quick steps came towards the bed-room.

'Oh God, he's here!' she whispered desperately, 'the count! Quick – you can slip out through the wardrobe. Don't betray me.'

Already she had thrust him among her robes, and he stood alone, fumbling in the darkness. From the room beyond, the count's loud voice was heard, with Agnes. He felt his way from gown to gown, gingerly, one foot before the other. Now he was beside the passage door, and gently tried to pull it open. Only then, as he found it locked on the further side, did he too start, and his heart stand still, then suddenly beat wildly and painfully. It might be by some unlucky chance that this door had been locked since he entered; he could not think it. He had walked into a trap, and was lost. Someone must have watched him creep in here. It would cost him his neck. He remembered her last words, 'Don't betray me.' No – he would not ... he set his teeth and waited. His heart still thumped, but fresh resolution steeled him.

All this had only lasted a few instants. Now the hither door was thrust open, and from Agnes' chamber came the count, with a torch and a drawn sword. Goldmund, in the very last instant, snatched robes and cloaks off the pegs, and huddled them together, over his arm. Let them take him for a thief; perhaps it would be a way out.

The count had spied him at once. He came on slowly.

'Who are you, sirrah. What are you doing? Answer me, or I thrust against you.'

'Forgive me,' Goldmund mumbled, 'I am a poor man, lord, and you are so rich, I'll give it all back. See here.'

He laid the robes on the floor.

'So – a thief. Is that it? You were a fool to lose your life for a few old cloaks. Are you a citizen here?'

'No, lord – I am homeless. . . . A poor man. . . . You will be merciful?'

'Silence. One other thing you shall tell me. Were you saucy enough to accost the gracious lady? But, since you'll hang in any case, we need go no further into that. Your theft suffices.'

He hammered on the locked door into the passage.

'You out there – unlock the door.'

The door was opened from outside. Three churls with drawn daggers stood in readiness.

'Tie him fast,' bellowed the count, in a voice hoarse with anger and disdain. 'This knave crept in here to steal. Lock him up, and, tomorrow at daybreak, set the cur dangling from the gallows.'

Goldmund's wrists were tied, without any protest from him. He was led off down the long passage, down steps, across the inner courtyard, with a varlet in front, bearing a torch. They halted at an arched cellar-door, thick-studded with nails, and began to gossip. This door had no key to it. One took the torch, and the varlet ran back to fetch the key. Thus they stood, waiting outside his prison, the three armed men and their prisoner.

The torch-bearer examined Goldmund curiously, holding the light close to his face. In that instant came two priests over the courtyard, of whom there were so many as guests in the castle. They had come from the chapel, and halted now before the group, drawn by the light, and this night-scene : the three armed churls with a bound prisoner, who stood there waiting for the key.

Goldmund did not heed these priests, or give any answer

to his gaolers. He saw nothing but the flame in the wind, held close before his eyes, and blinding him. Behind this waving light came glimpses of a terrible darkness, fading off into something huge and monstrous – a shapeless, horrible apparition; the hole into which he would fall, the abyss, the end. He was deaf and blind to all but that. One of the priests had begun to question a churl. When he learned that this was a thief, and must hang at daybreak, he asked if the fellow had had a confessor. No, they replied, he had just been caught red-handed. 'Then,' said the father, 'tomorrow I will come to him early, before first mass, with the last sacraments, to shrive him. You are to answer for his not being led out to death until I have seen him and done this. I will speak to my lord the count of it tonight. This man may be a thief, but he has the right of every Christian to confess, and make his peace with God.'

The gaolers dared no contradiction. They knew this priest for one of the embassy, and had seen him dine with the count, at the high table. Besides, why should this poor knave not have his priest and his assoilment?

The Paters went their way. Goldmund had heeded none of this. At last the servant returned, and the door was opened. They led the prisoner down to a vaulted chamber; he stumbled as they pushed him down the steps. A few three-legged stools stood round a table, since this was the outer vault of a wine-cellar. They pointed to a stool and bade him sit. 'There'll be a priest,' said one, 'in the morning to shrive you.' Then they went out, carefully locking the heavy door.

'Leave us a light, brother,' Goldmund begged.

'No, little brother, you might do harm with it. You'll be well enough. Be wise, and accustom yourself. And how long would a rush-light last you? In an hour it would be out. Good night.'

Now he sat alone in the dark. He laid his head down on

the table: it was cramped and painful to sit thus, and the thongs on his wrists seared like flames. But this he only knew much later. At first he sat, with his forehead on the table as though upon a headsman's block, striving to make his body and senses realize all that was now imposed upon his mind. He must bow his will, and give himself up to what would be — make himself know how soon he would be dead.

He sat on thus a long while, miserably cramped, and striving with all his might to take this horror into himself, and know it; breathe it, let it fill him from top to toe. Night was around him, and the end of that night would bring more darkness. He must strive to learn that tomorrow he would have ceased to be. There he would dangle, and be a thing, on which birds could perch, and peck their fill of it; he would be as Master Nicholas was, as Lene was, lying in her ashes, as all those many hundreds had been, at whom he had stared in empty, plague-stricken houses, or heaped, one over the other, on the death-carts. It was hard to make himself feel it deeply, let it become a part of his being. It was even impossible to think of it. There were so many things from which he had never managed to free his heart, of which he had taken no farewell. These night-hours were granted him for this.

First he must take his leave of Agnes. He would never see her tall beauty again, her sunny yellow hair, her cold blue eyes; nor watch the trembling pride die out of them, know the sweet, pale gleam of scented flesh. He had hoped to kiss her again so often. Ah, even today out in the hills, in the warm autumn sunlight, how he had thought of her; how he had longed for her, needed her. But hills, and sun, and blue, white-clouded sky — of all that too he must take his leave. No trees, no woods, no wandering, no day or night, no seasons any more. Perhaps Marie would still be waiting up for him, poor Marie, with her limp and her gentle eyes, dozing and waking in the kitchen, and still no Goldmund had come home.

Ah, and those sheets with all the drawings, his hopes of figures he would carve. Gone! Gone! And his other hope of seeing Narziss, St John the beloved – he must forget it.

Then he must take leave of his hands, his eyes; of thirst and hunger, food and drink, of love and lute-playing, sleep and waking: of all. Tomorrow a bird would skim through the air, and Goldmund have no eyes to watch it with, a girl stand singing at her window, and he have no ears for her song; the river would flow on and on, the dumb, shadowy fish swim with it, a wind spring up, and strip the yellow leaves to earth; there would be a moon, and glittering stars, young men would go out to dance at Christmas fairs, the first snows whiten the distant hills – and all these things would be for ever, each tree spreading out its shadow, men with joy or mirth in their living eyes, and all without him; none of it his! They would have torn his body away from it.

He seemed to taste the morning wind on moors, the sweet new wine, and young, firm walnuts, while into his fearful heart, like a memory, there crept the sudden realization of all the colour in the world, a dying pageant of farewells as the wild beauty of earth swept through his senses. He hunched himself up and broke into sobs, could feel tears scald and trickle down his cheeks; moaning, he let this wave of grief sweep over him, crouched, and gave himself up to endless woe. Alas, you valleys and wooded hills, you streams grown about with alders, you maids at night, on moonlit bridges, fair, glittering world of living things. How shall I go from you?

He lay and wept, bent far over the table, a child refusing to be comforted, called from his direst grief, in a sigh born of the deepest need: 'Oh mother! Oh mother!'

An image answered this magic name as he said it, her

shape, from the secrecy of his heart. Not the mother he had longed to carve in wood, the Eve of his craftsman's thoughts and dreams, but the very mother he remembered, clearer and more living than he had seen her since the dream he had had of her in Mariabronn. To her he complained, sobbed out this intolerable thought, gave himself over to her protection, gave her the sunshine and the woods, his eyes, his hands, his life, into her care again.

In the midst of his tears he fell asleep. Exhaustion enfolded him like her arms. Lulled by her, and rescued from his grief, for an hour or two he slumbered heavily.

Then he awoke in the sharpest pain. His fettered wrists still burned like fire, while down his back and shoulders ran darting agony. He sat up stiffly, and knew the reality that surrounded him. He was in the midst of utter blackness, could not tell how long he had been asleep, nor how many hours of life might still be left him. They might come any instant now! He remembered the priest who had been promised him.

Not that his sacraments meant much; nor could he tell if even the most perfect assoilment would bring his soul into a heaven. He did not care if any heaven existed, or the Father with His judgements, or any eternity. All this had long been hazy in his mind.

He had no care for any heaven. He wanted nothing but the passing, uncertain life of earth – but to breathe, and be at home in his own skin. He wanted nothing but to live!

Crazed with sudden terror he stood up, and fumbled through the blackness to the wall, leaned against the stone, and started to think. Surely there must be a hope. This priest might bring him a reprieve. Perhaps he was so sure of the prisoner's innocence that he had put in a word on his behalf, would manage a delay, and help his escape. He set his whole mind on this one thought, thinking it again and again. Even if all that should prove nothing, still his game was not lost, he would go on hoping. First, then, he must win over this priest, strain every nerve to charm, and flatter and convince him. Everything else was dream and possibility; the priest was the one good card left in his hands, though none the less, there were still hazards and chances. The hangman might be sick of a colic, the gallows break, some accident, none of them had foreseen, bring him his chance to get away. Never would he let them hang him! He had striven in vain to accept this destiny, now he would keep it off to the very end, trip up his gaoler, knock the hangman down, struggle to the last drop of his blood. Ah, if he could only bring this priest to the point of untying these cords!

How infinitely much would be gained by that! Meanwhile, not caring for any pain, he struggled to sever them with his teeth.

In a cruelly long time, with the maddest efforts, he managed to loosen them a little. He stood, panting in the darkness, with swollen arms, and throbbing hands. When his breath returned he crept further and further along the wall, feeling the damp stone, inch by inch, to make certain it had no jutting edges. Then he remembered the stairs down which they had thrust him, sought and found, and crouched down under them, to try and sever the thongs on the edge of a step. It was hard to manage, since his wrist-bones kept grating against the stone. It seared his flesh; he could feel his hands wet.

Still he persisted, and when at last a spare grey streak began to glimmer under the door, the cords were worn so thin that he could sever them. He had done it. His hands were free!

Yet now he could scarcely move a finger, since his arms were numb, and swollen to the shoulders. He tried to force the blood to flow back into them.

Now he had a plan which seemed good to him. If this

247

priest would not help his escape, and they left the man alone, even to shrive him, he would strike him down – one of the stools would serve his turn, his hands were still too weak for throttling – crack his skull with the stool, strip off his habit and get away in it. And then – run, run. Marie would take him in and hide him. It was worth trying. It was possible.

Never in all his life before had Goldmund awaited daybreak so impatiently, longed for it, watched for it and, yet feared it. He watched, with a huntsman's eye, the thin grey streak under the door as slowly, very slowly, it brightened. Then he went back to the table, and practised how he would sit, hunched up on the stool, in such a way that they should not see at once that his wrists were free again.

Now that he had his hands death seemed unreal to him. He would come out alive, if he shattered the whole world to do it. His body twitched with longing to be free. Who could tell – help might come from outside. Agnes was only a woman, and not very powerful. She might be afraid: she might let him die for her own sake. But still, she loved him, and something, perhaps, she would attempt. Her tire-woman, Bertha, might already be creeping to the door, and was there not a squire she had said was faithful? And if none came to him with a message he had his own plan, ready to execute. Should it go awry he would fell his keepers with a stool – two, three, or as many as they sent. He had this advantage – that his eyes were used to the dark. Now, in the twilight, he could see every shape and mass around him, whereas the others would be purblind.

He crouched behind the table, eagerly watching the spare increase of light under the door, forcing himself to plan out in advance each word he would say to the priest, since that at least must be attempted. The instant which he had dreaded an hour since, he longed for so that, now, he could scarcely wait for it. This strained alertness had grown un-

248

bearable. His strength, his quickness, his resolve, must gradually lose their edge if they kept him waiting. Surely this priest and gaoler would be here before the will to live had ebbed in him.

At last the world outside began to rouse itself, and so the enemy was upon him. Steps clattered over the yard, a key was thrust into the lock: it turned, and each of these sounds, after the long quiet and dark, seemed like a thunderclap.

Now the heavy door swung open slowly, on grating hinges. The priest came in to him alone, unescorted by any gaoler or serving-man, and carrying a sconce with double flames. Already something unforeseen by the prisoner.

And how strange and moving to behold: this priest whose invisible hand closed the door behind him, wore the well-known habit of Mariabronn, the habit of his home, the cloister; the habit worn by Abbot Daniel, by Pater Anselm, by Pater Martin. The sight of it stirred him so that he had to turn away his eyes. This might be the promise of rescue. Yet perhaps there would be no other way but to kill him. He set his teeth. It would be hard to strike down this priest.

CHAPTER SEVENTEEN

'Praise be Jesus Christ,' said the Pater, and set down his sconce on the table. Goldmund hung his head, and mouthed a response.

The monk said nothing. He stood expectant, without a word, till Goldmund, grown uneasy, raised curious eyes.

The prisoner's confusion increased, as he saw that this monk not only wore the habit of Mariabronn, but the abbot's cross and ring along with it. Then he looked this abbot full in the face, a spare face, firm and clearly outlined, with the thinnest of lips; a face he knew. Goldmund, as though enchanted, stared at this face, which seemed all formed of will and intellect. Uncertainly he put his hand to the sconce, raised the light, held it close to the stranger's eyes. He saw, and the flames were trembling as he set it back upon the table.

'Narziss,' he whispered, almost inaudibly. Everything swirled before his eyes.

'Yes, Goldmund, I was Narziss once, but now it is long since I laid aside that name. Have you forgotten that I took the name of John when I was consecrated?'

Goldmund was moved to the heart. For him the world had changed its aspect. The strain of the last hours suddenly loosened: he shook all over, and giddiness made his head an empty bladder, his belly heaved, hot tears scalded behind his eyes, sobs threatened to shake his whole body. To sink weeping to his knees, as in a swoon — everything within him longed for that.

But out of the depths, which this sight of Narziss opened up in him, there arose a warning memory of his boyhood.

Once, as a boy, he had sobbed, and let emotion drown him, before this fair, grave face, these omniscient eyes. That he must never do again. Here like a ghost, at this most crucial hour of his whole life, Narziss had come, and it seemed he brought him his reprieve. Should he stand again, weeping before his friend, sink down at his feet in a swoon? No! No! No! He must control himself, rein in his heart, and force his guts to obey him, sweep away the giddiness from his mind. No weakness now! He managed to answer, in a voice artfully controlled:

'You must let me call you Narziss still.'

'Call me that, *o amice*, But why not give me your hand?'

Again Goldmund forced his spirit to answer on a note of schoolboy mockery, just as he had often done in the old days:

'Forgive me, Narziss,' he said, a little coolly and wearily. 'I see they have turned you into an abbot. I am still nothing but a vagrant. And much as I would like a long talk with you, I fear we shall never be able to have it. For, listen, Narziss; I go to the gallows in half an hour! This I only tell you to make it clear.'

Narziss' expression had not changed. This grain of boastfulness and boy's courage still in his friend, touched him, and yet amused him highly. Truly he had imagined a different meeting, and yet this little comedy won his heart. Nothing that Goldmund could have said would have been a surer way back to his love.

'As to the gallows,' he said, as careless as Goldmund, 'make your mind easy on that. You are pardoned. I am commissioned to tell you this, and take you along with me. You must not stay here in the city. So there's time enough to tell each other this and that. Well, now, will you give me your hand?'

They clasped hands and stood a long while, their hearts stirred deeply by this touch, though their words, for a little longer, remained full of comedy and pretence.

'Good then, Narziss – let us leave this ignominious retreat. So I am to join you as a follower. Do we go back to Mariabronn? That's good. ... But how? On horseback? Better still. But then I shall need a horse to come with you.'

'You shall have your horse, my friend, and within two hours we must set out. Oh – but your hands. In Jesus' name – all gashed and bleeding. Ah, Goldmund, what have they been doing to you?'

'Let be, Narziss. It was I who wounded my own hands. I was bound, and wanted to break free, and it wasn't easy, I can tell you. Do you know it was very valiant of you to come in to shrive me, without an escort!'

'Valiant? But why? There was no danger.'

'Oh no – no danger at all – except that I might crack your skull. That was what I had planned, you see. They told me I should have a priest, and so I thought I would strike him down, and take his habit to escape in. It was a good plan.'

'So you wanted to live, then?'

'Assuredly. Though I never thought they would send me Narziss to shrive my soul.'

'All the same,' Narziss hesitated, 'it was an ugly plan to have in mind. Would you in truth have struck down the priest who had come to shrive you for your death?'

'Not you, Narziss – naturally I would never have struck you down. And perhaps not any of your monks. But any other priest – oh yes, believe me!'

Suddenly his voice grew sad.

'It would not have been the first man I had killed.'

They were silent. Both felt uneasy.

'As to all that,' said Narziss, in an even voice, 'we shall have the time to talk of it. If you like I will hear your confession. Or tell me of your life, if you would rather. I shall be glad to hear. Let us go.'

'One minute first, Narziss. I've remembered something. I named you "John" myself, once.'

'I don't understand.'

'No, how should you? It was many years since that I gave you the name of St John, and now you must bear it for ever. You see, I was once a carver and image-maker, and so I hope to be again. And the best statue I ever cut in those days was a young saint in wood, done in your likeness, though I called it St John, and not Narziss. It is St John the Disciple, under the rood.'

He rose, and went to the door.

'You've thought of me, then?' asked Narziss softly.

And Goldmund, in the same low voice:

'Oh, yes, Narziss – again and again.'

He gave the heavy door a shove, and the pale morning lighted them both. They said no more. Narziss led him on to his own guest-chamber. There a young monk was busy, packing their traps. Goldmund was given a meal, and his wrists bound up for the time being. Very soon the horses were led out.

As they mounted, Goldmund said:

'I have one more wish. Let us take the way across the Fish-Market. There's someone there I want to see.'

They all rode off. Goldmund looked up at every window of the palace, to make sure that Agnes was not in one of them. But he did not get another sight of her. They rode on, over the Fish-Market. Marie had been terrified for his safety. He took leave of her, and of her parents, promised to be back soon, and they rode away. She stood at the door looking after him till all the riders were out of sight. Slowly she limped back into the house.

They rode four abreast: Narziss, Goldmund, the young monk, and an armed churl.

'Can you still remember Bless, my pony, who had his stall in the cloister?' Goldmund asked.

'To be sure. You won't find him now, though, and I know you never expected you would. It must be seven or eight years now, since we had to slaughter him.'

'Ah, you remember that?'

'Oh yes. I remember.'

Goldmund did not grieve for his pony's death, but was glad indeed that Narziss should remember him so clearly — he who gave small thought to any animal, and certainly would never have known the name of any other horse in the cloister stall. This thought rejoiced him.

'You'll laugh,' he began, 'that first I ask for news of my poor little pony. That was uncivil of me. Indeed, I have better things to ask you, and would know first of Abbot Daniel. But since you are the abbot now, he must be dead. And I do not want to ask of nothing but death. This is a bad time to speak of death to me, both from last night, and because of the plague, of which I saw all too much on the roads. But all's one now, and we all die some day! Tell me when and how Abbot Daniel died. I honoured him greatly. And is Pater Martin alive? And Pater Anselm? I have had no news at all of any of you. But at least I rejoice that the plague has passed you by, although I never thought you could be dead. Always in my heart I knew that we should meet again. Yet beliefs can trick us, and this I know to my cost, since my master, Master Nicholas, the wood-carver, whom I never could think of as dead, and counted firmly on working with him again, had vanished for ever when I came back to him.'

'All's quickly told,' said Narziss. 'Abbot Daniel died so long as eight years since, without sickness or any pain. I am not his successor. I have only been abbot since last year. He was succeeded by Pater Martin, who governed the school, as you remember, and died a year ago, at close on seventy. And Pater Anselm is also dead. He loved you, and would often speak of you. In his last years he could not so much as walk any more, and to lie gave him great pain, since he died of the dropsy. Yes, and the plague has been with us, too. Let's not talk of it! Have you any more to ask?'

'Surely I have – and much. About everything. How came you here, to the Bishop's city, and the stattholder?'

'That's a long story and it would weary you. There is so much policy in it. The count is a favourite of the Emperor and, in certain matters, has full power from him, and at present there is much to set to rights between the Emperor and our order. The order gave me commission to treat with the count. My success was small.'

He was silent, and Goldmund asked no more. Nor was he ever to learn how when last night, Narziss had begged for his life he had had to pay for it with concessions, or the surly count would never have granted it.

They rode. Goldmund felt very weary, and soon had pains to sit his horse. After a long silence Narziss asked him:

'Is it true they took you as a thief? The count would have it you crept into the castle to steal gear from the inner rooms.'

Goldmund laughed: 'Sure enough that was how it seemed. I am not a thief, but I had a meeting with his leman. I am amazed he let me go so easily.'

'It wasn't so easy as all that.'

They could not do the stage they had set themselves. Goldmund was too weary to ride further, and his hands refused to hold the bridle. That night they lodged in a village, where he was put to bed in a low fever, and so lay on there, all next day. Then he could ride again, and soon, when his hands were better, he enjoyed the feel of his horse. It was a long time now since he had ridden one. He revived, and felt young and full of life, raced the groom for miles for a wager, and then, at times, assailed Narziss with a hundred impatient, eager questions. Narziss let him ask his fill. He had fallen under Goldmund's spell again, and loved this stream of doubts and demands, all made in the boundless trust of his own capacity to resolve them.

'One thing I wanted to ask you, Narziss. Did you ever burn Jews?'

'Burn Jews? Why should we? There are no Jews anywhere near Mariabronn.'

'Understand me, Narziss. I mean this. Can you imagine any instance in which you would give your consent to have Jews slaughtered, or command it? There have been so many dukes and bishops, and burgomasters, and other such lords, giving these orders.'

'I myself would not give such an order. But it might well be that I should have to stand by, and watch the cruelty.'

'You would bear with it, then?'

'Certainly, if I had not the power to prevent it. Did you see any Jews burn, Goldmund?'

'Oh yes —'

'Well, and did you prevent it? No? So you see —'

Goldmund told him the story of Rebeccca, and as he told, grew fiery and full of grief.

'And so,' he added angrily, 'what a world is this, in which we must live. Is it not a sort of hell? It is horrible, and fills me with rage.'

'Certainly. Such is the world.'

'Well,' cried Goldmund, 'how often did you tell me once that the world was divine, a great harmony of circles, so you said, in the centre of which the Creator sits on His throne, and that all which He has fashioned is good, and so on, and so on. And you said all that stands written in Aristotle and St Thomas! I am anxious to hear you unravel such contradictions.'

Narziss laughed.

'Your memory is admirable. And yet you have made a few mistakes. I have always honoured the Creator as perfect, but never His work. I have never denied the evil in the world. That man is good, or our earthly life just, and full of harmony – that, my friend, is more than any sound thinker has ever said. More it stands clear in Holy Writ that all the strivings and dreams in our hearts are imperfect, and this is proved every day.'

'Good. Now at last I see how you have learned to judge of it. So men are evil, you say, and our life on earth is full of meanness and horror: – that you admit, then. But somewhere behind, hidden in your thoughts and books of precepts, you discover a justice, and a perfection. They are there, and can be proved, but nobody uses them.'

'You have managed to store up much gall against us theologians, *o amice*. But with all that you are not a thinker yet. You confuse it all, and there is still a little for you to learn. Why do you say we make no use of the idea of justice? We do that every day, and every hour of the day. I, for example, am an abbot, and have my cloister to govern, and in that cloister they are just as imperfect and full of faults as any in the world outside. Yet again and again, unceasingly, we set the idea of justice against the original sin of our nature, strive to measure our imperfect lives by it, seek to arrest the evil, and keep ourselves in firm relationship with God.'

'Ah, no, Narziss – it was not you I meant. I never said you were not a good abbot. But I think of Rebecca, and the burning Jews, and the death-holes, and the great death in all the houses and streets, when plague-corpses rotted and stank, and all the horror and desolation! I think of the children straying the roads, without kith or kin, or any to shelter them, or yard-dogs, famished on their chains ... and when I see it all before my eyes again, it seems to me as if our mothers had born us into a world of fiends. It would be better if we had never been, and God never made this horrible earth, nor the Saviour hung uselessly on the cross for it.'

Narziss nodded gently:

'You are right,' he answered. 'Speak all your heart, and tell me everything. But in one thing you are very wide of the mark. You mistake all these for your thoughts, but they are your feelings — the feelings of a man stung to action by the cruelty of life. And never forget that other, very different feelings, may be set over against this despair. When you feel yourself at one with your horse, and so ride out through a pleasant country — or when, without knowing how it may end, you creep at night into a castle to pay your court to the count's leman, the world seems a very different place to you, and not all the burning Jews and plague-stricken houses can hinder you from seeking your desire in it. Is that not true?'

'To be sure it is. Yet it is just because the world is so full of death that I must ever find new comfort for my heart. I find a desire, and so, for an hour, I forget death. But, none the less, death is always with me.'

'You said that well. Good, then; you find yourself in a world of death and horror, and so, to escape them, you fly to lust. But lust soon fades; it dies and leaves you in the wilderness.'

'Yes, so it is.'

'And so it is for most other men, *amice*, though few care to feel it so deeply, or say it so vividly as you do. And fewer still have any need in them to make themselves aware of what they feel. But tell me this: besides this desperate running to and fro from horror to desire, and back again, this juggler's sport with your love of life and fear of death — have you sought any other way to happiness?'

'Oh yes, indeed. I tried to find my happiness as a carver. I told you how I had once been that. One day when I had been perhaps two years on the roads, I entered a cloister-church, and found there a Blessed Virgin in wood, who troubled my heart so much with her beauty, and held me so, that I sought out the Master who had carved her. I found

258

him, and he was a famous guildsman. I became his apprentice, and worked two years with him.'

'Later you shall tell me more of that. But what comfort did your carving bring you? What did it mean?'

'It meant the conquest of all that perishes. I saw that out of this zanies'-tumble and death-dance, something can remain of our lives, and survive us – our images. Yet they, too, perish in the end. They are buried, or they rot, or are broken again. And yet their lives are longer than any human life, so that, behind the instant that passes, we have, in images, a quiet land of shrines and precious shapes. To work at these seemed good and comforting to me, since it is almost a fixing of time for ever.'

'Your words delight me, Goldmund, and I hope you will carve many more of such fair images. My trust in your skill is great. In Mariabronn you must be our guest for a long while, and allow me to set you up a workshop there. It is years since our cloister had a craftsman. Yet I think that, by your definition, you have not exhausted all the wonders of art. I believe the truest images to have more in them than that something alive, and there for all to see, should be made permanent, and so rescued from death. I have seen many works of painters and carvers, many saints and madonnas, of which I do not believe that they are true copies of the shape of any single person, who lived once, and whose form and colour were caught and preserved by the maker.'

'You are right,' cried Goldmund, 'and I never should have thought you could know so well what a true craftsman can do. The pattern of any good image is no real, living form, or shape, although such shapes may have prompted the maker to it. Their true first pattern is not in flesh and blood, but in the mind. Such images have their home in the craftsman's soul. And in me, too, Goldmund, there live such images, which one day I shall hope to fashion, and show you.'

'I am very glad. But see, *amice*, how, without knowing it, you have strayed into the midst of philosophy, and given words to one of her secrets.'

'You should not mock me.'

'And I do not. You have spoken of "first patterns" — of images without existence save in the soul of the carver, but which he transmutes into matter, making them visible. So that, long before such a carver's shapes can be seen, and so obtain their formal reality, they are there already, as forms within his soul. And this same "first pattern" — this shape — is, to a hair, what old philosophers called "the idea".'

'That sounds true enough.'

'Well, but once you speak of ideas, you have wandered into the realm of intellect, into our world of theologians and philosophers, and so you admit that, in all this confusion and pain of the battlefield — this endless, weary dance of death of our living and corporeal substance, there is a spirit which fashions for eternity. Listen, I have always perceived this spirit in you, ever since you first came to me as a boy. But yours are not philosopher's thoughts, though they are that in you which has shown you your way out of the maze and sorrow of our senses, the restless tides of despair and lust. Ah, Goldmund — it makes me very happy to have heard you speak as you did. I have been waiting for that since those old days, ever since the night when you left your teacher, and found the courage to be yourself. Now we have found each other again.'

And it seemed, in that instant, to Goldmund, as though his life had taken a meaning — he seemed to see it all, as if from above, with a clear view of its three divisions: his dependence on Narziss; the time of his freedom and wandering; his return into harmony with himself, the ripening and fruitfulness of harvest.

The vision faded. But now he had found a worthy relationship with his friend. Narziss was no longer the master, he the disciple. They were free and equal, and able to help each other. He could be this abbot's guest without reluctance, since Narziss had seen in him his peer. As they cantered together along the roads, he dreamed, with evergrowing desire and happiness, of the day when he would reveal himself to Narziss, setting forth the life of his spirit, in many shapes. Sometimes, however, there came misgivings.

'Narziss,' he warned him, 'I fear you reckon without your host. Do you know whom you have bidden to the cloister? I am no monk, and never shall be. I know the three great vows, and though I have nothing to say against poverty, chastity and obedience I abhor. While, as for fervour, there is scarcely a grain of it left in me. It is years since I prayed, or had myself shriven, to take the sacrament.'

Narziss did not let this ruffle him:

'You seem to have turned into a heathen. But we have no fear of any such. You need not be so proud of your many sins. You have lived the common life of the world, and herded swine with all the other prodigals, till now you no longer know that rule, and good order, have any meaning. Certainly you would make a very bad monk. But I never asked you to join the order. All I ask is that you live with us as our guest, and let us set you up a workshop. And one thing more – do not forget that it was I who woke your senses, in your boyhood, and let them lead you forth into the world. You may be either a good man or a worthless, and I, after you, shall have to answer for it. I shall see what you are in truth, since you will show it me in words, by your life, and in images. If I find that our house is not for you I shall be the first to ask you to leave us.'

Each time that Narziss said such things as this they filled his friend with admiration. When he spoke thus, as an abbot, with this quiet certainty in his voice, his hint of mockery of worldlings and their life, Goldmund could perceive what his friend had made of himself. Here was a man

— a churchman, truly, with delicate, white hands and the face of a cleric, but a man full of courage and resolution, a ruler, who answered for all. This man, Narziss, was no longer the young scholar he had known, no longer St John, the gentle, tender disciple. He must carve another statue of this new friend; this knight and leader demanded his hands to fashion him. How many shapes were awaiting him! Narziss, Abbot Daniel, Pater Anselm, Master Nicholas, Rebecca, the gentle Agnes, so many he had hated or loved, living and dead. No, he did not want to be a monk. He wanted to carve, and yet it made him happy to think that his first home should be his workshop.

They rode through the cool, late autumn weather, till at last, on a day whose morning branches hung, white with rime, over the roads, they came out onto rippling moorland, with wide domains of russet heath around them, where the lines of the long, far hills looked oddly familiar, yet seemed to hold a kind of threat; on, along the skirts of a high oak-copse, by a running stream, and past a barn the sight of which made Goldmund's heart leap. Now, with joy and sorrow, he knew again those very hills on which he had ridden with Lydia, saw the heath over which he had trudged off, outcast and sad, through the thin snowflakes. Then came the alder-brake, the mill, the castle, and so, with aching delight, he saw the very window of the room in which, in his fabulous youth, long ago, he had heard the knight tell tales of pilgrimage, and helped fill up the gaps in his master's Latin. They rode on into the yard, since this was one of the stages of their journey. Goldmund begged the abbot not to name him here, but let him sup with the churls, at the lower table. So it was done. There was no knight now, and no Lydia. A few old servants and huntsmen still remained, and in the house, there ruled and lived with her husband, a very beautiful, scornful mistress — Julia, sitting beside her lord at the high table. She was still as lovely as he remembered her, radiant, and a little malicious. Neither she nor her knight knew Goldmund.

After supper, through the evening dusk, he stole outside into the garden, peeped over the hedge at already withered flower-beds, crept to the stable door, and peered through the chink at the horses. He slept with the grooms in their straw. Such a load of memories lay upon him that many times his sleep was troubled by it. How scattered and unfruitful had been his life, rich in the colour of its images, yet shivered into so many fragments; so poor in worth, so poor in love. As they rode off again next morning he looked up uneasily at the windows, since perhaps he might see Julia at one of them. Thus, only a short while since, in the courtyard of the bishop's palace, he had kept looking back over his shoulder, to make certain that Agnes had not shown herself. But she had not come, and neither did Julia come again! That had been his life, he thought, leave-taking, running away, being forgotten, being alone again with empty hands, and an icy heart. All day the thought of it poisoned him; he could not speak, but sat there, frowning in the saddle. Narziss left him to his mood.

Yet now, at last, they were near home and, a few days later, they had reached it. A little while before the cloister towers and roofs came into sight they rode over the same stony fallow-land where – how many ages ago – he had gone out plucking herbs for Pater Anselm; past the field where the gipsy, Lisa, had made a lover of him. They rode through the gates, and dismounted under the chestnut in the court. Goldmund gently stroked its trunk. He bent to pick up a split and prickly husk, which lay on the earth, brown and withering.

CHAPTER EIGHTEEN

At first Goldmund lived in a guest-cell within the enclosure. Then, on his own demand, they gave him a lodging, facing the smithy, on one of the many outbuildings which surrounded the great courtyard, wide as a market-place.

This return held such potent memories that sometimes he would feel himself bewitched. These folk, both monks and laymen, were at work, and left him in peace. They lived their own strong, well-ordered life around him. But the trees in the courtyard knew him, the arched doors and pointed windows, the flagstones in every passage, the shrivelled rose trees in the cloister, the storks' nests on refectory roof and granary. Every stick and stone held some gentle memory of his boyhood, and his love impelled him to seek out each, listen again for every cloister-sound, the Sunday bells, and bells to offices, the rushing of the dark millstream between its narrows walls, green with moss, the clatter of sandals, the evening jingle of keys, as the brother-porter went his rounds for the night. By the stone gutter into which, from the roof of the laymen's refectory, rain-water dripped, just as of old, there sprouted still the same small herbs, crane's-bill and plantain. The apple tree in the smith's garden spread wide, gnarled branches, just as before. But more than any other sound or sight, it rejoiced him to hear the little tinkling school-bell and, in a play-hour, watch the cloister schoolboys come clattering down the steps into the yard. How young and fresh and foolish they all looked. Could he ever really have been so young, so coltish, so apple-cheeked, so callow?

And, within this cloister he knew so well, he found

another, scarcely known to him. On the very first day he had been struck by it, and its beauty and significance increased, so that it took some time before it grew to be part of the other. This new cloister had no new features in it; each object stood exactly where he had known it as a boy, and where it had stood a hundred years before him. It was he who no longer saw with boy's eyes. He could feel and admire the massing of these buildings, the strength of the vaultings in the church, the beauty of the old paintings, of the figures in wood and stone on the altars, and in every niche above the doors. And yet he had known them all before. Now he had eyes for their beauty, and for the beauty of the spirit that had made them.

He would stand in the upper chapel before the old stone Mother of God. Even in his boyhood she had pleased him, and he had tried to copy her many times. But only now, with open eyes, did he grow aware that she was a masterpiece, such a work as he could never surpass, even with his best and happiest craftsmanship. And there were many more such wonders in Mariabronn, though none stood alone as a happy accident, and all were born of the one spirit. Each had its own place under these vaultings, between these walls and ancient pillars, as though they formed its natural home.

All that many centuries had built, chiselled, painted, thought, lived, taught here, sprang of one stem, was born of the one spirit, as related as are the branches of a tree.

Goldmund felt small indeed in this ordered world, and never smaller than when he saw Narziss, the Abbot John, his oldest friend, sway and control this mighty unity. Whatever wide difference between persons marked off this learned, thin-lipped Abbot John from the gentle, simple, homely Abbot Daniel, each of them was serving the same whole, the same thought, the same rule of life; had brought it his body as an offering, taken from it his dignity and worth. It made them as alike as did their habit.

Here, in the midst of his own cloister, Narziss grew to a giant in Goldmund's eyes, although he managed still to treat him as his pleasant host and good companion. Soon he scarcely dared to call him Narziss.

'Listen, Abbot John,' he said to him once, 'I shall have to learn to call you that in the end! I must tell you I find it pleasant to live with you. You almost tempt me to make my general confession, and then, when my penance is done, beg you to take me in as your lay brother. But hear me – it would mean the end of our friendship. You would be the abbot, and I the lay brother. And to live for ever as I am, and watch your labours, and be nothing myself, and do nothing – that is more than I can bear any longer. I want to work, and show you what I really am, so that then you can judge for yourself if you think me worth saving from the gallows.'

'I rejoice to hear it,' said Narziss, more formally and precisely even than usual. 'I will send for the smith and carpenter at once, and tell them they are to be at your orders. Use anything you can find in the cloister, and whatever else you may need, make out a list for me, and I will have it fetched for you by carriers. Now you shall hear what I think of you and your purposes. You must give me a little time to tell you my mind. I am a scholar, and would strive to set forth the matter as I conceive it, and I have no other language but the philosopher's. Will you hear me again, as patiently as you used?'

'I will try to follow you, Narziss.'

'Do you recollect how, even in our schooldays, I often told you you were a poet? In those days I considered you a poet, since both in what you wrote and liked best to read, there was always a certain sense of impatience with anything abstract and conceptual. Sounds were what you loved most in language, or any word which conveyed some sensible image; that is to say a word which could give a picture.'

'Forgive me,' Goldmund interrupted, 'but are not these concepts and abstractions which you say you prefer to images, pictures in their own way? Or do you really need to use words which can give no clear image of anything? How can you think, unless you picture something?'

'Good that you should ask! Most certainly we can think without images. Thought and imagery have nothing at all to do with one another. Thinking is not done in pictures, but in concepts, and formulae. There where poetry ends begins philosophy. That was what we quarrelled over so often, long ago. For you the world was composed of pictures, for me of concepts. I always said we should never make a scholar of you, and I said, too, that this was not a lack in you, since you were master in the realm of images. Now listen, and I will make it all plain to you. If you, instead of escaping into the world, had remained on here as a scholar, the end might have been your own undoing. You would have turned into a mystic. And mystics, to put it plainly and rather bluntly, are those thinkers who cannot free their minds of images, and so not thinkers at all. They are secret poets, poets without verses, painters without a brush, musicians without any notes. There are many good and highly gifted mystics, but almost without exception they are unhappy. You might have been just such a one. But instead, God be praised, you are a craftsman; you have conquered your own world, in which you can be lord and creator, instead of having remained an imperfect thinker.'

'I fear,' said Goldmund, 'I shall never have a right idea of your way of thinking without images.'

'Oh yes, I will give it you, now at once. Listen; a thinker strives to find out the essence of the world by means of logic, and so to define it. He knows that our understanding, and logic, its instrument, are imperfect tools with which to work – just as any skilled craftsman knows very well that no brush or chisel ever made, could give the perfect, shining

267

form of a saint or angel. Yet both these – the thinkers and craftsmen – strive to do it, each in his own way. That is all they can do, or dare to do. These are the highest, most significant human activities, since both are striving to fulfil themselves by means of the talents nature gave them. That is why I used so often to say to you: "Don't try to ape ascetics and scholars, but be yourself; seek to fulfil yourself".'

'I can half understand what you mean. But what is this saying – "fulfil yourself"?'

'That is a philosopher's concept, which I cannot express in any other words. For us, the disciples of Aristotle and St Thomas, the highest of all concepts is perfect being. Perfect being is God. All else that is, is only half. It is imperfect and for ever becoming, is mixed, and composed of possibilities. But God is whole. He is One, has no possibilities, but is all completion and reality. Men are transitory, we become, we are possibilities, and for us there is no perfection, no final being. But in all by which we pass on, from potentiality into action, from possibility to fulfilment, we have our share in this true being of God. That is what I mean when I say, "to fulfil oneself". Your own experience must have taught you this, and you have carved many figures in your time. Now, when any such work seems to you really achieved, when you have set forth a human shape, freed from its inessentials, and held within its own clear and perfect form, you as a craftsman have "fulfilled" the image of that man.'

'I understand you now.'

'You see me, *amice*, here in a cloister, in an office which makes it relatively easy for such a nature as mine to fulfil itself. I live in a community and tradition which further my effort. A monastery is not a heaven; it is full of imperfection and sin: yet none the less, for men of my kind, a rule well followed is far better than the life of the world. I do not merely speak of manners and customs, and morality, though, even in practice, abstract thought, which I, by my vocation, must use and teach, demands a certain protection from worldly things. So that, here in Mariabronn, I have had a far easier task to fulfil myself, than have you in the life outside. I much admire you for having found your way and made yourself a craftsman and an artist. Your life has been far harder than mine.'

Goldmund flushed to hear this praise, and yet it rejoiced him. He interrupted, to change their theme.

'Though I understood most of what you were saying, there is one thing I cannot get into my head. This thing you have just called "abstract thought" must be a kind of thought with nothing in it; or else in words conveying nothing.'

'Well, here's an example to make it clear. Think of mathematics. What pictures do you get from numerals? Or from plus and minus signs? Or from an equation? None at all. When you solve an arithmetical or algebraic problem no image in the world will help you to do it. All that you do is to carry out a formal task, by means of a certain method which you have learned.'

'That's true, Narziss. When you write me down a row of figures or signs, I can work my way through without any images, and let myself be helped by plus and minus, by square roots, and brackets, and so forth. That is to say I could once! Today I've forgotten all about it. But I can't see how such a formal task can be of use to any one at all except as a mental exercise for schoolboys. No doubt it's very good to learn to reckon. But I should think it senseless for a man to sit all his life doing sums, and covering sheets of paper with rows of figures.'

'You are mistaken, Goldmund. You imagine such a busy reckoner to go on and on, solving new school-tasks, set by a schoolmaster. But he can set himself his own problems, they can grow in his mind to mighty forces. A thinker must have worked over much real and imaginary space, mathematically, and planned it out, before he dares confront the problem of space itself.'

'Yes, but this problem of space, as a subject for thought, does not seem to me an object on which any man should waste his labour and years. To me the word "space" means nothing, and not worth a thought in itself, unless I can picture a real space – let us say the space between the stars. Though certainly to see that, and measure it, would not be a bad way of spending time.'

Narziss interrupted, with a smile:

'What you really mean is that thought itself seems useless to you, but not the application of thought to the visible and practical world. I can answer you there. We shall never lack chances, nor yet the will, to apply our thinking. This thinker, Narziss, for instance, has used the results of his thought a hundred times over, on behalf of Goldmund, his friend, and on that of each of his monks, and does every hour. But how can a thinker apply anything, unless he has learned it, and practised it first? Poets and craftsmen continually practise their eyes and fancy, and we praise their skill, even if they only use it to give us bad and unreal images. You cannot reject thought as such, and then only ask for its "practical uses". The contradiction is clear. So leave me in peace to think my thoughts, and judge me when I show you their results, just as I will judge your craftsmanship by your works. At present you are restless and moody because there are still obstacles set between you and your craft. Clear them away, then! Find, or build yourself a workshop, and set to work. Many cares will resolve themselves with that.'

Goldmund asked nothing better.

He chose a shed beside the courtyard gate, at present empty and good enough for a workshop. From the carpenter he ordered a drawing-table, and other furnishings, for which he set down the exactest measurements. He made out a list of all that the cloister carriers were to bring him, piece by piece, from the neighbouring cities – a long list. He picked out blocks, at the carpenter's shop, or in the forest, of every kind of wood already cut, had these set aside, and piled one above the other, to dry, on the grass plot behind his shop, where, with his own hands, he built a roof over them. To the smith also he gave much work, whose son, a young and dreamy boy, he had charmed completely, and won over to him. Together, for half the day, they would stand in the forge, at anvil or whetstone, hammering out all the many curved or straight-bladed chiselling-knives, gimlets, and shaving-irons they needed to work on the wood. The smith's son, Erich, a lad of twenty, became Goldmund's friend, and helped him in everything. He was eager to learn, and at times when the sight of Narziss and his cloister filled Goldmund's heart with shame for his idleness, he could always find his solace in Erich, who shyly loved, and made a hero of him. The boy would beg for tales of the Bishop's city and Master Nicholas, and these Goldmund told very gladly, until suddenly he would feel surprised to find himself sitting there, like an old man, full of tales of deeds and journeyings long ago, when his own life was only just beginning.

No one, since none here had known him before, could perceive how these last months had aged and altered him, making him far older than his years. The hazards and needs of vagrants' lives may already have begun to sap his strength, when he met the plague, with all its terrors, and experienced imprisonment by the count, with the horror of that night in the castle cellar. These things had shaken him to the depths, and many signs of his suffering still remained; grey hairs in his yellow beard, thin lines in his face, nights when his sleep was troubled, with, at times, a certain weariness in his heart, a slackening-off of desire and curiosity, the dim and drab sensation of satiety. But youth came back in all his talks with Erich, in the hours when he could loiter in the smithy and carpenter's shop. Then he was full of life, and beloved by them all, though at other times he would sit for an hour together, dreaming and smiling to himself, full of the strangest apathy and indifference.

Hardest of all was to decide which figure he should first set out to carve. This, the beginning of his work, done to repay the cloister's hospitality, must be no chance and idle product, quickly achieved to excite the curious, but must spring from the very heart and life of Mariabronn, and, like those ancient carvings in the church, be a worthy part of the very fabric. He would have liked best of all to carve a pulpit or an altar, but for neither was there need, nor any space. Yet he thought of something equally good. A high niche had been built into the wall of the Fathers' refectory, in which, at meals, a younger brother stood, to read out the Lives of the Saints. This niche was without any ornament, and Goldmund made up his mind to clothe the stairway up to the lectern, and the desk itself from which they read, in a wooden garment of decoration, with many figures, like those around a pulpit, some in half-relief, and others almost freed from the wood. He had told the abbot his plan, who praised and welcomed it. When at last the work could be begun, Christmas was passed, and the ground covered in snow.

Goldmund's life took on another shape. Now he might have left the cloister. None ever saw him now; no longer did he await the end of a lesson to watch the boys troop down into the court; he strayed no more in the woods, nor loitered idle in the cloister. His meals were eaten with the miller — though not that miller he visited as a boy — none now could come into his workshop, save only his assistant, Erich, though sometimes, for days together, even he would never hear a word from him.

For the winding gallery round the lectern he had thought out the following plan : of the two halves into which the work should be divided, one was to set forth the world, the other the word of God. The lower half, the stairs up to the desk, growing out of a strong oak, and winding about it, should figure all creation, the works of nature, the simple lives of patriarchs and prophets. The upper, the parapet of the desk, would have figures of the Four Evangelists. To one of these he would give the face of Abbot Daniel; another should be his successor, the dead Pater Martin, and in the figure of Luke he would carve Master Nicholas, for all time.

He had many stubborn obstacles to surmount, far harder than he ever would have guessed. This grieved him, but with a pleasant grief. He wooed and enticed his work, as full of despair and of delight as though he had been courting a difficult woman, struggling with it, tenderly and firmly, as a fisherman angles a great pike, learning from every difficulty, and making his fingers still more delicate. Everything else was forgotten – the cloister, and almost even Narziss. Though the abbott inquired several times he managed to see nothing but drawings.

But then, one day, in compensation, Goldmund surprised him with the demand to have himself shriven and assoiled.

'Till now,' he said, 'I could never bring myself to ask it of you. I felt small enough before you already. Now I am not so small. I have my work, and am not a cipher any more. After all, since I live in a cloister, I feel I ought to submit, like all the others.'

He would not wait, since now he felt that the hour had come for it. Moreover in his first weeks of meditation here, plunged as he had been in sudden memories, born of all these sights of his youth – and later, too, as he told his tales to Erich – he had seen, in looking back over his life, a certain shape and order in his days.

Narziss shrived him without ceremony. His confession lasted two whole hours. The abbot, with an unmoved face, heard all the adventures, griefs, and sins of his friend, asking many questions, but never breaking in on what he heard, listening, as unperturbed as ever, when Goldmund affirmed that he lacked all faith, admitting that he had ceased to believe either in God's justice or His mercy. He was struck by many things the penitent said to him; could see how deeply he had been shaken, how scarred he had been, how near at times to utter shipwreck. But then again he was forced to smile at the childlike innocence of this friend, whom he found so remorseful and afflicted, so full of despair at what he deemed his sacrilegious thoughts, though these were harmless enough, compared with some of those that haunted his confessor – to the dark chasms of doubt in Narziss's mind.

Goldmund was surprised, disappointed even, that Narziss should take his sins so lightly, though this priest admonished and punished him without stint for his neglect of prayer and of the sacraments. He laid on him the penance to live chaste, and fast for a month, before he took the Host again. He must hear the first mass every morning, and each night say a Pater Noster, and canticle to Mary.

Then he said: 'I beg and adjure you not to take this penance lightly. I do not know if you can still remember the text of the mass. You should follow it word for word, letting its sense sink into your mind. The Pater, and some canticles I will give you, we can go through together today, and I will show you passages and words in them whose worth to you I would have you mark very clearly. We should never speak God's words, or listen to them as we speak and listen to those of other men. If you find yourself saying them by rote (and this will happen very often to you) you must think of what I tell you now. Then you should start the prayer afresh, saying the words in such a guise that you feel them in your very heart. And now I will tell you how to do it.'

Whether by some fortunate chance or because the abbot's knowledge of souls went deep enough to contrive such an issue, his time of penance and assoilment brought Goldmund many days of peace and harmony, days which rejoiced his mind, in the midst of the cares and obstacles of his work. He would find himself refreshed each morning and evening by the light, yet precise and carefully chosen spiritual exercise : freed from the anxious striving of his days, his heart and mind drawn back from the dangerous solitude of his craft, into kinship with a higher order – to a certainty which freed his mind, and led him as a child into God's kingdom.

Forced as he was to struggle in utter solitude with his images, giving them his whole strength and his senses, this one hour's gentle withdrawal led him back, again and again, into contentment. Often, as he worked, he would chafe with rage, or else be filled with mad delight : this quiet penance laid on him by his friend was like a plunge into deep, cold water, cleansing him of the pride of his desire, the other pride of his despair. But it did not always succeed. Often, after a day of restless work, he could find no calm, and no appeasement. Several times he forgot these prayers altogether. Often, as he strove to plunge down again into their peace, he would find himself hindered and tormented by the thought that all prayers, in the end, are nothing but our childish striving to find a God who does not really exist, or, if He does, can never help us. He complained to his friend of it.

'Keep to it still,' said Narziss, 'you have promised, and you must stay it out. It is not for you to think whether God is listening to your prayers, or whether, indeed, a God exists at all, as you would imagine Him. Nor have you to fret or puzzle as to whether all this is so much child's play. In comparison with the God whom we petition all our human strivings are those of children. You must forbid yourself utterly all such silly, childish thoughts during your exercise. Say your Pater Noster, and your canticle, and give yourself up to the words, filling yourself, and letting them penetrate, just as though you were singing or playing a lute. If you sang or played you would not let your mind go hunting after clever thoughts and speculations, but would strive to give out each tone and fingering as clearly and perfectly as you could. When we sing we don't hinder ourselves with asking if our singing is really a waste of time. We sing, and that is all! That is how you must pray.'

It succeeded again. Again his fretful, covetous self was merged into the wide-arched hierarchy of this cloister, the fair words poured down into his heart, and ascended through his body like so many stars.

The abbot watched with deep delight how Goldmund, even after his time of penance, and now that he had taken God's Body, still followed the daily exercise he had set, and continued so for months and weeks together.

Meanwhile his work progressed. From the wide block, cut into spiral steps, there jutted forth a world of sprouting shapes, plants, beasts, and men, entwined together, and in their midst stood Father Noah, among his vines with clustering grapes on them – a picture-book and song of living thanks from all God's creatures in their beauty, each free after his own kind, yet led by nature and secret law.

In all these months Erich alone might see the work, who was taken to do prentices' labour on it, and so had now no other thought except to be a carver himself. But even he, on many days, was forbidden to enter the workshop, though on others Goldmund was his friend, instructing him, and letting him try his hand, delighted at heart to have found a pupil and disciple. When the work was done, if it were a good one, he meant to beg Erich of his father, and take him as his regular journeyman.

At the figures of the Four Evangelists he could only work on his best days, when all was peace, and no pain or scruple teased his mind. The best among them, he felt, was the figure he had taken from Abbot Daniel, and he loved it deeply, since innocence and gentleness shone in the face. His image of Master Nicholas pleased him less, though Erich admired it most of all. It showed too much grief and conflict, seemed full of noble projects to create, yet desperate with the secret knowledge that all our works are as nought, tormented for its lost unity and innocence.

When Abbot Daniel was quite ready he bade Erich sweep out the workshop. All the other figures he wound in cloths, leaving only this one full in the light. Then he went off to find Narziss, but, since the abbot had no time for him, waited in patience till the morning. Towards midday he led Narziss into the workshop.

His friend stood and gazed. He took his time, examining the figure before him with all the care and attention scholars use. Goldmund waited behind him in silence, trying to quell the storm in his heart.

'Oh,' he thought, 'if one of us fails now it will be bad! If my work is not good, or else he cannot understand it, then all my labour will have no meaning. I should have waited after all.'

These minutes seemed like hours. He remembered the day when Master Nicholas had stood there holding his first drawing, and waited, pressing his damp and burning hands together.

But when Narziss turned he knew he was safe. He could see how something had flowered in that spare, keen face; some blossom of delight he had never seen in it since their days together in his boyhood: a smile, almost shy and fearful, flickered about those eyes, all will and intellect, the smile of an undying love, a shimmer, as though its pride and solitude had been in that instant broken up, and only the heart, with all its love, were visible.

'Goldmund,' said Narziss, very softly, and, even now, weighing his words, 'you will not ask me suddenly to become a critic of statues. That I am not, as well you know. I could tell you nothing about your art which would not sound like prattle in your ears. But let me say only this – at my first glance I knew this apostle for Abbot Daniel, not only as he was, but as all that he meant to us in those days; his dignity, his gentleness, his simplicity. And even as our own dead Abbot Daniel stood before our eyes and our young reverence, so do I see him here again, and with him all that was holy to us in those days, all that has made that time so unforgettable. You have paid my friendship most richly, Goldmund, since not only have you given me Abbot Daniel, but have shown me your whole self for the first time, now. I have seen you as you are. Let us say no more of it – I dare not. Oh, Goldmund, that this hour should ever have come for us.'

The wide room was very still. Goldmund saw how deeply his friend rejoiced. Yet a kind of discomfort choked his answer.

'Yes,' he said shortly, 'I am glad of this. But now it is time you went to the refectory.'

CHAPTER NINETEEN

THIS work kept Goldmund busy for two years, and from the second of these he had Erich all day as his assistant. In the wooden balustrade of his staircase he had planted another little Paradise, carving with delight an innocent wilderness of leafy trunks and tufted herbs, with birds on branches, and the heads and bodies of lurking beasts peeping out everywhere through the stems. In the midst of this peaceful, sprouting garden he set forth scenes from the lives of Patriarchs. There were few days now on which he felt it impossible to carve, when restlessness and weariness of mind kept him away from the workshop. When such fits were on him he would set Erich a task for the day, and stray out alone into the fields, at times on horseback, to taste a little vagrancy and freedom, seek out a peasant's daughter in one of the villages, hunt, or lie for hours in the long grass, staring up at the vaultings of the forest, through a wilderness of fern and broom. Then he could work with fresh zest, carving with joy his plantation of herbs and trees, gently enticing men's faces out of the wood, cutting out a mouth in a few firm strokes, the line of an eye, or a folded beard. Apart from Erich only Narziss had seen the work, and he often came over to the workshop, which at times seemed his favourite room in the cloister.

Here he would sit and watch it all, amazed and delighted. Here at last, flowering in this work, were all the things his friend had kept so long in his child-like, defiant, suspicious heart. They blossomed here on every side — a creation, a little, sprouting world; a game perhaps, but certainly no worse a game than the one with grammar, logic, and theology. One day he said abstractedly:

'I am learning a great deal from you, Goldmund. I begin to see what it is that artists do. Till now it never seemed to me that their art, in comparison with my thought and science, was a thing to be taken very seriously. I would think more or less in this way: Since man, after all, is a dubious alloy of matter and spirit, and since his spirit can bring him to the knowledge of eternity, whereas matter can only draw him down into death, and fetter his soul to all that perishes, he should strive away from the senses, to the spirit, and so exalt his life, and give it a meaning. Only now do I begin to perceive how many paths lead us to knowledge, that study is not our only way to it, and perhaps not the best to follow. Certainly it is mine, and I must keep to it. But I see you by the opposite way, the way which leads through the senses, reach as deep a knowledge as any that most thinkers achieve, of the essence and secret of our being, and a far more living mode of setting it forth.'

'Now you understand,' said Goldmund, 'why it is that I cannot conceive of any thought without its image.'

'That I understood long ago. Thought is an eternal simplification – a seeing out, beyond the things of the eye; the attempt to construct a world of pure intelligence. But you craftsmen take the most perishable of all things to your hearts, and, in their very transience and corruption, you herald the meaning of the world. You never look beyond or above it, you give yourselves up to it, and yet, by your very devotion, you change it into the highest of all, till it seems the epitome of eternity. We thinkers strive to reach our God by drawing the world away from before His face. You come to Him, loving His creation, and fashioning it all over again. Both these are imperfect, human works; yet, of the two, art is the more innocent.'

'That I cannot tell you, Narziss. But it seems that you

thinkers and theologians can succeed far better than I do in coming to grips with life, and holding despair at arm's length. I have long since ceased to envy you your science, my friend, but I envy your calm, your peace, your even temper.'

'There's nothing to envy, Goldmund. There is no peace, in the sense in which you mean it. No doubt there is a peace, but not that peace which abides, and never forsakes us. On earth there is only that peace which we must conquer over and over again, from day to day, in ever fresh assaults and victories. You have never seen me assailed. You know nothing of my doubts at study, my torments in my cell at prayers. It is good that you do not. All you can see is that I am less subject to moods than you, and so you think I must be at peace. But like every true life, it is all battle and sacrifice. Like your life also, *o amice*.'

'We need not quarrel as to that. But neither do you see every struggle in my heart. I do not know if you understand what I feel when I think that soon my work will be finished. It will be carried away and set up, people will praise me for it, and then I shall go back to my empty workshop, sad for all its imperfections, and the many things others can never see in it, with my heart as empty and desolate as the place.'

'That may be so,' said Narziss, 'and neither of us can ever quite understand the other. Yet all men of goodwill have this in common – that our works in the end put us to shame; that always we must begin them afresh, and our sacrifice be eternally renewed.'

A few weeks later Goldmund's work was ready, and set up. All happened now just as it had happened years ago. The work became the possession of other men, was seen, judged, praised, and he was honoured for it. But his heart and workshop seemed deserted, nor could he tell if all his labour had been for anything of worth. On the day of its unveiling he dined in the abbot's refectory. There was a banquet, with the oldest wine in the house. Goldmund ate the delicate fish and the venison, but, more than by the rare old wine, he felt warmed and cheered by Narziss' pleasure, who honoured him, and acclaimed his work.

Another work, ordered and desired by the abbot, was already conceived, and the drawings made; an altar for the Lady Chapel at Neuzell, a cloister-church, served by a father from the monastery. For this altar he intended a Mother of God, whom he would use to rescue for ever one unforgettable memory of his youth, the knight's shy, lovely daughter, Lydia. For the rest the work meant very little to him, though it seemed a good opportunity to let Erich try his hand as journeyman. Should the boy succeed he would have a good workman to second him, one who could replace and set him free for such works as alone lay near his heart. He went with Erich to assemble wood for the altar, and let him prepare it. Goldmund would often leave him alone to work, and go off for a day in the forest. He had begun to stray far from the cloister, and once, when he had been gone for several days, Erich told the abbot of his absence, who began to fear that he had run away again for ever. He returned, worked for a week at the Lydia-madonna, and set out again.

He was restless. His life, since the great work was finished, had fallen into the old disorder. He no longer cared to go to early mass, and was deeply wearied and dissatisfied. Now he would often think of Master Nicholas, and wonder if he too would not soon have become very like him, busy, gruff, and skilful, and yet a slave, without youth in his heart. A recent experience set him thinking. One day in the woods he had met a little peasant, Francisca, who pleased him so that he did his best to charm her, using every device to make her his. The maid had listened to all his stories; she had laughed very happily at his jokes; but his love she refused, and so for the first time he perceived that, to a young maid, he seemed an old man. He had not gone back to see her, and had not forgotten it. Francisca was right; he had changed, he himself could feel it, and truly not because of his few grey hairs, come too early, nor the little wrinkles about his eyes – it was something deeper, something in his mind and spirit. He felt himself old, and grown strangely akin to Master Nicholas, considered himself glumly in the looking-glass, and shrugged his shoulders at the sight. He had become safe and tame like other burghers, no hare or eagle now, but a house-dog. Whenever he wandered in the fields he would find himself seeking out old memories, his mind full of thoughts of past adventures rather than new happiness and freedom – as mistrustful and eager as a dog on a false scent. A day or two of frolic away from the cloister was enough to make him feel a truant, remembering that wood stood ready in his workshop – uneasily responsible for the altar, for Erich, his journeyman. He was no longer free, no longer young.

And so he made a firm resolution. When this Lydia-madonna was finished he would take the roads for the third time. It was bad to live so long with men. Men were good enough to talk to, they could understand a craftsman's work, and reason cleverly on it. But for all the rest, for tenderness and delight, play and gossiping, pleasure, without need for thought – for these there must be women and vagabondage, the roads with their changes and adventure, and none of it all could prosper near a monastery. Everything here, and all the surroundings of the cloister, had made his heart a little grey and serious, a little masculine and heavy, had infected him and got into his blood.

The thought of another journey cheered him. He stuck hard to his work, to be sooner free of it, and, as Lydia's shape emerged by degrees from the wood – as he carved the long folds of the gown, in straight lines down from her delicate knees – a deep and poignant happiness shot through him, a melancholy devotion to her image, this firm, timid shape of a young maid, and all the memories it brought of her, of youth, first love, and first delight. He worked very slowly and carefully, feeling this shape at one with all the pleasure in his heart, with his joy and the gentlest of his memories. It was exquisite to shape the bend of her neck, her smiling, dolorous mouth, her lovely hands, the long fingers, and beautiful arched cups of the finger-nails. Erich, too, whenever he had time to look at it, would stare, in loving bewilderment, at the figure.

When they were nearly ready he showed his Lydia to the abbot.

Narziss said:

'This is your fairest work, Goldmund. We have nothing in the cloister to equal it. I must tell you that in these last months I have often been troubled about your happiness. I have seen you so restless and full of pain, and when you went off and stayed out longer than a day, I often feared you would never come back to us. Now you have made us this lovely figure. My friend, I am very proud and glad.'

'Yes,' answered Goldmund, 'the figure has turned out a good one. But, Narziss, listen. To shape that figure it needed the whole of my youth, it needed all my vagrancy and loves, and every woman I ever knew. That is the source of my work, and soon the fountain will dry up, for my heart grows withered. I will finish this Maria, and then I would beg for a long holiday – I cannot tell you how long. I must go out again, and find my youth, and all the things that made life dear to me. Can you understand? Well then, you know I am your guest, and have never taken payment for my work.'

'I have offered it you often,' exclaimed Narziss.

'Yes, and now I will take it. I will let them make me new clothes, and when they are ready I will come to you and ask you for a horse, to ride out again, and a few gold thalers for the journey. Say nothing against it, Narziss, and don't look sad! It is not that I have ever been unhappy here – I could never have found a better life – it is something else. Will you do as I ask you?'

They said little more of this. Goldmund had them cut him a plain jerkin and riding-boots, and, as summer approached, he finished his madonna, as though she were the last work he would do. As he set the careful finishing strokes to her hair and hands, and sorrowful face, it almost seemed as though he were delaying his own departure, as though he put it off again and again for one last delicate glimpse of Lydia's beauty. Day after day went by, and still he had this or that to set to rights. Narziss, though this parting grieved him, would often smile at Goldmund's passion, which seemed to hold him so fast to God's own Mother.

Then one day Goldmund surprised him by coming suddenly in, to take his leave. He had made up his mind overnight. In his new jerkin, boots, and cap, he came to ask the abbot's blessing. He had confessed, a while since, and received the Sacrament. This parting lay heavy on them both, though Goldmund pretended to more ruffling indifference than he felt.

'Shall I ever see you again?' asked Narziss.

'Oh yes, surely you will – unless your good horse breaks my neck. Why there'd be none left to call you "Narziss," and trouble your mind. You'll see me again, never fear. Don't forget to keep an eye on Erich, though. And let nobody meddle with my new statue. She must stand in my chamber, as I told you, and never let the key out of your hand.'

'Are you glad to set out?'

Goldmund screwed up his eyes.

'Well, there's no denying I liked the thought of it. But now that I start to ride away it isn't so good as I hoped.

You'll laugh at me, and say I'm a fool, but I don't find it easy to leave you all; and yet this dependence on you mispleases me. It feels like a sickness. Young, healthy folk aren't like that. Master Nicholas was, though. Oh, why do we waste so many words. Bless me, Narziss. I want to go.'

He rode off.

Narziss' thoughts could never leave his friend; he feared for him, and yet longed for his return. Would the golden bird ever fly back to his hand, the vagrant? God keep him, and bring him safe home. How many cares this yellow-haired boy had brought him, who complained all the while of getting old, and yet looked at him through such guileless eyes. How he feared for him now. This butterfly had gone his own zig-zag path, into danger perhaps, to death or new imprisonment. He trembled, yet he rejoiced. Deep down it filled him with delight that the forward child should have been so hard to curb, that he had such whims there was no holding him.

Every day, at one hour or the other, the abbot's thoughts returned to Goldmund, in care and longing, love and gratitude, at times in doubt, and self-reproach. Ought he not, perhaps, to have given more outward signs of his love, shown Goldmund how little he wished him other than he was, how both he and his carving had enriched him? He had said so little, perhaps too little, of all this. Who could tell if he might not have managed to keep him.

But Goldmund had not only enriched his life; he had made him poorer too, poorer and weaker, and certainly it was good to have kept that secret. This world in which he had his home, this cloister, his learning and his office, the whole well-grounded structure of his thought – had it not been shaken to its base, his faith in it almost destroyed, by his life with Goldmund? No doubt that, seen from a cloister, with the certainty of reason and morality, his ways had been better, and far more just: his ordered days of rigid service, his sacrifice, for ever renewed, his perpetual strivings after clarity, and the greater justice it would bring: a far better life than any this vagabond could boast, this artist and lecher.

But seen from above – as God might see it – were this patterned order and morality, this giving up of the world, and the joys of sense, this aloof withdrawal from blood and mire into prayer and philosophy, any better? Were men really made to live an ordered life, its virtues and duties set to the ringing of a bell? Was man created to study Aristotle and the *Summa*, to know Greek, extinguish his senses, fly the world? Had not God made man with lusts and pride in him, with blood and darkness in his heart, with the freedom to sin, love and despair? Whenever Narziss thought of Goldmund such questions were foremost in his mind.

Yes, and perhaps it was not merely simpler and more human to live a Goldmund-life in the world. Perhaps in the end it was more valiant, and greater in God's sight, to breast the currents of reality, sin, and accept sin's bitter consequence, instead of standing apart, with well-washed hands, living in sober, quiet security, planting a pretty garden of well-trained thoughts, and walking then, in stainless ignorance, among them – the sheltered beds of a little paradise. It was harder perhaps, and needed a stouter heart to walk with broken shoes through forest-glades, to trudge the roads, suffer rain and snow, want and drought, playing all the games of the senses, and paying one's losses with much grief.

Goldmund at least had shown him this – that a man born to noble life can plunge very deep indeed into the sea of blood and lust which men call living, spatter himself over with mire and gore, and yet never become deformed or dwarfish, never kill the God in his mind, and though he wander for years through the blackest darkness still carry, without risk of its extinction, the light which made him a creator.

Narziss had gained deep insight into the chequered spirit of his friend, and neither his respect nor love was in any way diminished by what he saw. Ah, no – and since, under Goldmund's sinful hands, he had watched the birth of all these marvels of still, yet living, form, each shape with its inner law and perfection, these reverend faces with deep-set eyes, through which the spirit shone in all its brightness, those praying or pardoning hands, all these bold or gentle, proud or holy images, he had known indeed how much of light and of God's grace had illumined this lecherous wastrel's heart.

He had found it easy enough to seem wiser than Goldmund in their talks, oppose to the passion of his friend the ordered clarity of his mind. But was not every gesture of these figures, each eye or mouth, each tendril, leaf, or folded garment, more real, more living, more irreplaceable than all that any thinker could ever furnish? Had not this vagrant, whose heart was so full of need and contradiction, set forth, for ever and for all men, the symbols of our human need, in shapes to which the longing and delight, the fears and hopes of countless humans would turn, to seek their comfort, strength and security?

Smiling, yet full of grief, Narziss remembered all the times since their boyhood, when he had seemed to guide and admonish Goldmund. And Goldmund had heard his lessons gratefully, never once protesting or growing angry at his easy assumptions of leadership and control. Yet now these works, brought forth so quietly, from all the storm and pain of this harassed life – no words, no preachments, no admonishments, but life itself, raised up and dignified? How poor he seemed beside all these, with his science, his dialectics, his monk's morality.

Such were the thoughts that kept recurring. Just as, many

years ago, he had laid warning hands on Goldmund's youth, shaking his purpose, and setting his life a new direction, so now his friend returned to trouble his spirit, forcing him to doubts and self-scrutinies. Goldmund was his equal. He had taken nothing from Narziss which he had not given again a hundred fold.

This absent friend gave him much time to think in; weeks passed, and the chestnut tree had long since flowered, the clear, milky green of its blossom had long since hardened and grown dark brown. The storks on the gateway towers had long brought forth their young, and taught them to fly. The longer Goldmund tarried his return the more acutely Narziss perceived how much he was losing by his absence. He had several learned fathers as guests in the house; one skilled in Plato, a good grammarian, a couple of acute theologians. And among his monks there were one or two good and faithful souls, to whom their vocation meant something serious. But none of all these was his equal, there was none with whom he could truly measure his spirit. Goldmund had this irreplaceable gift, and now it was hard to do without it. He longed for his friend.

Often he would go across to the workshop, to encourage the journeyman, Erich, who still worked on at the altar-piece, and who also pined to see his master again. Then he would unlock Goldmund's bedchamber, in which stood the new Mother of God, carefully raise the cloths that enveloped her, and sit awhile looking at the image. He knew nothing at all of her inspiration. Goldmund had never told him the story of Lydia. But he could feel it all, could see that the features of this girl had lived many years in his friend's heart. Long ago, perhaps, he had seduced her, deceived her hope, and gone his way. But in his heart he had taken her shape, and shielded it, truer than the best of husbands, till in the end, perhaps after many years in which he had never had a sight of her, he had shaped this gracious, tender, young girl's body, and in her face, her bearing, and her hands, set forth all the gentleness and wonder, delight and longing, of their love.

The figures round the refectory-lectern had also much, for Narziss, of Goldmund's history — the history of a lecher and a wastrel, a homeless, faithless, vagabond of the roads; yet all that he had left of it, there in the wood, was fair and true, and full of vivid love. How strange and secret life could be, how dark and muddy flowed the stream, how clear and beautiful what remained with us!

Narziss fought hard against himself. He won, and remained true to the way he had chosen, never abating a jot of his rigid service. But he suffered from the loss of his friend, and suffered too in the perception of how great a share, where all should have been given to God and his duty, that friend had taken in his heart.

CHAPTER TWENTY

THE summer ended; poppies and cornflowers, corn-campion and starwort, withered and vanished, the frogs in the fishponds ceased to croak, the storks flew high, preparing to depart. Then Goldmund came.

It scared Erich to see him. True that at the first glance he knew him, and his heart leapt with joy at the sight. Yet it seemed another man who had come back, older by many years, a counterfeit Goldmund, ailing and spent, with a dusty, greyish, sagging face, although there was no pain in his eyes, but rather a smile, an old, good-natured, patient smile. He dragged his steps, and seemed exhausted.

This strange, half-recognizable Goldmund took the young journeyman's hand, and peered into his eyes. He made no great matter of his return, behaving as though he were come from the next room. He held Erich's hand, but would say nothing, no greetings, no questions, no traveller's tales. He only said: 'I must sleep,' and seemed too weary, almost, to move. He sent Erich away, and went into his bedroom, next the workshop. There he pulled off his cap, and flung it down, kicked off his shoes, and lay on the bed. In the far, dark, corner of the room he could see his madonna, wound in cere cloths. He gave her a nod but did not go to lift her wrappings, or greet her. Instead he crept to the little window, outside which still stood the uneasy Erich, and called:

'Erich, don't tell any one I'm back. I'm very tired. There's time till morning.'

He stretched himself out without undressing. Soon, having found no sleep, he stood up again, and shuffled heavily to the wall, to peer into the little looking-glass that hung there. He stared very closely at the Goldmund who answered his gaze from the mirror's round, a tired, withered old man, with vivid white streaks in his beard. It was a rather unkempt old fellow who stared back at him from the small dim circle, with a face not his, although he knew it, a stranger's face, and one he could not feel to be really there, since it seemed to have so little to do with him. It reminded him of many other faces; a little of Master Nicholas, a little of that old knight in the castle who had dressed him once as a brown page, a little of St James in the church – old, bearded St James, who looked so very ancient and grey in the shadow of his wide pilgrim's hat, and yet a pleasant old man, with a good heart.

He read his face very carefully, as though eager to learn all he could of this queer old fellow. Then he nodded, and knew it again as Goldmund. Yes, it was he; it tallied with his feeling of himself. A very weary and rather dull old man, back from a long journey, a quiet greybeard, and, though nothing much could ever be made of him, he bore him no grudge, he found him easy to live with. This ancient had something in his face which the other handsome Goldmund had lacked. For all the exhaustion in these eyes there was a look in them of content – or of indifference. He chuckled gently, and watched the dim figure chuckle back. This was a fine old fellow to bring back home with him! His jaunt had left him spent and tattered indeed, with no horse now, and no travelling wallet, and no gold thalers in his purse. And, more than these, he had left his strength and youth, his trust in himself, the red in his cheeks, the light in his eyes. Nevertheless the image pleased him: this old weak fellow in the looking-glass was a better companion than the Goldmund he had lived with so long. He was feeble, pitiful; but more harmless far, and more content. It would be easier to have a quiet life with him. He laughed and blinked with one of his wrinkled lids. Then he lay down on the bed, and fell asleep.

Next day Narziss came to visit him as he sat, trying to draw a little, bent far down over the workshop table. The abbot stopped in the doorway:

'Thank God!' he cried. 'They have only just told me you were back. I am overjoyed. Since you did not ask for me I have come to you. Do I hinder your work?'

He came closer, Goldmund sat up from his drawing, and held out his hand. Though Erich had warned him in advance, Narziss' heart stood still at the sight of his friend. Goldmund smiled up at him:

'Greetings, Narziss. It's a while now since we had a sight of each other. Forgive me for not having come over to you.'

Narziss looked him in the eyes. He too saw deeper than the spent, pitiful weariness in this face, saw that strangely tranquil look of contentment beneath, – an old man's pitiful resignation. Expert in his reading of human faces, he knew at once that this broken, strange-looking Goldmund was indeed no longer his friend, come back to greet him – that either his soul had detached itself from reality and wandered along some far-off road of dreams, or already stood at the gate which leads out of life.

'Are you sick?' he asked him tenderly.

'Oh yes. I am sick, too. I sickened in the first days of my travels. But I didn't want to have you laugh at me, and so you see I couldn't turn back. You'd have laughed to see me again so soon, quietly pulling off my riding-boots. No – I couldn't do that. So on I went, and travelled a while here and there. I was ashamed to think my journey had gone so ill. I'd reckoned without my host, and so, you see, I felt a fool. Ah well, you're wise, you can understand. Oh, forgive me – what was it you asked? I might be bewitched, for I keep forgetting everything they say to me. That business with my mother, Narziss! – you did that very well, you know. It hurt me badly at the time, but –'

His mutterings ended in a smile.

'We'll care for you, Goldmund, you shall have everything. But, oh – why didn't you come back as soon as things began to go ill with you? Truly we would never have shamed you. You should have turned your horse.'

Goldmund laughed:

'Oh, yes – now I know what it was! I didn't trust myself simply to come back here. It would have put me to shame. But now I've come. I'm well again now.'

'Have you had great pain?'

'Pain? Oh yes, I have enough pain. But listen – my pain is a good one. It's brought me to reason, and I'm not ashamed any more – even with you. That time you came to the prison to save my neck ... I had to set my teeth then, Narziss, I was so ashamed to have you see me there. All's one now.'

Narziss laid a hand on his arm. He was silent at once, and closed his eyes with a smile. The abbot, with fear in his heart, hurried away to summon the cloister-leech, Pater Anton, and have him examine the sick man. When they came back Goldmund sat asleep at his drawing-table. They put him to bed. The leech remained with him.

He found him hopelessly sick. He was shifted into one of the cloister wards. Erich became his keeper, day and night.

No one ever learned the whole story of Goldmund's last adventure on the roads. Some he related, and much he left to be guessed. Often, as he lay in a half-swoon, his fever rose and his mind wandered. At times he was clear in his speech, and then, each time, the would send for Narziss, who set great store by these last talks.

Some fragments of Goldmund's story and his thoughts were set down by Narziss, others by Erich.

'When did my pains begin? That was near the beginning of my journey. I rode through a wood, and the nag stumbled and threw me, so that I fell in a stream, and lay the whole night long in cold water. Inside here, where my ribs broke, I've been feeling the pain ever since. And I wasn't so far from here when it happened, so I couldn't let it turn me back. I was like a silly child, that fears to look foolish. So on I rode, and then, when I couldn't ride because of the pain, I sold my pony, and lay a long while in a hospice. Now I'm back for good, Narziss: it's all over with riding. It's all over with wandering the roads, all over with dancing and women. Oh, if it weren't, I'd have stayed away a good while longer, years longer. But when I saw that, out there, there was no more pleasure for me, I thought: "Before I have to go underground I'll draw a little, and carve a couple of figures." A man must have some kind of pleasure.'

Then Narziss answered him:

'It rejoices me to have you back with me. I lacked you so, and thought of you every day. And often I was afraid you'd never come back.'

Goldmund shook his head:

'Ah, well, you wouldn't have lost much.'

Narziss, a fire of love and grief in his heart, bent slowly down over his friend, and did what he had never done till now, in all the years of their long friendship: he kissed Goldmund's forehead, and his hair. Amazed at first, and then enthralled, Goldmund took count of what he had done.

'Goldmund,' the abbot whispered, 'forgive me that I could never say it before. I ought to have said it that day in the Bishop's city, when I came to free you from prison; or here, when you showed me your first statue, or at any other time when I might. Let me say it now, and tell you how dearly I love you, how much your life has always meant to me, how rich you have made me. It will mean very little to you. You are used to love, for you it is nothing out of the common, many women have cherished you in their arms. For me it is different. I have missed the best, and my life has been poor in love. Our Abbot Daniel told me that I was proud, and it seems he was right in what he said. Not that I am unjust with men. I strive very hard to be just and patient with them. But I have never loved them. Of two learned monks in the cloister, the one with the more learning was the dearer to me. I have never loved a bad scholar in spite of his weakness. Yet if now, with all this, I know what love means, that is your doing, Goldmund. You I have loved, and you alone, of all humanity. You can never fathom what that means to me. It has meant the fountain in the desert, the one flowering tree in the wilderness. I have you alone to thank that my heart has not dried up and perished, that something in me can still be touched by grace.'

Goldmund smiled, happily but uneasily. He said, in the low, quiet voice of his lucid hours:

'After you set me free, as we rode home together, I asked you for news of Bless, my pony, and you told me his fate. Then I saw how you, who scarcely knew of any other horse in the cloister, have been keeping your eye on my little Bless. I was very glad, since I understood that you did it for my sake. Now I see that I was really as I thought, and indeed I know that you love me. I have always loved you, Narziss. Half my life has been a striving to gain your love. I knew you had always cherished me, but I never hoped you would say it – you proud one! You say it now, when I have nothing left but you, no life or freedom in the world, and women have turned their backs on me. I accept your love, and I thank you for it.'

The Lydia madonna watched them from the corner of the room.

'Do you still think of death?' asked Narziss.

296

'Oh, yes, I think of death. And I think of how my life has shaped itself. When I was a boy, and you a scholar still, I wanted to be as wise a man as you are. You showed me how little I was fitted for it. Then I took the other side of life, and followed my senses, and women made it easy enough to find joy in it, they were all so willing, and greedy. But I don't want to seem to despise them, or speak any ill of lechery. I was very happy in the flesh, and I had the happiness of knowing that the flesh can sometimes be the spirit. That is how craftsmen are made. But now the flames are all put out; I have lost the joy of beasts, and the longing for it. Today I should still not have it, even if women longed for me again. Nor do I care to carve more figures. I have done enough. What difference does it make how many figures a craftsman leaves? So it is time to die. I am willing enough. I am even curious for it.'

'Why curious?' asked Narziss.

'Well, I suppose you think me a fool – and yet I'm curious to die. Not for eternal life, Narziss. I think very little of that, and to put it plainly, I don't believe in it any more. There is no eternal life. A withered tree is dead for ever; a frozen bird can never stir its wings again. Why should a man be a better corpse? Folk may go on thinking for a while of him, but, once he's gone, that doesn't last so very long. No, I'm curious to die because it's still my belief, or my dream, that I'm on the way back to my mother; because I hope my death will be a great happiness – as great as I had of my first woman. I can never rid myself of the thought that, instead of Death with his sickle, it will be my mother who takes me into herself again, and leads me back into nothingness and innocence.'

At one of his last visits, when Goldmund had not spoken for several days, Narziss found him awake, and eager to talk.

'Pater Anton says you must be in very great pain. How

do you manage to bear it so quietly, Goldmund? I think you have made your peace at last.'

'Peace with God, you mean? No, I have not found that. I want no peace with God. He made the world too ill, we need not esteem it, and He will not care much that I praise or blame Him. He bungled the world! But you're right when you say I have made peace with the pains in my ribs. Once I found it hard to bear pain, and although I used to think it easy to die, I was wrong. That night when dying seemed likely, in Count Heinrich's prison, I saw that. I couldn't die, and that was all about it! I was far too strong and wild to die then: they would have had to kill every limb in me twice over. All that's changed now.'

It wearied him to speak and his voice grew feebler. Narziss implored him to spare himself.

'No,' he said, 'I want you to hear me. Once I should have been ashamed to tell it you. You'll mock me even now — but listen. That day when I straddled my horse and left you, it was not for any adventure I happened to find. I had heard a rumour that Count Heinrich was back in these parts again, and his leman with him, Mistress Agnes. Well now, all that means nothing to you, and today nothing to me either. But when I heard it, it fired me so that I could think of nothing else but Agnes. She was the loveliest I'd ever lain with, and so I longed for another sight of her. I wanted to be happy with her again. So I rode, and in a week I found her. She was beautiful still, and I managed to speak to her, and show myself. But think, Narziss — she wouldn't look at me. I was too old, she said, I was not fair or young or lively enough for her. She promised herself no joy with me now. So then my journey was really over. Yet still I rode on. You see I couldn't come back to you to be shamed. But even then, as I rode, my strength, and youth and cunning must all have forsaken me, for I fell down a gulley with my horse, into a stream, and broke my ribs, and I lay all night in the water.

Those were the first sharp pains I had ever known. In the very instant after I tumbled I could feel something break in my chest, and yet the breaking seemed a pleasure to me. I was glad. I felt it with delight. And so I lay there in the water, and knew that I should have to die. I had nothing against it now. Death didn't seem so bad as it had in that prison. I felt those same sharp pains under my ribs that I've had so often ever since, and they brought me a dream, or a vision – just as you like. At first the pain seemed like a fire, and I lay there, shouting, and fighting it off, till suddenly I heard a voice, laughing at me – it was a voice I used to hear when I was a boy. It was my mother's voice, a soft, deep, woman's voice, full of love and lechery. It was then I knew that it was my mother. She was with me, holding me in her lap, and she had made a hole in my chest, and set her fingers deep between my ribs, to loosen my heart, and draw it out of me. When I knew that, it didn't seem like pain any more. Even now, when these pains come back, they are not pains – not enemies. They are my mother's fingers, drawing my heart out. She's very busy at it. Sometimes she presses down and moans, as though she were in an agony of love. Sometimes she laughs and croons over me. Often she is up in the sky, and I see her face between the clouds as wide as a cloud, hovering up there, and smiling sadly at me. Her sad smile draws at my heart, and plucks it.'

He spoke of her again and again.

'Do you know,' he asked on one of the last days, 'how far I had forgotten my mother until you raised her up, and gave her back to me? Even that was a sharp pain. It was as though beasts' heads were gnawing my entrails. Then we were still young, Narziss – fine boys, both of us, in those days. But even then my mother had called me back. I had to follow. And she was everywhere. She was Lisa the gipsy, and the sorrowful madonna of Master Nicholas. She was life and wantonness, and fear and hunger, and love.

Now she is death, and she has her fingers in my breast.'

'Don't say so much, my friend,' begged Narziss, 'wait till morning.'

Goldmund smiled up into his eyes, with the new smile he had brought home from his travels, the smile which seemed so frail and old, uncertain, at times, and feeble-witted, and then again pure goodness and pure wisdom.

'My dear,' he whispered, 'I can't wait till morning. I must take my leave, and tell you everything in my leave-taking. Hear me a few minutes longer. I wanted to tell you of my mother, and how she keeps her fingers round my heart. For years I longed to carve my mother's statue, it seemed the most splendid of my dreams. That would have been the best of all my works, since always I had her in my mind, in a shape full love and secrecy. Even a short while ago I should have thought it unbearable to die without having carved my mother's image. My life would have seemed so useless. But now, see how well she contrives it. Instead of my hands moulding her shape, it is she who moulds me, and informs me. She has her fingers round my heart, and loosens it, and makes me empty. She has led me to death, and my dream dies with me – my statue of Eve, in wood, the Mother of all men. I can see it still, and would carve it, if I had any strength left in my hands. But she will not have it so. She will never have me disclose her secret. She will kill me rather. And yet I am glad to die, she makes it so easy for me.'

Narziss heard these last words in agony. To catch their sense he had to bend down close over Goldmund's face. Many he could only half hear; many he heard, and yet their meaning remained obscure to him. Now the sick man opened his eyes again. Their eyes took leave. He whispered, with a little gesture, as though he were striving to shake his head:

'But how will you ever die, Narziss? You know no

mother. How can we love without a mother? Without a mother, we cannot die.'

The rest of what he muttered was unintelligible. For the two last days and nights beside his bed, Narziss watched the light die out of his face. Goldmund's last words still seared his heart like a flame.

MORE ABOUT PENGUINS

Penguinews, which appears every month, contains details of all the new books issued by Penguins as they are published. From time to time it is supplemented by *Penguins in Print*, which is a complete list of all books published by Penguins which are in print. (There are well over three thousand of these.)

A specimen copy of *Penguinews* will be sent to you free on request, and you can become a subscriber for the price of the postage. For a year's issues (including the complete lists) please send 25p if you live in the United Kingdom, or 50p if you live elsewhere. Just write to Dept EP, Penguin Books Ltd, Harmondsworth, Middlesex, enclosing a cheque or postal order, and your name will be added to the mailing list.

Another Penguin by Hermann Hesse is described overleaf.

Note: *Penguinews* and *Penguins in Print* are not available in the U.S.A. or Canada

Hermann Hesse

STEPPENWOLF

Hermann Hesse's poetical novel, *Steppenwolf*, was written some twenty years before he won the Nobel Prize for Literature in 1946. This Faust-like and magical story of the humanization of a middle-aged misanthrope was described in the *New York Times* as 'a savage indictment of bourgeois society'. But, as the author notes in this edition, *Steppenwolf* is a book which has been violently misunderstood. This self-portrait of a man who felt himself to be half-human and half-wolf can also be seen as a plea for rigorous self-examination and an indictment of intellectual hypocrisy.

Not for sale in the U.S.A. or Canada